AIRLINE

AIRLINE

◆

a novel

Kevin Donovan

iUniverse, Inc.
New York Lincoln Shanghai

AIRLINE
a novel

Copyright © 2005 by Kevin Donovan

iUniverse books may be ordered through booksellers or by contacting:

iUniverse
2021 Pine Lake Road, Suite 100
Lincoln, NE 68512
www.iuniverse.com
1-800-Authors (1-800-288-4677)

Although this story references actual events and historical figures, it is a work of fiction, and any resemblance to actual or living characters is purely coincidental and unintentional.

ISBN: 0-595-33751-1 (pbk)
ISBN: 0-595-67001-6 (cloth)

Printed in the United States of America

To my colleagues, the people who get us off the ground.

1

Wesley Arnold was hot. He straightened his tie and discreetly rubbed his finger across his teeth. Here he was, squeezed into the back row of executives outside the red brick building unofficially known as mahogany row, and on this typically uninhabitable July day in Atlanta, it was scorching.

"You out front on the right, move to your left a bit. You over there on the left, come on, squeeze in there." And when that didn't work, and it never did, the man behind the tripod came right over and physically pushed them together.

Charles, the fastidious corporate photographer for the last three decades, seemed to take great joy in being the only man in the entire company who could literally shove the executives around as he tried to fit them into his frame. The company leadership, in both an acknowledgment of his seniority and peevish avoidance of his wrath, granted him the time he needed; this despite their power to toss him and his equipment out of the headquarters gate on a whim. The annual executive photo was, after all, a tradition, one of the hundreds of things that held the airline together.

But it was hot. Wesley could feel the sweat down his back and on his forehead. It gathered in the collar of his starched white shirt and rolled down the sleeves of his tensely straightened arms. As Charles fiddled with the lens and measured the light, drops of sweat began to slip into Wesley's eyes, burning like the pavement and brick around him. If only he could remove his suit jacket for the few minutes it would take Charles to shoot the photo. But this was unthinkable, one of the many "unthinkables" he had identified on his ride up the corporate ladder. For forty-three years, the executive photo had graced the inside cover of the annual report, a solid but symbolic demonstration of unwavering financial health to all the stockholders who were willing to take a chance on an airline. Now was not the time to be a nonconformist.

And then there was this strange tradition of the tractor. To his far left stood a crumbling reddish carcass of metal that only appeared once a year for the photograph. Wesley looked at it analytically, trying to decipher what it was that retained its perennial position in the annual report. It appeared as though attempts had been made to spruce it up, but they were quickly abandoned when it became clear that any rubbing of the exterior would destroy what was left of the rusted and pocked skin. The iron wheels appeared as if they were straight from a vehicle used in the First World War. The tangle of rotted pipes and cylinders looked ready to collapse in a heap of dust.

Wesley tried to recollect the founder's rationale for this creature; something about strength, perseverance, and the connection to the farming origins of the airline. *Get over it already*, he thought.

He let his mind wander as another aircraft rumbled into the sky less than a mile away, their aircraft, one of the hundreds that left Atlanta each day to one of the hundreds of far-flung destinations. In Atlanta they were not just the largest airline, they were an empire. They had literally carried their hometown from a bustling backwater to an "International City" and sprawling metropolis. And now he was one of the leaders of that empire.

Wesley recalled the last hour: eventful, satisfying, but in the overall context of his climb, not entirely unexpected.

◆   ◆   ◆

"MB needs to see you, Mr. Arnold."

Stacy didn't usually enter his office unannounced, but they had an understanding that this set of words did not require an announcement. Wesley sprung to his feet and grabbed his jacket off the hook at the back of his door.

"Thank you, Stacy."

MB, Morton Berenson, or M.W. Berenson as he was better known to the board of directors—all of the executive vice presidents had two initials preceding their surname. But MB was the president and chief operating officer now, and he had been the one who first spotted Wesley working in a department simply known as Methods. They were both Georgia Tech alumni, a fortuitous commonality to have with a mentor 15 years his senior. Although Wesley didn't report directly to him, MB would occasionally call him into his office, sit him down in one of the leather chairs and sound him out about various opportunities, difficulties, and most importantly, people. A probing question or two would be diluted with banalities so that MB could keep ahead of his rivals and enemies throughout the complex. Wesley had proven himself valuable in this regard, and there was no reason to expect this meeting to be any different.

MB's secretary greeted Wesley with just a bit more warmth than usual. She was as graceful as she was beautiful, a former flight attendant who had become

MB's executive secretary upon her marriage, fair compensation for the loss of sin-gularity that was a requirement for all flight attendants at the time she arrived.

"Hello, Wesley," she said. Executive secretaries retained the divine right to call anyone below the level of their boss by their first name. She came around her desk and pulled open the large oak door to Berenson's office with a smile. When Wesley entered, his boss rose to his feet from behind his desk, as did the seven other executives around him.

"Come in, Wesley," said Berenson.

Wesley was suddenly nervous. Why were they all there, all in their jackets, standing as stiffly as their smiles?

"Sit down, won't you?" as if this were a question.

"Thank you, sir."

"Wesley, we have some good news for you this morning."

Wesley Arnold knew from experience that this was debatable. Good news was relative, often meaning anything from an assignment that required 20-hour workdays, to the bestowal of a project with no known objective. But this particu-lar moment was unusual. He rarely saw all these men together; in reality, some of them hated each other, and all of them maintained a reasonable fear of each other, hidden behind the protective Southern hospitality of their lineage. Yet here they all were.

"We'd like to welcome you to our ranks as our newest vice president, the youngest in the history of the company."

These were the words he'd never forget. He would replay them in his head for months, if not years. At 43 years old, Wesley Arnold was the youngest ever! In front of all the other big heads, it was no wonder they smiled as they did. Sud-denly he was the one to fear. For now, though, there was a kinship with his cor-porate elders that he reveled in. He had arrived and was now among the keepers of the empire, an empire they all loved with a blind and occasionally twisted sin-cerity.

"Thank you, sir."

A mild applause erupted followed by handshakes from each of them.

"Okay, then," said MB as he clasped his hands together. "There's much to do. Your new secretary will show you to your office just down the hall. Legal will be meeting with you in about five minutes to go through your contract and then at noon we'll be meeting downstairs for the picture. Sorry for the rush on this, Wes-ley, but we needed to let you know before the picture so that you'd have a clue as to why you were going to be in it." The men forced laughter.

"Hi, I'm Diane Stevenson, Mr. Arnold. I look forward to working with you. Follow me." She wore a pleated peach colored skirt and a silk white blouse. A large gold and emerald studded pin in the shape of an airplane graced her heart. Simple pearl earrings shone brightly from the shelter of her long brunette hair. Her thick dark eyebrows revealed her youth, probably only about 25, but she carried herself with confidence, not like so many secretaries he had known whose often unfair burden had made a visible impact upon their posture. As Diane turned to lead him into his new office, the skirt made the slightest of elevations, and he noticed her heels, strapped nicely to the back of her bare ankles as if she were born with them on. She was the woman who would work for him, and though he considered himself happily married, this fact alone made him feel like so much more of a man than the one he had been only moments before.

The deeply cut carpeting in his office matched that of the rest of the row—a rich smoky brownish color. At the center of the office sat a dark wooden but well-worn desk with drawers. There were empty shelves to his right, and a wall of blinds in front of him. Diane reached up to open the blinds, revealing the long expanse of runway 9R and the sprawling concourses beyond. It was, even after ten years with the company, still a breathtaking view. The hundreds of aircraft, the thousands of workers, the millions of customers, all right before him as if it were his own model train set.

"Your calendar is right here on your desk. There are two moving men at your disposal to move your files over to this office. I'll give you a chance to get settled. Oh, and Legal will be coming in with your contract in just a few minutes."

"Thank you, Diane. Thank you." He didn't need to say it twice, but he couldn't help himself. He had to thank somebody for what he was feeling.

"You're welcome, Mr. Arnold."

She shut the door, and the tension left his body with an almost audible sigh of relief. He let his eyes scan the new world around him. Along the window stood four wooden model aircraft, as if at attention, all of them emblazoned with historical renditions of the airline livery. On the desk was a gift-wrapped basket of fruit from the chairman and CEO. Peach jellies from the south of Georgia, cheeses from the dairies of the north Georgia Mountains and breads from North Carolina flooded the basket. A handwritten note was pinned to the cellophane:

Wesley, Welcome to our world. We'll be expecting a lot from you, but we know you will deliver. Best regards, W.A.

He knew that W. A. Hartenfeld hadn't actually written the note. That was the job of any CEO's secretary, but it didn't matter. He had crossed a threshold, survived numerous petty rites of passage, navigated the shoals of the condemned in favor of the path of his mentor, and most importantly, made no enemies of significance. It was this last achievement that thrust him into the corporate limelight, safe from the blackballing and backbiting that had cast the more talented aside. If there was one undeniable pattern that led to the end of a burgeoning career, it was the correlation between the presence of youth and the absence of deference. But Wesley had broken the pattern and found the fine line between respectful acknowledgments and blatant ingratiation.

◆   ◆   ◆

Charles had finally finished testing the light, as if the blinding, burning brilliance of the Georgia sunlight was not enough. Wesley surveyed the other jacketed members of the executive leadership. None of them conveyed any sign of discomfort, perhaps by habit if not pure competitiveness over who could sweat and squirm the least.

"We're ready," yelled Charles. Wesley had no idea to whom he could be yelling, but then he realized who was missing.

To the right of the group in the small executive parking lot, a limo driver sprung from his quarters and pulled a folded wheelchair out of the trunk. A second bow-tied black man jumped from the far front door and came quickly around to the near back door. He pulled it open, allowing the aged and crumpled figure to stagger to a half stand before slumping backwards into the waiting wheelchair. Dressed like the others, Martin Willman, the revered founder of the airline, was wheeled proudly to the front corner of the pack of executives, a worthy bookend to the equally decrepit tractor on the other end of the front row.

"Okay, smile!"

PART I
1922–1959

2

Marty Willman was a failure, just like his father. He had tried almost everything in his short life and all anyone could ever say was that he tried. Granted, there wasn't a whole lot to try in the vast cotton fields of Louisiana, where farming was not only a way of life, but the backbone of what little economy there was. Cotton was king, and the few farmers who were responsible for the single industry that kept the small town of Oak Ridge on the map were the king's nobles.

There were three farmers within the town's five mile radius, and though they all shared a grudging and respectful friendship, there was a subtle competitiveness underlying the chats and gossip between them. By sheer default, they were the leaders of this town—without farmers you might as well board up everything—but they didn't flaunt it. Despite the wisdom that the townspeople attributed to them, each was smart enough to know that their destiny lay in the hands of nature. They were always a dust storm away from bankruptcy, so best not to tempt the winds of fate through unseemly acts of hubris.

Marty's father had tried farming and that's exactly what had happened to him. The drought-ravaged harvest of 1919 was far too meager to get the Willman family through the winter, and so he was forced to sell his thirty acres in September of that year when Marty was at the still impressionable age of 17. He remembered everything that led up to his father's eventual surrender.

"Willman, I have come to help you!"

It was the grating German voice of Owen Becker. He was banging on the door and shouting, just as he had each day for the past month to see if Marty's father was ready to sell. Each day he came offering an unreasonably low amount of money for the land—acreage that literally surrounded the Willman house—and each day, for the entire month of August, Frederick Willman would politely decline the offer. Until finally there was no alternative.

"That is good, Willman. You have made a wise choice."

But Marty's father would never be the same. At a time when the bond between father and son is so crucial, Marty watched his father fail and retreat into the shame of serving those who had survived.

Frederick Willman was always pretty good with the scissors, and so the proceeds of the sale helped him set up a small barbershop just off Church Street in Oak Ridge. Whenever Marty came in for a cut, he could see the gradual shift in his father's chats with the farmers; how he went from provider to servant, from peer to subordinate. First names faded from the salutations, replaced by "Mr." and "Sir."

"It's good business," he told his son. "You should always make your customer feel important, no matter what you think of them."

Marty wasn't usually conscious of the dissonance in his teenage mind, but he sensed the discontent in his father; the quickly fleeting smiles when the customer left the shop, the catatonic state at the dinner table and the overbearing orderliness of his mother, this being her attempt to find refuge in the safety of predictability. But he loved his father. It didn't matter if he failed, or at least not consciously. He reasoned that his father hated the farmers, hated their patronizing banter, and hated when they delved into their expertise about the land, always feeling the need to bestow a grain of their agricultural wisdom upon one of those who had failed. But then hatred was much too strong an emotion to ever reach the surface of his father, because the farmers were also his customers. Whatever the depth of his feelings, Frederick Willman managed to hide them behind a veneer of affability.

As the spring of 1922 arrived, it became apparent that this would not be an ordinary year. Larvae were slowly crawling through the fluffy fists of cotton, eating the buds, shrinking the bolls and killing the plants one by one. The boll weevil had arrived in Louisiana, and suddenly, the farmers' renowned wisdom was of little use.

At first, the townspeople saw little change in the farmers. There was some infestation the previous year just as there was every year.

"Nothing to be worried about," they'd say loud enough for the other barbershop patrons to hear. "Cotton is king. Plenty of cotton, plenty of money coming in. Just a little bug."

But as the spring began to wane, the chats were suddenly marked with tension. There was an edge to the conversation, a lack of hospitality that even among rivals seemed out of place. Despite the sultry blue skies of the impending summer, an unseen cloud was moving over Oak Ridge. A disaster was silently underway.

Meanwhile, 20-year-old Marty Willman was putting the finishing touches on his latest folly: Advertising delivered by rocket. He had read several books about rocket-powered flight and concluded that if you loaded a small rocket full of leaflets, they could be distributed across a large swath of land. Unfortunately, there were a few important concerns that Marty was unable to accommodate. First, there had to be people in the area, and there weren't that many in Oak Ridge. Second, the rocket needed some mechanism to release the leaflets at its zenith in order to maximize the number of people who received them. And third, one needed reasonably good weather to ensure the leaflets didn't get washed away or blown into a completely uninhabited field (which was very likely in Oak Ridge).

"How's the rocket thing coming, Marty?"

"Needs work, Dad. It would probably work in a city, where there are lots of people."

"Well, don't give up, Marty. If you think it'll work, then keep trying."

This was one of the reasons Marty loved his father. He knew how he felt when he saw his father fail, and there was something inside of the son that wouldn't let the father see him follow in his footsteps. How easy it would have been for his father to discourage him from taking chances after his own defeat. Nevertheless, it was clear that the rocket idea was not working. He needed a new one.

Now that Marty was out of his teens, the first set of high school dreams had long faded, and with so little family income, college was out of the question, but his ambition remained stronger than ever. He was going to make his father a success by being one himself. He just didn't know how he was going to do it yet.

◆   ◆   ◆

Every few days, Marty caught a sound in the air, a droning buzz of sorts. Whether he was helping out in the yard, visiting his father in town, or immersing himself deep in his projects within the garage, he would find a clearing and spot the source of the sound in the distance, an "aero plane" working its way slowly across the sky.

Flight was a growing fascination for Marty, especially since the Great War had been won largely because of the dominance of the skies and the bombs that had been dropped from above. Still, the sight of a flying machine was an incredible novelty in the Deep South, and airplanes on the ground in Oak Ridge were a rare sight. He had seen photographs, had heard that a few passed through nearby Monroe, but he had never actually seen one up close until one crystal clear breezy day in May when the drone was louder than usual. He ran from the garage in time to spot a biplane flying just a few feet off the ground, its wings teetering back in forth in the wind.

It occurred to Marty that a pilot would not have flown this way intentionally, but then he didn't know anything about flight, so maybe that was the way one was supposed to fly. At least this is what he thought, until the plane started flying right toward him.

Now just a hundred yards away, Marty was so awestruck he could not move his feet. Sputtering and dipping, the plane hit the ground with a crunch, bounced upward and then back down again, its left wing grazing the edge of the dirt road leading to the house. As the wing hit, the plane veered toward the left and cart wheeled violently into Marty's front yard, coming to rest only a few feet from where he still stood.

It took a few seconds before the shock of the event wore off. The propeller came to a slapping halt. The pilot sat like a rag doll, halfway out of the cockpit. The wheels, bent within the struts, spun to a clipping stop.

"Are you okay?"

No answer. Marty had the urge to jump up on the tattered wing and pull the pilot to safety, but what if the plane blew up? It was a frightening piece of machinery.

"Hey, buddy! You all right?"

The pilot's goggles were down over his nose. He was bleeding from his fore-head, which had smashed into the dashboard on impact. With a groan, his head fell back on the small headrest at the rear of the cockpit.

Marty finally reacted, stepping quickly up onto the edge of the wing. He reached in and tried to pry the pilot out as he regained consciousness.

"Yeah, yeah, I'm okay, son, hold on. Just hold on there."

Now the man was getting out under his own power. Marty backed away as the man missed a step and fell the three remaining feet to the ground. He staggered back up and managed a wobbly impression of composure by leaning against the fuselage behind him.

"Never again!" he snapped.

Simon Piersall was literally shaking, but in accordance with his personal cus-tom, he managed a firm handshake and introduction to Marty. Roundish and short, his jumpsuit seemed too big for him. He was in his late 40s with an elabo-rate handlebar mustache and grayish hair escaping from his flight cap. He blinked with more pronouncement and frequency than anyone would have needed to blink.

"Marty. My name's Marty Willman. Are you okay?"

"No. No, I'm not okay. Bit of a bruise on my head, I would say, wouldn't you? Flying wouldn't be such a bad thing if it wasn't for the ground."

"Come on inside the house. We'll get the doctor for you."

Simon was in a temporary state of stability, with the majority of his weight against the aircraft. As he pushed himself forward to follow Marty, he kept going and landed flat on his face on the sparse turf of the yard. Marty rushed to help him to his feet just as his mother came out of the house.

"Oh my God!!" she said. "I'll call the doctor!"

The next hour was spent nursing Simon Piersall back to some coherence—under the assumption that this was his normal state—with the doctor, Mrs. Willman and Marty alternating their watch. When he wasn't needed, Marty was out front inspecting the giant contraption that had literally dropped in on his home.

He found the latch to the wide sheet metal hood and pushed it open. The engine was so large. So intricate. Pipes and pistons and cables seemed to go in all directions. He had seen some large tractors before and they had always caught his interest. He studied them until he knew exactly how they worked, but this was far beyond the primitive gasoline-powered engines he had deconstructed. This was raw power—power enough to carry men into the air. A brilliant design in such a compact, circular space, it was the first time he had seen a piston engine constructed in this way. The wings, the tail, the propeller—it all seemed so much larger than he had envisioned. It was a foreign object that he just had to understand, completely.

Inside the house, Simon was now holding court on his back, describing the flight and how "…the extreme and unforeseen turbulence was driving the aircraft mercilessly into the earth. It looked like the squall was going to fly me right into your boy there; but fortunately, I tucked the wing into the ground and saved his life!"

"My God…Thank you, Mr. Piersall!"

"Instinct, Mrs. Willman. Pure instinct. No thanks are due."

The doctor placed a large cotton bandage over the gash on Simon's head and bestowed a few words of advice before he was on his way. There was a curtness to the doctor's words; he had listened to Simon's pronouncements throughout the treatment and his impatience with the man was about to overcome his professionalism.

"Stay off your feet, and do not do anything that either requires your attention or draws too much attention to yourself."

"Right, doctor. Thank you for your generous care."

He attempted to rise to his feet for one of his standard Simon Piersall handshakes, but he could only make it part way before slumping backwards again.

The doctor had said his piece and with a nod to Mrs. Willman, he grabbed his hat and headed out the door.

"I'm afraid you're not going anywhere this evening, Mr. Piersall," said Mrs. Willman.

"Simon, call me Simon, please. And if you insist, well, I'm afraid that I must accept your offer of hospitality. But the pain is awful. Might you have a touch of whiskey in the house to soften the discomfort?"

There was the slightest pause before Mrs. Willman responded. Alcohol was illegal, and though news would sometimes make the rounds that a still had been busted by the federal agents, almost every homestead kept a small but guarded supply for "medical emergencies and the like," to use a common excuse.

"Yes, let me get some for you," she said.

Over the next several hours, Marty's desire for more information from Simon bordered on rudeness. He could feel his mother's scolding gaze while he peppered Simon with questions.

"Marty, Mr. Piersall needs to rest," she said repeatedly.

But in fact, the attention, combined with the lubricating effects of "medicinal" alcohol, seemed to energize Simon, and before long, a bond had been forged between the eccentric pilot and the curious youth.

"How did you learn to fly?"

"Well, young man, obviously I could use another lesson. Actually, you don't just 'learn to fly.' You just do it. A plane like that? You're on your own. You just step on the throttle and do it by feel, and if you crash, well then, you're one of the ones that ain't *meant* to fly to begin with, know what I mean?"

"You mean you didn't know how to fly."

Simon took another gulp of the whiskey. He then pushed himself forward off the couch and brought his voice down to a whisper.

"Son, I still don't know how to fly. And I ain't never gonna learn because what you saw there was my last flight," he said, with a sharp point to the floor.

"Then why did you start flying to begin with?"

"Let me share another secret with you, Martin." Marty liked the fact that Simon called him Martin. It made him feel more like an adult, which was something he didn't totally believe of himself yet.

"I've got a little bit of money under my feet. Oil money. In Texas, everybody is looking to top the next guy, and flying is the latest way to do it. So I got myself a plane, got me this flying suit, only one I could find in Texas, and flew around and waved to the other oil guys on the ground. Just to see the envy in their eyes as I flew around their oil fields was rich enough for me. You see, these guys want to own everything, but they can't own the sky, and I proved it to them. I only got it to show it off!"

He paused and lowered his voice. "But I've had enough. By the way, what part of Texas is this?"

"This is Louisiana."

"Louisiana! Guess I had a bit of a tailwind there. Oh my!"

As his long walk back from the barbershop neared its end, Frederick Willman's eyes opened wider. There was something unrecognizable in his front yard. The fading light made it difficult to make out from a distance. Was it a tractor, or some other motorized vehicle that Marty had rescued from the junkyard? He gave it a quizzical look and a wide berth as he proceeded to his front door. When he came in, Simon Piersall attempted once again to rise and shake the hand of his unwitting host and once again the pain in his head pushed him back down.

Marty excitedly described the events of the day to his father and then after a pause, Mr. Willman gave a very simple but sincere "Welcome" to Simon. The conversation continued.

"So you're not going to fly again?" asked Marty.

"No, never again."

"What are you going to do with the plane?"

"I'm gonna sell it. Don't know how I'll get it to market, but I don't want it anymore. I'm staying on the ground."

"I'll buy it!" said Marty.

There was silence. Stunned shocked silence as Marty's parents looked at him with complete bewilderment.

"Marty!" But that was all Mrs. Willman could say. It was clear that she couldn't even begin to figure out what her son was thinking.

"How much?"

"Martin, your enthusiasm is commendable, but I think you should respect the will of your parents."

"Dad, I can make this work. I'll fix it and make it work."

"And then what will you do?" Mr. Willman restrained himself. His nature was not to dampen his son's excitement.

"I...I don't know exactly. Maybe my leaflets. I don't know, but it's not worth anything the way it is, and if I can fix it, then I should get to buy it!"

"You're not going to fly a plane!" The concern in Mrs. Willman's voice changed the entire tone of the discussion.

"I didn't say I was going to fly the plane. Mom, just let me fix it."

Simon Piersall was smart enough to recognize ambition but not tip off his appreciation in front of Marty's parents. The boy reminded him of himself, when he first got into the oil business in the 1890s and scraped enough money together to drill a hole in the unforgiving Texas prairie.

◆   ◆   ◆

The few days that followed only strengthened the connection between Marty and Simon, but now Simon was ready to return home. Although he could have ordered a truck to transport the ragged machine back to his Texas home, he begged forgiveness for his inability to do so as he was departing. In fact, he knew this was Marty's ultimate hope. Now Marty would be able to tow the thing into the backyard and pick it apart until there was nothing he didn't understand about it.

A long black vehicle arrived at the Willman driveway, summoned by Piersall Enterprises to carry their leader back by land. After expressing effusive appreciation to Mr. and Mrs. Willman, Simon pulled Marty aside.

"Martin, I would respectfully suggest that you do not share the following information I am about to give you with your parents."

Marty nodded.

"If you can get that thing to fly, it's yours. Here is my address. I want you to write to me, and I want to know exactly what you decide to do with it. I can help you, Martin."

"You already have helped me, Mr. Piersall. Thank you," said Marty, with tremendous gratitude but enough reserve that, from a distance, his parents wouldn't suspect anything other than a polite farewell.

They shook hands for a final time. A businesslike handshake, like the business partners they had now become. And with a final salute to Marty's parents in the distance, Simon hobbled into the rear seat of the vehicle.

The driver shut the door and returned to the wheel, and the car sped off, kicking dust into the cotton fields all the way back to Texas.

3

In late May, the government arrived in Oak Ridge. The boll weevil infestation had become a crisis, and agents from the Department of Agriculture were fanning out across the Mississippi delta to implement the only chance of overcoming the scourge. Each farmer had been allocated a supply of calcium arsenate, a newly created compound—an *insecticide*—that had proven successful in lab tests and on small plots of land. Whether it was strong enough to stem the destruction across the South was unknown.

All of the Feds had been trained to demonstrate the common method of application with expert precision. It involved a 40-pound cylindrical iron tank that was first pumped by hand to create internal pressure. A long spray wand was attached to the top of the tank and then the tank itself was strapped to the back of the farmer and carried into the fields. Farmers were to don a mask to minimize the ingestion of the deadly poison as they waved the wand and released the spray over each row of crops.

Grateful as they were, the job of applying the calcium arsenate to their entire farm was an overwhelming task, but the three farmers in the small town of Oak Ridge had no choice. They were on the verge of losing their entire crop, and so the unearthly sight of the masked and encumbered farmers became commonplace as they methodically attempted to complete a few rows of dusting each day in the growing heat of the late spring. It was not a good time to be a farmer.

Martin Willman remained joyfully oblivious to it all. He was making great progress, having completed the disassembly of the entire engine of the biplane and the cataloging of each part. Some of the parts were completely unrecognizable to Marty so he made up an easy to remember name. Then he cleaned and polished each of them to a perfect luster, completely removing any residue. His backyard had become a small construction site with a canopy fashioned out of a large canvas tarp to protect the engine from the spring rains.

One day a parcel arrived by mail truck. It was a small, but very heavy crate with a brand on the outside that said Piersall Enterprises. Marty pried open the crate with a crowbar and pulled out a metal box. He then opened the box to reveal a set of gleaming gunmetal tools. Aircraft tools, with a small note lying on top.

Martin,

These are for you, for the job at hand.

Best of luck,
Simon Piersall

The timing of this delivery was quite fortunate. Marty had begun reassembling some of the pistons, but tightening them was another problem he hadn't figured out yet. As he worked his way through his own analysis of the tools, he discovered that each of them was perfectly fitted for the various bolts, nuts and screws that solidified the machine. Beyond their functional purpose, the tools gave Marty an even greater sense of ownership of the aircraft. Now he was no longer just an aircraft hobbyist with a yard full of parts. These tools were valuable and unique, but most importantly, they were the necessary accompaniment to his most essential asset as an aviation businessman, this being the job title he had secretly bestowed upon himself.

"Businessman" was a fitting title for the young man, for Marty Willman was not an inventor, not an innovator and nowhere near an artist. His skill was in the application of innovations. He could take an entire engine apart and understand everything about it, but he was not capable of making it better. Still, with understanding came confidence and with confidence came vision. And he had just enough vision to figure out how to put the thing back together.

Marty faced numerous obstacles as he rebuilt the machine, but the most challenging was the final one: Getting the completed engine back inside the airplane. To accomplish this task, he first located a heavy length of rope from his father's dormant store of farming implements. Then he tossed one end of the rope over a massive branch of the large magnolia tree that stood in the center of their backyard. The engine sat on a heavy piece of tarp. Marty took the hanging end of the rope and looped it through three holes he had made in the corners of the tarp, creating a sling for the engine. Then with the help of his father, he took the other end of the rope and hoisted the completed engine a few inches into the air, just enough to swing it directly below the branch of the magnolia. But this is where his innovation ended and the obstacle began. The engine was far too heavy to lift it any higher.

"What now, Marty?" asked his father.

There were many times that Frederick Willman would ask his son a question even if he already had an answer to it. It was his way of generating thought and triggering ideas in Marty. But this time his son had no answer, just a grimace of frustration that only his father could resolve.

"I've got an idea," said the elder.

Deep among the refuse of farming equipment, far to the back of the garage, there sat a now obsolete tractor. Because of its obsolescence—its large metal rear wheels reminiscent of a tank from the Great War; its narrow width, capable of tilling no more than a seven-foot wide row at a time—it was of no interest to Owen Becker when he acquired the surrounding land. Just getting it out of the garage was a project in itself. It had accumulated a layer of mold and rot over its red rusting skin that seemed but one step away from turning to a pile of dust. Marty and his father looped a length of rope around the lone front wheel and pulled, dragging the beast toward the front door of the garage. Buckets, cans, hardware and other garage detritus clattered to the wooden floor as the tractor below them broke free from its long held resting-place.

Once outside the garage, Frederick stepped back and looked the thing over. So many years he had spent riding this tractor, filling the coffers with cotton for the country, a painful relic of a long lost livelihood.

"Start it up, Dad!" said Marty. He knew his father was thinking about the loss of the farm and he wanted to keep his attention on the immediate task at hand.

"You think this thing will start, Marty?"

"Why not? It's only been three years."

Frederick circled the tractor once, as if it were an ornery head of cattle that needed breaking. He mounted it and reached down to the choke, cranking it four times, the way he had always done it years ago. He stepped on the gas pedal. Nothing.

"Naah, she's dead."

"Try again, Dad."

He went through the same sequence again, and where before there was absolute rusted silence, suddenly there was a sputter and a jerk forward. Frederick pushed the clutch in, and another sputter, followed by two more very close together.

And then she was alive.

A broad smile worked its way across Frederick's mouth, his tongue protruding from his bout of concentration as was his habit when he cut the hair of the townspeople. But now, as the tractor roared to life beneath him, he was not cutting hair.

Marty laughed and then so did his dad as they looked at each other, father and son like children again. Dust and carcasses of long dead insects danced off the shaking rusted hood of the deafening machine. Frederick put the tractor in gear and it jerked forward again, resuming a methodical march that had ended with the buyout years ago. He pulled the large steering wheel to his right, taking it on a long circular loop toward the backyard and the magnolia, back in the saddle of his machine as if he'd never left. The noise brought Mrs. Willman out of the house.

"Frederick, what are you doing with that thing?"

"Thought I'd get back on to the farm, darling," he said with a smile, but she couldn't hear him. She looked on for a moment more and gave him a contemptuous wave for his foolishness before going back into the house. Once under the tree, Marty fastened the other end of the rope to the rear of the tractor and signaled his father to start forward.

The tractor strained at first, but its heavy rear wheels drove the machine forward and within a few seconds the airplane engine and the sling that carried it rose with a dangle into the air. Marty steadied it, and when it reached eye level, he signaled his father to stop. The tractor sputtered to a halt. They had done it. The engine was poised for placement.

Now they just needed to move the hollow biplane into position below the slowly twirling block of iron. This was the easy part. They each lifted one side of the rear stabilizer, pulled it backward so as to get the right angle for the magnolia, and eased it underneath the engine.

Marty had repaired the wing fabric and hammered out the dents in the metal surfaces of the fuselage. It was now fully ready to be reunited with its source of power. He opened the side engine cover and then neatly placed his wrench on a footstool along with the 12 bolts that would hold the engine in place. Then when everything was exactly where it needed to be, his father remounted the tractor. There was no need to start it up again; all his father needed to do was gradually release the brake. With a metal squeal, the tractor inched backward and the engine descended slowly into the nose of the plane. Marty guided it in, just barely avoiding the loss of fingers as it settled onto the metal framework that would once again support it. The holes in the engine block and eyelets within the frame lined up close enough for Marty to insert the bolts and tighten them halfway. He cut away the tarp with a knife and pulled it and the rope free of the aircraft. It wasn't lined up, but he was able slide the engine a minuscule amount with a shove in each direction, just enough to perfect the alignment for the bolts and tighten them down to the frame. He then connected the hose leading from the fuel tank and tightened the pedal rod that would feed the fuel into the engine.

The tractor had done its job. Frederick looked on with pride as his son put the final touches on the completed airplane.

Marty unwrapped the eight-foot span of wooden propeller that he had polished and covered in cloth to protect it from insects. Together, they placed it on the hexagonal shaft that protruded from the center of the nose. Marty inserted the single thick metal bolt that served as the pin, holding the propeller in place. He then replaced the cowling, a rounded three-quarter hoop of sheet metal that fit behind the propeller and protected the pistons from the elements.

The young man had not expected to accomplish this much in a single day, a day that was fast approaching its end. The sunlight was already grazing the cotton to the west, but his excitement would not let him stop. He directed his father back to the rear of the aircraft and together they pushed it into an empty swath of bare ground that connected to the road out in front of the house. A flicker of concern came across his father's face.

"What now, Marty? All finished, right?"

"I'm just going to start it up, Dad," he said.

"It's all done. You can sell it for Mr. Piersall now, Marty. You're done."

"Ain't no one going to buy it unless it works, right, Dad?"

"Marty."

"Dad, I'm just going to start it. Don't worry."

"Marty!"

But the moment they put the tail down, his son was up on the wing and vaulting into the cockpit.

"Dad, I need you to pull the propeller."

"Do what?"

"Just get out front and pull the propeller down hard so I can start it."

Frederick knew that if he didn't do it, Marty would find some way to have it done. Even if it was under the cover of darkness, he would rig up some propeller-pulling contraption that would allow him to start up the plane all by himself, and because he wanted to be present in his son's adventures, he knew that the boy's determination and excitement left him no choice. He came around to the front of the aircraft, and at Marty's signal, he pulled on one of the propeller blades with a downward thrust before jumping backward.

The engine sprang to life with no hesitation. It had been repaired as if new, and now every essential intent of every gleaming part was being perfectly met in unison. The propeller spun to a blur in seconds, and the engine roared with a powerful whine that brought Mrs. Willman back out of the house.

"No!!" she screamed.

Marty's intense study of the machine yielded a complete understanding of each and every control and gauge. He knew exactly what each lever and pedal was supposed to do, but what he didn't know was the level of responsiveness. His parents were yelling now, in a state of escalating panic for their son. He couldn't hear them, and he didn't look at them, well aware of what they were saying and what they feared. But he also knew that if he got out of the plane now, they would never let him back in. With all of his senses focused ahead, he eased the plane forward onto the road and pointed it toward the sun at the end of it.

Marty Willman had to fly. That was all there was to it. He throttled the engine, released the brake, and to the horror of his parents, began to roll forward. Fifty yards down the road the tail wheel bounced and then elevated. He felt the road bumping below, faster and faster, and then suddenly he felt nothing. He was off the ground, probably by mere inches, now moving at a speed he'd never experienced before.

The road was cresting ahead of him. He did not expect to reach this part of the road so quickly, but even worse, he had not expected an automobile to be approaching on the other side of the hill. A Model A was kicking up its own tail of dust and heading right for him, the eyes of the driver in a sudden state of absolute terror. Marty pulled up on the controls with just yards to spare, vaulting the biplane almost straight up. In the split second that followed he pushed the stick forward, easing the plane to level.

He was flying.

Flying over the cotton fields of Louisiana, flying over the scattered homes of Oak Ridge, flying high enough to keep the sun from setting.

He climbed higher and circled around. Down below, he could see the small figures of his parents; his mother hanging onto his father in a state of sustained panic. The garage to one side. The magnolia like a small umbrella over the backyard. The little red tractor and the dangling rope with a shred of tarp, all like little toys near a farmhouse. In the distance, he saw the breadth of the cotton farms, the domain of the farmers who ruled the town. Or at least, they once did.

He was flying a plane, his plane. And though he would manage to land it safely that evening, Martin Willman's soul would remain aloft for the rest of his life.

4

Marty flew a few more times in the days following his inaugural jaunt. He even took up some leaflets, a remnant of his rocket idea, and dropped them from the plane. It was a test leaflet, with the words "If found, return to Marty Willman, Oak Ridge—Louisiana." The results were disappointing, with a few of the prospective "customers" expecting some type of monetary reward for the effort of returning them. Regrettably, his return rate was too low to justify the cost in gasoline to fly the plane. On top of that, the local police had presented Marty with a traffic summons for repeated use of the roadway as an airplane runway. There wasn't anything on the county law books that specifically governed airplanes on the roads, so Marty was assessed a $10 fine for "speeding," which wiped out his remaining money for gasoline. By the beginning of June, his plane came to an extended rest under the magnolia.

Summer arrived, and as the plague of boll weevils overran the delta, the drifting smell of calcium arsenate became part of the Oak Ridge landscape.

On July 1st, 1922, the insects claimed their first casualty. Moses Parker, a large and proud member of the farming triumvirate, had succumbed to a massive heart attack in his fields. He was a big man as it was, but the people of Oak Ridge knew that the weight of his forty-pound iron tank and the stress of the battle were the true cause of his death. His son found him face down among the rows of struggling cotton, the heavy tank pressing his torso into the damp soil like a giant thumb.

The town was on edge. The death of Moses Parker was bad enough, but now economic failure was beginning to ripple slowly through the streets. The shops and services began to lose customers as everyone tightened their belts. Even Frederick Willman's modest little barbershop was not spared. People still needed haircuts, just not as often as they used to, or at least that's what they told him.

On a somber and sweltering 4th of July, the entire town turned out for the funeral of farmer Parker, a "man of dignity, well-known and beloved by many". The women and children sat while the men stood at the back of the filled-to-capacity Baptist church that marked the geographic center of Oak Ridge.

Marty found himself between his father and a federal agent who had come to know Moses over the last six months. He quietly introduced himself to the agent and started a conversation.

"How did it happen?" whispered Marty.

"Keeled over in the field. I know it was hard for him."

"Hard? What was hard?"

"The dusting. It takes its toll. Summer time. Those tanks. Not being able to breathe. Moses especially, being his size and all."

Application, not innovation; that was Marty's strength, and now the seed of an idea was planted and starting to grow.

"What if we poured the stuff out of a plane?" asked Marty.

"You can't just pour it out, you gotta spray it. And you gotta hit all of the plants."

"We could spray it. Somehow, we could spray it."

"We are spraying it. Whattaya mean, kid?"

"From a plane. We could spray it from a plane."

"Who's gotta plane?"

The sobs softly echoed through the church between the reverend's exhortations. The sermon reached a crescendo. Marty waited for the first pause. He lowered his voice and said with the confidence of a businessman, "I've got a plane."

Now, the agent made eye contact with him. He didn't say anything. His initial expression was one of skepticism, but it was fleeting, turning serious in response to Marty's look of determination. The agent was almost twice his age, but he had a need, and Marty might be the man—even if he was a kid—to fulfill it. The agent looked back up at the reverend and discreetly extended his right hand without making eye contact.

"Stanford Pate," he whispered. Then he handed him a business card with the U.S. Department of Agriculture shield on it.

"Be at this address tomorrow morning at nine."

◆   ◆   ◆

Within a week, Stanford Pate had secured funding from Washington to test the feasibility of "air-dusting," as he called it. But Marty was way ahead of him, having borrowed a nearly fresh tank of calcium arsenate, the one off Moses Parker's dead body, which he inserted lengthwise into the rear fuselage of the airplane. He then fashioned a rickety mechanism that would allow him to activate the spraying function from his seat in the cockpit. It was not the best engineering he'd ever done, but his purpose was not perfection at this stage, it was execution. If he could prove that it would work, there would inevitably be better ways to make it work. Application, not innovation.

His first flight with the spray was like his first ever flight: devoid of any intelligent planning. As had become his custom, he dragged the plane up the road to the top of the hill. This was the only way he could be sure there were neither cars nor police in sight. When he took off, he circled the area once and then came down toward Farmer Becker's field near the area that surrounded the Willman house. Becker was out in the field, underneath his mask and his tank, waving his wand with the diligence and calculation of a true German. Marty spotted him from high above, brought the plane down to just eight feet high and skimmed across the field toward the unwary farmer.

Becker had always been thorough, and as Marty approached, he was holding his wand pointed downward to a small but infested area of cotton just below him. The farmer could see the weevils coursing through the plant, and though this one was as good as dead, his obsession with killing the insects and watching them die had momentarily consumed him.

The plane came out of nowhere, unleashing a blanket of dust so thick that Becker didn't even see what had happened. The origin of the cloud around him was a mystery, until it settled and he saw the biplane on a steep climb, already hundreds of yards away, cresting the magnolia in the Willman backyard. Moments later it was coming back.

Becker's eyes widened under his mask as a tail of fog began to spew from the oncoming plane. He threw himself to the ground in fear and was soon covered in a second cloud that left him gagging and coughing in anger.

Aloft, Marty forgave himself for the mild pangs of revenge he let get the best of him. Besides, he was helping Becker save his farm. No harm in that. This thought triggered a bout of laughter as he circled for another pass to the now screaming farmer.

"Get off my land! You do not own this land. Get off it."

Such claims of ownership were forgivable in a day when air and land had yet to be customarily separated by the miracle of flight.

The days that followed brought engineers from Washington D.C. who arrived with custom-fitted calcium arsenate tanks based on the specifications of Marty's biplane. After they completed the modifications to the plane, under the careful supervision of its owner and Stanford Pate, Marty would no longer need to pull a cable to activate the spraying function. It was simply the flick of a switch that generated a liberal blanket of spray well beyond the volume that any wand could produce.

On a sunny July day, with the airplane ready for operation, a demonstration was held to show the farmers and other interested townspeople how dusting by air could save tremendous amounts of time. The test site was the farm of Moses Parker, now owned by his reluctant son. In attendance and full of skepticism was Owen Becker, despite being a witness to the very first aerial crop dusting in history.

"Interested Townspeople" was what the poster announcing the event had proclaimed, but this was clearly redundant. They were all interested. Stanford Pate opened up the festivities to the surprisingly large gathering of 80 townspeople, many still in mourning for the proprietor.

"Ladies and gentleman of Oak Ridge! As you know, the Mississippi delta is faced with a deadly infestation of the cotton crop, a bounty that is the very foundation of Oak Ridge and hundreds of other towns throughout the south land. We have devised a poison to ward off the deadly scourge, but the cost has been heavy."

He removed his hat and placed it over his heart, the message being that Moses was among the victims of the insect.

"Oh, so very heavy. But now we wish to demonstrate to you how the dusting of a field like this, which today requires the vigorous actions of three men working twelve-hour days for a total of four weeks to fully apply the poison, may now be completed by one man within ten minutes!"

Marty was already aloft, having taken off at the stroke of noon from his usual runway a few miles away. At 500 feet, he had seen Stanford remove his hat, the signal to begin his dive.

"Ladies and gentleman, behold the newest of agricultural technology."

The onlookers at the edge of the field turned toward the whine of the engines just in time to see the plane bearing down on them. They instinctively ducked as a group and watched in awe as Marty brought the plane into skimming distance of the crop; at the same time, he unleashed a blanket of arsenate dust. In seconds he had reached the end of the farm and brought the plane into a steep climb before diving back to the next row of cotton.

"That's the Willman boy, ain't it?" someone asked.

"Must be. He's the only one crazy nuf to do it! Look at 'em go!" said someone else.

The people's awe had barely subsided when smiles began to appear, all tilted upward toward the plane as it gracefully made its way back and forth across the Parker farm. It was like a miracle.

"A miracle for Moses!" yelled one of the townspeople.

The plane completed dusting the field, made a smooth landing on the nearby road, and was soon engulfed by the excited crowd with a joy reserved for the second coming. And for some of the more religious, it *had* come to pass; Marty was going to end the plague.

Only one of the flock did not smile. Owen Becker was still stewing about the "attack" the Willman boy had made upon him and his land. Steadfast in his denial, he finally walked stubbornly toward the plane behind the cheering townspeople.

The event was a success. Marty began to lay the groundwork for his enterprise. Negotiations between Stanford Pate and two of the three farmers started the following morning. Pate had blocked an hour's worth of time with each of the farmers at a small town hall office. Three hours, one for each of the farmers, with the last hour reserved for Becker.

On this most important day of his young life, Martin Willman rose with excitement before the sun. He dressed in his Sunday three-piece suit with a perfectly knotted bow tie. He generously wetted his hair and combed it back—anything to look older than the 20 years of age he had just turned—and borrowed a slightly weathered but still presentable straw hat from his father. Before walking out the door, he looked at himself in the mirror, and finally, after at least ten minutes and a few curious looks from his mother and father, he was convinced of his appearance as a businessman.

His first meeting was with the Parker boy, Joshua, son of Moses. Only 18, but growing daily in confidence amid the grieving of his family, Joshua Parker had confronted the inevitable; he would be the proprietor of the farm his father and grandfather had so devoutly tilled.

Pate wisely set up the meeting with Parker first, aware that both the boys were close in age, both on the verge of true manhood. If all went well, Marty's enthusiasm would inject Joshua with a seed of confidence, which in turn would give Marty the necessary boost for his later meetings.

"How are you, Josh? How's the family holding up?"

"It's tough, Marty. Mom's been waking up at night, worrying what'll happen next. She's still in a bad way."

"Well, we're gonna fix that, Josh. We're gonna make that farm of yours come around so you won't ever have to worry about it again."

Pate had expected to be running each of these meetings on behalf of the young aviator, but it only took a few moments before he realized he was in the midst of a natural salesman. He became as enthralled as Marty's customer, engrossed in a sales pitch full of comfort, security, happiness—an emotional message that conveyed everything that Joshua Parker and his family needed at that very moment.

"Stanford, why don't you give our friend Mr. Parker the details on the financing and subsidy."

Pate was shaken from his trance. He fumbled with his files before locating the draft of the agreement. Suddenly he was the willing administrative assistant to Martin Willman, sole proprietor of the first ever aircraft crop dusting operation. With the acceptance of the terms and the signature of Joshua Parker, a business was born.

The next meeting with Flanagan Otman was even more pointed. Marty was brimming with confidence, highlighting the schedule, procedure and terms of agreement from memory, but all in the homespun manner of the Oak Ridge way of life. His father's words came back to him now: "You should always make your customer feel important, no matter what you think of them."

Another signature, another customer.

Finally it was time for Becker. Marty was conscious of his own feelings about Becker and especially about the sudden shift of the ledger toward his favor. In spite of his underlying feelings of revenge toward the man who had humiliated his father, he promised himself that he would approach Becker as he would any other customer. He would not lower himself to that level; he would not initiate a feud. He was a businessman now, and the sweetest revenge would be to have Becker as a customer. But Owen Becker did not show up that morning.

"Two customers to start. Not bad, Marty. I think we're on our way."

"We need all of them, Stanford. All three of them. No reason for Becker not to show up, at least to discuss things."

"Do you think he's still angry with you?" asked Pate.

"He might be, but we need to put that aside, Stanford. This is business. He needs us and we need him. Let's close up shop and pay Mr. Becker a personal visit."

At the front door, Marty removed his hat in deference to the Becker household and so Pate did the same.

"Hello, Mrs. Becker, is Mr. Becker in?" Marty played the part of polite neighbor for Mrs. Becker.

"Oh hello, Marty. I'm afraid he is out on the farm right now."

"I see. All right, thank you, ma'am. I just wanted to personally apologize to him for the other day and make him an offer of compensation."

Marty had spotted the tractor behind the house, along with the spraying tank. He knew Becker couldn't be out in the fields, and a moment later he knew he was right. Becker was at the door in his undershirt.

"What offer are you talking about, boy?"

"Hello, Mr. Becker. Please accept my sincere apologies for my behavior." There was a long silence. Becker was waiting for the second part of the offer. Pate was ready to leave.

"Okay, and?" asked Becker.

"And, I'd like to provide you with a chance to save your farm. Get it back to profitability and increase its productivity. May we come in, sir?"

"What, with your damn airplane. No kid is coming on my property to fly a plane around it. I can do it myself. I don't need your help."

Becker slammed the door. Marty turned to Pate with a smile. "Well, what do you know about that. Our first dissatisfied customer."

"He really isn't much of customer, Marty," said Pate.

Marty smiled; a confident grin of certainty as he replaced the hat on his head. "If he ain't gonna be a customer, Stan, he ain't gonna be in business."

Two customers were better than nothing, and through the remainder of that summer, Marty began to see the slightest stream of money come from the government in support of the dusting. His new standing in the town had also allowed him to negotiate an agreement with local law enforcement to use the stretch of road in front of his house as a runway. In fact, the town had no choice; this was their only chance for survival. In exchange, he promised to schedule his take off and landings at opportune times and take off from the crest of the hill to avoid any unseen automobiles.

Much of the cotton crop had been destroyed beyond repair in the spring, but enough had been salvaged to get Otman and Parker through the winter and raise just enough hope among the townspeople that next year would be even better.

Becker was another story. He finished out the year on his own, continuing his stubborn refusal of Marty's services. He sprayed his wand as much as he could, but he could not compete with the blanket of dust that fell in minutes among his rival farms. His production crashed, and by the fall of 1922, he was on the verge of bankruptcy, his harvest virtually eliminated.

It was an early September morning when his wife came upon a ghastly and tragic discovery in their tool shed. Owen Becker had shoved the long wand of the sprayer down his throat and turned it on full force, filling his gullet with lethal concentrations of calcium arsenate.

Two months later, sufficient time for the shock to wear off, Marty tapped into his now substantial savings and quietly bought the Becker farm. On Christmas day 1922, he led his father toward the back door.

"I have a present for you, Dad."

"What is it, Marty? What you got up your sleeve, boy?"

Marty kicked open the back door and with a wave of his hand, presented the family farm back to his father.

"It's yours, Dad. Yours again."

Marty's mother collapsed in tears on her husband's shoulder.

"Frederick, the farm. Your farm!" she cried.

For the first time in his memory, Marty saw something new in his father. The man who had become known throughout the town for his unchanging state of stoic affability was now welling up in a joyous combination of tears and pride.

"Better get that tractor going again, Dad. And tell everyone they're going to need to find someone else to cut their hair!"

5

As Marty approached his second summer of business in 1923, it was clear that he could no longer get by being known simply as the local crop duster in Oak Ridge. The success of his operation brought him customers throughout central Louisiana. Now it was time to give his enterprise a name, and like most of his business decisions, Marty didn't dwell on this one.

"Alta Air Service," he said one day to his father.

"What does that mean?"

"It's the name off your old tractor, Dad. The one that helped us put the plane back together."

"Alta? You mean the company that made the tractor?"

"Yes. I like the name. It's a strong name, just like that little red machine."

"What about the company that already has the name? Don't they need to give you permission to use it?" his father asked.

"Long gone. Stanford Pate did a check for me. They went out of business in 1911. I own the name now." Frederick Willman could only shake his head and smile. His boy was hitting his stride and now all he could do was keep out of the way.

"Alta Air Service. Yes, it does sound kind of catchy," said the elder Willman.

◆　　　◆　　　◆

Marty's hard work and determination carried him through the 1920s. His fleet grew from the single plane that had crashed into his yard, to a robust fleet of 12 aircraft. But there was a flaw in the business that Marty recognized early on. The Alta Air Service crop dusting business was eternally seasonal, generating revenue in the spring and summer, but nothing through the fall and winter. This led Marty on the path toward alternate uses of his aircraft during the off season.

If his business was going to grow, crop dusting was only going to take him so far. The next logical step was to move into transportation, which would require the acquisition of a federal contract to deliver mail and with it, permissions to land in other towns and cities. Marty felt reasonably certain that Alta Air Service could handle the run from Fort Worth, Texas to Atlanta, Georgia and all points in between, but the two major air services in the country had already been fighting each other viciously for the right to secure this contract, with each effectively lining up allies in both political parties to the point of stalemate. Clearly, these airlines had a well-established lock on the postmaster general, which created a near hopeless cause for Marty's marginal crop dusting unit.

All of this haggling took place during the scandalous summer of 1924, when the story broke that money had passed from a few of the great oil barons of the West into the hands of President Harding's administration in exchange for the land they now drilled. Only two such land leases had been discovered, the more noteworthy being the one for the Teapot Dome reserve, the plot of land that leant the scandal its name. But these discoveries triggered a cover-up involving numerous arrangements between oil companies and the Republican dominated government that no one outside of Texas knew about.

Simon Piersall was in Texas, and he knew about them all.

Warren Harding was already one year in the grave, leaving President Coolidge in the unenviable position of snuffing out an inherited scandal during an election year. With a single phone call to the White House from Simon Piersall, Marty Willman had his mail route, and by the fall of 1924, two of the Alta Air Service biplanes were crisscrossing the south, each of their hollow fuselages stuffed with mail bags.

The pace picked up as the year drew to a close. The enthusiastic youth from Oak Ridge now entered the local bank in his newest three-piece suit, a man of burgeoning power, prestige and reserve. He had *the* federal contract and with it would come enough capital to purchase a fleet of modern aircraft that would carry not only mail, but people; *monoplanes* with twin engines.

After much research and observation he decided on Curtiss-Wright Aircraft, five of them, shiny and new. They were called Whirlwinds as a way of promoting their unique engine technology. Marty was particularly interested in one important feature: the first ever air-cooled engine, an important consideration for the southern route he'd be serving. He had all of them painted dark blue and orange, a balance, he felt, between visibility and conservatism.

In the spring of 1925, Marty's air service carried its first passenger, a federal agent assigned to assess the cotton industry that year. Because Alta was already an essential part of the upswing in cotton, Marty came to know all of the Feds who oversaw the farmlands of the Mississippi delta, and they knew him, if for no other reason than as the savior of an entire cotton crop just three years earlier. As passenger service grew, Marty retained the habit of meeting these men for many of their arrivals and departures, and coddling them with the help of the ground crews at each airport.

"Tommy, help this fine gentleman with his luggage, will you please?"

"Henry, please see that this fine gentleman receives a comfortable flight to Birmingham."

And with a wink to his subordinate, everything was understood, and all would be taken care of. Marty was, in effect, enlisting all of these "fine gentlemen" from Washington as his own lobbyists, knowing they would return to their various agencies, administrations and bureaucracies with nice things to say about the airline. It was good business; a lesson learned from watching his father in the barbershop. But in Marty's case, as the well-dressed and cordial founder of an airline, the shackles of subservience had been all but erased. Still, the most important business lesson Marty had learned from his father was the constant proximity to failure that any corporation faced. No business was immune, calling for the highest levels of conservatism even in the prosperous decade of the 1920s.

By 1929, Marty had a dozen aircraft serving eight cities between Fort Worth and Atlanta. With 55 people on his payroll, he had established himself as an important part of the community, if not the entire region. But October of that year brought a disaster of unimaginable force. The Great Depression blindsided the entire country, thrusting the business community into a new world of pain, bankruptcies and poverty.

The fledgling operation had moved to nearby Monroe, where they constructed a small whitewashed brick terminal (the white seemed to make it look bigger), that doubled as a headquarters. Out on the airfield was a large sheet metal structure that served as the airline's first hangar. Three of the Curtiss's were usually housed in the hangar at any one time with mechanics poring over each facet of the engines on a daily basis.

On October 30, 1929, Marty summoned his entire staff of 55 people to Monroe. All flights were canceled and all aircraft were ordered to return to the small headquarters. It was the night before Halloween, and people were scared for reasons that had nothing to do with costumes.

The purpose of the company meeting was twofold. First, a full inventory of the corporation's assets was needed so that Marty could have a clear understanding of the value of his enterprise. By bringing his entire fleet home to Monroe, he minimized the risk of seizure and repossession. Second, he needed to make an announcement to his employees or "his people," as he preferred to call them.

A hard rain fell in the afternoon as the employees huddled nervously in the hangar a few hours in advance of the 5:00 p.m. speech by their leader. The clatter of the downpour on the metal roof was deafening at times, increasing the sense of gloom. Rumors abounded: bankruptcy, mass firings, liquidation.

The rain slowed to a drizzle, and at precisely five o'clock, Martin Willman climbed onto the third step of a small stepladder used by the mechanics. The people hushed.

"Is everyone here? Steve, did we get everyone in okay?"

"Yeah, boss, I think we got everyone. Anyone know of anyone missing?" Steve asked the crowd.

No response.

"Okay then."

He paused, just for a moment, and shifted his feet slightly to maintain his balance. Marty liked to use his hands when he talked, and this ladder wasn't the best podium he'd ever had.

"As you all know, our country has fallen into a crisis of large proportion. President Coolidge once said, 'the business of this country is business,' but now our businesses are faced with a great depression in their value. And this means we face it too, because if they can't do business, they ain't going to be traveling anywhere. So what are we going to do about it?"

Marty made sure his emphasis was on the "we" as he said the word and waited a moment for an answer he knew wouldn't come.

"I got a call from one of my bankers the other day. Hal Davis, over at Great Plains National. They're good people, and they been good to us. But Hal says he wants to know how much that plane over there is worth." He pointed across the hangar to one of the Whirlwinds.

"He says to me, 'Marty, I know you ain't gonna be able to keep making those payments with all that's goin on, so I was just checking to see.'"

The people in the hangar were entranced, deeply under the spell of their leader.

"I says to him, 'Hal, if I give you that plane, what the hell are you gonna do with it?' He says to me, 'I'm gonna sell it.' I says to him, 'and who you gonna sell it to? An airline maybe?' Well, it gets real quiet on the other end of the line. Not a peep coming out of that horn. So I decide to let old Hal off the hook. I says to him, 'Hal, I know things are as tough for you as they are for me, and I'm not all that sure we're going to be able to make every payment exactly on time. But I'll tell you this. My people are the best there is, and if anyone is going to make the money to pay you for them airplanes, it's my people. So how bout you just let me hold on to them for a bit and we'll see what kind of money they can make for the both of us?'"

Marty stopped for a moment. Here stood a man, still well shy of 30, but with a seasoned charisma that made age irrelevant. There was total silence in the hangar. Each and every face was locked on his, each in a state of total and absolute attention to every word and nuance. He scanned his legions, looked humbly down at his feet again, and then back up before he resumed, his voice now lowered to a dramatic effect.

"I said, 'Listen, Hal, if you don't give my people a chance, this airline is as good as dead. You don't want that on your conscience, I know you don't.' Well, folks…" still another dramatic pause. "…he agreed to let us keep our planes."

This was followed by an audible expulsion of relief from the gathering.

"Just to put your minds at ease, because I know you must be feeling a tad uneasy coming here without knowing what for, I think you will agree with me when I say we are all in this together. This is why you should know that nobody is being let go here today, because we need all of you. Every one of you! But now, we've got to work harder than ever to make our airline the best there is. Now, we've got to make every single one of our passengers say they will use us whenever and wherever they can!"

His voice rose to a crescendo, igniting an evangelic devotion in his followers that grew from their momentous relief.

"Now, let me say this, and this is important. I just want to tell you all how proud I am to be working with you. And I want to thank you for coming, for some of you as far away as Georgia, to listen to me here today. Now go home to your families, to your husbands and your wives, to your children and your parents, and tell them that everything is going to work out. Everything is going to be okay. Go on now." And he waved them off with a paternal flick of his hand as if shooing the children out of the house.

They were standing already, but now they all stood a little taller as they clapped, during what would have been a standing ovation either way. As the buoyant crowd filed out of the hangar, the sun broke through the clouds just over the horizon. They were his for life.

It hardly mattered that there was no such person as Hal Davis.

6

The 1930s arrived with a cloud of dust, and Alta Air Service, or as Marty liked to think of it, the Alta family, was under siege. Naturally, like so many families facing the Great Depression, these challenges only drew them closer. Martin Willman's commitment to his employees flowed downward. He made a point of learning their names, all 55 of them, and then he tried to learn the names of their immediate family members.

"Bobby, how you doing today?" he would say to one of the cleaning crew.

"Oh not bad, Mr. Willman, thanks for asking."

"And how is Lillian?"

"She's all right, sir. Baby due next month."

"Ah, well that's wonderful, Bobby. You be sure and keep us up to date on that now."

"Yessir, Mr. Willman."

So maybe her name was Lila instead of Lillian, and maybe he'd forgotten about the baby, but it didn't matter in the least. Marty expressed sincerity every time he came across one of his people. And though he was sincere and heartfelt, his "way" with his people was as much good business as the purchase of a plane. While the country came apart around them, he was steadfast and plainspoken, standing by his pledge to keep his people employed in spite of the financial pressures.

Marty knew his role by instinct. He had long ago mastered the art of influencing people, and a fundamental basis of this was the ability to relate to his employees as if on an equal footing. He retained the modest title of general manager, delegating anything that required the sharing of unpalatable information to his second-in-command, a scholarly young man by the name of Winfield Neagle, his chief financial officer.

"A big title for a big man, Winn," he told him upon his promotion.

"Thank you, sir."

Winfield had been with him for just two years since he completed his post graduate studies at the Louisiana State University. Marty considered him a financial genius and that's exactly what he wanted. Winfield was younger than many of the employees who had been with the company for the last half decade, but

Marty was smart enough to know what he didn't know. He paid a personal visit to him in the spring of 1928 and signed him to a contract on the spot.

Soon after his arrival, Winfield Neagle's role expanded well beyond financial management. As the right-hand man to the founder, owner and general manager of the company, Winfield provided Marty with the perfect foil, the belt-tightening bearer of bad news whenever it needed to be borne. Though they were only a year apart, the perception was of two men representing different generations. Winfield, at 27 years of age, could pass for 21. In contrast, Marty at 28 years old when the decade turned looked older than his years. His gestures and language were naturally paternal, and this gave him increasingly greater influence with both his employees and his investors. And now more than ever that influence was being put to the test.

"Winn, how do you plan to squeeze us through the winter?" It was October 1930 when Marty posed the question during their daily closed-door meeting.

"Well, sir, I propose a fleet reduction to start. There is a carrier in South America that may be a good prospect to assume payments on three of the Curtiss's."

"We can look at that. What does that save us?"

"If they buy them, that'll take $10,000 off our books right away. Add to that the corresponding employee reduction..."

"There ain't gonna be no employee reduction, Winn."

"Sir, we can't keep all of our people if we don't have the flights for them to service."

"Winn, there ain't gonna be no employee reduction." This was the non-negotiable barrier between Marty and his financial officer.

"What else you got, Winn?"

"Let me work the numbers some more, sir."

"Work the numbers. Come up with something, but you know where I draw the line."

It was the fundamental clash of business and bean counter, but at Alta Air Service it was sharpened by the disproportionate influence of the founder over financial discretion. Fortunately, this is where Winfield's brilliance shone. Alta survived the early 1930s by applying what they had wherever they could.

First, they scaled down their passenger service, converting some of the aircraft back to crop dusters and expanding their operation as far south as Florida and Mexico, and as far north as Kentucky. Rather than selling planes, they leased four of them to other carriers at a slim margin of profit. People who lost their jobs with the planes were re-trained in other jobs and kept on in some capacity.

Meanwhile, Alta opened their hangar in Monroe to competitors and charged rent. They performed every manner of service for other airlines and aircraft, picking up a few dollars here and there for repairs and fuel. They even secured government contracts for aerial photography.

Alta also had the good fortune of picking up additional mail contracts in 1934 when all existing agreements were voided and renegotiated with the federal government. More than one of the established carriers had acquired their contracts through secret arrangements with the postal service, and when President Roosevelt ordered all of them to be thrown out, Alta stood as one of the untainted few. This set off a fortuitous chain of events that allowed Alta to pick up three more mail routes, enough to support a stock offering that helped pay off many of the small airline's existing assets and build a cash position that met the demands of the nation's collective rainy day.

Through it all, Martin Willman managed to maintain his pledge to his people. No member of the Alta family, his family, would ever be faced with the prospect of poverty and unemployment.

◆   ◆   ◆

Candace Hall knew she wasn't alone in her love for her boss, but she had an advantage. His life was his business, and she was his secretary, making her, by default, the most important woman in his life, except perhaps for his mother. Not surprisingly, she knew everything about him, including his yearning for a true family of his own, which in 1934 was only now beginning to slip out as the financial pressures began to subside.

"Good morning, Mr. Willman."

"Morning, Candace."

"How are the plans coming for the big day?"

Every year Alta would have a "family day" in the hangar, and parents would bring their children along, all of them awestruck by the size and breadth of the aircraft and the hangar that held them. Marty loved seeing the children. Their constant wonder and experimentation was a quality he'd never lost in himself, so family day was particularly joyful.

"We're ready for everyone, Mr. Willman. The hot dogs and balloons have all been ordered."

"That's great. Good job, Candace."

She could see it in his eyes, the twinkle of excitement that was every bit as childlike as that of their guests. At times his focus and diligence surrounding the airline were intimidating, but these were the moments, the windows into his soul, that bound them.

"I suppose some day your children will be joining us for family day too, won't they, sir?" she said. For all his ability to think on his feet in the business world, this was a question that he didn't know how to answer. A tension entered his smile.

"I suppose you're right, Candace."

She could see the stream of thoughts pass across his face, from joy, to regret to an awkward hope, and then what could have been the mildest touch of consideration—consideration of Candace.

Marty's overriding respect for Candace deemed any romantic inclination utterly unthinkable. She was taller than average, with square shoulders and the sharply defined face of her Irish heritage. Her manner of dress was impeccably conservative, her hair equally so, always tied back in a neat bun. Straight-laced as she was, this impression was well-balanced by her warmth and demeanor, and on the rare occasion that she missed work due to illness, Marty's workday would lapse into an organizational and emotional shambles. When she finally returned, in a humorous reversal of roles, he would dote on her.

"Are you feeling better today, Candace? Can I get you something to drink this morning?"

"No thank you, Mr. Willman. I feel much better today, thank you."

"Candace, I want you to know that if you don't feel tip-top, I will understand if you need to take another day off." Marty always said this when she returned, but his pained expression clearly conveyed that he was lost without her.

"Oh thank you, Mr. Willman, but you know I couldn't leave you alone for another day."

This was the response he was looking for, and although he didn't really know it, it had little to do with business.

7

She was a beautiful airplane, perfectly streamlined and already pointing skyward in repose. The first DC-3 in the fleet rolled triumphantly out of the paint shop hangar in the fall of 1938. Shinier and sleeker than anything Marty Willman had ever seen, the aircraft made the other planes he owned seem like Stone Age relics. This was a plane that brought the very essence of flight into tangible existence, as if all the other rickety fabric-covered monstrosities were impostors that happened to be able to fly. Two massive 1200 horsepower engines propelled the gleaming silver bird into the air; everything about it put everything before it to shame. She had power, beauty and undeniable prestige. The DC-3 didn't just fly; it was flight itself.

The inside of the aircraft was as compelling as the exterior. While the rest of Marty's fleet had one row of wicker seats on each side of a drafty cabin, the DC-3 had luxurious fabric seats, three across and 21 in all. She could fly 1500 miles at 10,000 feet! Marty knew immediately that the DC-3 would change everything about the modest little mail and passenger service he had nurtured. Even the language of it all; it was no longer "air service." In fact, it was an "Air Line," with routes and mail and passengers and cargo. He had his line and others had their lines, and all they could do now was spread their wings. The country was suddenly one vast expanse of opportunity to grow into, in which airlines would run in every direction to and from every city. But with the coming arrival of the DC-3, it was the "from" part that triggered Marty's acumen and foresight. He could not stay in Monroe and expect to capture his promising share of air travelers.

There was only one place to go in the South: Atlanta.

Terminus, as it was once called, had been a transportation capital from its earliest days. This is where the railway ended and then later began again. Portrayed as a Phoenix rising from the flames, Atlanta was a city with strong memories of a terrible war several decades old, a consequence that had generated its rise with a vengeance. As a Southerner, Marty was well aware of the magnetic appeal of the new south capital, the gravitation of industry, the strength and pride and growth of this city in this country. Atlanta, by its very nature—by the essential connotation of its name even—was a city that "radiated." And inevitably, the magnetic force of progress and prosperity captured Marty's imagination. He knew it was a perfect fit for Alta. Within its realm, this city had a network of investors, an abundance of space and a metropolis of people to carry back and forth across the South. There was no doubt in Martin Willman's mind.

"We're moving, Candace!"

"Congratulations, Mr. Willman," she said, but not with her usual warmth. She had heard the rumors and knew this moment would come. And despite her affection for her boss, she had grown impatient with him now. Many times she had felt he was on the verge of bridging the professional gap between them and looking at her as something more than his secretary and business confidant. But his work was his life, an ever-convenient distraction.

"Aren't you excited, Candace?"

"I'm excited for you, Martin." Though she could call him by his first name whenever she wanted to, she did so only as a signal that the conversation would be of a serious nature.

"Aren't you excited for us?"

"Us? Martin, what is 'us'?"

"We're a team, Candace. It won't work without you."

"I'm not moving to Atlanta, Martin. I'm a single girl, and until I get married, I'm not leaving my home and my parents." This was the sacred and undeniable custom of the time, and Marty could not argue against it. He had not courted Candace. She was already a part of his life as it was, and except for his repressed desire for children some day, there was nothing pushing him forward. Business was the ultimate obligation, until now.

"Candace, I can't…we can't make it without you."

"Oh stop it, Martin. You'll be fine."

There was an edge of resentment to her proclamation. He was trying to charm her the way he charmed his employees and investors. She had a seemingly endless reserve of patience for Marty when it came to her job, but it did not extend to her personal life.

Marty confronted the potential finality of losing Candace, who up to now, he had only thought of as his secretary. That night he dreamed about her and imagined what his life would be like without her. It was too much for him to bear. He woke up in a state of powerlessness that was like nothing he'd ever felt before. How could he go to work without seeing her there each morning?

It was certainly the most unconventional courtship that anyone had ever known, but Marty approached the situation in the only way he knew how. There was a business decision to be made, and since there was no distinction between his personal and his business life, there was no uncertainty about what he needed to do. At noon the next day he called his secretary into his office.

"Candace, I'm afraid we're going to have to let you go."

"Mr. Willman?"

"You heard me, Candace. You're fired."

"Martin? I told you I would be resigning when the company moves to Atlanta. Why are you doing this?" She was beginning to cry.

"Because I..." She could see he was struggling and her instinct was to be patient with him.

"Go ahead, Martin. Because?"

"Because I love you, Candace." She was silent. She regained her breath and gathered her thoughts.

"You love me?"

"Yes, Candace. I love you."

"Then...then why are you firing me?"

"Because I want to marry you."

She skipped a breath. Her hand came to her heart, her jaw dropped, and then she really did cry. Marty came out from behind his desk and dropped to his knees in front of her.

"Candace, I know I haven't paid much attention to you. I know this is...strange. But I can't live without you. I need you in my life."

"Yes," she said.

"We're a team, and I want you to come to Atlanta with me."

"I said yes, Martin."

"Yes?"

"Yes. I'll marry you."

And then he kissed her stiffly, because it was their first kiss, and because Martin Willman was far from practiced in this behavior.

The strangeness of it all seemed to hover over them in the day or two after the proposal, but then just as quickly, there was a sense of inevitability and excitement that made it all seem right.

Candace and Marty had a quiet family ceremony in the Baptist church in Oak Ridge. Though Marty was joyful, he was aware of the appearance of impropriety this marriage to his secretary could generate, and the tenuous economics of his enterprise could not afford any whiff of scandal. But his concerns were unfounded, and his extended family of employees was as happy as any family would be at the marriage of one of theirs. Now it was on to Atlanta.

◆   ◆   ◆

The move of assets and offices took place throughout the summer of 1939. At first Marty's parents were deeply troubled by their son's plans to move the business hundreds of miles away. Would they ever see him again? And if so, how often? Once a year maybe?

Their fears were soon put to rest. Marty visited them every few weeks after the move, flying in on the "Cross Southern Route" as it was marketed. The DC-3 went from Atlanta to Birmingham to Meridian to Jackson to Monroe. From there it was on to Shreveport before heading into Tyler, Texas, and finally on to Fort Worth and Dallas. Tyler wasn't an especially lucrative stop on the route, but it was the home of Marty's original benefactor, and so every few weeks he would take the flight a little further to Tyler and pay a cordial visit to Simon Piersall.

"What are yew doin here, boy? Get out of here—you got an airline to run!"

They both would laugh as Simon would recount the same story of the original crash each time he visited, always over the bottle of scotch that Marty brought along as a gift.

"I could see the whites of your eyes; you were so scared, boy!"

"Oh go on, Mr. Piersall. I wasn't scared."

"Luckily, I brought that bird down just in time to save your life."

"And I am forever thankful, Mr. Piersall."

Aside from the important visits to friends and family, Simon was right; Marty did have an airline to run, and run it he did. Though he had long ago proven his ability to deal with the unknown, Atlanta was a big town for Marty and his wife, well beyond the familiar environs of Monroe and Oak Ridge. Their arrival into this daunting and bustling city only served to strengthen their marriage. Together they would survive.

Marty purchased a small plot of land up on a hill, just north of Atlanta city proper. With the help of his new friends in the local banking community, he located a contractor and built a house. It was Candace's vision come to life, a two-story Victorian home with a wraparound porch, maple floors and heart-of-pine beams from the northern woods of Georgia. A large deck extended outward into the small backyard and from there they could see the blossoming skyline of downtown Atlanta. A narrow walkway led up to the front porch from the street below, giving it a sense of quiet majesty. Though it was not a big house, Marty and Candace felt a great sense of pride in their home. The pieces of their new life had settled nicely into place.

◆   ◆   ◆

From 1938 to 1940, the airline took delivery of eight DC-3s. By the end of the decade, over 200 people worked for Marty. He had successfully built relationships with two of Atlanta's largest banks, securing capital for the construction of two large airplane hangars and maintenance facilities. The fleet numbered 32 aircraft, with new ones arriving every other month. His route system spread; in fact it radiated like the railways that preceded him, outward from Atlanta. Northward toward Cincinnati by way of Knoxville and Lexington, east to Charleston, South Carolina via Augusta and Columbia, and west, all the way to Dallas on the Cross Southern Route. But gaining access to a new destination was never an easy task, and the lucky airline that was privileged to serve a city was often selected based on the whims of the federal regulators. For this reason, each of Alta's new destinations was preceded by a personal visit to the city by the general manager of the airline.

"A Mr. Martin Willman to see you, Mr. Mayor."

Well-dressed as always, Marty would be led into the inner sanctum of city leadership and given the few minutes he would need to make his case.

"Mr. Mayor, we're just a small operation right now, and like this great city of yours, we're like a family. But we're growing like a little boy who's constantly busting out of his britches. You know how it is. Soon as you get'em a new pair, it's like you gotta buy him another one," and they'd laugh about it because they both knew exactly what that was all about.

"So Mr. Mayor, I have come here to tell you that we want to serve your city. If we can fly to (Lexington, Charleston, Knoxville, etc.), I guarantee you that you'll see people coming and going like you've never seen before. Business trade will take off, and we'll make sure you get the credit for it come re-election time. And unlike those other airlines that are in Washington right now demanding the chance to send one flight here a week, we'll fly here *every day*. We'll stick with you too, that's my word to you, sir."

Mayors didn't necessarily have any official clout when it came to the federal government deciding which airline got which route, but Marty was clever enough to know that having them in his corner would certainly have some influence, especially in the home of the Confederacy. He knew how and when to pull the Dixie card from his hand.

"You don't want no Yankee bureaucrats telling you who's gonna fly here and who isn't, do you, Mr. Mayor?" More often than not, there Marty would be a month later at any given city, standing proudly next to the mayor, cutting a ribbon at the local municipal airfield for the airline's inaugural flight.

The interdependency between the airlines and government grew stronger as the United States entered the Second World War. Air travel had evolved into a fundamental mode of transportation and commerce through the 1930s, and a small but thriving contingent of airlines entered the 1940s with little threat from anyone but each other. Still, even that threat was muted by government regulation. There would be enough of a market to go around for all of the established carriers, and Alta was one of them. As long as they managed their operation with reasonable financial foresight and safety, they were essentially guaranteed a profit. When war struck, the government deployed passenger aircraft as troop carriers to the European and Asian theaters. Alta Airlines, with its close personal associations so ably fostered by its leader, was a willing contributor to the war effort. Patriotism aside, this was a political investment that could only pay off down the road.

Christmas 1941 was a dark and anxious time for the country, but on Christmas Day, Martin and Candace Willman received their greatest gift ever: A baby girl. Her first name honored the distant American harbor that had been attacked just a few weeks earlier, while her middle name memorialized the land they had left behind.

They named her Pearl Louise Willman.

8

Throughout the 1940s and 50s, Alta Airlines continued to grow and prosper. The formula that Marty's father had taught his son continued to work: always make your customers feel important. From its humble beginnings in rural Louisiana, Alta had now become the major airline of the southeast, with routes stretching north to New York and Chicago, west as far as Los Angeles and south to Florida, Cuba, Jamaica and Caracas.

Martin Willman was a rich man, but he never forgot that his success was a function of relationships, a tenet that served him well from the day he made his first sales pitch to a farmer. These relationships grew like the cotton he had dusted long ago, branching outward and upward until they yielded a wealth that could be woven into enduring value. Alta was a player in the industry, an airline whose best sales representatives were its customers, especially in the emerging city of Atlanta. Now wealthy and comfortable in his late 50s, Marty's energy never waned. His marriage to Candace was strong and joyous, and their only child, their daughter Pearl, was nearing the end of high school, soon to be the star debutante among the denizens of Peachtree Street.

By 1957, Alta Airlines dominated most of the routes radiating out of the city of Atlanta. They had established a centralized headquarters complex, and a "hub," the first of its kind, that had ingeniously allowed it to serve numerous smaller cities and towns that on their own would never be able to fill the 69 seats of a DC-7 to an individual city. The brilliance of the hub was that everyone on a single plane could be coming from or going to one of several destinations, allowing Alta to increase their "load factor," the fundamental measure of success for a particular flight.

Still, no year was without its rounds of turbulence. There were nearly constant battles for route authorities as Alta vied with competitors for government favor. Fortunately, in most if not all cases, Marty came out even or on top. Martin Willman was who he was, a common man whose charm shone through to even the most jaded of bureaucrats. He made a point of developing sincere personal friendships with government regulators that overcame the most blatant bribes of his less authentic counterparts. With Alta, there were no intermediaries, no exacting payments requiring reciprocity, only the handshake, the promise and the human touch of a human enterprise. When Alta won authority to serve cities they'd never dreamed of in the early days, the large dominant carriers of the North and Midwest would fire their lobbyists in fits of frustration and anger. Nevertheless, as well as the formula worked through the fifties, change of unprecedented proportions was suddenly on the horizon.

◆   ◆   ◆

"What is it, Winn?" answered Marty through the intercom.

"I need to talk to you, Mr. Willman."

"Come on in."

Marty had honed his ability to read the nuances of Winfield Neagle's face through the many years they had worked together. The man was a barometer, a perfect finance man whose tenure had earned him a place of permanence at Alta. When his face was scrunched and tense, this was usually a sign that there was important work to be done, yet there were varying degrees of this condition and Marty knew not to become overly concerned when Winfield was agitated. But this time was different. Marty could see there was a weighty matter at hand the moment Winfield entered his modest office at the Atlanta headquarters.

"We need to move to jet aircraft," Winfield said calmly to his boss.

Marty reclined in his high back chair and smiled. He rarely answered Winfield right away out of respect for his financial acumen, but in this instance, he almost let loose an involuntary laugh until the look on Winfield's face reminded him that this was important. Marty had heard about jets, but nothing compelled him to take them seriously. Alta was consistently profitable with their piston aircraft, and jets were not only expensive, they had been involved in a string of deadly crashes in recent years.

"Why do you say that, Winn? Why would we want to spend that kind of money and take that risk?"

"We really don't have a choice, sir. The industry is about to undergo a dramatic transition."

"Since when has that been a problem, Winfield? We've had transitions before. We've got a great thing going with our Douglas aircraft. We're making money hand over fist. Why should we mess with that? I'm not ready to spend all of our profits just to say that we fly a jet airplane."

"Mr. Willman, this is not like anything in the past. This is…this is…"

Winfield started breathing heavily to the point of being unable to talk. Marty had never seen him this way, as if some kind of force had taken control of his lungs and induced hyperventilation.

"What's the matter, Winn? Are you okay?"

"I'm, I'm okay, Mr. Willman."

"Hang on there, Winfield. Let me get you something to drink."

Marty ran to the door of his office and ordered his secretary to bring a glass of water for his tormented chief financial officer. When she returned, Marty tenderly handed the water to Winfield. He pulled his chair around to the same side of the desk, and when Winfield had fully regained his breath, Marty gently continued the conversation.

"Why should we fly jets, Winn? Why not go to turboprops?"

Winfield took a deep and thoughtful breath, aware that the next thing he was going to say would determine the fate of the entire airline.

"Jets will be more productive, and they will also be what our customers demand. They're much faster than props and turboprops. It's a risk that everyone will take because the risk of not doing it is higher. That's what it comes down to, Mr. Willman."

Ever since the dark days of the Depression, the principals of fiscal restraint and frugality had infused the culture of Alta Airlines and provided the locus of common ground between the leader and his loyal accountant. Marty had been known to retrieve a wayward paper clip or the stub of a discarded pencil from the hangar floor, always in pursuit of saving an extra buck. Now he was being asked to spend tens of millions of dollars on something he knew so little about. There was a tremendous urge to shut down the entire idea, an overwhelming drive to deny that Winfield Neagle's thinking held any shred of intelligence. But the physical state alone of his right-hand man was just enough to hold back and hear the story, even if it wasn't a particularly encouraging story.

"We need to transition from piston to jet aircraft to compete. Jets will be able to fly farther and faster, with more people, meaning we can fly more flights each day."

That was the kick-off, the preview to Winfield's best performance as an employee of Alta Airlines. His research was characteristically thorough, touching on every possible and previously inconceivable cost and benefit, all of it culminating in a decision to move forward. At the end of the three-hour presentation to Marty and the rest of the board of directors, there was no doubt on the direction of the enterprise. They would surge full speed ahead into the jet age.

By late 1959, Martin Willman was on the verge of his 60's, but he'd never lost his youthful excitement or his human touch. On the day the first four-engine DC-8 jet settled softly on to the tarmac, there was in him something of a confirmation. He had built a company of nearly 7000 employees, an airline with 80 aircraft that now flew to over 60 cities in the United States and the Caribbean. And somehow Alta Airlines had once again come through a period of great upheaval that just ten years before would have been well beyond the imagination of even the most experienced airline executive.

As was his nature, Marty recognized and credited his people for the success. The loyalty he received and the devotion he returned to them seemed to be absolute. By the time the transformation neared completion in the early 1960s, Martin Willman harbored no concerns about the future of his enterprise. He would gradually hand the reins of his company over in the next few years without regret and take an increasingly passive role as chairman of the board. His faith in the spirit of Alta Airlines and the traditions he had built among his people would undoubtedly carry them through the challenges that lay ahead in the decades to come.

PART II
1987–1990

9

Daniel Woodson had no idea what to expect. The employment agency sent him to some 40th floor office in a nameless Manhattan skyscraper to interview for one of the jobs he had circled in the newspaper. He didn't know what the job was, only that it was with an airline. It was the "*AIRLINE*" in big bold letters of the New York Times want ad that prodded him to call the number, for no other reason than he liked to travel. But the reality was he had no direction and needed to start making money. He was five months out of college with a liberal arts degree that was proving both expensive and worthless in the tight job market.

The woman who interviewed him was cordial and to the point. She handed him a ticket to fly to Atlanta the following day to meet with the personnel department of a company called Alta Airlines. Early the next morning he found himself at LaGuardia Airport for the first time in his life. He made his way to the Alta ticket counter and then to the gate at the new and ultra-modern terminal. Just as he sat down in the gate area, he heard his name.

"Passenger Woodson, please check with the agent at the podium."

He had the urge to run up to the gate, as if the plane would leave without him if he didn't hurry. He fumbled his entire ticket over to the agent and with a professional half smile, she gave him his boarding pass—Seat 2D, First Class.

He had to be pointed toward the jetway. As he entered, he caught the faint smell of jet fuel creeping in from the tarmac below. There was something about this smell, something exciting that seemed to signify escape and the privilege of a long journey in a short time. He was the last person to board the flight and as he stepped on to the aircraft, two smiling flight attendants greeted him, glanced at his boarding pass and pointed out his seat.

"Can I take your coat?" asked one of them.

"Would you like something to drink?" asked another.

"Um, yes. Orange juice?"

He sat down and looked out the window at the scurrying ramp agents while the attendant delivered his drink. A light rain had begun to fall and the last few bags were being loaded from a covered cart below his window.

Twenty minutes later as the jet sped down the runway and climbed into the air over the New York skyline, Danny had already made a decision. He wasn't quite sure why he wanted to work for this company, whether it was the fascination of flying or the desperation of not having a job, but he had been seduced.

The flight attendants doted on him. Maybe it was because that's what they always did for first class passengers, or maybe it was because Danny looked younger than his age, and they felt protective. He had grown accustomed to this and the occasional comments about his "cute" dimples and blue eyes. Now, at 23 years old, he hadn't quite mastered the subtle art of wearing a jacket and tie with the demeanor that it required. His occasionally unruly shock of black hair would curl with length and humidity, but to a good number of women, this only added to his boyish attraction.

The interview turned out to be a formality, and Danny received a job offer a few days after his return. Three weeks later in early November of 1987, Danny and the other new-hires came to attention in their training class. Each had in front of them a plastic bag with their Reservations Training manual and an assortment of company trinkets: a bumper sticker, a plastic set of wings and a small metal ashtray with the logo emblazoned across it.

"Let's introduce ourselves," said the instructor. "Tell us your name and why you wanted to work for Alta Airlines. We'll start over here with you."

Danny usually picked a spot on one side or the other of a classroom—anything other than the middle—but in this situation, it meant he'd have to go first.

"Daniel Woodson. I wanted to work for an airline because I like to travel."

It sounded as good as any explanation. He wasn't interested in telling the rest of his classmates that he had a college degree, nor that he needed a job bad enough to take one that didn't need a degree. The assumption that working for Alta Airlines was his goal struck him as funny and he wondered if those around him were now on the verge of fulfilling their highest aspirations.

"Joanne Weir. I've been a schoolteacher for five years, but I got tired of it. This was my chance to get into the corporate world and see what else I can do."

Prim and proper, the marrying type, Danny thought.

"Jeffrey Palmer. I'm a Navy pilot, but Alta isn't hiring pilots right now. I figure this will give me the inside track once they do start hiring because Alta is the best of the bunch to work for."

Swaggering fella who knows where he's going, which was better than Danny could say for himself. Girls must love this guy.

"Caroline Douglas. I've been in school for a few years and needed a change."

Cute, but kind of glum. She didn't seem as excited as the others about working for Alta Airlines, which meant he already had something in common with
her. As the round of introductions continued, Danny's attention to Caroline
gradually tuned out his other classmates. He made his introduction during a
break.

"So where'd you go to school?"

"Brooklyn. And you?"

"Pennsylvania. But I didn't get tired of it; I just, kind of, graduated. Where in
Brooklyn?"

"So they threw you out?"

"Yes, I guess you could say that."

"And you like to travel and so now you're here?"

"I couldn't think of anything else to say."

"Yeah...me neither."

He knew he wasn't going to get any further with Brooklyn, but it didn't matter. The ice had been broken.

The three weeks of class were devoted to learning how to book a reservation.
Among the prerequisites was the memorization of hundreds of three letter codes
that represented every city in the world served by Alta Airlines. This was followed
by the mastery of intricate formats that accessed flight availability and the thousands of published airfares from the computer system. Finally, at the completion
of training, they faced the punishment they had unwittingly signed up for as they
were thrown to the wolves, on the phones taking calls from customers.

As the lowest in seniority, Danny and his fellow classmates developed bonds
similar to those of any group that shares the experience of struggling together, but
this was especially true of his friendships with Caroline, Joanne and Jeff. The four
of them were firmly stuck on the late shift, working from 3:00pm to midnight
with three weekends off out of every eight. While New York flowed around
them, through its Monday-to-Friday-Nine-to-Five world, Danny and the other
three occupied their own isolated layer of time and space. The cold of a Gotham
winter set in upon them, and they became a nocturnal contingent, meeting
almost every night after work at a bar downstairs on a midtown corner. There
they'd drink away their pain and lapse into semi-serious hook-ups in the dark
corners of the establishment.

Inevitably, the foursome gravitated into a pair of twosomes: Jeff and Joanne,
Danny and Caroline, with the latter relationship the less serious of the two.
Joanne's pursuit of Jeff became ever more obvious, eventually wearing down Jeff's
resistance, which proved easy to do. The job called for distractions and demanded

stress relief. None of them were satisfied with their lives, nor were they capable of changing them, so each day's struggle was made slightly easier by the companionship. Danny and Caroline's relationship became a function of their youth and proximity, and because the office never closed and they had no seniority to get holidays off, their first kiss came after midnight on Christmas morning in the bar.

But only two months into his "career," with the arrival of 1988, the monotony of Danny's job had already overcome the novelty. This, he concluded, was a painful and unforgiving occupation with a never-ending flow of calls from a never-ending string of people whose distrust of airlines seemed a part of their eternal nature. Sure, it was a paycheck, something not to be taken for granted in this economy, even by a college graduate. Still, Danny had the most difficulty of the four. He had graduated from a well-known east coast university, yet here he was, working nights and weekends, catering to the masses and their significant abuse. He could rationalize the effort to some degree—free travel was a great perk—but the trade-off seemed foolish at times. By February, he began to hate what he was doing with every fiber of his being.

"Meet you downstairs," he said to Caroline late one night as he ripped off his headset. Half an hour later, in the dark corner they often reserved for their personal conversations, he told her.

"I'm quitting. I can't talk to these people anymore."

"None of us can. So talk to me," she said.

"I'm still quitting."

"Don't. Not yet!"

"I've got to."

"But I need you!" They had only known each other for a few months, but in the depths of a New York winter night, her outstretched hand was a safety net of sanity.

"Let's go to the beach this weekend," she said. She pulled him toward her, and they each rose a bit off their seats to kiss each other across the narrow table. If he did end up staying, Caroline would be the sole reason.

On a sunny morning two days later, their flight broke through the billowing clouds over the ocean off Fort Lauderdale. It was a spectacular sight: the aqua blue, the white strip of sand, the tall palms and taller hotels in the lower distance. This was one of those moments when Danny remembered why he put up with the job. The world was his to discover, and Alta was his chariot. He turned to Caroline and remembered the other reason he persevered. Caroline had a way about her, a strength of character that he hadn't seen in any girl during his college years. Her appeal to Danny was all the more powerful in its meaning simply because it seemed out of character for someone like her. She was not a needy person by nature, and nor should she be. Her personality was endearing, and she was a natural beauty. She had dark brown hair that grazed her shoulders and light blue eyes that always carried a spark of skepticism; a quality to her eyes that continually reminded him that her trust was a gift. During the flight, when Danny leaned in close to kiss her, he could see the fleeting traces of childhood freckles.

That night, they sat together in the hot tub facing the moonlit ocean off in the distance. As the last few patrons made their way out of the bar area near the pool, Caroline gave Danny a smile that he hadn't seen before.

"What?" he asked.

She didn't answer. Instead, she very casually slid her leg over Danny before shifting her weight on top of him, and that's when he realized she had removed the bottom of her bathing suit.

"Caroline?"

"What is it, Danny?" Her eyes were half closed.

"What if someone sees us?" She put her hand over his mouth and giggled, then tilted her head back and took a peek behind her.

"Just shut up and everything will be okay," she said.

So maybe she was a bit needy, in her own special way. The jets of the hot tub were loud, white noise for their little adventure. Her other hand was busy below the surface, pulling, almost ripping until Danny was free in the swirling pool of warmth. She pressed her body against his, sliding upward until her breasts brushed his chin. And then very slowly she slid back down, until he was completely inside of her. Only then did she remove her hand from his mouth. Her hands found his shoulders and her fingernails began to dig in.

"So, Danny."

"What?"

"You're leaving the company." Her tone was suddenly conversational, as if they were having lunch together.

"That's what you said, isn't it?" she asked him.

"Caroline...we're having sex," he whispered.

"Yes..." She rose up and down slowly; slow enough to mask the purpose.

"...I'm sure going to miss this," she whispered. A pair of half intoxicated couples strolled into the pool area only a few feet from the tub.

"Hi!" she said to the group

"How yew?"

"Great!" she said. The foam of the whirlpool was sufficient cover, and the guests paid no further notice. They were just having a conversation and so she continued as if they were.

"Where were we?" she asked, squeezing him with her thighs, digging with her nails.

"Yes. We were...having sex."

"Oh, I know that. And you were thinking of leaving the company."

"I was."

"You were. But now you're not. Right?" She bobbed just a bit faster, a mild threat of pulling off him.

"Right," he said.

What else could he say? This woman enchanted him, and at least for the moment, leaving Caroline was the farthest thing from his mind. He had given in on everything. It was one of those nights where you fold your cards and succumb to the more powerful forces of the moment.

"I don't want you to leave, Danny. Can you tell?"

"I had a feeling."

◆   ◆   ◆

Of course, they had to return to their dreary daily world up north. For Caroline and Danny, the winter was cold, dark and barely tolerable. She would stay at Danny's small New Jersey apartment once or twice a week, and this helped them both forget their dreaded days of a hundred or so nagging phone calls. They looked for every diversion to shake them from their daily dread, and as spring turned to summer, one of their favorites became the Cyclone at Coney Island.

"If we ride this enough, maybe it will shake all those phone calls loose from our heads," he told her.

"Sounds like something has already shaken loose in yours."

"Come on, let's go!"

"Let's!" she said, the sarcasm apparent.

They squeezed in tightly next to each other, and she dug her fingers into his arm, and then they laughed all of the stress out of themselves as the roller coaster whipped them up and down and around. Then they did it again.

But these escapes were only short-term remedies for Danny. He always had to go back to doing what he hated, and gradually the job resumed its erosion of Danny's spirit. When an internal job opening became available in the late summer, his mind instantly wrapped around it. It had been eight months that seemed like eight years, leading him easily to the conclusion that being a reservations agent would drive him insane, but he didn't want to leave the company, just the job he'd been burdened with.

The open position was for a marketing representative, a highly sought after job that involved socializing with travel agencies, chaperoning them to tourist destinations and most importantly, the opportunity to leave the job he had without leaving Alta. He was confident he could get the position, but there was one problem: it was a million miles away in Salt Lake City.

Caroline, his confidante, lover and best friend, would have to understand. Sure, there was always the question of why to stay with the airline. It seemed as though the job had managed to drive everyone's self-esteem, including Danny's, into a gradual decline that clouded their ability to visualize any alternatives. For Danny there was no other option. He put in for the job without telling Caroline and soon after being interviewed two weeks later, he received an offer.

His first reaction was physical, a sharp pain in his stomach, entirely related to Caroline. But in a moment there was no doubt; this was something he had to do. There was no lack of intensity to their feelings for each other, but right or wrong, Danny's state of mind quickly became one in which he could not imagine turning the job down.

That night, down at the bar, he broke the news.

"I've got to take it, Caroline."

"Why? How can you leave me here?"

"I'll come back…every week if I have to."

"No, you won't. Maybe a few times in the beginning, but you're leaving. You'll be thousands of miles away."

"Don't you think you're important enough to me?" he asked.

"It's not as important as getting out of town, obviously."

She was right. In truth, it was the job that was more important. Even though he cared deeply for Caroline, he was excited about the end of his daily pain and all the newness ahead.

In late August of 1988, Danny came into Manhattan on his first day off between assignments, the first day of the drive to Salt Lake City, to give Caroline a final kiss goodbye. It was tearful for both of them. She alternated between anger and sadness, and he allowed her the entire range of emotions before a final friendly hug. But he knew, or at least convinced himself, that Caroline was strong. A hug, a kiss, and then she abruptly turned to head back into the building. It was as if she had shaken off all of the emotion of the moment, although he couldn't see her face as she walked away.

When he got in the car, the pain in his stomach returned. As confused as he was, he couldn't deny that he was willing to accept the loss, but he realized he would also have to deny what might have been. He wasn't ready to settle down and get married, that he knew, and if he didn't leave, he would have an even greater "might have been" to deal with. The months they spent passed through his mind as he sped through the Lincoln tunnel. He reached the sunlight at the end of it and found himself on the road west.

10

She didn't need him. She didn't need anybody. So what if she screwed up by falling in love with him. It was just another mistake that could be corrected, or maybe it was just meant to be. In either case, Caroline Douglas was not going to give anymore, or even look like she wanted to, so when she finally turned her back on him, that was it. Yeah, it hurt, but fuck him. Let him head out to Utah and try and find someone like her.

Caroline had known pain before and battled through it every time. She was the youngest of three, the other two being drug addict brothers who were achieving great success following in the footsteps of their drug addict father. The ragged upbringing of her Queens borough childhood was marked by regular rounds of parental screaming, visits by the police and clouds of uncertainty that seemed to come at the end of every month. Why were they moving again, she'd asked her father, until it became apparent that they were always one dark night ahead of an eviction notice.

As a teenager she had already become hardened to uncertainty. Her self-image was formed by her grandmother, who provided a single strain of predictability, and her friends, whose "normal" parents served as healthy reference points. But her method of escape was always work, any kind of work. She waitressed, she cashiered and she delivered pizzas, sometimes all at the same time—anything to keep her out of the house. She put money in a passbook savings account that her grandmother had started in her name and gradually her deposits of ten and fifteen dollars began to amount to something.

And then when she was sixteen, she was asked if she had ever modeled before. She was waitressing in a diner when a customer pitched the idea to her as she served him breakfast. He was a photographer, or at least had the requisite accessories: camera, a leather bag and a foreign accent. He said he worked at the Brooklyn Institute of Beauty.

"Can I shoot you?"

"Shoot me? Like with your camera?"

"Yes. Will you model for me?"

"How much?"

"We would need to do a test shoot first, but models can make a couple hundred an hour, and you may have what it takes."

"Okay, yeah sure, I'll letcha do a couple shots. Where is this place?"

"Bensonhurst. Just take the G train down from here. Or better yet, I can pick you up."

"No. Just tell me where to go and when and I'll be there."

She had low expectations that this was legit, but she had to at least check it out. She felt better once she got to the studio. He seemed to be a real photographer. He had a large fan to create wind, and a bunch of bright lights inside of what looked like umbrellas. There was also a makeup artist, a woman, which made her feel even better.

She didn't know what to wear so she wore jeans and a tank top, figuring if she was really model material, then he'd have clothes for her anyway. He said what she had on would be fine.

He held a light meter near her face.

"Very nice, Caroline. You do have a lovely structure to your cheeks." That's what they're supposed to tell all models to feed their ego, she thought. The makeup artist suddenly proved her point by brushing her cheeks with enough well-placed blush to make the fantasy a reality.

"Splendid, Vanessa, thank you," he told the artist. She left abruptly, and the door slammed shut.

"Great, Caroline, okay, smile," he said.

"How long is this going to last?"

"Why, are you not liking being beautiful?"

"Yeah, right. I'm not beautiful." He kept snapping photos, stopping her in mid-sentence to catch her 'attitude' as he put it. And her attitude was certainly beginning to show.

"You didn't tell me how long this was going to take."

"We're making progress, Caroline, great, all right, now on your knees, please."

"What?"

"For the angle." She grudgingly complied. He came closer and began to shoot photos from above. Soon he was shooting straight down at her, into what little cleavage she offered.

"Now, I want you to pull your top back, just off the shoulder." He lent an encouraging hand. "That's it, good!"

This was as far as she was going to let him go, and she didn't care if he was Cosmo/Vogue/Sports fucking Illustrated photographer of the year. He hovered over her for one more shot and then slowly placed his camera on the nearby stool.

Even if he was legitimate, Caroline didn't like the way he was smiling at her. She braced herself, her body now taut with more tension than she'd ever felt in her life. Just as his hands touched each of her shoulders, she screamed.

And screamed and screamed and screamed.

It was a deafening, bloodcurdling massive howling elicitation that echoed throughout the studio, throughout the building and well into the academic quad. Whatever he might have planned to do, he never had a chance.

◆   ◆   ◆

The negotiations were simple. A full three-year scholarship to the Brooklyn Institute of Beauty in exchange for a simple signature on a single piece of paper that would likely never see the light of day. There would be no public accusations, no charges, no media, no need to make a big deal out of this.

"Mom! I gotta scholarship!!"

"To where, honey?"

"To this School of Astrology, or something like that. It's in Brooklyn."

"That's wonderful? Astrology?"

"Yeah, well, I gotta figure out what to major in anyway. But it's all free!!"

When she went to enroll, she found out the entire school was devoted to makeup and manicures—the correct term was cosmetology. Each student was required to purchase a personal toolbox of makeup and manicure supplies to be used through their course work, something that took a good chunk out of her passbook savings. It didn't take her long to realize that the Brooklyn Institute of Beauty was not a stepping stone to fulfilling whatever lifelong aspirations she would some day have, but it would serve a purpose. It would give her a degree, and even if it was meaningless to her, it would be her ticket to something else.

But in the spring of her second year, she couldn't wait any longer. She started sending primitive résumés to companies whose names she had heard of and got a response from an airline that didn't even require a degree. Just "some college" and that was something she could say she had, even though she considered it bogus.

As soon as she got the call from Alta that she was hired, she stopped going to class and tossed the stupid toolbox into the incinerator of her parents' latest apartment building.

11

On a perfect desert summer day, Danny took his first drive to work in Salt Lake City, a unique experience after a year of mass transit commuting. The highway led him cleanly to the airport office through sparse traffic. His building was a sandstone block with horizontal lines of varying color, designed to mirror the geology of the nearby terrain. The upper level was dedicated to reservations, the airline's western regional reservations office. The lower level, where he would be working, was the marketing office.

He entered the coolness of the lobby and politely waited for the receptionist to complete her call before introducing himself.

"Daniel, yes, welcome. We've been expecting you." She rose quickly, with a deference that up to now he had never experienced from the company he worked for.

"I'm Patricia. Welcome to Salt Lake City." She extended her hand.

"Thank you, Patricia."

"Follow me." She led him down the corridor past a row of vacant cubicles.

"Where is everyone?" he asked.

"Oh, they're probably all out on calls," and then she turned and smiled at him. "Just like you will be. I'm going to introduce you to Reid." Her expression changed and her voice descended into a whisper as they walked down the corridor. "He likes me to call him Mr. Nielson since his promotion."

She poked her head into one of the offices and led him in. "Mr. Nielson, Daniel Woodson is here," she announced. It was a large office, with a long window facing the terminal, a glass-top desk and a wall of plaques and community service awards.

"Daniel, welcome! Reid Nielson. Come on in! Great to meet you!" He stood and gave a warm handshake. "Take a seat."

Nielson was slightly taller than most, dressed in the requisite button-down shirt and tie. His appearance was neater than it was stylish, his hair parted perfectly with a bit of gray skirting his ears. The tie was diagonally striped, a design long gone from the east coast. He had nicely shined loafers with small tassels and a belt with an oversize rodeo buckle that wouldn't go with anything other than chaps. Daniel guessed that it was a gift from a travel agent that he was scheduled to meet with that day.

They talked, or rather Nielson talked, running through every aspect of the local economy, the airline industry and travel agency community in granular detail. He had a habit of tilting his head slightly when he was emphasizing a point, something Danny caught himself mirroring unconsciously.

"The job involves long hours out of the office, calling upon travel agents and corporations and selling them on the benefits of the airline for their clients," said Reid. He sounded like a handbook.

"You'll need to go to a lot of these cocktail parties and conventions. We'll also be sending you on fam trips."

"Fam trips?"

"Familiarization. We give tickets to groups of travel agents so they can fly Alta to various destinations and familiarize themselves with the city and its attractions. We always assign a rep as a chaperone. Then this winter, we'll also need you to host the inbound fam trips. Agents will be coming into Salt Lake from around the country to spend a few days skiing at the resorts."

"Which resorts?"

"The big ones: Park City, Deer Valley and Snowbird. I hope you know how to ski. If you don't, you're going to have to learn," he said.

Danny was trying to understand what the catch was. They were going to pay him to travel to cities with large groups of travel agents, mostly women, and then pay him to go skiing with them in the winter. He wanted to explode in a fit of lottery winning laughter, except for the fact that the man speaking to him seemed devoid of any humor. He was a pleasant but vacuous fellow, probably trustworthy, certainly quirky; his dominant quality appeared to be a rigid seriousness, where laughter was a curious behavior but perpetual explanation was not. Naturally, the man felt obliged to go deeply into detail on his own background.

Reid Nielson had made it to his regional manager position, he explained, by thoroughly researching his accounts, identifying their needs and targeting them with relentless politeness. Twenty years later, he had made it to his new position from the one that Danny was now filling. It was the two decades in the same job that struck Danny as incomprehensible. Where do you draw the line between patience and stupidity? he thought.

"...I was never much for the cocktail parties though. But, Daniel, it's part of the job. You've got to do it, and there may be some times when you don't want to do it again. You just don't feel like going to another cocktail party, but there you are again, and you have to be at your best and show them the Alta way. You've got to be at the top of your game and…"

On and on he went. Danny's attention waxed and waned through what felt like hours of near monologue. Finally, when Reid asked him if he had any questions, he lied and said no, simply so he could break free.

When he walked out of the building, he could honestly say that he had never felt freer in his life.

◆   ◆   ◆

As Caroline predicted, Danny flew back a few weeks in a row at first, and then every two weeks. When it got to a visit a month, she told him that was enough. At first she didn't want any part of him, then she did and then she didn't again. Their status was ambiguous. They were still "seeing" each other, but when he flew back into town and touched her, it was like being touched by a stranger.

"It's like we've got to start over every time I see you," she told him.

"Not for me," he said. "For me it's like we're picking up right where we left off."

"Well, it's not that way for me," she said.

"What's the problem?"

"You're not here," she said. "You're not a part of my life."

When he did come back into town, they slept together out of custom. They hugged and kissed and held hands. They went out for cheap meals followed by drinks into the night, but it was clear there was a barrier between them now, an emotional separation that overwhelmed whatever physical closeness they hung onto. Back when they worked together, they needed each other, but now the distance between them was proof enough that the need was not real, and so they looked at each other across the table as if they were looking across a canyon. The touch was hollow, the love had dried up like a flower that only gets watered once a week, then two weeks and then once a month. And then it is dead.

Each of them had their own way of dealing with the job that dominated their soul. While Danny escaped, Caroline descended into a state of zombie-like behavior. She'd take the E-train in from Queens every day, take her hundred or more calls, have a few or more drinks at the bar downstairs and head back out to Queens. She became cold to those around her for fear of being warm. Pain was all that waited at the end of any relationship, and since they always ended, why begin?

She became the third wheel to Jeff and Joanne, who announced their engagement that fall of 1988, and this isolated her even more. On the surface, there was no one reason for this downward spiral. It was more the cumulative effect of several minor assaults on her self-esteem that had begun with Danny's departure. She took less time to get ready for work and gave less consideration to her appearance. She started smoking as an excuse to get out of the building once an hour.

Socially, she was her own worst obstacle. She was still a beautiful young woman, but "droopy" as Joanne finally confessed one night, with Jeff sitting beside her, his arm possessively around her shoulder. Caroline looked at them with secret contempt. The "couple" she thought, well coupled, doing "couple-y" stuff that only couples can do. She still cared for her friend, but she was aware that Joanne had now become a complete product of her relationship with Jeff. Joanne's strength was dependent on someone else, which she knew from experience was ultimately precarious.

And then there was Jeff, whom she didn't trust for a millisecond. During the rare times Caroline found herself alone in the same room with him, even for the few moments when Joanne had to go to the restroom, there were looks from him covered by benign chat. Nothing obvious enough to raise a flag to Joanne, but she knew he was casting a line to see what he'd catch from her. Still, even if she had evidence to pass on to Joanne, what good would it do? There would be denial, accusations of jealousy, and a friendship jettisoned. Joanne would always choose Jeff over her; there was too much invested already. All Caroline could do was deal with it.

So she was droopy, so what? She didn't do anything with her hair anymore; it dropped straight down around her head. So what! Take it or leave it, this is who I am, she thought. Fuck the world.

In the broadest sense, Caroline began to lose feeling. The job and the coming winter had ground her down to a state of sensory deprivation. The smoking had clouded her sense of taste and smell. Her field of vision was limited to the oppressive reservations office, the E-train and her parent's shag carpeted Queens apartment. And her hearing was dominated by the endless stream of incoming calls for flights to Florida. She'd go down to the bar after her shift as a matter of routine, but the work-obsessed conversations with co-workers annoyed her. The bitching might have helped some people, but she was at least conscious of the need to leave work at work. In the meantime, there were many guys who would have asked Caroline out if it wasn't for the scowl that served as her default expression. But one of them saw this as an opportunity.

"Caroline, you and I need to go out."

His name was Peter. Tall, lanky and good-looking in a dangerous way, he had a strong jaw and dark hair, a portion of it draping perfectly over his forehead every once in a while. His movements were taught, confident, assertive, almost dominant. Peter seemed to have a different girl with him every week, but never a girlfriend. He dressed well, in an uptown way. He wore one of those long leather jackets, its dull shine reflecting the dim lights of the bar. But it was his eyes that controlled the conversation. Elbow on the bar next to Caroline, he leaned down slightly to bring himself within her eye level.

"Yeah, why's that?" she asked him.

"You look like you need something."

He was talking to her as if they were best buds, longtime friends who had been through much together. It was unnerving to Caroline because it was so far from the truth, even though there was no legitimate reason why it couldn't be true. On some level, they could probably skip all the steps between building a friendship, or even a relationship, and it would be immediate gratification.

"What do you think I need?"

"Oh, I don't know. A friend maybe," said Peter.

He said this with just the right level of distance and sincerity, definitely enough sincerity to threaten the comfort of her cynicism. What could be wrong with a friend? He looked great. This guy always looked great. Why would *he* want her as a friend? Especially her? It was time to get her guard back up. She took a swig of her beer and turned on her stool to face him.

"So, what do you mean by a friend? You know, if you need a friend, there's a bunch of them waiting out there on the corner just before you head into the Lincoln tunnel." She glanced at his jacket. "Looks like you can afford it," she added.

"Oh Caroline, that's not what I mean."

He was smiling at her with a lightness of mood that seemed foreign to her, something she hadn't felt herself in months. She had yet to reciprocate the smile, or even the tone of his voice. It occurred to her that he was resistant to her magnetic pull of gloom. He was not going down with her.

"Caroline, look, I've just seen you around and thought to myself 'what's she thinking?' I wondered if I could be one of your friends and find out." She noticed that he used her name a lot and realized that she couldn't remember when she had heard her name spoken this often in such a short period. He offered her a cigarette.

"You want to be my friend so you can know what I'm thinking, is that it?" she asked.

"It's chicken or the egg. A good friend already knows what you're thinking, but that's also probably why they become good friends," he said.

"So then, if you don't know what I'm thinking now, we probably shouldn't be friends."

"Right. Yes, I think you're right about that." They each took a drag of their cigarettes. "But I knew you would say that," he added, and she let herself laugh just a bit.

He was good. Despite whatever pitfalls lay ahead, she was enjoying the stupid conversation. Her guard began to slowly drop. The music in the background was adding to the mood, and the other people around her began to fade away.

"So what *am* I thinking?" This time he took a long drag, pulled the ashtray over and lodged the cigarette before bringing his eyes back to hers.

"You're thinking that you're a machine, a soulless piece of machinery that comes to work, works, and then goes home from work. You hate this fucking job, but you do it. People suck and you don't care what they think of you." Even if he didn't know what he was talking about, he spoke with authority. She held her cigarette aloft, and her eyes narrowed.

"Well, that's very interesting, Dr. Peter. Here's my question for you." She pointed her cigarette at him as she spoke. "Who the fuck *doesn't* feel that way?"

"Right, right! Caroline, you're right. But so am I."

"Yeah, so?"

"So as your friend, I'm even going to tell you what you *should* be thinking," he said.

""*Should* be thinking? You're going to tell me what I should be thinking?"

"No charge. This one's on me," he said. This made her laugh again. As much as she thought she was on the verge of finally putting a torpedo through the conversation, he still managed to keep it afloat.

"You need stimulation." He let the three words stand on their own as he snuffed out his cigarette.

"Ah, of course. What are you selling, vibrators inside your damn leather jacket?"

"Well, if that's what you're into, maybe so. Caroline, we all need stimulation. We need variety in order to feel things. Anything that makes us more sensitive is a good thing. That's what makes us alive."

It was nearing 1:00am, and she had a train to catch, the last train back to Queens with enough passengers to keep it relatively safe.

"I gotta go or I'm not going to be alive no matter how much stimulation there is." He nodded and lifted his beer in a toast.

"To friends," he said, and she complied, even though she noticed that there was no beer left in his bottle.

12

Peter Owens had stepped from the mottled background of human machinery to the foreground of friendship in Caroline's life. He was not what she expected. He might have been just another New York reservations agent like her, but he was good at his job. Polished and engaging, Peter knew his stuff, rolling through call after call with grace and ease. He was fast but polite, and he almost always got the sale.

It was a Friday night in November on the week of Caroline's one-year anniversary with Alta Airlines. Every employee who made it through their first year of service received a small pair of metal wings to replace the plastic version they had been given on their first day. And certainly this was a case where it was the thought that counted. The reservations general manager proudly pinned the wings on Caroline, Joanne and Jeff with uninspired pomp and circumstance. When Caroline got back to her desk, she took the pin off and looked it over: the small "A" logo in the middle, the dark silver of the wings and on the back, a tiny safety pin clasp with the barely legible words "HONG KONG" underneath.

"Let's celebrate," said Peter over her shoulder as she fingered the piece of scrap metal in her hand. She laughed.

"I've got my wings! My wings! I can fly!" she said with mock excitement.

"I'm taking you downtown," he said.

She wasn't sure at what point their relationship had crossed over to where he could tell her what they were going to do, but she went with it. The declaration triggered the slightest bit of excitement in her, mostly because so little else did.

"Where we going?" she said.

"To the Village. Maybe catch some blues."

"Who else is going?"

"Let me see, there's you…and me." She raised an eyebrow, and a call came in, pulling her out of the chat.

The city was alive that night. The holiday season had just arrived and as they left the heat of the building, the only thing that softened the bite of the midnight November air was the friendly herd of yellow cabs making their way down 7th Avenue. Tall and striking, Peter commanded a cab in seconds and guided her into the warmth of the back seat.

"Village Gate," he said.

He knew where he was going and what he was doing. He knew the city because he was one of those people who *was* the city. The cab carried them swiftly downtown, slicing past the other cars, 23rd, 22nd, 21st, catching every green light before finally being held up at 14th. Then another stretch of speed until they descended into the tangle of streets that is the West Village. People were out, filling the sidewalks and clogging the crosswalks when the Walk signs blinked on. The cab crawled and maneuvered its way deeper into the Village until Peter gave the command.

"This is good."

He left him a ten on a seven-dollar ride and extended his hand to Caroline as they slipped out. The crowds on the street gave Peter excuse enough to keep hold of her hand as they briskly made their way through the bundled packs of night-lifers.

He knew where he was going.

Though they were moving quickly, it was sub-freezing and there was a line at the door. Without a break in his stride and Caroline still in tow, Peter caught the eye of the bouncer, who tilted his head in acknowledgment. In they went through the out door, to the muted disgust of the freezing patrons to be.

A blast of warmth, the smell of smoke and the sound of a sax filtered up from the stairs they were heading down. Inside, there was the feeling of exclusivity that is the nature of a perfectly sized crowd with tables for each. Peter continued to lead Caroline toward the front and against the wall, to the single empty table; a booth with a small scripted tent card on it that said "Reserved."

They slid into the booth and began peeling off the layers. A waitress arrived immediately.

"Hi-ya, Pete."

"Hey, Tanya, how you doin this evening?"

"Good, Pete. The usual? Martini?"

"Yeah. Caroline, what would you like?" She was still processing her surroundings so she just said the first thing that came to her mind. "Beer."

"Got it," said Tanya.

"Thanks, Tanya," said Peter. She winked at him as she left.

"Beer?" he asked Caroline with a smile as he pulled out his cigarettes. "What kind of a celebration drink is that?"

"All right, then I'll have what you're having."

Peter's hand went up, and Tanya made a beeline back to them, ignoring the summons of the other tables.

"Let's give the lady a martini as well."

"Got it," and she was gone again.

A spell had taken hold of Caroline. The past week had been better than average. Peter was now a part of her daily consciousness, something she couldn't say for anyone else she worked with. She was just starting to care about how she looked again. Her skepticism, cynicism and determination to keep her distance had now melted in the warmth of her surroundings. The band finished their show and when the headline act—a blues band straight from Chicago—took the small platform of a stage, Peter left his seat and joined Caroline on the same side of the booth.

The second martini made her pliable. His hand found hers, and he pulled it, along with all of their elbows, onto the table. He massaged her palm with both hands and stared at it as if searching for clues to the mind of its owner.

"What now, oh great reader of minds and palms?" she said with her usual edge, but this time with a drunken smile.

"You've got a long lifeline."

"Oh gimme a break!" she said, pulling her hand free. She was brutal, but at the same time she had to know if Peter was even capable of being hurt. He gave her a jaw-drop look, as if she had wounded him, but it was all still a joke. They didn't know each other well enough yet to cause each other pain.

"Yeah, go ahead, play the 'hurt' card," she said. He pulled back, sliding apart from her in the booth with a pout.

"Oh cut it out," she said, and she grabbed his hand again and pulled him back over.

Although the booth made it impossible to face her directly, he could face her just enough to kiss her. Caroline knew "the kiss" thing would probably happen at some point during the night and she wasn't opposed to it. She wanted to kiss him, but she also wanted to be ready for it, and she hadn't been. The thought of pulling back was fleeting, and when he did kiss her, it was clear that he knew how to kiss. He knew what he was doing. He always seemed to know what he was doing.

Aside from her growing attraction to Peter, the kiss brought forth a sensation that ironically had nothing to do with him. She hadn't kissed anyone since Danny had left five months ago. She had shut down all channels to physical enjoyment until they were safely dormant. The kiss created a spark—not a spark of love, or even of friendship, but of the physical. He was right about stimulation. It made you feel alive, even if it wasn't necessarily the right thing. She at least had a right to feel alive after feeling so dead.

By 3:00 am the band began to work their way through a long string of encores that would have never ended if the crowd got their way. Caroline was beginning to tire, but Peter seemed tireless.

"Let's get outta here," he said. There was no bill. They just left the booth and headed up the stairs. Their cab headed east through the now emptying streets, and then uptown, catching every light on First Avenue on the way north. She was groggy now. She should have stuck with beer. Martinis were not her thing.

As she began to doze off, Peter came close, and with his arm tightly around her, he placed his fist below her nose.

"Have some. It'll wake you right up," he whispered.

A small line of whiteness ran from his knuckle to his wrist.

"Just sniff it. Sniff a little."

"Ugh, no. Peter!"

"It's stimulation. You'll feel alive."

She was at a crossroads, wanting to like Peter and hoping the night would be perfectly aligned with what she wanted, but that meant being in his hands. So she did it. It was wrong, nasty bad stuff, she knew, but now she was becoming one with him and that was exciting. She had never done this before, so when she inhaled deeply, she wasn't even sure if she had gotten any. She could feel something, liquid, like candy, making its way through her sinuses and down the back of her throat. Then she could feel her eyes opening, as if stretching to a new day in the middle of the night. Then she felt awake, and then she wanted more.

54th, 59th, 61st, the streets flew by faster.

"Where we going next?" she said.

"Home, darling. We need to get you some rest," and she thought, 'how protective of him.' If he was really a bad guy, he would have kept her out, or let her get out of control.

74th Street and the cab pulled up suddenly at Peter's signal. He led her now as he had the whole night, her hand in his, to the elevator, to the button marked P.

"Parking?" she asked, laughing. "You live in the parking garage?"

He looked at her with a chill, the first time she had seen him with any shred of a negative word or action. It scared her. So unusual, so "un-Peter," she thought, as if she really knew that much about him.

"Penthouse, darling."

Darling. At least he was still her darling, even if he had been mad there for just a moment. So then he wasn't mad. She was his *darling*. That was a good thing because right now at this moment she wanted him to like her more than ever. She had been bad, worse than she had ever been, doing cocaine like this, so she needed to be forgiven, or at least accepted. At the same time, she felt so good. She crowded him into the corner of the elevator and kissed him.

They got to the roof and looked south to the Empire State and the twin towers, standing at attention way off in the distance. A spectacular sight that Caroline felt compelled to enhance.

"One more," she said.

"No."

"One…come on Peter!" She had become childish, a baby voice asking for a lollipop. After no response, she turned the adult back on.

"One more and then you can fuck me."

She couldn't believe she was saying this, like it wasn't her voice that said the words, words that came out quickly and decisively, as if she were closing a business deal.

But it was Peter all along who had closed the deal.

13

Joanne was worried. "He's bad news, Caroline."

"How do you know? You don't know Peter."

"I don't want to know Peter."

Caroline knew what Joanne was talking about, but tough luck. She wasn't backing down, and she was sick of Joanne's judgments, as though Caroline weren't worthy of someone like her own precious pilot fiancé.

"Well, maybe I don't want to know *Jeff*!" said Caroline. This drew the line between them.

"That's it. See-ya, Caroline," said Joanne.

She got up and left Caroline alone in the breakroom. Fine. If Joanne didn't want to know anything more about Jeff, if she didn't want to know the cold truth, then maybe they weren't meant to be friends. Joanne could have at least tried to understand how she felt about Peter, how she had a right to "be alive" as he liked to say.

But the reality was that Caroline had descended into addiction for a drug that she mistook for an addiction to Peter. He would take care of her; that was all that mattered. She deserved that, or at least something. She deserved to feel alive. To be alive!

Whatever the clouded source of her needs, she couldn't get enough of Peter. They went out every night. He paid for everything, and whenever they flagged just a bit, there was always a steady source of energy available to snort into their skulls. She was at least conscious of the danger and rationalized her addiction with the belief that she was in a transitional state, "just having fun." This was an easy leap for her; she truly did feel more alive, on the cutting edge of life itself and as much in the flow of the city as the cabs up and down the avenues.

Peter seemed to know everything. They had laughed at their own routine, just as they seemed to laugh at everything these days. They had their own mini language of acronyms; their favorite stood for dinner, drinks, drugs and sex. "DDDS," she said. This sparked a fit of laughter in them that only they could share. It wasn't even funny, which made it funny, and so they laughed, and then laughed at their laughing until they couldn't breathe. It was stupid, she knew, but oh, how she loved to laugh, and he was good at making her laugh, even if an altered state was required for it to happen.

As 1988 drew to a close, they wrapped around each other in the bundled New Year's throng of Times Square, drunk, stoned and high all at once. There was no one else with them—she no longer had any friends other than Peter, and he never seemed to have friends to begin with—only "intimate acquaintances," as he liked to joke, before qualifying the meaning of this to save his one friendship.

All through January there was an endless supply of cocaine for both of them. The thought had already run through Caroline's mind that as long as they didn't have to worry about running out, everything was absolutely fine. She convinced herself that she wasn't doing that much anyway and all seemed okay with her world. She couldn't deny that she felt much better than she had a few months ago, except for when she was crashing. She was also proud of the fact that, despite his seductive ways, his money and the desire that he had ignited in her, she had managed to mirror the emotional distance that Peter had kept from her. She didn't think she loved him, but she did love to be with him and hated to be without him. He was danger, excitement and "life." One Thursday afternoon he caught her in the midst of a call at work.

"Gotta go outta town this weekend," he said.

She could only look at him, surprised, but more disturbed by the breaking of their routine. Her caller was a gravelly voiced man haggling ferociously over the airfare. She snapped back at the shopper, and before it could escalate any further, she hung up on him. She had never done that before, not even with the worst customers, but something had spun out of control for the moment. She went over to Peter, who was now seated and on a call of his own.

"Where are you going?" He covered up the speaker on the end of his headset.

"I'll tell you later. I'm on a call," as if that ever mattered before.

She returned to her seat and toughed out the next few hours, certain that Peter would meet her downstairs at the end of the shift, just as he had each night. The comfort of the routine was the greatest assurance that they'd see each other almost every night, but as she got ready to leave the building, he was gone. She headed down to the bar, thinking he'd be there. He wasn't. She was unprepared for the sense of total emptiness that she felt. After spending virtually every night of the last two months together, he was gone. Completely gone.

The next afternoon he was a no-show at work. No sign of him, nor did anyone know where he was going. She started checking flights from LaGuardia, searching for him on the standby list. Miami, New Orleans, Chicago, San Francisco, until finally she came across his name. Los Angeles, with a return the next day, Saturday—not bad, she thought. She could survive a couple days without him. No big deal. And she was working Saturday, so she would be able to see if he got on his flight.

When she got into work Saturday afternoon, she logged in and went right to the standby list for his flight, but he didn't get on. According to the record, he didn't even show up for the flight, which was strange. She frantically checked the other flights, but he wasn't on those either. She checked Burbank and Orange County to see if he might have flown out of there, but he hadn't. She was left with her emptiness and a long day of agonizing phone calls ahead.

Monday came, and so did the news. Bulletins were "flashed" to the workforce each day with updates about new fares and promotions that everyone needed to be aware of. But sometimes the bulletins were more of a tragic nature and this one fit that description. The stark capital letters on the green screen overwhelmed any attempt at sympathy. It was plain, blunt and painful, like a full force kick to Caroline's stomach.

WE REGRET TO INFORM YOU THAT PETER OWENS PASSED AWAY ON FRIDAY JANUARY 29TH. FUNERAL ARRANGEMENTS WILL BE FORTHCOMING.

14

Caroline sat stunned, staring at the words on her computer screen. The hand on her shoulder nearly made her scream.

"Caroline, we need to talk to you." It was Donna, her manager. "Follow me."

She was led into one of the small "QC" rooms—for Quality Control—as they called it, which were normally used for monitoring calls. The room was small, barely big enough for its table and two plastic chairs. A well-dressed man she'd never seen before sat in one of them. There was one other man standing behind him. Across from him and right in front of Caroline was the empty chair.

"Caroline, this is Detective Murphy of the NYPD," said Donna. He rose politely and extended a hand to her.

"Hello, Caroline. Please take a seat."

Caroline was lapsing into autopilot, taking directions as if she were disembodied, severed from her will by the low-level state of shock that had overtaken her. She could barely make eye contact.

"Did you know Peter Owens?"

"Yes, I know him…knew him."

"Do you know anyone who would want to kill him?"

"*Kill* him? What happened?"

"His body was found on the beach in Santa Monica. He was beaten, and from the reports we have, it appears he was shot and killed execution style."

Caroline began to get sick. Murphy's style was not to sugarcoat anything. This was the cold reality he knew so well, and the biggest mistake he could make was to shield the victims from it. Donna grabbed a wastebasket just in time for Caroline to let loose: tears from her eyes, her last meal from her mouth, and under Murphy's trained eye, blood from her nose. He waited until she had wiped her mouth and her nose with the fistful of tissues that her manager placed in her hand as she spit her mouth clean.

"Caroline, how well did you know Peter?"

"We dated."

"Who do you think would have wanted to kill him?"

"I don't know. I have absolutely no idea. I mean, I knew him, but…I didn't really know him."

She had regained some composure. She wanted to help, but she was also scared. Murphy spent the next half hour asking the same questions in an endless variety of ways, but in the end he was satisfied that Caroline really did know nothing. She was as much in the dark as they were, thousands of miles away from the murder. The LAPD would need to fill in the blanks.

But one thing was obvious to Murphy: Caroline was just another coke whore, one he sympathized with on some level but knew was of little help in the investigation. Hits like these were precise because the drug culture of millions relied on the activities of a relatively few, and a clean hit never involved others. It just removed the cancer. This was a self-regulating world, Darwinian in every sense, where the strong survived, and the weak—those who lost control of either their addiction or the money to pay for it—were systematically eliminated. People like Caroline were simply collateral damage. He'd seen it so often that he felt like a typical underpaid social worker, especially when he'd end the conversation just like he did this one, with a coded phrase that was meant to go over the head of management and under the skin of his witness.

"Look at me, Caroline," he said. She finally made full eye contact. "You've got a very important decision to make. Don't make the wrong decision."

If she didn't know what he was talking about, there was probably no hope for her anyway. He spoke with the intensity of someone handing down a death sentence and that was the feeling he wanted to create before he returned to his civilized world of the non-addicted.

"I want to thank you both for your time," he said as he stood. His sudden politeness was his way of implying that she still had a chance to be a part of this world, however distant it might seem at the moment. He led his fellow officers out of the room, and Donna offered to escort them to the elevator.

"I'll be right back. You stay here," she said to Caroline.

Alone in the room, Caroline pulled out a mirror from her purse and looked at herself. She was crashing, a cumulative crash that left her too apathetic to be disgusted with her appearance, but aware enough to know she should be. She wiped her nose again, rubbed the tears out of her eyes, smoothed her hair and tried to regain some posture in the sterile plastic chair.

When Donna returned, Caroline became conscious of the differences between herself and her manager. Donna was all about appearance, propriety, and a quality that management liked to call "shininess." She wore a brightly patterned dress in the tradition of her African heritage, perfect makeup, every hair in place and a sense of command of her surroundings. Donna was power on the rise. She shut the door, pulled the seat over next to Caroline and resumed the interrogation.

"What's going on, Caroline?"

"Donna, I can't talk about it. I can't."

Caroline was starting to cry again. She knew not to talk to management. They were seductive, taking every intimate disclosure and documenting them one by one until they had enough on you to show you the door. A tap on the shoulder, a directive to gather your personal belongings and there you were out on the street. She'd seen it happen more than once.

"Caroline, I'm not going to ask you a bunch of questions. The airline doesn't want to know about this either. But I do want to make sure you're not heading down the same path as Peter."

Caroline looked at her now, her expression reaching for some shred of trust in her manager. Donna was right on it.

"I been there, honey. I know, I know! You're looking at me like you think I'm gonna get this all down and fuck you over, but I'm not Caroline, I'm with you. Nothing leaves this room. I just want you to be okay."

It was the "fuck you over" phrase that threw Caroline. It never seemed as though it could possibly be in Donna's vocabulary. This was an extension of trust via intimate profanity. Not that drug addiction was perfectly balanced with saying 'fuck' to a subordinate, but now they both had something on each other. It was a gift from Donna to Caroline that said trust me because I'm going to trust you.

"Here's a number for you. Call them," Donna said. It was a business card for a rehabilitation center in Pennsylvania.

"How do you know about this place?" Caroline asked.

"I know about that place because they saved my life."

15

"Congratulations, Ms. Douglas. You have made it through the first stage."

They didn't call them nurses in rehab, but that was for legal reasons, and the first stage only meant she'd completed Alta's mandatory cleansing and counseling program at the facility in the Pennsylvania mountains. There was no disputing that the next stage would last the rest of her life. She was a recovering cocaine addict and always would be.

But Caroline was a receptive patient. She had half tricked herself into believing that Peter wasn't real and could be blamed for everything, even if that wasn't the whole truth. Her responsibility now was to keep getting better and start looking forward, something that fully occupied her mind on the long bus ride back to New York.

Donna had described the airline's two-strike rule in detail. It was more a product of capitalist pragmatism than corporate altruism. A previous policy had served only to draw the company's legal department into endless harassment hearings in the city court. The deliberations were often inconclusive no matter how at fault the plaintiff was. Termination was much easier the second time around, after the corporation had made a good faith effort to rehabilitate their laborer, as if "corporation" and "faith" could ever really be used in the same sentence. But none of that was important to either Donna or her subordinate. All that mattered was that Caroline was clean.

"Welcome back, Caroline." Donna had been waiting for her.

"Donna, you are such a...*friend*." She said the word as if she had never used it before, but also because, recently, she had so often misused it.

"Now we gotta get you out of here," said Donna.

"What do you mean?" A fleeting thought of termination crossed Caroline's mind. Why should she be surprised? What recourse would she have if they could claim they saved her life and then fire her?

"I mean we've got to get you out of Reservations. You can't do this all your life. I know you're very smart, Caroline, and I know you're not using your brain. I see that in you, and you and I both know you can't go very far here in Reservations. You need a fresh start."

Caroline was stunned. No one had ever told her she was smart. Where did that come from? Why would anyone think that about her?

"When I said I've been there, I wasn't just talking about addiction, Caroline." Donna went on about her life, her frustrations, her inspirations and her successes. Caroline listened as best she could, still distracted by the declaration that kicked it off.

"You really think I'm smart?"

Donna just smiled at her. She took a quick look at the door of the room and made sure it was closed before she answered.

"If you don't think so, then you *are* a dumb ass, girl!"

They laughed the way friends should laugh, but the moment was a watershed for Caroline. Here was a pledge of faith in her abilities that carried forward the momentum of her recovery, beyond what she ever was and toward what she could be. A rebirth? A resurrection? There were no words to describe the confidence that was now steadily flowing into her soul. This was new ground for her, and Donna was going to kick her ass to make sure she did something.

It had been a long and cold winter, but now in April, New York had its first mild day of warmth, a spring day that Caroline felt with its full force, and it buoyed her. She had stopped smoking and had tuned into her restored sense of taste and smell. At lunch time she headed down to the street to pick up a few plain slices of cheese pizza from Don Pepe's, a small pizzeria lodged conveniently below Madison Square Garden and above the tracks of Penn Station. With both hands, she cradled the fat triangles of cheese, crust, tomato sauce and a perfect sheen of oil on flimsy paper plates. She was alone, on a stool at the counter against the wall. It wasn't as if she'd never had pizza before. It was a staple. But on this day, when she bit off the tip of her first slice, the mixture of thick mozzarella, firm crust and a touch of tomato suffused her mouth with a blissful richness. She was alive again.

She *was* resurrecting herself. Her health, her head, her body, and her senses were reawakening. And now it was time to resurrect her friendship.

"Joanne."

Joanne was thumbing through a bride magazine as she finished a sandwich when Caroline came up behind her in the break room. She didn't answer, but her body language conveyed a whisper of revulsion.

"Joanne, I'm sorry."

"Caroline..."

"I'm sorry, Joanne. I'm sorry for the way I've acted—for how I treated you. It wasn't...I wasn't myself."

"No kidding."

"I know. No kidding. My fault. *Me*. It was me, and I'm truly *truly* sorry." There was silence. Joanne looked at her with a blend of sympathy and disdain.

"Okay," she finally said.

"Okay. You forgive me?" she asked with a smile.

"Yeah, sure." But Caroline picked up the indifference and her smile faded. More work to be done.

"Hey, let's get a drink after work?" said Caroline. Caroline had actually stopped drinking. A soda in front of Joanne would prove her resolve to her friend and give her enough one-on-one time to thaw out the friendship. And Jeff had temporarily moved to Atlanta for pilot training, so she wouldn't have to compete with him for Joanne's time. Or so she thought.

"I can't, sorry. Got a lot to do. Wedding stuff."

Retreat. She had given it her best shot for now, and accepted that this might be one of the unavoidable punishments of her addiction. It would take time, a lot more time.

She felt a familiar pang of loneliness, something she had last felt when Danny vanished to Salt Lake City, but this time she embraced it, building on the momentum of her personal resurrection. If she was alone, then that's the way it was going to be. This time she would refuse to cloud the pain of being alone with drugs or sex or alcohol. She would feel it fully and confront it as a much better version of hell than the one she nearly fell into.

16

Everything was falling into place for Jeff Palmer. He would complete his pilot training in September, marry Joanne in October, and start flying a few weeks later. His decision to get in to the airline first, before he got on as a pilot had finally paid off. The months of aggravation he had spent in Reservations were now at an end.

But why shouldn't everything fall into place, he thought. He had controlled his destiny ever since he entered the Navy five years earlier. Sure, the path hadn't been a straight one, but that was his choice, because Alta was his chosen airline, the best in the country, the one his father had flown for and the one he had grown up on, traveling almost every month of his childhood between his father in Pensacola and his mother in Philadelphia.

The months of flight training down in Atlanta were a welcome break from the preparations for the wedding. He had no problem leaving all of that to Joanne and her mom. Let them put the whole thing together while he stayed out of the way, down in Atlanta, immersed in his training.

Although he had weekend breaks from the instruction, he decided to spend his last one before his final written exam in Atlanta. Training was rigorous, and a weekend of studying would be helpful. So he would study…a little. Joanne didn't need to know anything more than that. It wasn't really any of her business anyway. His last simulator session came to an end on a Friday in mid-June, and when he left the training center, he felt a rush of excitement that he hadn't experienced since before he met Joanne.

He met his buddies in the lobby of the hotel just an hour after class broke, and soon they were in a cab, heading up to an area in Atlanta known as Buckhead. Although he had been in Atlanta for the past few months, Jeff had only seen the skyline from a ten-mile distance. He had no concept of it as a city; to him it was just a far off cluster of buildings. But as the cab sped up I-75, the modest set of downtown skyscrapers rose before him. They were bigger than he had expected, and he had a mild revelation that Atlanta *was* actually a city.

He opened the window all the way. The air had just a touch of humidity, a smell of heaviness, of anticipation and the warmth of the setting sun. The highway snaked around downtown and into midtown, where he recognized some of the landmarks others had told him of. Georgia Tech on his left, the famous Varsity, Atlanta's glorified hot-dog stand, on the right. Soon they were following the sprawl toward the mansions and groves of the village north of the city. He had heard so much about this place called Buckhead, but never any real descriptions. Usually when he asked a native about it, they would just roll their eyes and shake their head.

The cab came off the highway and went down West Paces Ferry Road, a residential wooded community of the upper class. Then they broke through the trees and entered a different world.

It was teeming—a playground of spring breakers shorn of their beach. Glittering clubs, bars and discos in three directions, each with clusters of "wanna-get-ins" outside their doors, heels and skirts and hair and earrings, breasts that would cause accidents if it weren't for the prevailing gridlock. A cacophonous mix of music from doorways and cars with sound systems that made them shiver for attention, because attention was what everyone demanded.

The cab wasn't going any further without a struggle, so the four pilot trainees paid their $19 cab fare with a twenty and jumped into the plodding traffic. Their first stop was a place called Lulu's Bait Shack. Jeff was handed something called a fish bowl, a massive quantity of punch in a glass the size of his head with a plastic alligator in it, whatever that meant. Lulu's was rustic, like an old fraternity that hadn't yet trained the pledges how to keep the place clean. The drink was like candy and went down dangerously easy. They chased those with some shots—kamikazes, since after all, they were pilots—and then they were on to the next establishment.

This one was an Irish place, a pub in every possible way it could be, full of bricks and nooks and crannies, shelves full of Irish artifacts, stone and wood, slate and iron, and decades old ads that said 'Guinness, For Strength!' It was a veritable museum of unnatural history.

"Sure is a lot a crap in this place," one of them said.

The actual bar was in the center of the space, facing outward toward sections that were actually life-size dioramas of Irish history. The patron side of the bar was partitioned into small cubbies for the twosomes, mixed in with broad arcing expanses for the convivial. The first few minutes after their arrival were devoted to reconnaissance. They circumnavigated the bar with relative ease at the early hour of 9 o'clock. After a lap and a half, they found a worthy indentation along the bar and ordered pints of Guinness because that's what they figured they were supposed to do.

Jeff felt at home. They swung their stools around so their backs were to the bar and they could watch the flow of patrons parade past them on their own circumnavigations. No need for discussion among this foursome; these were not the types of guys who needed to have a whole lot of conversation and that made Jeff feel comfortable. It was just like the Navy; these were his fellow warriors, his buddies that he would die either for or with. Who the fuck needed to talk so much, to analyze things? Others might, but that's because they had little else in their life. These others certainly didn't have what it took, the "right stuff" as someone had said, although he was never very clear about what that meant. Thing was, there were always lots of terms like that flying around to describe pilots and almost all of them were complimentary. The one he liked the best was alpha male. He knew what that was.

Pilots were alpha males. They were the male-est of males, the fittest that survived, the ones that led the way for the species. Who else would have the guts to take hundreds of human lives in their hands every single day? Pilots were the dominant males, and he was one of them. He loved that feeling, that fundamental certainty of his dominance, of his superior position in the hierarchy of maleness.

They watched the flow of humanity thicken in front of them, but it never stopped moving. Occasionally a breast would inadvertently brush against a shoulder as they leaned forward into the flow. Or the eye contact would cross a threshold of time that warranted some comment, however trite it might be. Jeff winced at the beauty of the Buckhead blondes and pitied the lesser men who accompanied them. After two more pints of Guinness, pity turned to contempt. They were worthless, weak, meaningless carcasses of supposed manhood that happened to get lucky, but this kind of luck was threatening to screw up the gene pool.

The parade of women became ever more enticing, growing in numbers, attractiveness and variety. Some were statuesque and flamboyant, others seductive and submissive, most tending toward the unnaturally blonde and nearly all with the common quality of irresistible beauty. Now he knew why people rolled their eyes and shook their heads. He had never seen anything like this, not even in New York.

As much as Jeff loved every moment, there was something troubling him. Why were so many loser men with so many beautiful women? There was something wrong with that and he was having a hard time letting it sit.

An older guy with a slight hunch led his girlfriend by the hand through the slower moving patrons. The girl's body had an almost imperceptible arc to it, the upper half like a taut bow with breasts. Her hair was a perfect blonde wave, her eyes a perfect combination of shadow and darkness, her cheeks a perfect beckoning blend of pink and tan. She wore a white top, low riding jeans and a too-long belt of small gold hoops with the excess dangling to the split of her legs. The density of the crowd forced many people to wriggle sideways, sliding upstream past the bar into ever denser schools of humanity. The girl's tenuous grip on her boyfriend's hand and the flow of people around Jeff gave him a full frontal view of the girl. Perched on his stool in his own little eddy, he waited to catch her eye. The proximity forced upon them left her no choice. There she was, right in front of him, face to face, eye to eye, and body to body, inches apart.

It only lasted about a second, but it was so fully charged with electricity that it ended in the slightest half smile for each of them before the firm tug of her boyfriend's hand pulled her onward upstream with a jerk that tossed her blondeness. She followed with obedient high-heeled baby steps. The other three saw it all.

"Whoa, you might-a caught something there!"

"Who's the guy she's with?"

"Who's the asshole she's with?" They all chimed in, all charged and stoked and wanting some of it themselves.

"She wanted you, man. She wants noooo part of him."

"The guy's gotta fuckin' drag her through the place. He's a fuckin' pussy."

"Matter of time. She'll be back for you. If he lets her."

"You might gotta rescue that damsel, Jeffrey."

He smiled and laughed and peered over the heads, trying to spot their upstream destination. That look had touched off something in him, something he hadn't felt in a while. It was a sharp burning in his gut that he detested because he couldn't control it. This was something he had to put out, but just as it had been in the past for Jeff Palmer, the only way for him to manage it, to control it, was to get what he wanted, and what he wanted was her. The thought of it started off as ridiculous, but that disappeared after another shot with the boys ("to Jeffrey's one-that-got-away"), followed immediately by another Guinness, which were now going down faster, followed by a reconnaissance walk to the rest room, where he spotted her long legs crossed atop the stool next to her preoccupied boyfriend. No, not preoccupied. Rude. The guy was being rude to her. You don't ignore a woman like that. That's wrong.

One of the others began to gradually lapse into belligerence.

"So, Jeff-rey…"

They occasionally mocked him with his full first name because they were certain that that's what his 'mommy' called him, but this time it was more cutting than usual.

"…When are you going to step up to the plate and get that woman?"

"Yeah, yeah," said Jeff.

"When are you going to rescue her, eh?" He was a local—a true Southerner and proud of it. Not someone Jeff ever really liked that much, but just as it was in the military, you didn't have to necessarily like your brothers in arms anyway. Still, he was leaning in way too close.

"What happens if you've gotta rescue someone in trouble. You gonna be able to do it? You gonna step up?"

"Shut the fuck up," said Jeff.

"No, Jeffrey, hey, no problem. If you don't got it in you, you don't got it in you. Not everyone does. It's not your fault."

"Fuck you."

"Whoa, we're buds, man. It's okay."

"Fuuuuuck you."

The guy raised his hand for a high-five, submitting to Jeff, who complied in a haze of drunkenness.

"Fuck me. You got it, man," said the guy. And for no apparent reason, they toasted. But Jeff was past the point of wanting to kick the shit out of the guy, whatever the fuck his name was. At the moment he couldn't remember; Bobby Ray some-fucking-thing-or-the-other. Revenge would taste better if he proved him wrong, and that's what he was going to do, right now.

The look in Jeff's eyes was enough to tell the others that something was about to happen. He finished his beer and slid off his stool. He started pushing his way upstream, bumping people without a care; Jeff was too big for them to say anything more than "asshole" under their breath.

"I gotta see this," said one of the others, and they were quickly following in his wake. The couple was deep in conversation now, but Jeff went right up to the guy.

"You with her?" He was standing right over him, teetering forward in his face.

"Yeah, yeah, I'm with her," he said.

"No, I mean, are you *with* her?"

"Hey," she said, but that was all she could say. Jeff didn't wait for an answer.

"Like what I mean is, are you fucking her?"

"What the fuck? Get outta my face!" said the guy as he pushed him back. In seconds, the bar turned into a swirling pandamonius cluster of arms, fists, screams and women running for cover.

Two bouncers were on the scene in seconds, joined by a surprisingly agile bartender who had vaulted the bar in an instant. The three of them managed to continuously push Jeff backward toward the rear door with the force of a defensive line. The crowd parted, except for the other three pilots, who fell in behind their comrade. Already off balance, all of them were too drunk to throw a punch with any force. They were easily thrust into the rear parking lot with one final massive proprietary shove.

"Get—the—fuck—outta—here!!"

"Fuck you!!"

There was an uncomfortable moment of defeated silence until one of them laughed and the others joined in. But an undercurrent of anger was still simmering, hanging overhead and threatening to turn them into a dangerous foursome.

Their next stop was a place called the Buckhead Saloon. They pushed their way through the door and to the bar, bumping the more passive patrons on the way. They had smiles on their faces, devilish smiles that had nothing to do with happiness. Nobody was going to stop them for the rest of the night.

"Fuckin' assholes. We oughta go back there and kick their asses." After four or five variations of the same statement among them, they were distracted by a pair of women playing pool by themselves. They weren't quite as striking as the fish in the previous stream, but their handling of the cues, and body language as they rounded the table, put all previous thoughts to rest. Jeff moved first before anyone could question his courage.

"You gals any good at pool?"

One of them, the blonde, was about to take a shot. She looked up at him and then over to the other, the brunette, to see if this guy was worthy of an answer before answering.

"Yeah, as long as no one breaks our concentration with stupid questions like 'You gals any good at pool?'"

Jeff squinted in mock pain and stepped back from the table. She refocused on her shot, a long one, the target perfectly centered between the cue ball and the far corner. With silence and then suddenness, she cracked the ball into the pocket with a rumble.

Jeff was systematically assessing which of the two would be more receptive, filing his flight plan through the path of least resistance. The blonde's shot alone drew her down a notch. Not very feminine of her to slam that ball in so hard; she would be difficult to break. Plus she seemed to have an attitude problem. His eyes gravitated toward the brunette. Her eyes were already on him.

"Now, what was your question?" she said. The blonde circled the table with absolute indifference, lining up her next shot.

"You wanna play pool?"

"Yes, I think we do want to play pool. Oh look, we already *are* playing pool!" she said. Another attitude.

"Like, with us?"

"Hey, Deb, do we wanna play pool with these guys?"

She slammed another ball into the side.

"Yeah, whatever."

One of the foursome brought a fist full of tall necks over, and Jeff drafted Billy-Ray-whatever as a partner. The table was clear now. They set about preparing—chalking and racking as if they really knew what they were doing. The question in Jeff's mind was how to gracefully clue these women in that they were pilots. That was the one thing that would undoubtedly set them apart from the losers around them.

"Hey Billy Ray, I thought that L-1011 simulator was a little rocky."

"Did you do the emergency sequence?"

"Passed it."

"Yeah, me too, but it wasn't easy."

It went like this for a few minutes—pure bullshit, simply for the sake of strategic disclosure. Soon, he thought, these girls would have to ask them what they did for a living. In the meantime, it was clear that the piloting skills learned over the last five weeks did not translate well to the pool table. Jeff had a marked propensity for sinking the cue ball and then looking as if he meant to do it. It was all over in less than ten minutes.

"You win, we buy the beers."

Not once did the blonde make eye contact, nor did she say anything to any of them throughout the game. She was off to the bathroom moments after the eight ball fell, leaving the brunette in the unfettered thrall of her opponent.

"My name's Jeff."

"Sharon."

"You're pretty good at pool," he said.

"Thanks. You're not." She smiled.

At least Jeff got a bit more warmth from Sharon while blondie was absent, the chill of peer pressure having vacated. She was wearing the same thing as the girl in the last place, sprayed on blue jeans and a high riding white top. The only difference was a black braided belt to go with her brunette hair. But it was her eyes that dominated the package, eyes that were a lovely mix of passion and amusement; humanity that softened her face, if not the entire surroundings.

"You're a pilot."

"How did you know?"

"Because you made sure we knew, you and your silly conversation about simulators and check-offs and shit."

"Check *rides*," he corrected.

"Yeah, whatever."

She was leaning on the pool table, cue in her left hand, beer in her right and he with the same, just a foot away from her. Maybe she was a bit snotty in her banter, but there was interest in the way she looked up at him. The blonde came back and it all fled away. Sharon returned to her friend, leaving him to the inevitable interrogation.

"What's the deal?"

"You gonna get some of that or what?"

"Yeah, if you guys don't fuck it up," he said. Sharon was stealing glimpses.

"That blonde is something, isn't she?" Jeff said to the other three. The flight plan called for a diversion. Someone had to unburden his target or this wasn't going anywhere.

"Why don't *you* guys play now," said Jeff. Billy Ray was drunk and on the sidelines. The other two looked at each other with hesitation, leaving the door open for Jeff.

"Whattaya chicken? Get your asses out there and play some pool with that babe! Come on, you gonna step up to the plate or what?"

He grabbed them by the shoulders and pushed them over, then grabbed Billy Ray.

"Do me a favor and make it a foursome," he said into his ear.

The three of them plodded over to the girls. Jeff caught Sharon's eye again and gestured with his head toward the back of the bar. She said a few quick words to her friend, and just as the pilot contingent encircled them, she slipped free to join Jeff.

The chill had lifted again, and so the smile returned as she led him back into the caverns of the saloon. There was a heavy wooden door at the rear of the place that opened up into a long narrow pub, a treasure chest of semi-privacy. They found a pair of stools at the end of the bar, ordered a few more beers and started fresh. She tossed him softball questions about his training, about his time in the Navy and about his personal life, in that order, and with each change of subject, she drew a little bit closer until they were only inches apart.

"No girlfriend?"

"Nope. No girlfriend." He wasn't lying.

"There's a lot of pilots that live here and they're all married. What's the deal with you? Are you gay?"

"Gay? Me? You think I'm a faggot?"

"Well, I don't think so, but I guess there's no way of knowing, is there?"

"There's one way."

He kissed her. She let him. It was a kiss fit for a saloon, a sloppy, slippery kiss. She had an active tongue—more exploratory than he had ever known Joanne to be. Her hand came up on his back, and he could feel her nails biting through his shirt and along his spine, and then up his neck and into his hair. Her lips ground into his, her nails stabbed at his scalp. She grabbed a clump of his hair and pulled him away with a gasp, as if she had lost control and regained it just in time.

The rest of the conversation was purely for display, simply to prove to the people around them that they were capable of being civilized in a public place. Now they needed to work out their escape.

"I'll be right back," she said.

She coyly touched the back of her neck as she got up and discreetly looked around to see who was looking at her; force of habit to preserve an image of modesty, when in fact she hoped that everyone was looking at her. She was gone for only a few minutes, but it seemed much longer to Jeff. He considered that she might not be coming back. Maybe her bitch of a blonde friend had talked her into leaving. It had happened before—before he was a pilot. He looked up at the door, begging it to open, hoping for her to return to him. Return to him! He should be able to command it, to will it, to make it happen with the pure power of his alpha maleness. And then there she was.

"Let's get out of here," she said, grabbing his hand.

They walked a few blocks down Peachtree Street where they flagged a taxi. The driver made a daring U-turn and they headed south towards the high-rises until they were dropped in front of the lobby of one of the tallest. Although he extracted enough crumpled singles to cover the cost of the cab, she was now in charge, taking his hand and leading him to the plush elevator. The ride upward seemed endless. Thirty something floors to her apartment, which she unlocked with a fumble of her keys.

If she had been a New Yorker, she would have been a multi-millionaire with this kind of place. Carpeting, strange artwork and the glowing Atlanta skyline to the south were all he would remember about the apartment. As he looked out the window, her hands wrapped around his waist and slid down along the front of his thighs before moving inward. Sharon led the way and did everything, serving him well beyond his expectations with a writhing enthusiasm he had never known. It was sex with someone he hardly knew, but he could only conclude that this was one of the perks of his job. She had drawn him in, she had brought him home and she was the one who had recognized the alpha male and everything that went with it. This was nature at work, something that, for the good of his species, he best not fight.

When it was over and she was sleeping beside him, he considered how the constraints of society sometimes failed to accommodate all that someone like him was entitled to. They would never understand, never completely accept that this was the way things really work. He was one of the dominant ones, and perhaps this was the curse of being a leader. He might one day be called upon to save hundreds of people with a split second decision, and if so, who could deny him that which he, the hero, desired. Isn't this exactly what they meant by "the spoils"?

Content and at peace, he drifted off to sleep.

17

Caroline had completed six months of abstention by the time summer arrived. This had been a personal test for her, a test of both her strength and her smarts. It didn't matter how hard her job was right now; her company had stood behind her and she was going to give them her best.

"Good news, Caroline" said Donna, radiant, professional Donna, the bearer of positive energy. "You got the job at Kennedy."

It had been weeks since they last discussed the idea of even putting in for a ticket counter position, but Donna had submitted Caroline's name and pushed hard.

"I got it?"

"Yeah, you got it! You start on Monday!"

With that, Caroline sprung to her feet and gave her manager a long and loving hug. Donna had become more savior than manager, not because working at Kennedy Airport would be the job of a lifetime, but because this was a woman who believed in her when she needed it most. It had been almost two years since Caroline first walked into the building and now she was ready to remove the little plug from her ear for the last time and take the next modest step in her career with Alta.

Even though it was barely ten miles distant, there was no easy way to get to Kennedy from her home in Jackson Heights. On her first day, Caroline was late. She'd taken the E train to the G, to the L, and then finally to the A train into the airport. It took her almost two hours and replaced all of the first-day excitement with anxiety. On the positive side, she was given a small salary increase and was on the path toward saving enough money for a deposit on her own place. Still, it would be several weeks before she could leave the cramped quarters of her parents' apartment, meaning each day until then promised to be an adventure in commuting.

The training program at the airport was very simple: there was none. You learned by drinking out of the fire hose. When Caroline walked in, the ticket counter was in full swing, a madness of sorts, with lines of people winding in and around every patch of bare floor space that didn't have a pole and a rope guarding it. Massive piles of bags upon bags were slid with kicks and shoves toward the counter as the customers inched their way to an agent.

"Get over here. Right here, help this guy."

This is what Caroline heard the moment she told someone behind the counter that this was her first day. She didn't know his name, she didn't know what to do, she didn't even have a uniform yet.

"What'll I do?"

"Just help him," he said as he helped someone else.

The customer handed her his ticket and she instinctively smiled.

"Thank you, how are you today?"

"Very well, thank you," said the customer, an elderly man with a cheeriness about him that Caroline immediately appreciated, maybe too much.

"And where are you going today, sir?"

"Yo!" said her co-worker. "Why don't you take a look at his ticket and maybe you'll find out." He was a tall guy, black, nice looking but not very nice at the moment. Didn't matter. He knew a hell of a lot more than she did and that's what mattered.

"Oh, yeah, good idea," she answered.

She was conditioned for phone conversations and so the question she asked the customer came naturally, but at least the man was patient with her. Of course, that didn't mean she knew what to do with his ticket, so she made a show of taking it out of the envelope, looking it over pensively and straightening it before replacing it in the envelope.

"Okay, whatta we got?" The black guy snatched the ticket out of her hand and nearly bumped her out of the way of the computer. Within seconds he was logged in and looking at the customer's reservation.

"Aisle or window?"

"Window," said the customer.

Caroline watched the guy type in the commands. He was faster than anyone she'd ever seen, even in Reservations. And he typed loudly too, with big thrashing pecks that echoed in the cavernous terminal.

"All set, there you go. Gate B8," he said. He gave the guy a tight-lipped grin as he handed him his ticket. At the same time, he reached up with the other hand and flipped the "Position Closed" spindle into place.

"Follow me," he said to Caroline. She trailed him back through an unmarked door behind the ticket counter. As soon as they were out of public view, his entire personality transformed.

"How you doin, my name's Shawn."

"Caroline. This is my first day."

"Yeah, no kidding." He was smiling so she did too.

"You didn't know what the fuck you were doing out there, did you?" He talked fast.

"Well, how am I...?"

"Taking the ticket outta the envelope and putting it back in. That's a good one," he said laughing.

"How am I supposed to know!?"

"I'll teach you everything you gotta know. You just watch me, Caroline, and everything is gonna be all right."

He seemed like a bonehead. Kind of stupid, but Caroline was well aware that she was more stupid, and even in his boneheadedness, he was strangely charming.

"Lesson number 1: Try not to be so nice."

"Whattaya mean? You don't want me to be nice?"

"Not too nice. They sense that, that niceness thing. I'm not sayin' don't be nice. I'm just saying if you're too nice, they're gonna start asking you for things."

"Yeah, like what?"

"Like an upgrade, or a wheelchair or a special meal, or a free ticket. Whatever, you name it. I seen people ask if they can carry their friggin steamer trunks on board."

"Oh. Yeah. That's not good."

"Right!" he said, pointing at her. "So, what's Lesson number 1?"

"Don't be too nice!" she said.

"You got it. But something tells me that's gonna be a hard one for you." He flashed a smile. Acceptance.

"What's Lesson number 2?" she asked. She wanted to be a willing student.

"Lesson 2 is it's time to go back to work. Follow me."

"What? Wait!"

She followed him around for the rest of the day. Abrupt as he was, he was also gracious and patient with her, passing on tips between customers as she looked over his shoulder. Time permitting, she would make every attempt to ask questions that showed some thought behind them.

"Shawn, why'd you give him a refund there? Isn't that a nonrefundable fare?"

"I gave him a refund because it was the right thing to do. Gotta keep the customers happy. Make'em feel important, but never let them take advantage of you."

"But that's not what we tell them in Reservations."

"We ain't in Reservations, sweetheart. This is the airport. A *totally* different world."

He was right about that.

John F. Kennedy International Airport was exciting and tumultuous—a constant stream of people arriving from and flying to distant lands. There was an energy at the airport that her previous job could never match. This was a place of palpable emotion and anticipation, the closest thing to an Ellis Island of the airways.

Alta's terminal at JFK was ancient by airline standards, accidentally retro in its appearance with flamboyant mid-60s décor. Psychedelic mobiles hung from the high ceiling, relics that were meant to greet the modern jet age. Linoleum stretched from the ticket counter to what was probably the first baggage carousel ever built.

Caroline got a break in the early afternoon and took a stroll with a cup of coffee. The lack of a uniform allowed her to avoid the assault of questions from the lost and confused, which was a good thing because she would have only added to their confusion.

She noted the historical quality of the vast space. The intent of its original design was clear: wide open whiteness, a theme of airiness upheld by thirty foot walls of window, framing the newest jets of the period and the novelty of air travel. But this probably lasted no more than ten years before another surge of construction was thoughtlessly overlaid, this being a cluster of free standing shops in the middle of the floor that managed to impale the space and suck the air out of the airiness. And then the remaining space simply evaporated. Jets got bigger, gates were added, budgets got tighter and the terminal remained, treading water in a flood of people, in a city that was and always had been a gateway. A city that once swallowed immigrants and visitors from ocean liners was now being injected by narrow metal tubes of them on an hourly basis.

Caroline bumbled through the rest of her first day with Shawn's help. By the end of the shift, he was her friend and a mentor, this at the expense of knowing every other person she would be working with.

"Tomorrow, if you can get your ass here on time, I'll take you around and introduce you."

"Okay. I'll be here."

"I dunno, Caroline. First day and you don't show up. Not good."

"I showed up!"

"Luckily, I covered for you. I had a word with a few people so no one should give you any shit for it."

"Yeah, except maybe for you."

"Hey, if I cover for you then I got the right to give you shit."

"Nobody's got the right to give me shit!" she said.

"You're pushing it. Using profanity in front of me like that. Disrespecting me. It's your first day! You're just a rookie, little girl. On probationary status."

"Probationary status!? I'm not on any probationary status."

"'PS'. That's what we call the rookies. But I have elected to make a special exception for you and decided to call you Caroline."

She was sure he was full of shit, but she felt out of breath. Without a comeback from her, he changed his tone.

"You gonna get here tomorrow okay?" he asked her.

"Yeah, I'll get here. Somehow," she said.

"Where you live anyway?"

"Jackson Heights."

"Oh yeah? How'd you get here?" he asked her. She didn't answer immediately. "I took the train."

"The train?!" he said, on the verge of laughter. "You took the train? What train? The Jackson Heights to Kennedy express?"

"I'd rather not get into it."

"Hey, I live in Elmhurst. I gotta find this train!"

She knew he had figured out what she'd been through and it was embarrassing. He could have laughed, could have mocked her all the way back to Jackson Heights, but he picked up on her shame and restrained himself.

"Caroline, come on, I'll take you home. It'll take fifteen minutes."

Normally, Caroline would have immediately rejected this offer, but this was someone she would be working with every day. The risk was minuscule. There was also a strange sense of having known him for much longer than one day, maybe because it had been a very long day. She accepted the offer with relief, and the banter continued all the way back to her home, along with negotiations for one-sided carpooling; Shawn would pick her up the next morning, and every morning that they had the same shift.

"Just don't be nasty like some of the other girls we work with."

"Maybe that's because you told them not to be too nice."

"You know what I mean."

That, and some occasional gas money, he said, would be enough compensation for her daily lift to work.

It may have been a lopsided arrangement, but a friendship took hold between Caroline and Shawn. Now he was both mentor and chauffeur, laying a path toward routine that Caroline easily followed. In exchange, she dutifully gave him gas money every payday.

Though she did get to know her other co-workers—winning their respect with her work ethic and resilience in the face of demanding customers—Shawn might as well have owned her social life. Still, she drew a firm line around herself. In spite of his chivalrous and occasionally profane affection, Caroline did not let Shawn distract her from the very specific goal she had set for herself: the escape from her parents' apartment and acquisition of her own living space.

By the end of July she was finally ready to move out, with just enough in her tattered passbook savings account to make the deposit on an apartment and just enough cash flow to cover her monthly rent. After several wasted off days of apartment hunting, she finally found a studio in Long Beach, just a short train ride from the airport. It was on Beach Street, on the top floor of a two-story house turned into apartments. Caroline conceded to herself that it was probably a bit out of her price range, but the landlord, an affable old man, seemed to like her and offered her a break on the rent. That settled it.

The place was modest and constricting, with a ceiling that slanted down around dormers that faced the Atlantic Ocean. Outside the door there was a common area balcony, a widow's walk of sorts, that also looked out over the ocean, but since Caroline was the only upstairs resident, this was effectively her space. She probably could have had a much bigger apartment somewhere, maybe even one with a bedroom rather than a living room that doubled as a bedroom, but this is what she wanted. A year earlier, in the wake of Danny's departure, she had let her loneliness get the best of her. But now she was welcoming isolation and this was the first time she had a space she could truly call her own. Now her independence was everything—no boyfriends, no parents and no distractions. This apartment would be her sanctuary, her corner of peace, her shield against the uncertainty and insanity that had trailed her through so much of her life.

On the summer day when she was handed the keys, when she unlocked her door, entered *her* apartment and shut the door behind her, she realized that she had never been this excited before. Caroline was home.

18

"Caroline, it's Joanne."

"Joanne! How's the wedding coming?"

"I'm looking forward to it, but I'll be glad when it's over. Listen, let's not talk about that. You want to get a drink?"

"Absolutely!"

It had been a while since they'd talked, and though Caroline had sensed some warmth on occasion, their friendship wasn't quite back to its original form. They picked an evening and met at a pub in Queens under the tracks of the Long Island Railroad. There was an immediate lightness to their conversation, a long-lost-friend atmosphere that neither wanted to ruin.

"You look so good!" Joanne said.

"Thank you. You think so?"

"You really do."

"I've been...behaving myself."

"Did you ever find out what happened?"

"You mean to Peter?"

"Yeah."

"He must have been dealing. That's what I think. Some of the things he had, like where he lived, and of course the drugs, there's no way a piddly airline salary would have paid for it. I'm guessing even the deals couldn't pay for what he owed. But that's all I know. That's all I want to know." She paused but only for a second.

"So you're getting married!"

"Yes, believe it or not. It all seems to be coming together. Will you be there?"

"You want me to come?"

"Yes, I want you to come. I know we haven't been real close lately, but I want to get back to where we were."

"Are you inviting Danny?"

"I was going to, yes. Should I not do that? Jeff wanted him to come, but I make the final decision, so..."

"No, that's fine. No problem at all. Invite him."

"Are you guys okay and all?"

"I haven't talked to him in a while, but we're fine. I'm fine. I'm so over it, Joanne. Invite him. You can even stick him at the same table with me."

Caroline was so pleased with having her friendship with Joanne back that she was in an over-conciliatory mood. They were drinking daiquiris, a virgin for Caroline. The new job and her new home had restored her confidence and her near death experience made everything else seem trivial.

"How's Jeff doing?" she asked.

"Great. He's doing check rides now. He finishes training in September."

"Are you excited?"

"Yeah, except, like I said, I'll be kind of glad when it's all over."

"Yes, but are you excited about marrying Jeff?"

Caroline made a conscious effort to ask this question tactfully. She would ask it once and only once. She didn't trust Jeff at all, but in the warmth of her resurrected bond with Joanne, now was not the time to probe any deeper than this, nor would she mount a soapbox to bestow warnings. Joanne took an extra moment to assess the question.

"Yes, I am excited, Caroline. I'm very excited. I love him."

Caroline raised her drink and Joanne joined her, clearly relieved by the show of approval.

"Let this be the first of many. To Joanne and Jeff."

◆   ◆   ◆

The weekend of the wedding arrived. Danny had been back to New York for the holidays to see his family, but it had been over a year and a half since he'd seen Caroline, and he was nervous about this. His dominant memories of the great city were of her, and he was deeply in tune with the sense of loss that he now felt as his arrival neared. He'd had a flurry of meaningless relationships, and now he couldn't help wondering what would have happened if he'd stayed.

The plane approached from Sandy Hook over the Jersey shore before making a long slow circle over Brooklyn and Queens. They would have dinner together. She would meet him at the gate at Kennedy and they'd head into Manhattan. They were both going to the wedding, and this evening together would allow them to diffuse any tension that remained. He convinced himself that it would be fine once they started talking, but he couldn't figure out why he was so nervous. There was nothing to be nervous about. He missed her, but more than that, he missed the whole New York experience: the city, the nights together with her and the bond they had developed in the very early days of their careers. Their favorite roller coaster—which he spotted on final approach over Coney Island—brought back the best of his memories with her and he realized he hadn't laughed as hard with anyone since those days. Maybe they weren't so miserable.

It was fall in New York, the time of year that he felt most drawn to his old home. In contrast, the desert valley of Salt Lake really only had two seasons: summer and winter. Just a few weeks before, it had snowed a day after it had been in the 70s. No transition, no warning. But autumn in New York was intoxicating, and the skyline—the unfathomable pride of that skyline—seemed more unreachable than it had ever been. He wasn't from here anymore.

"Hi, Danny." She was waiting at the gate and managed to sneak up on him from behind.

"Caroline! Hi." They hugged, and he kissed her on the cheek. He had that pain in his stomach that he always had when he was nervous.

"You look good, Danny," she said. It occurred to him that this was something she wouldn't have said in the past. She didn't seem nervous at all. Her body language was assertive.

"Thanks, so do you."

"Yeah."

"No, you really do. You look great. You look like you lost weight."

"I have, but for all the wrong reasons."

"What do you mean?"

"Never mind. Follow me. My car's out here."

It was actually Shawn's car, but he'd lent it to her for the evening. She led Danny through the catacombs of their terminal, through tunnels and secure doors to the employee parking lot. During the ride they talked about the innocuous, the jobs, Jeff and Joanne, the company. It was almost midnight so traffic was thin, and within a half-hour they were in lower Manhattan and on to a bar in the West Village. They had considered going back to the bar near the reservations office, the place where the sparks first flew, but when Caroline suggested otherwise, Danny quickly consented. This was not an evening to cultivate regrets.

They decided to sit at the bar rather than a table, on stools that would allow them to swivel away if things got too intense.

"I think this was a good idea," said Caroline.

"What was?" asked Danny.

"This meeting, between us. We need to feel comfortable together."

"I agree. Do you feel comfortable?" he asked.

"Yes, I feel much better. I was a little nervous about it, but I knew it would be okay once we got past the first few minutes," she said. This was not the Caroline that Danny had left behind. Though their relationship had lasted less than year, it had happened during an impressionable time for both of them. He remembered how she always needed him, always gauged her own self-esteem by her proximity to him. But she had something of her own now—a confidence, a strength that he had never seen before. Now there was the hint of age in her face, around her lips and her eyes, and all of these minor details contributed favorably to her new demeanor. He saw it immediately in the way she carried herself. She was not the freckled girl he said goodbye to less than two years ago. She was a woman.

"How about you? Were you nervous?" she asked.

"I'm still nervous. I missed you." He hadn't planned on saying this because it wasn't until he saw her again that he *really* missed her.

Oh, he missed her all right. He missed her ride to hell and back, her transition from girl to woman. There was no reason that Caroline could think of to share the details with Danny. He was looking at her differently now, which made her smile.

"You missed me? Why did you miss me? Aren't you dating those Utah girls now?"

"Yeah, right. Utah girls."

She probed him for details, and this took them off on a tangent of strange experiences and provincial humor until they both almost fell off their barstools in fits of hysterical laughter. Now Danny's stomach hurt not from nerves but from laughing, and Caroline was experiencing her own pain. It all seemed so much funnier from 2000 miles away. When they finally regained control, took a sip of their drinks and looked at each other in repose, Danny realized something he wasn't prepared for. He knew he could fall in love with this woman.

"Are you dating anyone?" he asked.

"No, not right now."

"No?" Danny's curiosity was suddenly unrestrained.

"Listen, Danny. Maybe this is something we should just keep off limits for us. Whattaya think?"

"Caroline, I never stopped feeling the way I do about you."

"Oh bullshit, Danny. You left! You left me for...for fucking *Utah*, and all I know is that I wasn't part of that plan, so stop right there and just cut the crap."

"I'm sorry."

He hated the weakness he heard in his voice. This was the last thing he wanted, Caroline thinking he was an asshole and him proving it on demand.

"Danny, let's just go to the wedding, smile for the pictures and make sure Joanne has the best day of her life." He was nodding before she finished her sentence. He wanted nothing more now than to realign with her, so he dropped it. But there was something about her statement that triggered a question.

"What about Jeff?" he asked.

"What about him?"

"You said let's make this the best day of Joanne's life? What about Jeff?"

She took another sip of her soda, finishing it off before answering. She looked at him in a way that was completely transparent. Danny knew that she was calculating, deciding whether she should confide in him.

"Come on, tell me. Tell me what you're thinking."

"No."

"Caroline, come on, it's me. I'm still Danny. Still the Danny you knew."

"That's what I'm afraid of. No, Danny."

In the past, Caroline might have actually gotten some enjoyment in the gossip, in the confidentiality, the secrecy of sharing with Danny the flaws of both Joanne and Jeff, but now there would be nothing good to come from conveying her own distrust in the marriage. Danny was no longer an intimate. He had forfeited his right to her thoughts.

"Let's just go and have a good time, Danny," she finally said.

"Let's," he said. No more disagreements.

"We'll have fun," she said. She softly tapped her hand on his, but it was a friendly gesture.

19

The wedding was great—a joyous event that Jeff was sure he'd always remember. He cherished the chance to have his family and all of his closest friends there. Danny and Caroline, the other two of their original foursome, brought back surprisingly warm memories of their shared struggles. Caroline may have been gruff to him once in a while, and he wasn't as close to Danny as he had been, but they were as much his fellow soldiers as the Navy guys. They had suffered together just like he had with the plebes years earlier.

He never could figure out why Caroline and Danny didn't make it together, but he knew from Joanne that she had already gone off the deep end a while back. Still, just because Danny went to Salt Lake City didn't mean they couldn't have taken a crack at a long-distance relationship. It was working for him. With Joanne in New York and his new base in Dallas, he was now in a long-distance marriage and he loved it.

The wedding followed the completion of his training, and the honeymoon in Maui followed the wedding. It was a week of candlelit dinners, beachfront balcony views, snorkeling, whale watching, and a sunrise climb up Haleakela, the enormous volcano that once spouted the mass that made the island. Throughout the trip, Joanne always managed to work into her conversations—with waiters and waitresses, cab drivers and tour guides—that Jeff was a pilot. All through it, Jeff played a good romantic, but his idea of romance had little to do with passion and more to do with association. She was an important piece of the puzzle, the one that would be there for him and give him children.

When the trip was over, he was glad to be home and ready to get to work. Although he didn't share it with Joanne, he bid for Dallas as his base because it offered a better ranking than New York. He could have gotten New York, but that would have left him on reserve, the pilot equivalent of being benched for who knows how long. And he didn't want to move her out of New York, not with the possibility that he could be changing his base two or three times in the next few years. He set himself up in an apartment in Plano, a high-end suburb outside of Dallas, but he didn't spend a lot of time there. Once he got his monthly bid, he and Joanne would do their best to coordinate their schedules. She would swap days, sometimes working seven days in a row just to string two days together that coincided with Jeff's off days. Then one of them would head east or west, and they'd pretend they were a settled married couple. He had no friends in Dallas, so the commuting neatly filled a void for him.

But it was only one of many voids.

His career kicked off with a position as a second officer on 727s, the work-horse of the commercial skies through the 70s and 80s. He didn't get to actually fly the plane in this assignment, but at least he was in the air a lot, and that helped because the initial pay was minimal. Seniority, and the pay scale that went with it, was everything to pilots, and the guys on the low end usually paid the price for the guys on the high end. But if he stuck with it, he'd be one of those high-end guys too, well into six figures for two weeks of work a month. He signed on to the union and joined his brethren, many of them fellow Navy men.

Jeff could tell right away who the Navy guys were because they were just like him—always the most competitive. They were the ones who looked at the others and sized them up for a fight, even if they were the best of friends. It was a sur-vival instinct that had been bred into him and the others who had followed the same path. They'd peek across the cockpit at the other pilot, the guys who weren't Navy, and check their reflexes, their reactions, their demeanor, their cool, and almost always conclude that they couldn't hit an aircraft carrier with a heli-copter.

But Jeff was an alpha male, comfortable that he was one of the few men of exceptional quality, and so he was willing to wait his turn as a bow to pilot civili-zation. This was a highly stratified society, this system of seniority, in some ways like the military in that it conformed to a framework for the common good, the unionized good. He conceded that natural selection would wreak havoc on the system; the supply of the superior was limited by its very nature. It wasn't long before the culture and customs found a place in Jeff's consciousness. There weren't a lot of opportunities to prove superiority in this job, 90% of which involved cruising through clear air on automatic pilot. But the act of landing served as something of a competitive arena.

For the pilot, a smooth landing was an affirmation to the guy next to him that he had what it took. Who cared what the passengers thought; it was the cockpit audience, the harshest of silent critics that would render the meaningful judg-ment. And if after a particularly cataclysmic meeting with the tarmac, a flight attendant let slip a reference to their "eventful" arrival, no matter how casual or humorous her tart little declaration, the castration might as well have been in the Town Square. This sometimes brought to mind stories like the one about the elderly lady who approached the pilot before deplaning and politely asked him, "Captain, did we land, or were we shot down?"

It was also an unfortunate circumstance that Jeff would have to accept the injustices of inferiority by seniority, the primary reason why Alta was unable to hire him right out of the Navy. But now he had signed on and that meant a stoic acceptance of all the rules of the game. Sacrifices had to be made, yet it still irked him when he witnessed a lack of discipline in the cockpit, no matter how small. From where he sat there were far too many of these anomalies. A scuffed shoe, crooked wings, a wayward shock of hair—it annoyed him, because in Jeff's mind, there was no room for error as a pilot, and a lack of discipline was the start down a slippery slope. Discipline was everything. Perfection, or at least a constant striving for it, was the price of admission. They were not bus drivers; they were shepherds of commerce and community, literally defying gravity to keep the country running

Jeff was a good pilot, maybe even a great pilot, but that meant little. Unlike the Navy—a beautiful performance driven pilot factory where the best rose to the top and survival was truly a function of the fittest—there was no such thing as a "top gun" at a commercial airline. An airline was more like a digestive tract in reverse: you entered from the ass and over time, you worked your way up to the mouth, where eventually you could speak your mind and have some influence over your future. Progression was a function of time rather than ability. His entire future, the next 35 years, was completely mapped out. The only unknown was how much money they could get out of management with each contract negotiation.

A pilot is married to his career and to his airline, and naturally demands a "return" on this investment that is financial, but analogous to the emotional and sexual return of a marriage. Where the two marriages diverge is in the cost of divorce. A pilot who divorces his airline goes to the back of the pack, the ass of the next airline. This is not the case with the other marriage, and very often, as the soul seeks passion in a too predictable world, one marriage pays the price for the other.

Jeff was very clear on this, very precise, very calculating and very pragmatic, and he had absolutely no intention or desire to ever divorce his wife. Joanne would bear his children, be his wife, his spouse, his companion. But it was unfair to expect her to satisfy everything that he needed. He had no disrespect for the many thousands of competent pilots who were loyal to their wives. Good for them, he thought. That was who they were—easily satisfied, accepting of their own world of monotony, with their houses in Peachtree City, their perfectly manicured lawns, their corner of perfection. Fine, but in Jeff's mind, he was diametrically different, on a higher level in terms of proficiency, perfection, and humanity. He was a leader who could not be fully defined or understood within the oppressive limits of current society. He considered himself on the cutting edge, with passions and feelings that were absolutely natural. He accepted that 20th century society would damn his behavior, but perhaps in a hundred years people like him would be understood.

PART III
1990–1994

20

Wesley Arnold was a king yet to be crowned. By the end of the 1980s his role as the vice president of personnel allowed him to vanquish rivals and place himself on the next and most appropriate rung on the corporate ladder. He was now the recently anointed executive vice president of marketing and sales. And since he was still the youngest of the VPs, it was just a matter of time. The airline stuck to tradition, never going outside the company for their leadership. Assuming no major slip-ups, this meant that those above him would either have to give way or die off.

But Wesley left nothing to chance. He had even schmoozed the revered but now powerless and wheelchair-bound Martin Willman. Every quarterly board of directors meeting had a stiff social event, and always during the evening, Wesley made it a point to take a seat next to Willman. He'd make wistful comments to the founder about the perennial tractor that appeared in the annual executive photo, and how his father had a tractor like that once—a complete lie. Willman's eyes would light up, and nobody in the room missed it when he'd slap an appreciative hand on Wesley's shoulder. This also served as a convenient exchange for Wesley, because with Willman's memory all but shot, he could tell the same story every quarter and get the same reaction.

The executive vice president of marketing was also the plum position, full of more perks than all the others combined. Whatever Wesley wanted, he got, but sometimes he needed help getting it. Only when it was absolutely necessary would he pick up the phone to make a special request. His secretary Diane would take care of that, but she couldn't handle all of it. He needed a "boy." Someone besides a secretary, someone who could handle the crap while he concentrated on putting the hammer down on all of his division VPs. With reservations, marketing, advertising, sales and now international sales all under his domain, Wesley was responsible for well over eight thousand people.

◆   ◆   ◆

The ascendance of Wesley Arnold coincided with the descent of Danny's sanity. In the three years that he'd been in Salt Lake City, he never quite made it out from behind his desk. Danny had fulfilled the role of safety net for the incompetence of Reid Nielson, becoming the classic corporate scapegoat for failures and the ghost for successes. Each day brought a new pile of paperwork, and ironically, his high proficiency only served to solidify his position. Or so he thought.

He did have one advantage over the other reps: he was constantly interacting with the corporate offices. This allowed him to cultivate a rapport with many of the managers, directors and VPs back in Atlanta, and the result was a Friday afternoon phone call from the executive VP of marketing.

"Danny, Wesley Arnold, here."

"Hello, Mr. Arnold."

"I'm going to get right to the point, Dan. You've done some good work out there, and we'd like to have you do the same for us here."

"In Atlanta?"

"That's right. Now I haven't talked to Reid about this yet, so I want you to think about it over the weekend. Give me your answer Monday morning."

"What's the position?"

Wesley paused for a moment, and immediately Danny thought he might have crossed the line. Did it matter what the position was? Wasn't he supposed to just leap at it like a hungry corporate climber before someone else did?

"It's a new position: Administrative assistant to the executive vice president of marketing. That would be me. We've got a lot of plans, a lot of opportunities this year, and I need help. Let me just say this: if you have any long-term plans to stay with Alta Airlines, this is an excellent chance for you. That's all I'm going to say right now."

The standard practice would have been to interview a battery of candidates, whittle them down to two or three, conduct a rigorous panel interrogation of each, and make a final selection, but that wasn't Wesley's style. Speed was of the essence. He didn't care about personality nearly as much as proficiency, and word had gotten to him that this guy out in Salt Lake was good.

When Danny called back on Monday with his acceptance, it was only a few minutes later that he heard Reid's door slam shut in frustration as he took the call advising him of the loss of his most important employee. This led to a grudging congratulations and a curt farewell. Danny was given the rest of the week off to move east.

It was the fall of 1990. After living in the high desert, he found the greenness of his new surroundings striking. Atlanta was tropical in contrast to Utah, with mildly rolling hills of tree filled apartment complexes and neighborhoods. He had no problem finding a comfortable apartment with all the amenities he'd had in Salt Lake. Exactly a week after he accepted the position, he found himself in Wesley's office for his first day of work.

"I need you here at six thirty every morning. That okay with you?" said Wesley. It wasn't really a question. He had offered Danny a seat but didn't sit down himself. Instead, he was strolling around his office, tinkering with his golf clubs, straightening a picture and wiping some dust off one of the many plaques with a finger.

"No problem, I'll be here."

"And you'll probably find it hard to get out of here before 8:00 each night." He was watching Danny's eyes for a twitch, a sigh, the slightest show of weakness.

"That's fine."

"Good. We'll have fun. It's a great job that will pay off for you if you play it right."

So much for introductions. Danny was told to get a new daily planner, the same brand and model that Wesley had so that pages could be inserted if necessary. He wrote as fast as he could as Wesley reeled off one task after another.

"We need a memo to the Field about expense reports. Get a hold of the corporate card terms and conditions and make sure we hit the high points. We had to let a few of the reps go for charging personal items and we can't let it get out of hand. You don't have to mention the firings; just write something that lets them read between the lines.

"Next, we'll be going to the London office next week. Have Diane get me a seat up front. You normally would have to go in coach, but I need you up front next to me. Also, make sure she's got us booked at the Mayfair and that they know it's me. There shouldn't be any charges.

"Get with Veronica about the new phone system."

"Veronica?" asked Danny

"Veronica Stapleton, VP of Reservations. Nice lady. You'll probably be working on a few things with her. They've got a system they're putting in that times everybody's calls and monitors their performance. We've got to get it up and running right away. Too many people sitting around on the phones not taking calls when they should and that's not good. We need to squeeze out a lot more pro-ductivity."

"Got it. What else?"

"Get the latest data on the load factors out of Atlanta and the other hubs. This will be one of your daily routines. I need to see it before it goes anywhere else. You'll want to master the revenue spreadsheet program."

"What else?"

"Guy in the Atlanta office, sales rep, made an ass of himself at the last sales conference. Call the district sales manager and tell him to let him go."

"Just tell him to fire him?" Danny asked.

"Yeah. Just handle it. I don't want to deal with that one anymore so make it go away."

This should be wrapping up soon, thought Danny.

"Okay, is that all?"

"No, Danny, that's not all." He was clearly put off by the question. This was one of the many first-day lessons in the understanding of Wesley Arnold. The subtle tones, the subtext of conversation, the body language—it was as if every-thing had a dual message and he'd better be tuned into it. The boundaries and irritants of the executive vice president of sales and marketing were very slowly coming into focus, and this, Danny would find, would be the core knowledge base for the job. All of the other stuff didn't matter. Knowing what ticked off Wesley Arnold mattered. He handed Danny a small yellow piece of paper.

"Take this, its dry cleaning, and pick it up sometime today, but let me know when you're going in case I need you. Also, I need you to get a gift for Diane. It's her birthday. Get her something girly. She likes soap and bath stuff. Don't go over twenty bucks if you can help it. Might not seem like much, but the expense report doesn't have a category for these things, and Berenson could make a fuss."

"Right." There was nothing more spewing from Arnold's mouth, but Danny wasn't about to ask him if that was all. He waited while the man looked over his putter in silence.

"That'll do it for now, Danny. Have a good first day."

"Thank you, Mr. Arnold."

"Wesley, Danny. First name basis here. That's my rule, for you and me at least. We're going to be working too closely together to use this 'Mister' stuff."

Danny carried his scribble-filled notebook out the door and to his small office down the hall. It was windowless, but it was an office, an office in the heart of the headquarters, on mahogany row, in the largest hub of the largest company in the entire southeast. If he could put up with the hours, the dry cleaning, the gift shopping and the other silly tasks, maybe he could actually work his way into something he'd really like.

21

He made it through that first day and many days to come. Atlanta offered much more of a social life, and though he cultivated some scattered friendships, his job afforded him little time to socialize.

By the spring of 1992, Danny had gotten the hang of his boss, though not without some bumps. The egomaniacal behavior that flowed up and down the executive hierarchy presented him with a political minefield, but he managed to negotiate it by not questioning the inane chores that were dumped upon him. The one certainty that guided him was that Wesley Arnold expected to get what he asked for. The network of relationships that Alta had with hotels, resorts, cruise lines, rental cars and a host of other travel industry players elevated Arnold to a position of undeniable, if not unaccountable power. If they didn't fulfill his requests "as a courtesy to Alta Airlines' executive vice president of sales and marketing," there would be a penalty to pay, an exclusion of sorts, perhaps at the next airline managed junket. There might be a commission cut or an elimination of familiarization trip privileges or a reduction in the reciprocal discounts that hotels and airlines offered each other. Whatever the punishment, it was clear to the other travel suppliers that a failure to give Wesley Arnold what he wanted was a bad business decision, and Danny's own circumstances were no different.

The summer marked the second full year in a row that the airline industry had faced financial struggle, with annual losses that numbered in the hundreds of millions of dollars. The previous year's Persian Gulf War threw the oil markets into peril. Fuel prices went up, passenger traffic went down and profits went down with them. The margin had become so thin that any depression in passenger numbers translated into million-dollar-a-day bloodletting. The nature of the industry, limited to a few major players, a few second tier airlines and a flock of start-ups, always seemed to win or lose in lockstep. There was one exception to this; Southwest Airlines appeared to have achieved virtual immunity with its simple business model, single aircraft and modest number of domestic point-to-point routes to smaller airports. In contrast, Alta Airlines was entrenched in a mammoth hub-and-spoke system, with nine different aircraft and excessive operating costs. At some point, the hub-and-spoke carriers would need to take dramatic action or they would fail. A few of the players would either "eat or be eaten" as Wesley Arnold liked to say. He said this in confidence to Danny, behind closed doors, and only a moment after Danny signed a non-disclosure agreement, a document from Legal that had begun working its way down the row all morning.

"What's up?" asked Danny. Although Danny never expected to escape the workplace tension of his job, he never hesitated to diffuse it with casual verbiage. Not 'What do we need to do, Mr. Arnold', but instead a simple 'What's up?' and Wesley usually welcomed this.

"We're going after Global, Danny."

"Global Airlines?"

"Yes. An acquisition. They've got what we need."

"You mean the routes?"

"That's the big prize, yes. It's going to be a poker game though. There's a few other major players involved. Very high stakes so I don't need to remind you of the importance of keeping this totally under wraps."

"You got it."

This was exciting. Global had been a dominant carrier for most of the century, the first airline to cross the oceans in their giant "flying boats." They flew all over Europe and even as far as the Middle East and India. For so many years, Alta had been perceived as a southern backwater operation. It didn't matter that they had cobbled together a few international routes to London and Frankfurt; Alta still had no name recognition in Europe. But getting Global's routes would make them the largest of international carriers. They would have more flights between New York and Europe than any other airline, over a hundred flights a day out of Kennedy Airport alone!

"I've got a meeting with Global's leadership that I need you to set up. Get us into the Ventana in Tucson. We're going to play a few rounds of golf. Talk to Diane about how that works. Here are the dates and a phone number to call at Global. You can only talk to this person. Don't talk to anybody else, got that?"

"Yes, got it. Does Diane know about this?"

"No. We'll let her in on it when she needs to know. Right now, she doesn't need to know."

Danny was energized. If there was one thing about the airline industry, it never stopped changing, and now he would be in the thick of one of the most dramatic acquisitions in decades. He caught Diane between calls.

"I've got to set up a trip. Wesley and Berenson," he told her.

"Sure, where are they going?"

"Tucson."

"The Ventana?"

"Yes. He told me to tell you it's a golf trip." Her expression suddenly changed, and she lowered her voice to a near whisper.

"I'll meet you in your office in a few minutes." She arrived with a folder and a one-page list of "requirements."

"Here's what you need to know," she began. "Wesley and Berenson will play as part of a foursome. Tee times should be nine o'clock. You'll also need to block the tee times before and after nine."

"For who?"

"For no one."

"What's that about? Is that so no one can hear their conversations?"

"No, it's so no one can see them play golf. Mr. Arnold is a very bad golfer." She smiled, and he laughed, causing them both to check that the door was closed.

"Really bad?"

"Atrocious. I saw him play once at a secretary day outing. He didn't want to go, but Berenson made him. He hits this tree, the ball ricochets and almost takes our heads off." They shared a conspiratorial laugh.

"But seriously, this information doesn't go anywhere else or we're both through. Write this all down. Did you want me to set it up?" she asked him.

"No, for some reason he wants me to handle it. How do you pay for this stuff?" he asked.

"Corporate card info at the bottom. Put everything you can on that account. If Berenson is on the trip, you don't need to worry about the cost."

"Got it, thanks."

Danny spent the next hour on the phone with the Ventana and the assistants to the VPs at Global Airlines. The hotel was booked and so were most of the tee times. He had to go through several layers of management before they were able to confirm anything. The people holding existing reservations would be compensated appropriately for the inconvenience of losing their rooms. Four rooms at a rack rate of $400 per night for three nights. Tee times—$180 per person times four: $720. Then another $720 x 2 to block the times before and after nine o'clock—$2160. Then $2160 x 3 days, bringing the total to $6480. And that was just for the golf.

When he finished all of the booking and all of the phone calls, he didn't have to say a thing to Diane. The expression on his face was the same as hers—quiet disgust with a dash of amusement.

"How much money are we losing per day?" he asked her. She laughed. "Are you going to caddie?" she asked.

"Caddie? Me? I reserved carts for them. That's what they wanted, right?"

"Yes, but Mr. Arnold likes a caddie too. He gets off on someone handing him his clubs."

◆　　◆　　◆

"Five iron please, Dan," Wesley said.

The request followed a round of brief introductions to the Global Airlines executives and a surprisingly passable shot off the tee. One of them, the Global CEO, was a polished New Yorker by the name of Joseph Egan, stylishly dressed. Polo by Ralph Lauren. The other was the Global chairman of the board, a Frenchman named Jacques Dion. Izods.

Berenson wore a floppy hat and a too bright patterned golf shirt with the Alta Airlines logo on it, but at least it all fit. Arnold wore a yellow shirt with a hotel logo on it that was too tight around his abdomen, and plaid pants that were just this side of cartoonish. Probably his standard golf attire that hadn't been worn since the last time he played golf at least 20 pounds ago.

The course was spectacular, with crystal clear desert vistas of saguaro's stretching into the distance. Once they made it out onto the fairway of the par four 1st hole, the only animated living thing within sight of the foursome was a roadrunner skittering across the green in the distance. The intended perception had been created for the Global executives; it was as if Wesley and his boss owned the course, which was one of the reasons why Berenson consistently took his protégé on these trips. Normally, the chief operating officer, the number two man in the eyes of the board of directors, would be along for the ride, but Wesley Arnold was his man, the one who stood to run the operation well into the distant future when the appointed time arrived. The COO was a lame duck. He just didn't know it yet.

"Nice shot, Morty," said Wesley to his boss.

Danny watched Wesley closely. He rarely saw him and Berenson together back home, since most of the time, their meetings were behind closed doors. But here they were in plain view, in a seemingly casual atmosphere, with their counterparts from one of the largest airlines in the world. Danny picked up the subtle changes in the body language of his boss: a near submissive state, peppered with strategically placed "Great shot, MB," or similar. Arnold was not the same person when in the company of the man who held the key to his future.

The round moved slowly, but they kept a comfortable two-hole lead over the next foursome. Though Berenson was easily the elder of the group, his form was fluid, an obvious product of a battery of expense account paid lessons over the years. Wesley was nowhere near as proficient, but he also wasn't nearly as bad as Danny had expected. He would swing way too hard, probably thinking that anything less would reveal weakness, but then when the ball rocketed off into the cacti, he managed to reveal himself anyway. Still, there was something about hitting the ball hard, no matter where it went, that was more acceptable to the group than leaving it short of everyone else's drive.

By the time they made it to the back nine, it occurred to Danny that no one in the group had brought up the purchase of Global. He asked Wesley about this when they were out of earshot of the others.

"Not the time for it, my friend. We've got to get to know each other, build a rapport. You don't ask a girl to sleep with you before you dance, do you, Danny?" Wesley smiled, his mood lightening. He was half sitting in the cart, fishing through the basket behind the seat for a cigar.

"No, I guess not."

"A good lesson for you to keep in mind: don't negotiate until you know your opponent."

"Opponent? Isn't this a friendly acquisition?" asked Danny. Wesley paused for a moment to light and kindle his cigar before snapping his lighter closed. Then he took the cigar between his fingers and used it to emphasize his next point.

"No acquisition is friendly, Danny. Once the ball starts rolling, things can happen fast, and they can get very messy. You'll see when we start the real work back in Atlanta. Boy, are you going to be busy."

A sadistic smile wrapped around the cigar.

22

News about Global being in play leaked to the press two weeks after the Tucson trip. This accelerated the discussions, putting Danny on call virtually around the clock. Most of what he needed to come up with had to do with statistics related to assets and costs, both fixed and variable. As the senior management of Alta became aware that they were the leading candidate to buy Global, Danny's position took on a new level of prestige. When he called a director or VP within another department, they didn't make him wait. His name and status as Wesley Arnold's right-hand man had an immediate impact as department heads scurried through their files to deliver key information in time for the next discussion.

The discussions themselves were held in New York and included Berenson, Wesley and four of the active board members. The chief operating officer, a man named Higgins, was once again shut out and told to stay in Atlanta to "mind the store." Danny had also been ordered to remain at the headquarters, with his most important assignment being the protection of all of the information related to the acquisition. Not even Higgins, the de facto leader of the company while Berenson was away, could see these files.

◆ ◆ ◆

Wesley Arnold led his team of negotiators into a room that was already occupied by the Global Airlines leadership. It was a standard boardroom overlooking lower Manhattan, in a skyscraper that straddled Park Avenue. The Tucson trip, in Wesley's opinion, was a great success. He had downed more than a few cocktails with his counterparts, and as far as he could tell, he had won their trust. But time was working against them. The stock was beginning to spike on news of the acquisition, and the competitors had already begun sniffing around the Global headquarters, requesting just the type of high level meeting with them that was about to get underway. On this day, Alta was the suitor, but everyone in the room knew how quickly that could change if a more appealing offer were to be put on the table.

The agenda began with an exchange of asset data and a short presentation by each airline. While Global clearly had an advantage in terms of international route structure, Alta had been consistently profitable up until the past year and a half, with a superior domestic route system and much lower operating costs. Global had 747s, behemoths that Alta had long ago disposed of because of their lack of fuel efficiency. Global chose to keep theirs if for no other reason than the pride of flying the largest commercial airliner in the sky.

Global had a heavily unionized workforce with sometimes shady connections at Kennedy Airport. With the exception of their pilots, Alta had a non-union employee base, allowing enough flexibility to trim wages and reallocate headcount without one of the work stoppages that had devastated so many competitors.

Global had a worldwide name, often called the most recognizable brand in the world.

Alta's solid domestic network was so dominant in the South, that they called their Atlanta hub a "fortress," and with good reason. Competitors had tried to break into Atlanta for years, but when Alta matched their fares, they would soon lose whatever small shred of market share they had gained as a novelty.

When the presentations were complete, Alta's legal counsel outlined the basic terms of the proposed deal, including, for the first time, the stock purchase price. A counteroffer had already been prepared, leading into several hours of debate about the alleged value of each airline's assets.

As night began to fall, Wesley and Berenson asked their two counterparts to dinner. This was part of the plan. Endure a long day's struggle of debating, offering and counter offering. Although the other board members had grown weary and pushed for conciliation, this ran counter to Wesley's plan. Once they got them out to dinner in a weakened state, just the four of them, he was certain they'd have a signed deal early the next morning.

Danny had reserved them a corner table at The Palm, a favorite of Wesley's when he was in New York. This table was off the main dining room, shielded from the commotion, but without the stiff formality of a private room. Waiting for them was a bottle of Maker's Mark and a box of Dominican cigars, Joseph Egan's favorite, all as planned. Wesley took a moment to point out the caricature of himself on the restaurant wall as they sat down. Now the real negotiation with Egan and Dion would take place.

"Joe, I don't think we've given you all the details of the proposal," said Wesley to the Global CEO. "You realize that you both get the buyout if you approve this." Wesley made it sound as if the guy should have already known what he was talking about.

"What buyout?"

"We didn't tell you guys about the buyout?" he asked with fake incredulity.

"No. Tell us about the buyout." Egan was considered a straight shooter in the industry. He had no patience for this kind of tap dancing.

"You get a 50% increase in your current pay until retirement age. You can retire if you want to or stay on as a consultant. Fourteen thousand stock options with Alta. Flight benefits for life, of course. Confirmed first class."

"I want a title," chirped Jacques Dion.

"You would both be on the board. We've got two of our members ready to step down. We would reserve one of those slots for each of you."

"I want it in writing," said Egan.

"We can do that. Give us until the end of the week and we'll have something for you. In the meantime, let's close this deal. Your option strike price is going to be the share price on the day we sign, so the more it goes up, the more you're going to lose."

Wesley had studiously observed Egan's affinity for material wealth—the finest of fine things, the Rolex, and the diamond ring with the small globe on it. It was clear he was the decision-maker of the two. He remembered the gold-faced golf clubs and tailored clothing and that's when he knew that Egan's expensive tastes would be in jeopardy if his cash flow was cut off. He also knew he was on his third wife, and that in itself had to be a financial drain. This was a deal Joseph Egan *had* to support.

In the meantime, Wesley's lifelong plan was sliding nicely into place. He was two short steps away from heading the largest and quite possibly the most powerful airline in the world. Nobody would ever look at Alta the same way. No more laughter, no more backwater jokes, no more stupid southernisms. Wesley was about to show all those Northerners, if not the entire world, that his airline was a player. But not only was he representing the airline, he was leading the newest of the new South by bringing Atlanta into the true realm of an international city.

Morton Berenson had remained relatively passive throughout, letting Wesley hold the reins during the negotiations. Despite the respect he had for his mentor, Wesley had begun to question whether Berenson was the right man for the Alta Airlines of the 90s. Like all of Alta's leaders, Berenson was handpicked by Martin Willman years ago, a product of the paternalistic genealogy of leadership that had followed nobly in the footsteps of William Hartenfield. Certainly Wesley had descended from the same forces of power, but he, unlike the rest, was recognizing that a new age had arrived.

His other observation, one long ago understood within the highest levels of corporate leadership, was the "passivity play," something he detested and took as a sign of weakness. This involved restrained observation of crucial decisions for the sake of self-preservation. As the number one guy, Berenson was entitled to the luxury of passivity. If the deal failed, Wesley would be responsible for its demise and ordered to fall on his sword. He could keep his job, but he would be in a weakened state, something Berenson could exploit in the future if he so desired. Conversely, if the deal went through, Berenson would get the credit. Berenson would be the hero, the corporate power broker, the guy with the balls that clang. Wesley had seen this happen time and again on his climb up the ladder and so the potential dynamics of the deal did not escape him. He also suspected that Berenson knew what he had in mind. How could he not know? He was too smart to be that ignorant, Wesley thought. No matter how chummy you were, how influential your mentor might become, there were strict limits to trust that became more defined as one ascended the food chain. You could mentor the finest most trusting soul, shepherd him to the inner sanctum of power, godfather his children and sponsor his club memberships, but then you must be prepared for him to destroy you if the opportunity presents itself.

Wesley balanced his conscience with a doting appreciation of Berenson—a nice old man whom he would always remember, someone who had always looked out for him. But as the deal progressed toward consummation, Wesley became more comfortable with his own destiny, and now the time had come. Berenson had to go.

"Excuse me for a minute," said Berenson.

In more ways than one he had to go. He had bladder problems. It was embarrassing. In the interest of the fifty thousand people who worked and sweat for the airline, this was not the kind of man who could represent the youthful face of the enterprise with maximum effectiveness. In that respect, Wesley Arnold was only doing what was good for the company.

He tried not to change his tone while Berenson was gone, but his next few words were crucial to his plan. They needed to be pointed and confident.

"I'll need your votes on the board, and I'll need them immediately."

"What do you mean?" asked Joseph.

"Morty will be leaving us. He hasn't announced yet. I know he wants to keep it confidential, so let's not go into it. With his departure, I'll need your vote to assume the CEO position. That way you can be certain that our promises to both of you will be kept."

This was as hard as Wesley could push in his own favor. There was simply no way to guarantee that a particular board member would vote a particular way. In fact, many board members seemed to take a twisted pride in being hard to pin down, changing their votes on a whim to fulfill their perverted desire to watch people squirm.

"But even if you don't vote for me, I want you both on the board. Us good ol' boys don't always understand the international markets, so we need you more than you need us." He said this with a wink and a tilt of his head toward Berenson's vacated seat, effectively canceling out the "we" in his deprecating statement. They smiled with a nod, a knowing nod of successful Northern aggression that Wesley secretly hated but knew it was key to closing the deal on all levels.

Joseph Egan took a puff on his cigar and let loose a smoke ring. He'd been around long enough to recognize the smell of blood in the water.

"We're with you," he said.

23

Martin Willman, Founder of Alta Airlines, Dead at 90. Created Family Atmosphere.

On September 11th, 1992, Marty Willman died in his sleep. The Atlanta Journal ran a special section about his life with pages full of pictures through the decades: the first biplane trailing a spray of crop dust in Oak Ridge, Marty in his proud youth standing in front of his fleet of Curtiss-Wright Whirlwinds, a ribbon cutting in Atlanta for the new General Office building, Marty on the ramp in front of their first DC-8, Marty at another ribbon cutting, inaugurating service to Cuba. Each photo a little less grainy than the one before it, until the final photo of Martin Willman, in color, in front of the executive team, seated proudly in his wheelchair just two months earlier. And even then, with his body worn and broken, there was still the twinkle of eternal optimism in his eyes, of pride in what he had accomplished and determination to prove over and over again the legitimacy of his guiding principle: Take care of your customers, make them feel important, and there are no limits that can't be overcome.

Of course, life itself is limited, and to this, Marty had finally succumbed. Berenson declared a company day of mourning. Flags were lowered to half-staff at all facilities throughout the country, and condolences came in from around the world. Candace Willman fielded a call from the President, the details of which were passed on to the local media by the President's press secretary. In accordance with his wishes, Martin Willman's ashes were scattered from a biplane as it flew over the cotton fields of his family farm, now in the hands of a distant cousin.

Loyal airport staff, including those who had known Marty personally, began donning black armbands until politely told to cease because it was unnerving the customers. There were stories of flight attendants whose effusive crying led passengers to ask them what was wrong. This provided the necessary opening for them to recount the wonderful memories of their revered founder, even if they had never met him.

The leader of the pilot union put out a rambling eulogy on the call-in phone line, saying that Martin Willman was long a friend of pilot labor who had stood by them and recognized the value of their leadership. He was "one of our own."

In truth, the union leader had long ago named Marty as an enemy of labor, but contract negotiations were approaching and it was important to leverage the collective sympathies of the enterprise and board of directors as much as possible.

Meanwhile, the acquisition of Global Airlines was nearing completion, and while the death of the founder was in itself a minimal distraction, it did begin a string of events unlike any the airline had seen. Marty had retained a ceremonial seat on the board, passing on meetings but always voting his inclinations. Word was that he had "concerns" about the acquisition, and there was speculation that he would have voted against it, which would have led an unwavering share of loyal board members to join him. Wesley knew there was not a very big margin in favor of the deal to begin with, but now with Willman gone, the success of the proposal was almost assured.

After a week of solemnity, Wesley promptly raised the flags and set to work on the next phase of his plan. He began by reviewing the by-laws and confirming his understanding of the voting rights. A clause allowed the acceptance of board members prior to formal confirmation, and since the awarding of two directorships to the Global executives was a contingency of the acquisition, now was the time to move them in. Next, he contacted each board member without Berenson's knowledge and outlined the specifics of the deal. He did this in a manner that gave each director the sense that they were being brought into an exclusive circle of confidence. As always, Wesley was cordial and deferential, seductive in his patronage and respectful of Berenson's legacy.

"Jack, need your thoughts on this one," he would start off. He would then generate a flurry of facts and figures that overwhelmed his audience as it demonstrated his command of the acquisition's complexity. The numbers were fictional—for demonstration purposes only—but he delivered them as if the board member already knew and understood as much as he did. He knew they had no idea what he was talking about, but their egos would never let them admit it. Then, with an intimacy of a fellow soldier in a heated battle, he would say politely: "How's this sound to you, Jack. Would you give it a thumbs up or no?" Each director thought they were the only one being asked this question, a question that would determine the fate of nearly 100,000 airline employees around the world. Regardless of what they said, Wesley would agree with them, because nicely buried in all the details was another play.

"When Morty steps down next month, we want to be moving on the consolidation plan."

And before a question could be raised, he had already moved on to describing the plan. Fiction again, but each director would have been just as embarrassed

not to know about the retirement of their chairman. In the corporate strato-
sphere, few things were more shameful than being left out of the loop.

Wesley played their vanity to perfection. Not one admitted to being ignorant
of Berenson's departure, despite Wesley's complete fabrication of it. He also
sprinkled the entire pitch with an air of impending turmoil. The death of the
founder, the change of leadership, the acquisition—in Wesley's words, all of this
required the stability that only he could provide.

"I hope I can get your support on this, Jack. We've come such a long way
together and we need the stability of a smooth transition to carry forward the tradition of Alta Airlines."

With egos thoroughly stroked, they could do nothing more than pledge their
full commitment to Wesley Arnold.

By October, a week before the quarterly board meeting, word leaked to Berenson that a coup was underway, but it was too late. There was too much momentum to turn back the clock and erase the doubts that had already been firmly
planted in the heads of each director. Wesley had lined up votes in his favor and
baked them into the acquisition deal. Berenson passed through all of the stages of
death-to-his-leadership within a few days: shock, denial, anger, negotiation and
then finally acceptance. There was nothing he could do. Wesley had accounted
for everything. The acquisition would pass and so would the vote for his ascen-
dancy to the throne of Alta Airlines.

Although Berenson had every intention of staying on for the next three years
of his contract, his legacy suddenly moved to the forefront of his concerns. His
path to acceptance of the ouster was quick, primarily because that was the only
condition under which he could leave the company with any dignity, and dignity
was the key to his legacy. Like Martin Willman, he wanted to be remembered as
a revered leader who oversaw great periods of transition. He did not want to be
remembered as a deposed geriatric who could not change with the times or control his bladder. Wesley had calculated that his mentor would reach this conclusion. The path and the script that went with it were clearly defined.

"You did it, and I'm proud of you," Berenson told his former protégé. Of
course he hated him profusely, but he wasn't going to show it. Wesley knew he
was hated. There was no need to make it worse. Don't rub it in. Be as conciliatory as appropriate. Be professional and businesslike. Minimize his pain and be
civilized. Respect his legacy.

"Thank you, sir. I owe so much of this to you."

Then have him removed from the premises.

The conversation lasted all of 30 seconds. Wesley would give him a few days, but more than that might make things uncomfortable, and now was no time for distractions. Fortunately for Wesley, one day was more than enough. Berenson would not endure the humiliation of being removed; he would remove himself first, and Wesley would have Danny deliver his personal belongings the following day. MW Berenson was gone by lunch.

The board vote was a formality. With Wesley in and Berenson out, Higgins—the lame duck chief operating officer—was asked to stay on to help with the transition, but the subtext of the request was *get out now*. If he had any brains, thought Wesley, he wouldn't be staying. There was no place for him to go with Alta, and within a week, Higgins had jumped to another airline.

Wesley's control of the airline was now total.

24

Change was in the air, literally. Wesley immediately set about making his mark on the enterprise, and that included a change in the corporate identity: a new livery, new logos, new advertising and a completely new branding campaign. The board embraced Wesley's leadership as "bold and refreshing," and this was the salient quote used in a full-page profile in the Wall Street Journal.

But at a time of financial duress in the industry, the multi-million dollar rebranding initiative set off waves of discord among the workforce, many of whom believed their annual raise to be an entitlement that went with everlasting job security. Alta was losing a million dollars a day and this would increase as the airline proceeded to slowly digest the considerable assets of Global Airlines. The official "Acquisition Day" was set for November 1, 1992, a day that would be granted all of the fanfare of a national holiday at the Alta headquarters. On this day every Global Airlines employee would immediately become a member of Alta Airlines, but there were still many details to work out with the employee units, particularly the unions, or at least what would be left of them.

Alta always paid as well if not better than the unions, but nobody could argue that the unions of the other airlines didn't have an influence on salaries. Martin Willman's legendary immunity to the unions had died with him, and now they were beginning to sniff dissension in the air. In the meantime, Wesley had no doubt that the world had changed, and the airline industry had to change with it. The only question was who in the industry would lead the way? The needle of decision-making was biased clearly in favor of action, and Wesley's victory in the Global Airlines poker game was an undeniable sign of successful leadership.

◆　　　◆　　　◆

Caroline's stint at JFK was comfortable, but it was also growing tiresome. She knew her job well now, perhaps too well after more than three years. Normally, she was not easily bored, gravitating toward the stability of routine, but she was no match for her peers in this regard. Still, she loved her lifestyle. It was hard for her to imagine being without her beachfront home and the comfort of her now familiar neighborhood. There were certainly positions open in Atlanta that she could grow into, but that would mean leaving New York and her widow's walk view of the ocean. Shawn had recently been selected for a sales representative position in Atlanta and that triggered some envy, but then Shawn was a natural for the job. She thought back to her first impressions of him, how she thought he was dense and goofy, but it wasn't long before she saw how smart he was and how good he was with people. He was also her best friend and now he was leaving. "Abandoned again," she jokingly complained to Joanne, but she was sincerely happy for Shawn.

She put in a bid for flight attendant on a whim—something she could do and probably still stay in New York—but then she forgot about it. Then the merger was announced and that generated a wave of excitement throughout the Alta workforce at Kennedy.

Alta's building was one shuttle bus stop away from the massive Global Airlines terminal, a giant disk shaped pinwheel of gates that dispatched and welcomed hulking 747s from every corner of the world. Alta had a modest set of six gates in their decrepit monument to the early jet age, whereas Global had the aviation equivalent of Penn Station. A week after the merger, the Alta airport staff hosted an after-hours party in their airport lounge for the Global people, an advanced welcome to all of their counterparts weeks before the deal was consummated. It was an eye-opener for Caroline.

"Not going to happen! Not going to go through!"

The guy was a lifer, graying hair, glasses with thick black frames and a slight hunch in his shoulders. Caroline listened politely, just out of spitting range.

"Why not? Hasn't it already gone through?" Caroline asked.

"On paper maybe. But no one's talked to us about it yet."

She noticed the redness of his nose, the spidery capillaries of a weathered drinker. He didn't make eye contact with her. He just held his drink and stared straight ahead before the next outburst, when he bent his head ever so slightly in her direction, as if that was a polite enough acknowledgment of her presence.

"They think they know what they're doing, those hick Southerners. They just better not fuck with us."

"You don't seem too happy about this." This finally brought eye contact from him.

"Sweetheart, Global Airlines practically invented the airlines. We ain't going down without a fight. You all seem like real nice people, but this is a business. Anyone who thinks Alta is just going to slap their logo on our uniforms and send us on our way is fucking nuts!"

His spitting range was increasing. She slowly withdrew, and as soon as he broke eye contact, she excused herself and slipped away.

Caroline began to put feelers out over the next few weeks, chatting with the Global people, the Alta people and some of her old friends in Reservations. By the last week of October, she had a pretty solid understanding of what would be going down. As part of the terms of the agreement, the Airport Workers' Union (aka the AWU), would be effectively dissolved on the day of the acquisition. Caroline's intelligence work had uncovered a counterattack by the union. Over the weeks leading up to Acquisition Day, her general perception of the Global people had gone from warm and knowledgeable veterans of the industry to cynical curmudgeons bent on sabotage. On October 30, two days before the changeover, she called Danny.

"Hey, how's it going up there?" he asked her. They hadn't talked in a few months, but it was still a surprise whenever Danny heard from her.

"Not as good as you probably think, Daniel. Does Arnold know about the Global people here?"

"Yeah, of course. They're all going to be working for us. No layoffs planned."

"You think that'll cover it?" asked Caroline.

"Why not? We promised them job security."

"Danny, you've been out of New York too long."

"Whattya mean?" His New York accent was still fading.

"Not everything is so rosy up here. Is it possible that anyone in Atlanta knows that working for Alta is not nirvana?"

"No, not possible. They all think it's nirvana."

"Oh my God, you're one of them! Like one of those mints!"

"You mean, like, I'm an 'Altoid'?"

"Yeah, you're a goner," she told him.

They could laugh about this, but there was still a problem to be solved, and she wasn't sure exactly how to do it. She was *not* an "Altoid"; her bond was not so much with the company as it was with the people of the company, the people she worked for and with, her friends who struggled alongside her. Yeah, it had been a long time now and so maybe she was becoming the female version of the "company man," but that term was abhorrent. She was not a corporate person and never would be if she could help it. Danny on the other hand had drunk the Kool-Aid and that's what made him a goner.

Motivations aside, there was no doubt in her mind that she had to do something. In her discussions with her Global counterparts, she saw a level of anger and cynicism that bordered on danger. The union was powerful and connected, and they would be vengeful if not brought to the table. Her suspicions were confirmed in her conversation with Danny; these people had never been taken seriously, and now they were going to make Alta pay.

"They're going to shut everything down, Danny. Do you hear what I'm telling you?"

"You mean when we transition on November 1?"

Transition, she thought. He had even adopted the corporate-speak for the acquisition. They really had their heads up their asses.

"Daniel! There will be no *transition* if Alta doesn't talk to these people. They're pissed off!!"

"For what? They should be grateful. What did we do?"

"It's what you didn't do, Danny. You gotta understand, these people are different than us. Their life is all about a contract. They need it in writing."

"But we have a verbal contract with all of our people. It's the Alta way."

"Danny, are you fucking on drugs!! The Alta way?! I'm telling you right now, you've gotta problem!"

This was exhausting her. Over the years, the North-South thing had ranged anywhere from an amusing set of backward customs to the most dug-in stubbornness she had ever experienced. Alta was a Southern company, and like its hometown, there was always the need to prove that it could handle "the North." What exactly this meant was never entirely clear to her, but this ambiguous chip on the shoulder of the dormant confederacy would manifest itself in the strangest of ways, and the most damaging was through ignorance. In general, the leaders of Alta could never quite understand why their thousands of workers up north could be so ungrateful, and worse, impolite about everything they were trying to do for them. Little did they know that on the other side of the trenches, where the militant union forces festered and broiled, the "Alta Way" was the equivalent of a benevolent plantation owner letting the slaves come into the house for a spell.

Grateful. Oh, that was a good one!

25

Wesley had little reason to worry, or so it appeared. The entire merger task force was rapt in the belief that all the people of Global Airlines were eager and excited to become Alta employees. This presumption was a legacy of the founder, hard-wired into Marty Willman's corporate descendants with the persistence of a genetic code. It was outside the realm of Wesley Arnold's thinking that Alta could be anything other than the safest of safe havens for these "other" airline employees. Though there may have been some truth to that in years past, the presence of conflicting loyalties and cultures was a blind spot rooted in "southno-centrism." In forty-eight hours, the prestigious company known around the world as Global Airlines would cease to exist.

October 30, 1992—4:30 p.m.
"Wesley, need to have a word with you when you have a chance," said Danny through the foot-wide gap in Wesley's door, his nod to the Willman tradition of the "open door policy." Diane was sitting across from Wesley in her standard pose of corporate submission: pad and pen in hand, her stockinged legs together, angled slightly from the floor and curling under her seat. Wesley's reaction was one of restrained disgust at the interruption.

"Sure, Danny. Give me a few minutes."

5:30 p.m.
Much more than a few minutes later, Wesley stopped by Danny's office, his briefcase in hand as he pulled on his suit jacket.

"What did you need to discuss?" he said. Wesley always left the office before Danny for no other reason than Danny could never leave before Wesley. But now he was leaving and the jacket thing was his way of telling Danny that he better make it quick, and if he had any control over what he was going to say, he would also be better off making it unimportant.

"I think we might have a problem up at Kennedy."

"What kind of problem?" asked Wesley.

"Not sure. One of my contacts says there's a lot of unhappy people there."

"There's no reason they should be unhappy. Find out what the problem is and fix it. It's probably the squeaky wheels, always a few of them. Happens in every merger."

"I think it might be bigger than that."

Wesley was growing impatient. He considered himself an open-minded person, and when someone presented him with a compelling case, he listened, no matter if it was a lowly cabin service agent or a senior vice president. He took pride in what he considered a Willman custom of egalitarianism, but the common denominator was the strength of the appeal, and Danny, who had the privilege of working with the elite of the company, should know better than to throw some half-baked problem at him and waste his time. Normally, Danny would pick up the signals. His failure to do so irritated Wesley.

"Danny, if there's a problem, solve it. Find out what it is and solve it. And if you can't solve it, make sure you understand what you're talking about when we get together tomorrow. Goodnight."

6:22 p.m.

He knew Caroline was working an afternoon shift and would be on until at least nine that night, but calling people at the airport wasn't an easy task. Normally, you would leave a message for them and they could call you back when they got a break. Danny put in his call to Caroline minutes after Wesley stormed out, but it was nearly an hour before Danny's phone rang.

"What are they planning on doing, Caroline?" he asked her.

"I don't know exactly, but it has something to do with the kitchen. You know they're all union here. I think they're just going to stop catering. This way it doesn't look like the Global people are striking."

"What do the caterers have to do with it?" he asked.

"They're also AWU."

"AWU?"

"Airline Workers' Union! Don't tell me you haven't heard of them yet?"

"Oh, yeah, I think I've heard of them."

"This is what I'm talking about, Danny. How can you guys go through with this deal if you don't even know who the real players are?"

"All right! I can't help it. No one tells me what's going on, so don't blame me. What are they going to do?"

"They're just going to stop delivering food to the planes. And you damn well better believe nobody's crossing the pond unless we feed'em."

"How are they going to get away with that?" Danny asked. Caroline had a flash of memory, of when she liked Danny in what seemed like another life. Why, she thought, was he so unable to connect the dots? She had no choice but to plow through his denseness.

"Here's how I think they'll do it. Alta thinks they're replacing Global as the owners of the catering contract, but the caterers are going to say that Alta is a third party that they've never negotiated with. They'll just blow off the contract. And they've got a case. No one talked to them, right?"

Danny didn't say anything. For the first time he was beginning to understand the enormity of the impending catastrophe. Caroline's suspicions were likely correct. They had only talked to Global management, only worked with the highest levels of their target, completely missing the power of the masses underneath, because in the culture of Alta those masses were essentially powerless. Or so they thought.

"Danny, are you still there?"

"Yeah, Caroline. I'm here. I'm thinking. So what do they want?"

"Not sure, but I at least know they want to get Wesley's attention. My guess is they want a pay-off, but I don't know."

"Can you find out?" he asked.

"Me? You want me to find out what they want? What am I, your chief negotiator or something?"

"Caroline, you're right, we're clueless. So now we're desperate. You don't want people who can't get to Europe screaming in your face two days from now, right? What else do you suggest? We need your help."

Now Caroline needed a moment. She wasn't really sure where to start. Plus she actually had a job to do that evening.

"If I can pull something off, then you owe me. And not just you, but Alta will owe me big."

"No kidding. I got Wesley's ear and he usually has me pull the strings for him. Whattaya want?"

"I put in for flight attendant, and I think after this, I'm going to need to get the hell out of here."

"Shouldn't be a problem. Go find out something for me. I'll be here as long as it takes."

9:07 p.m.

Caroline ended her shift and walked over to the Global terminal. She saw some of the faces she had seen weeks earlier, hammering away at their computers with barely a smile. Not that Alta was all smiles all the time, but these people seemed to have a gruffness that permeated every tiny element of their behavior. She felt out of place in her navy blue Alta uniform, in the sea of Global workers in their powder blue shirts (blue was the dominant color in the airline industry). At an opportune moment, she caught the attention of one of the agents and, with a charming smile, told him that she was sent over from Alta and had a meeting with the kitchen. Unfortunately, the kitchen was three miles away, off the airport grounds in a separate building. One of the gate agents agreed to call a catering truck that was loading a flight on the tarmac. She took the stairway down from the jetway and caught a ride.

9:26 p.m.

The flight kitchen was a vast warehouse of gastronomic assembly. She didn't know who she was looking for, but she needed someone in charge, someone whose ears would prick when she told him or her why she was there. After several go-rounds with various workers, she was sent upstairs to a glass enclosed office that overlooked the entire premises. The sign on the door said: "Anthony Gaylord—General Manager—Flight Cuisine." The door was open, but he was on the phone. He saw her and her uniform, and his eyes lit up slightly. Not many women strolling around Kennedy Airport this time of night. He waved her in as he tried to wrap up his phone call, but it would be another minute before he hung up and turned back from the window to face her.

"What can I do for you, young lady?" he said. Tony Gaylord was a man whose age and weight had just overtaken his polished good looks. He still looked good for a man in his mid fifties, but it was clear that he recently looked better. After some exceedingly polite introductions, she got to it.

"I'm with Alta. I wanted to talk to you about the Global acquisition."

He smiled and held back a belly laugh. She smiled back reflexively but kept talking.

"So are you looking forward to it?" she asked. At that, he could not hold back the laughter and let loose.

"Oh, yeah. Yeah, we're looking forward to it all right!" he said, laughing harder. She laughed a little with him and abruptly stopped.

"So what's Flight Cuisine going to do after the acquisition? Do you have any other airlines lined up to make up for the loss?"

Now he stopped laughing.

"What do you mean, what are we going to do? We're going to cater the Alta flights just like we catered the Global flights."

"Well, that's not what I heard, Anthony. Or can I call you Tony? How bout I call you Tony, okay?"

"Yeah, okay. What did you hear?"

"I heard you're all walking off. Flight Cuisine isn't going to raise a finger because Alta didn't talk to the AWU before they cut this deal."

"Yeah. So, what if you just happen to be right about that? So what? What's Alta going to do about it?"

"Oh, it'll be fine. They got it all worked out. They're going to cater from Atlanta." She let that sink in for a second before continuing. "The flights are going to start there and stop here before they cross the pond. But they're already going to have all the food on board that they need. They're also going to put some of the Atlanta caterers on the planes to supervise. Just in case."

Tony's eyes grew a little wider and then narrower as he tried to calculate the logistics of Caroline's claim. He'd only been down to Atlanta once, as a spy to tour a competitor's operation, and he remembered it well: huge kitchens that cranked out tens of thousands of meals a day, five times the size of Global's Kennedy operation. She was probably telling the truth.

But of course she wasn't. In fact, Caroline was making this shit up as she went along. The last few weeks had given her enough of an understanding of the union mind to know what buttons to push, and Tony was clearly beginning to feel some heat, so she turned it up, but with a twist.

"Anyway, I thought you should know about this. I didn't know if you guys were really going to go through with your work stoppage, but in case you were, this is what was going to happen, and I didn't want to see you get screwed."

Tony was quiet, staring down at his note covered desk blotter. He started cracking the knuckles of one of his hands, one finger at a time. Then he looked Caroline firmly in the eye.

"Well, you tell those guys we're professionals! We're going to be on the job and working as hard for Alta as we have for Global."

10:40 p.m.

"Danny, it's Caroline."

"What's the deal?"

"I think we might be okay," she said.

They got their stories straight. Tony Gaylord would probably buy the tale if it came from one other source. The ruse would require an additional piece of documentation: A "secretly" faxed copy of the "Global Acquisition Catering Contingency Plan." Danny wrote it over Wesley Arnold's signature, a memo confirming the arrangement that Alta had with Flight Cuisine's competitor to cater flights from Atlanta. It was one of Danny's finest pieces of plausible fiction, with minor references to aircraft weight and balance measurements (due to the extra meals), and waste disposal.

October 31, 10:17 a.m.

Caroline came in well before her shift to pick up the fax that was waiting for her. One thing she couldn't deny about Danny: the man knew how to write fiction. She folded it into a company envelope and stopped off at the kitchen for her final visit with Tony.

"I got this from the headquarters office." He snatched it from her hand and fumbled the letter as he unfolded it. Caroline provided background to his reading.

"You know they want you to walk-off tomorrow. They'd rather hand it to their slave labor in Atlanta, pay'em minimum wage and tell you guys to have a nice life. But they can't do that if you stay. Last thing they want is to fire you guys and have it go public. You'd have to fire yourselves and that's what they're counting on."

Tony looked up from the memo. He was turning red with anger now.

"Yeah? Well screw them! We're not going anywhere! They're not moving us out. Not now, not ever!"

Caroline gave him a collaborative smile, rewarding his determination as if she were providing a food pellet for a pigeon.

"That's right, Tony. I've been with this company long enough to know you can't let'em push you around. Don't let'em fuck with you."

"No way," he said, and then he smiled too, warming to her.

"One other thing, Tony. They don't know I got a hold of this memo, so keep it to yourself or I'm screwed," she said.

"You got it," he said. She turned to leave.

"Hey, Caroline?"

"Yeah?"

"Thanks for the heads up. You know some of you Alta people aren't so dumb after all."

26

When Danny got back into the office early the next morning, there was no word yet from Caroline. He took a gamble and told Wesley the problem had been solved. It was just a matter of poking his head inside the head-sized open door and telling him he was right—just a few "squeaky wheels," but nothing to be concerned about. This was not Danny's preference, but he had nothing to report, and if you had nothing to report, then there better not be a problem. Still, until Caroline called him, the worst case scenario was still out there and all he could do was reassure himself that there was no way he could be blamed for not blowing a loud enough whistle.

Caroline's call did finally come into Danny at 10:42 a.m., as noted in his call log.

"He bought it," she said.

"How do you know?"

"They'll be there. Believe me. Great memo by the way."

"How do you know he bought it?"

"I know. Don't worry. Those Alta passengers will be fat and happy across the Atlantic."

"So he believed it?"

"Danny! What did I just say? Yeah, he believed it! It's a done deal."

"Great! Caroline, you saved our ass."

"Why, I'm not sure. When are you going to tell Arnold?"

"Tell him? Why should we tell him?" asked Danny.

Caroline took a deep breath. This was so 'Danny' of him—so self-absorbed, so 'path of least resistance.' She knew she had to restrain her anger if this bozo of an ex-boyfriend was going to do his part for her.

"Because, Daniel, I saved your ass. Remember? I want in-flight. They're hiring. I'm here. I may not be part of the next crop of southern belles who have it handed to them, but I'm ready for a change, and I expect you to pull some strings."

"Okay, I'll tell him. I'll tell him tonight on our way up," he said.

"Good. Otherwise, my new Mafia friend Tony might just find out about the real source of that memo."

"Did I say, okay? Yes, I think I did. Caroline, I'll take care of it." The conversation had grown testy; they both knew it was a good time to end it.

That night on the flight up to New York, Danny and Wesley went through the next day's routine. It would be another ribbon cutting, not that an acquisition had anything to do with ribbons. Alta had a team of event planners responsible for all public ceremonies, and because of the nature of the industry, this almost always involved the cutting of a giant ribbon with a pair of giant scissors, commemorating the start of service to a giant new city. The media loved ribbon cuttings; they offered the perfect combination of still life and action, with all of the key players tightly bunched somewhere along the breadth of an oversized swatch of cheap fabric, if not paper that looked like fabric. And always, just beyond each side of the frame were the two excited volunteers, usually gate agents, holding each end of the ribbon as if they had been selected to sign the Declaration of Independence.

But this wasn't new service to anywhere. Danny thought the plan was cliché, a typical demonstration of Alta's lack of imagination. Yes, it would be a ribbon cutting, but the ribbon would be wrapped around one of Global's planes, the first of their flights taking off to Europe under the Alta name. A large decal with the Alta logo would be placed on the tail fin in the morning, and hopefully it would stick long enough for the reporters to leave, before peeling away somewhere over the Atlantic.

Then there was the ribbon itself, which was supposed to read "ALTA TAKES YOU OVER TO EUROPE!!" Somewhere in the hasty design and development of the ribbon, the vendor omitted the "you" and the "to," or at least that's who the Alta event planners blamed (because you can always blame the vendor). The result was a ribbon that literally rippled with arrogance:

"ALTA TAKES OVER EUROPE!!"

And of course it was huge—huge enough to drape the bulging forward fuselage of a gleaming white Global 747.

Wesley didn't know anything about the ribbon fiasco. Like so many of these events, the logistics were in Danny's hands. His boss's only demand was that it include the words Alta and Europe, so technically Danny had fulfilled the requirements. He had no idea how Wesley would react to the final version, so now, on the flight up to New York and with less than 24 hours to the ceremony, it was time to give him the details. The more matter-of-fact, the better, he thought, but once again he hated not knowing what the reaction would be.

"The ribbon will be across the front of the plane," Danny explained.

"Not across the front windows, right?"

"It'll cover some windows," Danny said.

"But not the cockpit."

"No. Not the cockpit."

"Because then they wouldn't be able to see. It would look stupid," Wesley said.

"It's not going to cover the cockpit."

"Good. What else?"

"It says 'Alta takes over Europe.'"

Regardless of the consequences, Danny wanted to get this out of the way; weave it in quickly with the other details.

"'Alta takes over Europe.' I like it," said Wesley with a nod.

"You'll take the podium first and last, and you'll introduce the Global CEO."

And on Danny went, over the hump and beyond to the other meaningless ceremonial details, each full of their own pomp and protocol. Wesley liked the ribbon. No need to dwell on it any further. If he had to, Danny was prepared to go on about the boldness and confidence of the statement. Spin it away from presumption and toward decisiveness. But inside he knew it was quite possibly the dumbest and most obnoxious statement, so characteristic of Alta's southnocentrism. The blind spots were bad enough when dealing with the Yankees of New York, but now they were about to expand their blindness to the far corners of the world.

Danny ticked off each piece of choreography in the timetable. As he approached the end of his list, he sensed a new level of appreciation from his boss. The coming day appeared to be very well organized, and Wesley liked it. Whatever the real source of his gratitude, Danny considered that he was benefiting more from Wesley's excitement and pride over the acquisition. The mood of the Alta CEO was triumphant. Perhaps he liked the ribbon because he really believed it, that Alta was in fact taking over Europe, or at least New York, and there were all sorts of subconscious joys that could poke through the surface with the South taking over something, anything, that belonged to the North.

They were in the front row of first class; Wesley always boarded last and sat in an aisle in the front row, minimizing the chance of passengers recognizing him and becoming overly chatty. More than once, Danny had to call a passenger who had booked the seat that Wesley wanted and "negotiate" a seat change, even if it meant giving the person a free first-class ticket for a future trip.

The crew wasn't crazy about this either. What could be worse than having your CEO peering straight into the galley, literally watching your every move over your shoulder? Wesley resisted the temptation to micromanage during the flight, but he would still scribble a few indecipherable comments after every trip for Danny to send on to Barbara Lewis, the VP of the in-flight division.

"Send this on to Babs," he would say, though Danny had never heard anyone else ever refer to Barbara as "Babs" either publicly or privately. Barbara knew that Wesley liked to call her that, but there was nothing she could do, and Danny, in sympathy, always treated her with the highest level of respect, calling her Ms. Lewis until she insisted on Barbara. She came to like Danny, and they developed an affinity for each other, sometimes laughing together at the superfluous detail within Wesley's scribbles. *"Napkin not properly creased"* or *"Alta logo not prominently displayed when setting glassware down on tray."* In fairness, Wesley also shared compliments, or rather, bestowed kudos from on high.

They approached LaGuardia from the East, toward the sun setting beyond the New York skyline. He looked down to his left and spotted the gaping mouth of Shea Stadium, the U.S. tennis center, and the span of the Whitestone Bridge. Everything seemed clearer than usual, even though darkness was settling over the city. Even now, after so many years of being out of New York, it was still and would always be his home.

The flight made the sweeping turn over Long Island Sound and settled into the typically exciting final approach that makes LaGuardia the special airport that it is. Just when you're certain the wheels are about to submerge themselves in the Sound and throw the aircraft nose-first into the rotting piers, a tongue of tarmac shoots below and you speed to a stop just before spilling off the other end of the landfill. Danny looked to his right and caught the landscaped shrubbery spelling out "Welcome to New York" in a bluff along the runway. The plane pulled into the Alta terminal, and Wesley sprung to his feet the split second the seat belt light turned off.

"Great job, crew. Have a wonderful evening," he said in the galley. The single glass of wine on the way up seemed to have added to his good cheer.

"Thank you, Mr. Arnold," said the head flight attendant as they took their positions for the string of goodbyes. The cockpit door opened, and the captain quickly placed his hat on just in time to tip it for his CEO.

"Thank you for flying with us, Mr. Arnold," said the captain.

"No, thank *you* for a very nice ride," he said with a smile.

On went the love-fest, spurred by the momentous events that awaited them. It was clear that pride ran from top to bottom at Alta, and the chance to show it to the people who pulled the strings was a chance not to be missed. The continuing chat with the hometown crew was cornier than Danny could ever have imagined, but what made it all tolerable was its sincerity. Everybody in Danny's midst really *was* very proud and he could not fault them for their feelings. Still, he peered out the small round window of the cabin door, wondering when the jetway would finally kiss the plane so they could get out of there. When it did, and the cabin door was lifted open, a perfectly groomed customer service agent met Wesley and Danny and led them down the exterior stairs to the tarmac and their waiting limousine. It was a stretch, but they were the only passengers. Their carry-on bags were snatched from their hands and loaded in the trunk as the agent swung the passenger door open. Diane had obviously set it up, and Danny could imagine her written reusable instructions with the all-important phrase, "only stretch limos."

Danny looked up in time to see the limo exiting the Midtown tunnel into Manhattan. About forty minutes later, they were pulling up to the Waldorf Astoria, and the limo door swung open toward the lobby. Following in Wesley's wake, Danny's eyes were drawn immediately to a tall brunette, standing alone with a small backpack hanging over one shoulder. She was well-dressed—a long satin (or was it polished leather) dress, low cut but informal. She had bracelets on, maybe a few more than she needed. But the strangest part of her ensemble was the mask she was wearing, a too small plastic mask of a blonde princess with a tiara—strange, but not quite so peculiar once Danny remembered that it was Halloween night. She was almost directly between them and the elevator, which is where they were going since Diane had called in an advance check in.

"Hello, my king," she said as Wesley walked by. He smiled bashfully as they passed by her and took a quick look back at Danny. It was a curious look, a smile of embarrassment, but also one that attempted to diminish the incident, to put it aside and stamp it as trivial. As they neared the elevator, the manager handed each of them their keys. Wesley inserted his, activating the button for the top floor. Danny was on the third floor, probably a standard single facing the dumpsters.

"Who was that?" he asked.

Wesley's head snapped a bit at the question and then he looked at Danny. He didn't say anything, but he didn't need to. The look was stern and cold, a flash of evil, warning him not to go further with the inquiry. But then it disappeared in a second and the tone was once again cordial.

"See you for breakfast downstairs. 8:30."

"Right," said Danny. Relief again.

That night, as Danny fell asleep in the Waldorf, he realized that his job had taken on a pattern. His was a life devoted to the constant pursuit of relief.

27

Danny hardly cared what Wesley did behind closed doors. He had worked for him long enough now to limit his trust in him and lower his expectations. His strategy could be summed up very simply: Keep your distance, play the game, stay out of trouble and pretend you really gave a shit. While there was a certain ego boost to a lofty title atop a powerful company, Danny reached one conclusion early on in his Atlanta tenure: He did not want to become Wesley Arnold. The fact that the "happily married" Wesley likely managed to arrange one of his favorite call girls for his trip to New York was not in the least a fall from grace, because to Danny, there was nowhere to fall from. His boss was a beautifully honed product of the system, the Darwinian outcome of corporate inbreeding, and for Danny it generated more fascination than envy.

After breakfast, the limo carried them from the Waldorf, out through the Midtown tunnel and on to the Long Island Expressway, then to the Grand Central Parkway and the long access road to Kennedy Airport where the ceremony would be held. The inaugural flight didn't leave until 4:00 p.m., so there was some downtime, giving Danny a chance to find Caroline in the break room.

"Did you ask him?"

"Ask him what?"

"About me! In-flight, remember?"

"No, not yet. He wasn't in the best of moods yesterday. I want to make sure I time it right," said Danny.

"Just fucking ask him!"

"Caroline, don't worry about it. I'm going to get it done. I am absolutely going to get it done for you!"

There was no lack of sincerity from Danny. He had a need to prove himself to her, and this was a task he would follow through on. His determination was evident so Caroline backed off.

"Okay. Good."

"I'm going to talk to him on the way back."

After an agonizing couple of hours waiting around for the press to gather and the ribbon to be put in place, the event finally commenced just before 3:00 p.m. A platform was placed right below the front fuselage of the enormous 747.

Except for a very short period before the novelty wore off, Alta had never had a plane quite this large, and Danny marveled at the pure mass of the aircraft. It bulged and towered over everything in its midst.

The weather was overcast and gusty, but there was no indication of rain. A chilled and volatile wind had arrived, along with the conquering airline and the month of November.

On the platform there stood the requisite podium with the Alta logo on its base. A row of eight chairs lined the back of the platform, but nobody wanted to sit down first. Distinguished guests included the manager of the Port Authority of New York, the superintendent of Kennedy Airport, the deputy mayor of New York, the Queens Borough president, Joseph Egan—the CEO of Global Airlines, Jacques Dion—the chairman of Global, the chief marketing officer of Global, and the senior vice president of marketing for Alta. Wesley had resisted all efforts to install a chief marketing officer. His new official title was president and chief executive officer, and as long as he was CEO, there would be no other "chiefs." His senior VP was a pliable veteran whom he privately deemed non-threatening, and as a tip of the hat to loyalty and seniority, he installed him in the vice president position despite, or perhaps because of the man's complete lack of influence.

The ribbon was colossal, with bold lettering that shouted its proclamation: *"ALTA TAKES OVER EUROPE!!"* A giant bow sat near the crest of the fuselage, obscuring the once renowned but suddenly defunct Global logo. Danny watched Wesley's eyes, looking up with pride. He half expected him to finally get it, but instead a smile formed as he scanned the breadth of the plane and its haughty adornment.

The press trickled in, and slowly the dignitaries made their way up to the platform. Wesley shook all of their hands with both of his and a tilt of his head, suggesting heartfelt sincerity, as if they were all brothers in arms who'd come through Armageddon as one. About thirty Alta employees, including Caroline, were directed by their managers to fill out the audience and provide applause on cue.

Music had been arranged: Sinatra's *New York, New York*, on a continuous loop, as if this had any prodigious meaning to the 95 percent of New Yorkers that comprised the participants and audience. Danny thought they probably should have been playing *Dixie*.

Finally, the music was cut and Wesley strode to the podium. As per protocol, Wesley graciously introduced the deputy mayor, the Port Authority management and "most importantly, my distinguished colleagues from Global Airlines, whose perseverance and determination in the name of our beloved industry should be commended." Cue applause.

Essential to the success of the event was the portrayal of a strong unity between the leadership of the two carriers. This was part of the deal, and for the Global CEO and president, it was intimately understood that this was the only way they could cover their tracks. For the public's consumption, they were part of a single airline, and their continued leadership would be "an integral part of our future success." But, in fact, the Global leadership was about to plunge to earth via their golden parachutes and fulfill the barest of minimums in their role as board members. That was mutually understood and desired by all of the principals in the deal. Make it look good. "Stay on board and guide the ship on the path to *winning*."

On went the festivities, until finally, Wesley and Joseph Egan each took a handle of the giant scissors and began cutting. The last thread was the toughest, especially since Egan had decided to let Wesley finish the job on his own once the cameras stopped clicking.

Just at the moment of complete severance, a gust of wind blew up and caught the bow as the tension of the ribbon was released. Up it went, unwrapping the plane and wrapping Wesley across his face and around the neck. The blast whipped the bow like an errant kite, outward into the press gallery, pulling the rest of the ribbon behind it. The ribbon then caught the upraised microphone on the podium, dragging it just enough for the entire podium to teeter and fall sideways onto the platform before rolling forward to the tarmac. Wesley's head was suddenly gift wrapped, and in his surprise, he lost his grip on the giant scissors and they too clattered to the ground.

It all happened in seconds—seconds that were caught in a rejuvenated cacophony of whirrs and clicks from the flock of cameras.

Out of boredom, Caroline had retreated to the relative seclusion of a ground floor entrance to the terminal, but she was glad she caught the end of it. She quickly shut the door because she was laughing too hard.

28

Wesley Arnold was not pleased. Danny could already imagine the next day's headlines: "While Alta 'takes over Europe,' Giant Ribbon takes over their new CEO." As it were, the new CEO was seething over the embarrassment and his entourage did their best to stay clear of his wrath.

Mixed in with the gusts blowing through the microphone, the amplified roar of jet aircraft and the smattering of laughter, a small pack of disgruntled (former) Global workers had gathered to heckle their new CEO during the conference. Wesley and Danny quickly slid into a limo parked on the other side of the aircraft, and the barrage began.

"Who the hell picked that ribbon? Find out!" Wesley shouted.

Danny had managed to get in his share of laughter out of earshot, but if a snicker escaped now, it would be time to send out résumés.

"What the fuck are we doing out on the tarmac anyway? How were they supposed to hear us? Who were those guys yelling at me? If they're Global, they're gone!"

"I think they've already quit," said Danny. But the situation was actually much worse than that. Caroline had estimated at least 50 of the Global people had no-showed for work, possibly because they were counting on the meal embargo to freeze Alta in its tracks, but when the meals showed up and they didn't, their leverage was gone. They were effectively terminated.

"Fine. Then we don't have to interview them. Global assholes! They're lucky we saved them and their shit airline!"

It occurred to Danny that Alta had just consummated a mammoth transaction amounting to several hundred million dollars for what their leader was now referring to as a "shit airline." No doubt the coming months would uncover just how much shit there was, including the disturbing revelation that Alta was bidding against itself with each counteroffer. For the last two months, speed was essential. The mission was to get the deal done, but who knew for sure what was under the hood. Now the real work would begin.

The limo took them back to the Alta terminal where they boarded the 4:30 p.m. flight back to Atlanta from the tarmac. Once he got his Maker's Mark on the rocks aboard the flight home, Wesley's mood lightened, but his motivations remained dark as he outlined his vendetta.

"We'll interview each and every one of the Global people. They've got to be up to Alta standards, right?"

"Right," said Danny. What else was he going to say?

"Get with Wilson in Personnel tomorrow. I want an employee-screening plan by close of business. It doesn't have to be final, but he should have something underway already. We're just going to have to turn it up a notch."

Danny hadn't a clue what that meant, but that was Wilson's problem. He would huddle in his role as messenger until he figured out what Wesley wanted, but somehow he knew it wasn't anything of high moral standing.

"Also, get me the latest acquisition status report. Now that it's done, let's step back and make sure we've done our due diligence."

Somewhere between the giant carrot of 'taking over Europe' and the giant stick of due diligence, the center of gravity had shifted, and it was at the expense of prudence, something that Alta Airlines had been known for since the first crop was dusted. There was a clear and genuine euphoria among the inheriting work-force and an excitement that drove the leadership forward to this day of acquisition, but it also pushed a cloud over their judgment.

As the flight ascended over Jamaica Bay, Danny looked back at the chaotic assemblage of terminals and runways that made up Kennedy Airport. Atlanta was so organized, so predictable and so southern in its controlled bustle. Kennedy and everything that went with it struck Danny as a bureaucratic minefield, and now Wesley was about to walk through it with snowshoes.

"Tech Ops, In-flight, Reservations, Airport Customer Service, Field Sales, and Flight Ops. Especially the front line. They all need to know what to look for. We don't want any of these *Global* people dragging down our reputation."

Danny pulled out a pad and scribbled notes. Wesley rambled on, and Danny was soon scribbling for the sake of appearance—he had given up on keeping pace by the second bourbon.

"And let's get that place cleaned up! Why is New York so fucking dirty? They're a bunch a pigs."

As the third drink was drained, the ramblings turned to blurtings, with inter-missions of tortured thought, or at least that's how it appeared to Danny as he waited for the next blurt. He watched Wesley sidelong. The man's eyes were focused straight into the bulkhead, his chin doubling, his eyebrows knit, his nose scrunched in pain as he recollected the ribbon incident and then regrouped into the next angry blurt between sips of his drink.

"Marketing! What do they have in Europe? We've got to get over there and shut down some of those offices. They've got offices in every fucking country in Europe! Even the ones they don't fly to."

The attendants working the flight were now well aware that their leader was front and almost center, and they were tuned into his behavior. Of course, you don't cut off the CEO unless you're ready for another career, so all they could do was keep their distance.

"I can't make those calls, and I don't want any of the other VPs over there. They've got to look at their own shops, so I'm gonna send you."

"Me?" Danny asked.

"Yes. You can handle it. You know what we need to do. You can be my eyes and ears over there."

"In Europe?"

"Yes. Let's see what we got waiting for us back home, and then set yourself up to leave next week."

Danny stopped scribbling and started writing. This was going to be a massive undertaking, overwhelming for a single person, but at the same time he couldn't think of anything quite as exciting.

"Got it."

That appeared to be the end of the blurting. The only thing hanging over him was the final task at hand. He needed to call in his favor; it was time to get Caroline an in-flight job, but first he would venture to the restroom, if for no other reason than to allow his boss to wind down in his absence.

For the sake of a walk, Danny went back to the coach compartment and the aft restroom. The flight was about half full, not characteristic of their New York—Atlanta flights, and this gave the flight crew a bit of a breather. As he made his way to the rear, he spotted a single flight attendant seated in the jumpseat of the galley, deeply enthralled in a paperback novel. Her legs were crossed, a heel dangling off her stockinged toes. Her shoulders were slightly hunched, her hair was long, straight and blonde. Danny had to smile—she was the once iconic flight attendant, a typical Miss America in waiting.

With just a few rows to go, she looked up from the book. Why she did this, he didn't know. His stroll was soundless beneath the white noise of the flight, but she looked as if she had heard him, and then, as he pulled the door open to the lavatory, she smiled at him. He smiled back in pure reaction. She was naturally attractive, but her smile dominated, a radiant affirmation of the humanity it shone upon. It was a smile that granted power.

He was mildly shocked, making the lav something of a sanctuary that would give him a chance to figure out what it meant. He looked in the mirror. This was the face she had smiled at? Was he worthy? Was it some mistake? Was it just a high point in the book she was reading and he had happened along?

Of course, he did have to use the bathroom, but as he did, he leaned over enough to see his face in the mirror again, still wondering if there wasn't some mistake. A mild pain in his stomach replaced the shock. Now he was nervous, and he was running out of time (he was almost done peeing). She seemed at first glance to be too attractive to be interested in someone like him, but now, suddenly, absurdly, there was this opportunity, this "possibility" that had so rarely been available up to now as he toiled his days away in servitude. Why should he care? It was purely physical, just a look. Or was it? Isn't a smile more than physical? Whatever it was, it had nudged him beyond any rational assessment of its meaning.

He washed his hands much longer than he needed to, brushed his hair back, straightened his tie and fidgeted with the rest of his appearance. And then he turned the knob of the lavatory door and pushed it open.

29

She was already looking at him and smiling. He held the eye contact a little longer than he normally would have before becoming conscious of his stupor and the person trying to get around him to the lavatory. Without thinking, he was suddenly walking back up the aisle, and with each step, the weight of regret became heavier. He'd blown it. He hadn't even said hello.

When he got to the front row, Wesley was fast asleep, head back, mouth open, the fingers of his hand still curled around his latest glass of bourbon. Danny stood in the aisle, looking straight down at him, straight into the upturned nostrils of his esteemed leader. He considered how so much of his job had become unconscious, how his behavior had evolved from judgment to instinct. He acted to avoid wrath, to prevent calamity, to maintain equilibrium, but none of his actions had anything to do with a rational decision process. And now he was standing here out of concern that his absence from his seat would be an issue.

He looked back down the aisle and at the small flood of light from the rear galley through the crack in the first-class curtain. And then he started walking back, tentatively at first, and then with resolve.

"Hi," he said to her. She wasn't looking up this time, so Danny's voice brought her back out of her book.

"Hi," she said. She was slightly startled, but the smile came back right away. "Danny."

"Cathy. Did you have to go to the bathroom again?"

"No. No, I just came back to say hi."

"Hi!"

"Hi." He had about three seconds to avoid looking like an idiot.

"Are you based here?"

"Here? Where? We're probably somewhere over Virginia."

"Atlanta?"

"Yes. Just transferred from Dallas," she said.

"Really."

"And you? Aren't you sitting up there with Arnold?"

"Yeah. I'm his AA?"

"AA?"

"Administrative assistant. Basically, I'm his gopher."

"Wow. So you must know everything that's going on. Do you like it?"

"Sometimes. Not all the time."

"Would you like to sit down?" She pulled down the jump seat next to her and put her book on the floor beside her feet. Her blonde hair spilled over her shoulder, her eyes stayed on his.

"Sure."

Now they were close to each other, closer than any two people would normally be so quickly, but that's the way jump seats were built. Their faces were barely a foot apart as they continued the conversation, but it was surprisingly comfortable, forced intimacy that was in no way disturbing to either of them.

"Can I get you something to drink?"

"Yeah, okay."

"How about a beer?" She reached into one of the metal compartments near her feet and pulled out a can for him.

"Great, thanks. Guess you can't have one with me, can you."

"Not this time," she said. Her smile nearly guaranteed a next time.

The conversation was chatty, with no major revelations on either end, but the tone was one of growing warmth. He told her the story of Wesley's golf, and then she leaned closer to him and shared her horror stories. Whispers and laughter, especially over the one about the passenger who stuck the audio headphones in her nose because she thought it was oxygen. It was a conversation that made him lose track of time, an easy flowing discussion that drilled slowly down into each of their thoughts and towards their beliefs. And with strange appropriateness, the conversation ended with an audible "ping." The seat belt sign went on, bringing them back to awareness that they were on a plane. Their time was up.

"Can I call you?"

"Yes."

Her smile energized him. It had been so long since he had had anything resembling a social life. She pulled out a pen and a business card—he didn't realize flight attendants had business cards—placed it on her knee and jotted down her home number. He watched her in profile, her hair hanging down in front of her shoulders, her pensive eyes, her eyelashes. She took the card and pressed it into his hand. He almost felt as though he could have kissed her, but instead he squeezed her hand and rose to leave.

"I'll be calling you," and then he left before he could screw it up.

Meeting Cathy was a rush—an awakening that made him realize that his life had put him to sleep. As he walked back up the aisle, he suddenly felt good. He took one look back down the aisle, almost as if to confirm that he'd really met her. She gave him a friendly backhand wave, shooing him to his seat before final approach.

◆   ◆   ◆

A day out of the office for Danny was like leaving the water running. He routinely returned to a mess that was usually triple the size of what he left behind. Everyone who needed to talk to Wesley would then call Danny if Wesley was unavailable. So when they were both out, the backlog was unmanageable, requiring prioritization based on each caller's known threshold of impatience. But it was still a no-win situation, with the large majority of people demanding immediate return phone calls and prompt action.

Diane helped all she could, but most of her day was spent putting together Danny's upcoming itinerary. Despite the workload, Wesley still wanted him in Europe within 48 hours. It would be a three-week trip, starting in London and covering the 15 different destinations that Global Airlines had just passed to Alta Airlines. After London, it would be on to Dublin, Lisbon, Madrid, Barcelona, Munich, Paris, Rome, Florence, Milan, Zurich, Prague, Stockholm, Moscow, St. Petersburg, and Budapest.

Much of the first day back was spent handling the flood of congratulatory notes and calls that were coming in about the acquisition. Wesley insisted that each one be acknowledged and replied to. The new innovation of e-mail presumably increased the efficiency of these tasks, but with everything forwarded to Danny, it felt like just another water cannon pointed in his direction. He was leaving the following night and had four crucial things on his list before his departure.

First, he had to train his replacements for the next few weeks. There were two contractors being brought in to do his job at probably twice his salary. Second, he had to somehow get home and pack. Third, call Barbara Lewis and get Caroline an interview for in-flight. Calling in a favor from Wesley was onerous, even though there was nothing more appropriate. Caroline had saved the deal, but Wesley would never grasp the importance of her role, nor would he want to. Anything that supplanted Wesley as the engineer, mastermind and savior of the Global acquisition, whether it was true or not, would be considered a threat. And except for internal PR opportunities, Wesley was not a "front-line" kind of guy; he didn't know Caroline or anyone else at Kennedy Airport. A request on Caroline's behalf would not have a basis to Wesley; it would be creating a debt rather than repaying one. Danny would take it to Barbara as a "respected colleague" and see what she could do.

Finally, he had to call Cathy. The glow of their conversation would dim with each day, and he was determined not to miss this opportunity. As illusory as it might be, the idea of settling down with someone and actually having a relationship was suddenly very appealing.

Danny put in his call to Barbara and she called him back as darkness fell.

"Barbara, need a favor."

"Sure, Danny, what's up?"

"I have a friend at Kennedy. She put in for in-flight, and I need to see if we can get her an interview. She worked behind the scenes on the acquisition and..."

"Done. Give her my number and tell her to call me."

Danny had even made notes in preparation for this conversation, ready to reel off Caroline's fine qualities to make his case, but Barbara had cut him off. He didn't know what to say.

"Tell her interviews start next week. We'll get her in there."

"Barbara, thank you! This will mean so much to her."

Danny was relieved, but also proud, not of his clout, but of the precedence that friendship had taken over politics. This was his own moral victory. He didn't need to put pressure on anyone. His judgment was respected, and Barbara was there to help him.

He made his call to Cathy and left her a message. That was okay; he had made contact. Still, he was definitely not going to see her before he left, and the intensity of his conversation with her was such that he had neglected to mention his assignment in Europe to her.

She called him back in the office just before midnight.

"I'm going to be gone for three weeks," he told her.

"Where are you going?"

"Everywhere. All of our new cities in Europe."

"Which one are you looking forward to going to most?" she asked.

"Oh, I don't know. I haven't even thought about it. I don't know anything about these places. Why, do you get a lot of trips to Europe?"

"A few. I speak German and Italian so I'm a backup on those routes."

"I speak...English."

"You'll be fine. So does almost everyone else." Her assurances were both surprising and calming.

"Did you still want to get together?" she asked.

"Yes, absolutely, but I won't be back until the end of November."

"How about I meet you over there. Florence is a good spot." She might as well have been referring to Buckhead's latest hip restaurant.

"Florence? You mean like, in Italy?"

"Yeah. Good food. Nice people. See you there?"

Although his mind was consumed with his own logistics, he couldn't think of any reason to say no. He remembered how good flight attendants had it, how many of them had plenty of days off and the flexibility to swap trips, and suddenly the idea of a rendezvous in Italy seemed totally plausible. They worked out the details. He gave her the date he'd be there, and she gave him the name of a café.

"Florence. I'll see you there."

30

By the time of his arrival in Italy, Danny had found his rhythm. The headquarters office was far behind, and each day when he dropped in on the sales office of a different country, he was greeted with a level of warmth that belied the fears of the local staff. His position as assistant to the chief executive officer of the acquiring airline generated much more deference than he was comfortable with, especially when meeting many of the old guard Global reps who had devoted their lives to their now extinct airline. For this reason, he kept the interactions cordial and reassuring wherever possible. He was only there to assess their needs, not to shut down their office. His report would be thorough and descriptive rather than analytical and financial, and once this was understood, the conversations became lighter. More than once, the relief of his hosts spawned a camaraderie that carried them out the door and on to one of the city's finest restaurants. Wesley had emphatically directed Danny to spare no expense toward building the rapport with the managers of each sales office, and even if this mandate was a bit patronizing, nearly every night of his journey was filled with the rich experience of a unique European metropolis.

But tonight he had managed to defer the same activities with his Florentine hosts in favor of a woman. The sensory overload of the last ten days had blurred his physical memory of her. He remembered how he felt, and he remembered the power of the smile, but theirs was one of those first encounters that needed a second one to set the image in the mind for good. She had been to Florence several times and knew exactly where he was staying and where they should meet. A fax arrived in the hotel with directions that were not just step-by-step, but step for step, like something a spy might receive or perhaps a courier dropping off a ransom payment.

It was late afternoon when he paused on the balcony of his hotel room to take in the sweeping view of the central city on the far side of the Arno River. The hills were a darkish blue beyond the thousands of terra cotta roof tops stretching into the distance. The red half circle of the Duomo rose proudly above it all, declaring this as a place of enduring civilization that prized beauty. The waning sun turned the river into a field of sparkling light and there was a murmur in the soft air, not one of traffic and horns, but of people. People walking, talking, living—a car-less rush hour of sorts, perhaps no different in tenor than one that would have occurred in the same place seven hundred years ago.

Danny thought the view looked romantic, but then he realized he wasn't quite sure what that meant. How could something *look* romantic, especially since romance was all about a feeling? How could such a thought be running through his head, especially since his idea of romance, at least up to this point, was strongly, if wrongly, associated with pain? For Danny, romance was, by its very nature, something that women felt much more than men, but the cold reality was that romance never endured. When the passion was gone—and he believed he understood passion—the romance inevitably went with it. Every flame went out when the fuel was exhausted; every climactic, romantic high seemed to be destined to be pulled back to earth.

A feathery gust of wind carried the smell of fresh pasta up to him from a street side restaurant below. He caught glimpses of aproned waiters and clinking glasses of wine under the corner of a white awning. Another breeze and he could smell the bread, and he realized he was hungry. Then he remembered Cathy's face, her smile. And all at once the breeze turned his sails away from cynicism and toward a revelation, a crystallized understanding of romance and the possibility that it could be as enduring as the radiant city in front of him. For once there was a possibility.

He headed down the steps and on to the street, walking up along the Arno. His directions were specific: he was to walk up river to the Ponte Vecchio, the 14th century bridge with markets and small shops that girdled its arc across the river. Then onward into the heart of oldest Florence to the Piazza della Repubblica, the square where he would meet her, and finally to a cafe called Giubbe Rosse.

He was early, but still concerned. It seemed as though it would be a miracle if she actually found him, but then they were *her* directions, and after he settled into a prominent outdoor table just inside the rope, he reviewed them just to make sure he was in the right place. A red-vested waiter came out and said something to him in Italian as he handed him a menu.

"Vino," he said, conveying both his desire and his nationality in two syllables. The waiter nodded and returned with a slight bow as he handed him the list. Danny always felt a pang of guilt when he couldn't speak the native language. He was hopelessly concerned about presumption among his hosts in every country where his ignorance was unavoidably on display.

The square was winding down from rush hour, the pedestrians and Vespas crisscrossing with diminishing urgency. The tables around Danny began to fill up. He looked at his watch and just as the minute hand grazed 7:00 p.m., their meeting time, he saw her in the distance, weaving through the masses. She strode confidently toward him, slipped beneath the rope and sat down across from him at what he then realized was just a very small bistro table.

"Sorry I'm late," she said.

"You're 45 seconds late," he said.

"I'm usually on time." It didn't occur to him that she was serious. Instead, there was an immediate pause in their conversation, and because it was a bistro table, he only needed to lean over from his seat, and she to him, to kiss her on the cheek.

"You're not done."

"Huh?"

"We're in Italy. You're supposed to kiss both cheeks. Haven't you learned that yet?"

"Let's try that again," he said. "I'm going to have to start over."

This time he got it right. It seemed so natural, as if they already had a bond between them that went far past their little in-flight conversation. Maybe they had, or maybe it was just the sight of a familiar and beautiful face in a faraway land among cobblestones and cathedrals. Maybe it was the *romance* of the place? He still didn't like the word. It was too mushy for him, but passion wasn't the right word either. This was something bigger than passion, as big as the spires of cathedrals that lined the square. He finally conceded to himself that romance was as much a part of life as pain was and he was willing to accept the latter if he could truly have the former, now that he was beginning to understand what it was.

"You look beautiful tonight, Cathy."

"Grazi."

"Grazi?"

"It means 'Thank you.'"

"Oh. You're welcome."

"Prego." And then he finally started to catch on.

"Prego," he said, stretching out the word.

"Very good," she said.

"Graaazzziiii."

"Try not to over do it," she said.

He asked her about the city, about what she liked and why, and she carried the conversation with vivid descriptions of the charms of "Firenze." After a glass of wine for each, she led him to a taxi that swept them out of the city and into the hills beyond. The driver was daring, dipping over hills and wrapping around turns along the increasingly narrow roads as if he were driving a Formula One. He came within inches of some twilight cyclists, passing them before swerving back into the lane to avoid an oncoming vehicle. And quickly they were in a mountaintop hamlet, with deeply weathered cobblestones and hilly streets barely wide enough for a pair of Vespas. Cathy grabbed Danny by the hand.

"I'm going to show you one of my favorite restaurants."

They climbed up a hill. No sidewalks, just a street within a cavern of medieval buildings. A yellow glow and a joyous gush of spirited Italian conversation escaped from the open-air window near the top. They entered a full restaurant, but with a few words in the native language from Cathy, the host waved them back to a small square table against the wall beside the arch of another open window. Off in the distance, they could still see the Duomo lit up and framed by purplish clouds that bounced what was left of the sun from beyond the horizon.

The wine, bread and pasta tasted different than back home, as if some barrier had been lifted that had, up to now, repressed Danny's ability to taste and smell. All of his sensations were suddenly fuller and richer. The wine, for instance: it was deeply red against the amber light that surrounded them. When the waiter pulled the cork, the presence of the bouquet was immediate. When the wine flowed into the depths of his glass, it curled around the bowl and crashed in upon itself in a miniature breaker that was wonderfully audible. And when he tasted it, there were portions of his tongue and mouth and throat that seemed as if they had never been touched before and were now so noticeably awakened.

"This is...fantastic." He couldn't think of the right word to describe what he was feeling, but he also knew such a word might not exist, at least not in his language.

"I thought you'd like it. Florence is a wonderful city, but this is true Tuscany, where the good food really is."

"How do you know so much about this place?"

"I have a relative from here, my grandfather's sister. I had a trip to Rome and came up for a few days about two years ago. Then I just kept coming back when I could. It feels safe here for some reason."

The bread crackled as they broke off pieces and softened when they dipped it in the plate of fresh virgin olive oil. The pasta seemed to make him hungrier as he ate it.

"Do you feel unsafe in Atlanta?" he asked.

"Yes, sometimes. I don't always feel like I have much control over what's happening. It's kind of funny, but I feel more in control when I'm working a flight than when I'm on the ground."

"Do you feel like you have control here?"

"No, but I don't feel like I need to." Her face was deeply expressive, flashing a moment of anxiety when she described Atlanta and contentment when she talked about Florence or her job. He felt the need to protect her, take her home and shelter her from her fears. His hand reached across the table, and she locked her fingers into his.

"How do you feel right now?" he asked.

"I feel...fantastic," she said, mocking his opening statement with a softening smile.

"Seriously, this is nice," she added, in case he had any doubts.

When he kissed her goodnight out in front of her hotel, the arc of the evening was perfectly complete and the mutual anticipation of their next meeting back home was ever more exciting. The memories of Florence carried Danny through the rest of Europe on a cloud of happiness.

31

Jeff and Joanne had a baby boy within days of their first anniversary in 1990, but now, over three years since their wedding day, their marriage had crumbled.

From his point of view, she had failed to appreciate her husband's role in her livelihood. He didn't really try very hard to hide his infidelity. That's who he was and she needed to accept that. At first, Joanne lived with it, but over time and after months of counseling on her own, she got up the will to end it. Not that it wasn't already over. It certainly wasn't marriage as she envisioned it anyway. There was neither sexual nor conversational intimacy between them, and so it wasn't long before her bitterness rose triumphantly to the surface during a routine phone call.

"Jeff, you don't need to come home from Atlanta. Why don't you just stay down there and we'll get a divorce."

It sounded so matter-of-fact that at first Jeff thought she was joking. How could she divorce him? As far as he was concerned, the marriage offered him everything he expected. Why wasn't it the same for her? He had a wife, a child, a house and all the stability he needed without the stigma of being single. How could she have the nerve to take this all for granted? What was she thinking?

"Are you crazy? What are you talking about? Divorce?"

"We don't have a marriage."

"Well, I think you're quite mistaken and I have the papers to prove it," he said.

"Jeff, I have the papers to prove you're an adulterer," she said, referring to a stash of suspicious receipts she had socked away. This was not like her. Not his wife. She knew better than to rock the boat. He began to feel his anger rise. If she tried to use his personal life against him he'd destroy her. She had challenged him before but not like this. This time she had stepped way out of line.

"I don't know who you've been talking to or what you've been taking, but you get your act together right away, woman. I will call you back in an hour and I expect you to straighten yourself out!" he yelled.

This method had worked in the past. He would cow her into submission, because for Jeff, this was just another form of corrective action in the face of turbulence. They would pass through it and he would get them back on course, and then, once he was certain they were "stabilized," he would forgive her for this outburst and that would be the end of it. But when he called her back exactly 60 minutes later, she was not answering. This left him seething, on the threshold of full-blown rage.

He had a trip that afternoon, one that he handled with a level of professionalism beyond his normal perfection. He was exceedingly nice to all the passengers as they came on board; he delivered a charming rendition of the route of flight and he generously complimented the rest of the flight crew. But underneath his facade of professionalism he grew angrier at the foolishness of his wife, as if his perfection was a continuing reminder of how stupid she was, ready to throw her marriage away in a tantrum of selfishness. He thought it might be a PMS thing. She had blamed that in the past, but he was getting sick of this.

The flight crew was Atlanta based, and he recognized some of the faces. A girl named Jeanine in particular. He engaged her in a solemn but friendly conversation, his face conveying fleeting moments of pain, prompting her to ask him what was wrong.

"It's my wife. She wants out of the marriage."

"Oh, I'm so sorry, Jeff. That must be so difficult for you."

Of course, she wasn't sorry at all. The trip was an out and back journey—no overnights. Jeanine observed him, his professionalism in the face of domestic crisis, and it wasn't long before she had also demonized the ungrateful wife. Who says pilots aren't sensitive, she thought. And how could his wife put him through this?

Jeff was fully conscious of the impression he was building for Jeanine and he sensed her growing attraction. When their return flight arrived back in Atlanta that evening and all the passengers had deplaned, she got her nerve up and asked him.

"Where are you staying tonight?"

"Not sure. Wherever they put the crews up I guess." This despite the fact that he now had his own apartment in Atlanta.

"Why don't you stay at my place tonight? We can talk. I've got a bottle of wine we can share." After a nicely performed bout of ambivalence, he accepted.

◆　　　◆　　　◆

Joanne called a phone number that a friend had given her for a divorce lawyer. Jeff and Joanne's house was located in one of the finer middle-class neighborhoods of Long Island, and ownership was in both their names. She didn't really want to stay there, but according to the lawyer, it might end up being her only asset with any value, so she would fight for it. She would also demand full custody of their son Jamie. At two years old and with a father who was away more than any pilot should be, Jamie probably wouldn't even notice a difference for a few years. Still, the trauma of irreversible change was setting in quickly for Joanne, so she called Caroline for support. They arranged brunch the next morning.

"So he comes in and says he had to stay in Atlanta for union work. I ask him about it and he gets mad at *me!*"

"What did you do wrong?" asked Caroline.

"I questioned him, that's what I did wrong," said Joanne

"Yeah, but you were right, weren't you?"

"Doesn't matter. That's not the issue, according to him."

"I don't get it. What's not the issue?"

"I'm not supposed to *question* him. He will do what he wants and I can take it or leave it."

"Asshole," said Caroline. She continued, "Was he surprised when you decided not to 'take it'?"

"Yeah, I think he was surprised. Then he got mad. *Really* mad. I almost backed down, but when he hung up I felt, like, relieved."

"Relieved?"

"Yeah. I felt okay about it."

"What does that tell you, Joanne?" Caroline could have made the case with Joanne months, even years before, but the ebb and flow of their friendship taught her the importance of letting Joanne make her own discoveries.

"I know. I don't need him. I really thought for a long time this could get better, but it's only gotten worse. I think I was kidding myself."

Caroline grabbed her friend's hand across the table and squeezed. It was almost as if she were squeezing the tears out of Joanne's eyes as she began to well up.

◆　　　◆　　　◆

Jeff and Jeanine had met before on a trip months earlier, but now as he slept next to her in the late morning hours of the following day, he looked different to her, like a little boy who was wayward and lost. This activated a maternal instinct of sorts, a need to take care of him so he could "get back on his feet." He was a pilot, but at this very moment, as he slept naked in the fetal position beside her, he seemed anything but the strong solid model of integrity that all pilots aspire to. He needed to be stable and content. She considered that if she took him on, she would not only be fulfilling her own needs, she would be performing a service for her company. It was the right thing to do.

With that rationale solidified, she switched perspectives and looked him over as the sexual being that he was. Muscular and square shouldered, his hands were large, his fingers thick and softly bent around her wrist. He had light colored eyebrows and a shock of tousled blond hair with a few locks hanging across his forehead. His chest was rock solid, well defined under a fine layer of chest hair. Was she good enough for him? In the past, she would have said never. She was not unattractive. Rather, she had often been told that she had a beautiful face, nicely framed by her short dark hair, but she conceded to herself that she'd never be the trophy that most pilots seemed to gravitate toward. It all came down to her hips, something she had been told about point blank by another pilot "friend."

Would he recognize that she was right for him and stay with her? After a few moments of self-doubt, the plan formed in her head. She would meet his every wish and demand until he had no choice but to choose her. She would make him deliciously dependent on her. With that, she pulled herself from bed while he still slept, wrapped herself in his shirt and set about making him breakfast.

32

A month after he'd met Jeanine, Jeff broke the lease on his Atlanta apartment and moved in with her. The woman was amazing, so incredibly thoughtful, supportive and helpful. Here was someone who knew the value of a man like him and never took it for granted. She did everything for him with girlish enthusiasm, and before he knew it, she had won the right to return him to the stability he required.

As the divorce hearings approached, his conversations with his wife alternated between volatile and businesslike. He agreed to the divorce, but now he hated the fact that it wasn't his idea. The thought of not bringing up his son in a stable two-parent family was unacceptable. There was, it turned out, an inheritance at stake. His aging grandfather had mandated distribution of his estate to his grandchildren contingent on their upholding "family values" as he defined it, and that meant a traditional nuclear family with a male heir. Well, Gramps didn't have to know all the circumstances, thought Jeff. As long as he could occasionally see his great-grandson in the flesh, that would be enough to ensure the windfall when he kicked. And so Jeff arranged to take Jamie down to Florida at least twice a year to his grandfather's nursing home. The divorce would not interrupt this routine, and since Joanne had yet to gain sole custody, there was nothing legally preventing him from doing this. As much as Joanne hated the charade, she knew she had to choose her battles carefully and she didn't put up a fight. Doing so would only give her soon-to-be ex another method of irritating her and another small source of sadistic pleasure.

Behind the scenes, Jeff found himself an attorney through the pilots union, an experienced bulldog of a divorce lawyer who had handled several other pilot cases with great success. His perspective was absolutely clear: Wives of pilots were simply out for the money and everything that went with it. Pilots deserved whatever they could get and that was almost always better than what they had. His name was Trent Graham (Esq.), and he was young and arrogant. Like Jeff, he would not accept losing and their initial consultation was an exercise in male bonding that took on the air of a locker room pep talk.

"First of all, be prepared. She's gonna want the house. They always want the house," said Graham.

"She hasn't said anything to me about it yet."

"Yeah, and she's not going to. She's going to try and blindside you with this. Trust me." Jeff was feeling his anger rise, and Trent Graham was establishing a steady fuel line for the fire within.

"What about my son?"

"That's a tough one. These women don't have a clue about the importance of a father in the household. Most of the time the guy gets screwed. I'm going to need to know what you know about your wife. Everything, no matter how embarrassing. In fact, the more embarrassing the better. Is she mentally stable?"

Jeff smiled. "Well, she's a woman, you know." Graham returned the smile. Now they had misogyny in common to strengthen their bond.

"Yeah, I know. But as *you* well know, some of this just can't be helped. Aside from that, has she ever hit the child? Or freaked out in a restaurant? Any kind of incident that we can disclose?"

"She has a hard job and sometimes she comes home crying."

"Good. Okay, we might be able to use that. What does she do?"

"She's in Reservations. At the airline."

"Has she ever told a customer to fuck off?"

"I don't know, probably. I used to do the job too, and I told people to fuck off once in a while."

"Yeah well, this isn't about you so let's just forget that one. This is about the mother of your child and establishing a pattern of erratic behavior."

"She threw a dish once when I came home a day late."

"What the hell are you supposed to do about late flights? What was it, weather? Mechanical problem?" Jeff paused before answering, but Trent cut him off. The pause told Trent what really happened and that this was something he was better off not hearing.

"Did the dish come close to you?"

"No, she threw it on the floor," said Jeff.

"So it shattered."

"Yes."

"And did the shards of the dish come anywhere near you? Like near your eyes?"

"They could have. I don't really remember."

"If they came near your eyes, they could have endangered your career. It could have grounded you. Wiped out your entire viability," Graham said. He was good.

"They might have come close, yes."

"What about the child? Was the child in the room?"

"In the dining room in the high chair, just off the kitchen where she threw the dish."

"So the child could have been hit by the shards of the dish."

"Could have, yes. It was a big dish."

"And the child could have easily had pieces of the dish go in her eyes."

"His eyes. Yes, I suppose that's possible."

"Of course it's possible. She's a woman. Anything could happen!"

Graham tossed his pen on the desk in disgust and reclined in his high back chair, letting the opening foray sink into his client. Like so many of those before him, he simply needed to light the fuse and the rest would ignite by itself.

In the coming weeks, he would manage to uncover a string of Joanne's behaviors from Jeff that he would bless as sufficiently erratic. The teamwork between Jeff and Trent was powered by a vengeance that went well beyond the courtroom—a vengeance that the highly skilled attorney adeptly channeled into their immediate purpose.

On the day of the divorce hearing, in the city courthouse in lower Manhattan, the judge wavered—a judge who in the past had been exceedingly sympathetic to the wives of estranged husbands—and this forced suspension of a decision on the question of custody until more information could be obtained to validate or refute Joanne's "grossly erratic behavior."

33

Jeff had other more important things to think about. There was an acquisition in progress, and he had worked his way into a key position. His seniority and new base in Atlanta yielded him a captain's seat for 757s. Not a widebody yet, but close to it—a workhorse of an aircraft, graceful and beautiful and one that gave him enough prestige to take a leadership role within the pilots' union. His professionalism in the cockpit won him additional respect among his fellow crew members.

The union whetted Jeff's appetite for power and control. He was the executive secretary of the Alta chapter of the union, which included responsibility for internal communications. Each month the union newsletter included a "Letter from the Secretary" penned by Jeff himself. The theme was fairly consistent, centering on the importance of unity in the face of management's subversive efforts to derail that unity. In one letter, Jeff warned his brethren to keep diligent track of every hour they were away from home because "management is diverting the off-hour pay to their own fund. Every penny out of your pocket is a penny into theirs!"

Another one espoused the potential danger of hypoglycemia if pilots no longer received their first choice of meals on their flight:

This overreaching management cost-cutting initiative ignores the pilot whose unpalatable meal could lead him to lose consciousness in the cockpit, putting at risk the lives of our very own customers.

The urgent recommendation was that pilots should always get a choice of first class meals before the customers do. The key to unity, as Jeff rightfully saw it, was the calculated fomenting of anger towards a common enemy. As long as management could be clearly identified as this enemy, the union membership could be counted on to fall in line. Nevertheless, the acquisition of Global was wholeheartedly endorsed and supported by the union because it meant bigger aircraft, higher pay, longer routes and a much larger membership that would generate over a million dollars a year in additional dues for the Alta chapter.

Jeff praised Wesley Arnold in his monthly letter for his astute leadership of the acquisition; a deal that would quickly vault Alta into position as a "premier air carrier in the world." But even the compliments implied a presumed equal partnership between management and the pilots. The installment that followed bestowed evenhanded credit for "this bold step we've taken together," when in fact the pilots had nothing to do with it. And on it went:

We have been deeply involved in the negotiations with Global Airlines and although these confidential discussions do not allow us to share details, we will protect the interests of our membership and ensure that whatever agreement is reached, it will guarantee that Alta's pilots are the highest paid in the profession.

One might easily assume that Jeff was at the table, shoulder to shoulder with Wesley Arnold as details were hammered out, and that was exactly the image that he intended to convey. But soon after the deal was announced, the tone suddenly changed. The president of the union was too passive for Jeff, too uninvolved. This incensed him. Now that the deal was done, it was time to step up and either approve or decline the acquisition, as if the union actually had approval rights. But they didn't, they weren't at the table, and nobody had made the formal request to the union to okay the deal. This alone was offensive to Jeff, but there was the added concern that Alta had made a deal that did not appropriately consider the interests of their most important employee group.

We are awaiting the release of the acquisition agreement document to your union board for review, however management has missed the original deadline, raising concern among your leadership. Let us be clear that no acquisition will be approved by the union if it in any way diminishes the standards of our existing contract.

"Management" was not taking him seriously, and as the deal came to fruition, Jeff's anger began to spiral upward. They were going to pay for this lack of respect.

Jeff hadn't talked to Danny in over a year, but now was the time. He left him a rambling message with a thin layer of friendship over words of ominous warning—a message he was sure would get him a prompt return phone call.

"Danny, its Jeff. Hey man, howzit going for you? Great to hear you're at the top of the food chain there, or at least close to it. Listen, we've got some issues I want to share with you about the acquisition before things get out of control. We're not getting a whole lot of response here from Flight Ops or Corporate Comm, and I just wanted you to be aware of what's going down. Maybe you're in a spot to send it up to Arnold and keep the shit from hitting the fan, I dunno. But let's talk. Gimme a call when you get a sec. Okay, talk to you."

Danny had gotten periodic reports on Jeff's progress over the years through Caroline. He knew the marriage to Joanne was ending, and he'd just heard about the impending custody battle. The type of minimal friendship that Danny had with Jeff called for staying clear until the dust settled. But small talk would probably carry him through and obviously there was something on Jeff's mind that sounded important, so he dialed him back later that day. Might as well get it over with.

"Jeff, its Danny."

"Hey man! How are you?" Jeff sounded friendlier than Danny could ever remember him being. "So you're doing well up there, are you?" asked Jeff.

"Doing all right. How about you?"

"Excellent. Doing great!"

"Great!" Oh how "great" things could be. They covered a few other details and touched on their recollections of Reservations, but nothing about their divergent personal lives, and so the small talk quickly drained away.

"Listen, the reason I'm calling is to get the word out about the acquisition. There are some problems."

"Problems? It's all done," said Danny. Jeff bristled and the tone of his voice darkened.

"Yeah, well, it's not quite done yet, buddy. You know there was no union rep at the table, right?" It was a menacing non-question.

"Yeah, that's what I heard."

"Well that's fucked up. Pardon my French."

"But the deal went through okay," said Danny. He was trying to lighten things, but he noticed that he was suddenly gripping the phone a little tighter than normal.

"The deal went through for management. But we didn't get a look at it, and Arnold needs to know that was a mistake."

"A mistake?"

"Damn right it was a mistake. Since when do you cut a deal like this without talking to your pilot leadership? All due respect, Danny, but did they have their heads that far up their asses that they couldn't see what a shit storm this could cause?"

"Obviously not." This was a dig that Danny couldn't help. Jeff picked up on it and moved into belligerence.

"Obviously fucking not is right, my friend! Listen, Arnold better take this seriously or this whole goddamn airline is going to come to a full stop!"

"Jeff, easy man. Talk to me."

Danny remembered Jeff's anger, how it could easily catapult out of control, and he wondered how the man managed to keep his cool under the stress of a difficult flight. He heard a deep breath of exasperation on the other end of the line, perhaps something a counselor, or maybe even a lawyer, had told Jeff to do when he verged on being apoplectic.

"Jeff. What's the biggest issue? Let's start with that."

"Seniority. That's the deal. It's very simple. Like in real estate. Location Location Location. Same with us. Seniority is our location and Arnold better not mess with it."

"What have you heard?" asked Danny.

"Danny, what's important here is not what I've heard but what you've heard. No one has given us any answers…"

"What's Dugan telling you?" asked Danny, referring to the union president.

"I'm calling on behalf of Dugan. We got nothing from you guys."

"Alright, let me check into it," said Danny, interrupting him. "Honestly, Jeff, I don't know the details, so let me do some investigating."

"Okay. Yeah, check on it for me."

"Okay," said Danny, and he hung up.

The moment Jeff put the phone down in his barren union office, he went ballistic. Why the hell had he let him off the hook so easily? Why hadn't he pressed him more? He'd shown his cards and got nothing back. He hadn't even gotten a commitment to call him back by a certain time! He'd been talking to a friend and forgot the importance of the business at hand and now he'd screwed himself. He picked up the cheap pencil holder on the desk and flung it against the wall, shattering it into tiny slivers of plastic. Jeff had always prided himself on his perfection, on never letting his guard down, but this time, this one time, he'd fucked up and the cost as he saw it was grossly unacceptable. He'd give Danny two hours, call him back and do his best not to sound like one of the blithering peons that made up ninety percent of his goddamned company.

34

It had been just four months since the acquisition, and Danny seemed to be fading slowly into the background of Wesley Arnold's day-to-day life. But he wasn't the only one. Alta's new CEO had completely transcended and distanced himself from every principal at Alta, including the other executive VPs. He was now an isolated command-and-control leader, in part because he had managed to consolidate his influence under one giant umbrella title: chairman of the board, president and chief executive officer, and that put up a major barrier against any threats to his leadership. He literally held the number one, two and three positions at Alta Airlines—an unprecedented position of power in the industry.

There were some efficiencies: he was the only one who had a clear view of the big picture both inside and outside the enterprise, so if something needed to be done, he had all of the buttons and levers in front of him. But it was just as clear to Danny that his leader's corporate vision was dwindling within what was becoming an impenetrable fortress of power. For that reason, he dreaded the task in front of him as he entered his vast office.

"Whattaya got?" Wesley asked him. He was genial. Must have seen his name in the papers again.

"Pilot seniority. Where does it stand right now?" Danny asked.

"I wanted our pilots to have full seniority. Complete preservation of their seniority. Their employee dates will not be affected by the acquisition. That should have been communicated by Yarman," Wesley said, referring to the executive VP of flight operations.

"I think he did. But does that mean that Global pilots with previous employee dates will have higher seniority?" Wesley didn't have an immediate answer to this one, and within the two extra seconds that it took him not to answer the question, Danny knew they were in trouble.

"Why wouldn't they? Of course, anyone with an earlier employee date is going to have higher seniority," Wesley said.

There was nothing to be gained by pressing Wesley on this. It was clear he didn't really know what he was talking about, and they needed to get to a solution. The *relative* nature of seniority had escaped him. Danny decided to lay out the problem.

"The issue we're facing is the merging of the seniority lists. Our pilots don't want to lose their position on the Alta list, and if we weave in the Global pilots with their hire dates, our pilots are not going to be happy."

"How the hell are we supposed to make everyone happy!" said Wesley to his messenger. Another pause as Danny let it sink in. This is the way he had to play his boss. Throw out enough food for thought that he would eventually 'eat.'

"Let's get Yarman in here," Wesley said.

He yelled an order to Diane, and 30 seconds of silence later, a dignified old soldier of a pilot walked into Wesley's spacious office. Henry "Hank" Yarman was a pilot who'd worked his way into management when he knew his eyes were going. The clumsy way he wore a suit was a constant reminder that he belonged in a uniform, even if he couldn't fly anymore. As he stepped on the carpet, Danny could almost see him stifling a salute.

"What's going on with the pilots?" Wesley snapped.

"I'm not sure what you mean, sir."

"The, pilots, uh…" Wesley forgot the issue long enough for Danny to fill in the blank.

"Seniority, Hank," said Danny.

"Ah, yes. It's being looked at carefully. We are trying to optimize the seniority lists," said Yarman, hoping the word "optimize" would carry him through this little bout of turbulence.

"Whattaya mean, optimize? Siddown," said Wesley. He was out of patience.

"What did the agreement say?" asked Wesley.

"It didn't specify, sir," said Yarman.

"Okay. That's good. That means we can do anything we want then."

Yarman and Danny looked at each other helplessly. Yarman slowly began a gesticulation that would have gone with some sort of convoluted statement, but he was too slow.

"We can't do anything, Mr. Arnold," said Danny. The rule was Danny couldn't call him Wesley if someone else was in the room.

"Why not?" asked Wesley.

"The pilots want complete preservation of their positions on the list. Isn't that right, Hank?" Danny suspected Yarman was clueless, but he wasn't trying to trap him, just get him to follow along on the path to the truth. The worst thing that could happen was a piece of fiction from Yarman that would only lay a blanket over the bomb. He nodded.

"Are you telling me that our pilots, our lowest seniority pilot wants to be higher on the totem pole than their highest seniority pilot?" asked Wesley. Yarman had become a complete spectator.

"Yes," said Danny. "That's what I'm telling you, but even they know that's ridiculous. A 30 year 747 pilot is not going to come down to fly MD80s, and we're not going to give a seat in a widebody to someone out of training ahead of someone who's been flying them for years."

Danny had picked up enough over the years to understand the dynamics of pilot seniority; however, the problem at hand wasn't dynamics but mentality. How to broach that as an issue without enraging the king of the airline was now the present challenge.

"So if they know that, what do they want?"

"I think what they'll demand is a bump in their contract to compensate for their loss in position," said Danny. If he could just get Wesley to consider a pay raise, or even just say they were considering it, it might diffuse some of the union anger.

"Don't these guys get it? We just spent half a billion on this acquisition and they want more money!"

Yarman was getting a little squirrelly in his seat. He was at least three exchanges behind in the conversation, but the pressure to say something was apparent.

"Here's what I recommend," said Danny. "You first give them credit for supporting the acquisition. Usual statement about how this is going to make us a leader and one of the reasons we are in this position is because we have the best pilots in the world. Something that taps into their ego and lets them know they were partners in this. Right, Hank?"

"Right," said Hank, now immediately relieved of his obligation to speak.

"But they didn't do shit!" said Wesley.

"Doesn't matter. We've got to find a way out of this."

"What if we just tell them to bite me!" said Wesley. Yarman started getting squirrelly again.

"Then they *will* bite us." Danny spoke in measured, authoritative tones. He was commanding in his delivery because, unlike the king in his fortress, he now had a very clear understanding of the dangers they faced.

"They can't strike, but they may slow things down."

"They can't do that. That's illegal," said Wesley.

"True, and we may win in court, but we'll have lost millions along the way just from the customer service issues. We've got to deal with them." Wesley reflected on this. He put his head in his hands and looked up at the ceiling in wonderment.

"These fucking guys don't know when to quit!"

"With all due respect, sir..." and that was the last thing that came out of Yarman's mouth.

"What do we have to do? Continue, Danny," said Wesley. Yarman had about as much clout in the room as the occupants of the fish tank along the wall.

"Do a pilot presentation. A 'we did it together' show of unity first. They'll like that. Then talk to Dugan directly. Concede that there is no perfect way to do this, but we need a short-term solution and so we'll merge the lists based on position and seniority, whether they're Global or Alta. Discrepancies will be addressed in the contract negotiations next summer and leave it at that. No need to go into detail. We just need to get things off the ground and have a few months of normal operations under our belt."

"Good. Good work, Danny." Yarman gave a nod of satisfaction, as though his blessing held any weight, and they both left the office.

It was 6:30 in the evening but dark outside, quicker than he'd expected. December had arrived, and the days were rapidly growing shorter. Danny got back to his office and tried to return Jeff's call, but he got voice mail (In a second episode of fury, Jeff had ripped his phone out of the wall, causing his calls to be diverted directly into the pilot union voice mail system.)

"Jeff, listen, I talked to Arnold. He was pretty clear on the fact that he dropped the ball on this one. He's going to be in touch with Dugan tomorrow and he'll be making a presentation to the pilots next week. Listen, between you and me, this is going to work out fine. Not everyone is going to be happy in the beginning, but you guys are the best and everyone knows that. You should hear something through the chain tomorrow, but gimme a call by Friday if not."

One more call for the night.

"Cathy, its Danny."

"Hey, stranger."

"I miss you."

"You do?"

"I really miss you."

"Bad day?"

"Not too bad. Just insane."

"Well at least it wasn't bad."

"When's your next trip?"

"Tomorrow night."

"What are you doing tonight?"

"Nothing."

"I'll pick you up in half an hour."

35

Danny would normally be tired, wrung out by this time of the day. Typically he would head out of the office no later than 8:00 p.m. if he was lucky, but if he got out of there earlier, he might even squeeze in a workout to jettison the day's stress and recapture some of the energy he'd lost. But not tonight. On this cold early December evening, Danny felt energized, both by his performance that day and in the knowledge that he would soon see Cathy. He recounted the discussion in Wesley's office: his boss's eyes and concentration on Danny's every word. He'd never seen him listen so intently. Most of the time he *didn't* listen, but here Danny was, suddenly the wizard to the king.

Cathy lived in midtown Atlanta, near the city's Piedmont Park on the second floor of an aging two-story house. It was an apartment, one of four converted from a single family house. He found a parking space a few houses down and bounded up the steps to the door. An apartment doorbell with four numbers and four buttons was clumsily bolted to the doorframe, conspicuously out of place on what was once a stately dwelling. Her name was barely legible next to one of the buttons. He pressed it and heard a muffled buzz before she answered.

"It's Danny. Let's go, I'm taking you out!" He thought for a moment that maybe he was taking this wizard thing a bit too far until he heard laughter on the other end, and in a few seconds she was in his arms and they were on their way.

"Where we going?"

"You hungry?"

"I will be."

"I gotta place."

They headed up Peachtree, first through midtown, past the art museum and the symphony hall, each festively lit for the holidays, then crossing over the highway into lower Buckhead. The traffic seemed to swirl up and down Peachtree, and Danny wove in and around the slower traffic, catching every light until they arrived at a restaurant, a place called Café Intermezzo.

"I've never been here," she said, looking around. "This is nice."

"I don't come here much. It's kind of a date place, and I haven't had one in a long time," he said.

"That's good. So no one is going to pop in from your past and say hi to you?"

"Not likely," he said.

"Where do you usually go for a drink?" she asked.

"My refrigerator." She laughed at this.

"I can just imagine your refrigerator."

"What do you mean?"

"I mean I can picture it. Beer. An old jar of mayonnaise. Two half filled bottles of catsup. Peanut butter."

"Whattaya mean? Where are you getting this from? You're totally wrong!"

"Really?"

"Yes. I only have one bottle of catsup."

The refrigerator as a topic led them to talk of where they lived, and then where they used to live. And that led to family, to siblings and parents and warm memories they shared with laughter. The embarrassing moments, the highs and lows. They worked their way back to their origins together, covering the basics, and then they turned a corner and wandered ever so slowly back to the present on a more intimate path, covering the less than basics, the pain of past romances, the role models, their inspirations and then, when comfort had set in fully, their aspirations.

Danny caught himself looking at her and thinking. The way she looked at him, deep in conversation, was almost distracting, as her smile was when he first saw her. There was that need to remind himself that he was the one she was looking at, talking to, and hopefully, falling in love with. Because that was clearly happening to him. As he recounted the last few years to her, he realized how tiresome his life had become. He was burnt out, lonely, and long past the need for conquest of any kind.

"Do you like kids?" he asked. It just came out, right past the brain filter and off his lips, but she answered immediately.

"I love kids." She smiled and then he smiled back, with a silent nod. He thought that might be enough for the moment. She seemed to read his mind and laughed at him.

"You're a funny guy, Daniel."

"You think? Wanna see my refrigerator?"

"I'm not ready to make that kind of commitment," she said, before adding, "But I'm willing to let you see mine."

He would see more than her refrigerator, but not much more. The house was creaky, and poorly heated. When they got up the stairs, Cathy grabbed his hand and didn't turn on the lights.

"My place is a mess so you can't see it," she said. He had no choice but to follow her lead. From all indications, it felt as though he was in her bedroom. Piercing streams of chilled air flowed in through the over-painted gaps along the sill of a window. She turned to him and hugged him, and then they kissed. It grew more intense, and she started pulling his shirt out from his pants and sliding her hands underneath. He started to do the same.

"Oh, your hands are cold!" she said.

"They'll be warm in a minute." As he began to pull off her top, a frigid blast of air hit them, and she squealed with laughter.

"Hurry, take everything off so we can get warm," she told him.

"Am I missing something here?" he asked.

"Hurry!" She got her clothes off first, and he caught a glimpse of her nakedness as she slipped into bed. She had one of those giant comforters that he remembered from his trip to Europe. A giant bulging white cocoon. He got everything off and slipped in just as another whistle of air knifed him in the lower back.

"Ohhhhhh!! This feels great!"

They giggled and snuggled—two sticks building a fire. He pulled one of his legs up and rubbed it against hers, and let the arch of his foot slide down along her calf. He could feel the slightest of stubble and it made him feel even closer to her, made her more human. And then his foot came to something else.

"Hey!!" he said.

"What?"

"You cheated!"

"What do you mean?"

"You're wearing socks!"

"So."

"You said take everything off."

"Yeah, to you. I didn't say *I* was going to take everything off."

They were face to face in the dark, lips inches apart talking in near whispers, intimate, warm, comfortable. Joyous. They both knew they were going to make love—that was understood. There was no rush, no emotional tension that so often clouds the delight of physical tension, and they knew this.

"How do I know you're not wearing something else?"

"I guess this is the place to find out, isn't it?" she said.

They made love in their little sheltered world of the comforter, a delightful shared womb that cradled the parts of their bodies that weren't touching each other. And then they talked some more in whispers.

"I haven't seen your refrigerator yet."

"Be my guest."

"Actually, the whole place is a refrigerator." She pinched him hard for that.

It was midnight now and the wind was romping outside. Their second round of sex was heated and vigorous, so much so that the comforter came off. When they finished and collapsed in a tangle, the chill dried the sweat from their bodies. Just before they drifted to sleep, Danny pulled the comforter back over both of them.

He woke up in the early morning grayness and made a quick exit—he still had to beat Wesley to work as his routine dictated—but soon after he was out the door, he thought that maybe he should have awakened her. He could see her apartment now and it was actually very nice, perfectly decorated and extremely neat. He couldn't figure out why she said it was a mess. Maybe she just wanted to get right into bed. Whatever the reason, it didn't matter. It was one of the better nights of his life, if not the best.

36

A week after the acquisition went through, Caroline had a surprisingly cordial conversation with Barbara Lewis, the VP of In-flight Service. The air of suspicion at Kennedy toward all forms of corporate leadership had no doubt generated her prejudice. But when Barbara Lewis picked up her direct line, Caroline discovered that she was not the elitist she'd expected.

"So you want to be a flight attendant, do you?" Caroline could hear the smile in Barbara's voice and it immediately put her at ease.

"Yeah. Why, am I crazy?" Barbara laughed at this.

"Let me be the first to tell you, Caroline, that yes, you are crazy. You've got to be a little crazy, but you come highly recommended from Danny, and he's got Mr. Arnold driving him crazy every day, so I trust his judgment." This made Caroline laugh. Maybe they weren't all subservient Barbie dolls after all—another prejudice she had fallen victim to. She was instantly drawn to Barbara; her comfort amid her power was both surprising and beguiling. Barbara Lewis might actually be someone she could look up to. Here was a woman in a position of leadership, but with perspective. Caroline had always made the unfair assumption that these two qualities could never go together, especially for those ascending the corporate ladder.

"We've had to push back the training classes and we won't be starting interviews until the first week of January. We have a lot of Global people we need to bring down here and talk to, but we're not ready to interview them yet. Doesn't make a lot of sense, I know, but that's what Mr. Arnold wanted, so I'm afraid we're going to have to wait to bring you down here too."

"That's okay. Do I need to call anyone?"

"No. They'll be talking to the station manager at Kennedy, and he'll tell you when you're scheduled. Do this for me though. Call me after the interview and let me know how it went. This will just remind me that your name is in."

Caroline never liked to make assumptions about her future, but Barbara came about as close as humanly possible to making an offer right there. She suspected that, unless she bombed in the interview, the follow-up call was going to be Barbara's trigger to make sure that Caroline was a successful candidate.

The next morning Caroline's manager stuck a folded note next to her keyboard as she was handling a customer.

Interview for In-flight in Atlanta, January 4, 1994, 10:30am.

She took the first flight out of LaGuardia on the morning of January 4th, giving herself a two-hour buffer to make the interview. All interviews were at the training center within the General Office complex, one of the many red brick buildings that made up the headquarters.

When she stepped off the shuttle bus for the terminal, there was an interesting, if not obvious divergence of two groups of women about thirty yards in the distance. One was a gaggle of perky overly made-up youth. The other was a slightly hunched contingent of weathered middle-aged women whispering in a cloud of cigarette smoke and cynicism. Was it possible to "see" cynicism from a distance? The body language and the occasional head wag were enough to confirm to Caroline that those were the Global women, and the others were the "virgins."

A slightly overweight but attractive lady came out of the building, hands in the air, to gather the disparate groups. She had the demeanor of a housemother.

"Hello everyone! Welcome to Atlanta! We'll need the new-hire candidates over here to my right, and other employees, including the Global people, over on this side if you don't mind. Thank you!"

The last syllable of each of her statements was always the loudest. Maybe this was a technique she learned for in-flight announcements, but outside in front of the building like this, it struck Caroline as bizarre. She couldn't help reaffirming to herself that she never wanted to live down here.

Caroline fell in with the Global women as instructed and then noticed that there were actually two men who were part of the group, but with identical body language (maybe that's why she hadn't noticed them from a distance). She also noticed the tension. Some were forcing smiles, rigid long lost smiles from the earlier days of the jet age, smiles that seemed to crackle audibly like a canvas being reframed after decades.

The two groups were led into a classroom and seated apart, one on each side of the classroom. Paperwork was distributed. Caroline noticed that her side of the room received an extra form to fill out. Among all of the forms, one of the applications appeared to be a new one. At the bottom, almost microscopic, was the notation "rev/11–15–93." This one had an extensive list of questions, an addendum of sorts, with inquiries that went well beyond anything she'd seen in a job application:

1) Have you ever been convicted of a misdemeanor? If yes, explain.
2) Have you ever had your wages garnished for any reason?
3) Have you ever declared bankruptcy?
4) Are you married?
5) If you are not married, are you divorced, widowed or never married? (circle one)
6) Do you have children?
7) If you do not have children, do you plan on having children?
8) If you do have children, do you plan on having more children?
9) If you do not plan to have children, do you use birth control? If "Yes" what type?
10) Do you smoke?
11) Do you exercise regularly?

And this was just the beginning. The entire questionnaire numbered 87 questions. The only thing that made it tolerable was that it was mostly multiple choice or yes/no.

Caroline snuck peeks at the various groups taking the test. The virgins appeared to be breezing through their paperwork as if they were doing a word search puzzle. They all seemed to have the same mannerisms, pausing between questions to touch the eraser of their pencils to their glossed lips. The Global women showed signs of struggle, not so much with the answers but with whether they *should* answer. A few minutes into the "test," housemother lady stood up at the front of the room and began to speak.

"You have 30 minutes to complete your paperwork, and then you'll be called in individually for your interview. Any questions at all?"

"I have a question," asked Caroline. She was pretty sure that no one else in the room would be compelled to ask a question, even if they all wanted to know the answer. The lady acknowledged her with a point of her chin and raised eyebrows, but no words.

"Why do you need to know about birth control?"

"Some forms of birth control pills can affect the drug testing and we just need to have a record of this." The answer was clearly rehearsed. It wasn't necessarily implausible, but then, what if it was true and it did affect the drug test? Would they get to take it over?

36) Have you had any moving violations in the last three years?
37) Have you ever been subject to a real estate foreclosure?
38) Have you ever used illegal drugs?

No, no, and despite the lie, no. It was easy for Caroline to rationalize lying once she moved further down the questionnaire. This was bullshit.

Three of the Global women got up and walked out. Caroline watched without looking, her head down but tilted to peek as they exited. She could hear the sniffle of impending tears, the premature realization among these veteran flight attendants that Alta's standards would be too high for them to meet. Another one threw down her No. 2 pencil when she was done and shook her head with pursed lips, as if to say, 'I might as well stay and see what happens.' Caroline caught her eye and gave her a very discreet thumbs-up. In return, she got an exasperated smile of sisterhood.

A head poked out through a door to the classroom.

"Caroline Douglas," said housemother lady.

Caroline followed her through the door and into an auditorium. It had a stage, like in high school. What the hell did they do in here? Skits?

"Hello, Caroline, thank you for coming down."

Scattered among the first two rows in front of her was an assortment of mostly women and a few men. Some of them were in uniform. The woman addressing her sat just off center. She had a legal size clipboard and what looked like a fountain pen. She was a big woman, but it was clear she knew how to dress well enough to minimize her size. Her voice was husky, but friendly.

"You'll have to excuse me; I've got a bit of a cold."

"No problem," said Caroline.

"So you work at Kennedy?"

"Yes."

"And now you're with Alta?" said the woman.

"Actually, I've always been with Alta."

"You're not one of the Global people?"

"No, I'm just in for a transfer."

"Oh! Okay. Well…welcome." The woman did some shuffling of papers. She seemed to be switching to a different list of questions.

"How long have you been with Alta?"

"It's been about seven years now. I started in Reservations."

"Reservations! I started there too! Tough job, isn't it?"

The conversation was chatty, and contrary to Caroline's expectations, it never quite became anything more than that for the next 20 minutes. The hardest question the woman asked her was why she wanted to be a flight attendant. Caroline was brutally honest; she told the woman she needed a change and felt this might be a good career path. She wanted to slip in the phrase "career path" somewhere. It had been shared with her that in-flight management liked this terminology. It seemed to lend dignity to a long-ridiculed occupation, but for Caroline, there was actually some truth to it.

When it was over, they thanked her and she was led out of the auditorium through another exit. Caroline speculated that the stage was used to assess things like appearance, presence, posture, and perhaps even an estimate of weight. The virgins probably loved it. Nothing like being put up on a pedestal if you're young and attractive. The only thing they wouldn't be able to do was tell the panel how they were going to end world hunger and save the whales. At the same time, she felt certain that the stage was an exercise in humiliation for any experienced Global woman who'd made it that far. Why should they, after decades of experience, have to prance out onto a stage to justify the career they already had?

Caroline had some time before her flight back to New York. She left messages for Barbara Lewis, ("Just wanted to let you know I had my interview"), Danny ("Thanks for getting me in the door, I think it went well") and Shawn ("Hey, your protégé is back. What's up with you, dude? Sorry I missed you"), before she caught her flight that afternoon. The next morning, another folded note was placed on her keyboard.

Training begins on February 10th

37

Caroline was both excited and scared about the new job. She knew she'd be able to handle it. That wasn't the problem. Her fears were rooted in ambivalence; she wasn't totally sure she'd made the right decision. There was a comfort level at Kennedy that she knew she hadn't fully appreciated, but the excitement she was also feeling told her it was time—time for a new and long overdue challenge. She had never really traveled that much for an airline employee, and now just the fact that it would be part of her job gave her a burst of energy.

Coupled with that was her near non-existent social life. She'd succeeded at the independence thing, gotten her own place and managed to isolate herself. Since Shawn left, she had retreated into her own little world of her beach house balcony and the ticket counter. She'd go out once in a while, see Joanne every few weeks as part of a routine, but beyond that, the joy and security that her structured surroundings had given her had now taken on a stale quality, and the sudden draw of the new job confirmed this. It was time to start another chapter.

Caroline didn't know what to expect from flight attendant training, but as she sat quietly in the classroom of the Atlanta training center, she was aware of her own attitude—an attitude about the company, about the South, about the virginal girls (they were *not* women) sitting around her. She promised herself that she would keep an open mind and approach it as if it was not just a new job, but an entirely new company.

"Welcome to in-flight training everyone!!"

It was the first thing out of the instructor's mouth, in the twangiest Dolly Parton-ish accent she'd ever heard, prompting Caroline to consider whether her new attitude resolution had immediately been blown to bits. They'll never take me alive, she thought.

"Alta flight attendants have the most rigorous standards in the industry. Many candidates do not make it through the training, and none of you should feel bad if you realize during the instruction that this is just not for you."

Caroline surveyed the classroom. The virgins were sitting at attention, shoulders back, breasts out as if in some kind of position that maximized their chance for reproduction. Unconscious of course. Perhaps even a matter of instinct. Most other women who did not sit this way by nature were, naturally, deselected. And the rules of the jungle for in-flight candidates were at least aligned and at most identical to the rules for successful reproduction. It was *natural.*

"The first week will provide an overview of the airline and our standard practices."

But why was that natural? Caroline's mind was only half tuned in to the instructor as she worked through the curiosities of it all. The business world was also a jungle—a jungle with its own set of rules. If an airline wasn't profitable, it died a nasty death. Profitability was elusive, naturally weeding out the weak.

"During the second week, we will discuss safety procedures. You will be tested every day on this. This is the most important part of your training."

But what made it profitable? She had always been amazed at how an airline could make money with planes and airports and all the other crap that costs so many millions of dollars. What was the edge? How did an airline even hope to eke out a profit with all of the expenses?

"The third week will cover processes. How our meals are served. What you need to know about first class and coach…"

Could it be that the whole concept of a flight attendant was one of the places in the universe where the characteristics of business and reproductive success intersected?

"The fourth week will be devoted to appearance. All of you will get a makeover, a color analysis and access to a nutritionist. As you know, there are weight requirements that you must meet each and every month."

That sealed it. It was so logical that it had to be true. Men were the ones who most often flew the airline for business, they were the ones who paid the highest fares, they were the bread and butter. If they had a good flight, which often could amount to nothing more than a soft touch on the wrist from a "reproductively qualified" flight attendant, they would most certainly fly that airline again.

Caroline had a fantasy. She considered raising her hand and asking a question.

"Why not just call us sky whores? We could increase revenue if we just gave all of the first-class passengers blow jobs!" She wouldn't put it past some of the virgins. They were pathetic. But she had to brace herself for this. Why should she be surprised? Isn't this exactly what she expected?

One of the women in her class was an ex-Global flight attendant, the one who had smiled at her thumbs-up as she completed her application. Not many of the ex-Globals were in the class, so this one was easy to pick out, her body language alone a complete break from the rows of Barbie dolls that surrounded her. Caroline immediately gravitated toward her, and at the first break, she introduced herself.

"Hi, I'm Caroline."

"Yes! I remember you. You..." She didn't quite know what to say, but it was instantly clear to Caroline that she remembered the moment. "...You're really nice," she said.

"Thank you. What's your name?"

"I'm sorry. My name's Paula." They shook hands. Caroline knew right away they'd be friends.

"What do you think so far?" Caroline asked.

"Oh, I don't know. It's okay I guess." Caroline could see her reticence. She was scared to talk, convinced she was under some type of all seeing company surveillance. Caroline picked up on it right away.

"Paula, listen, I'm not...one of them. You can talk to me. Come on, tell me. What do you think so far?" Paula's relief came through in her laughter.

"You really want to know?"

"Yeah, damn it. Why the hell do you think I asked you?" The choice of words was a lifeline, an assurance that she wasn't 'one of them.' Another giggle from Paula.

"Alright. I think it'll be okay. I do." She paused. "But you know, it's kind of hokey," she added.

"You're damn right it's hokey. No kidding!! Paula, are you holding back on me or what?" And then they both laughed. Paula was under Caroline's spell.

"And how about those virgins! You'd think they were auditioning for friggin' Miss Universe!"

"Yeah!!" Paula was beginning to come around.

"God, I'm so glad I met you," she added.

"I'm with ya, Paula. We'll get through this little debutante ball together!"

They picked each other's mood up through training. The funniest moment was the makeover. Caroline had always mused over the whole deal with rouge. As a cosmetology school dropout, she had never been a big makeup person, and when she worked at Kennedy she and her co-workers would silently rank various flight attendants on a "rouge scale" of 1 to 10, but there was no reason to discuss anyone below a 7. Once in a while they'd spot a 9 or a 10, someone who looked as if they had stuck their head into a vat of rouge and arisen with a face so cartoonish that it warranted calls ahead from the ticket counter to the gate.

"You gotta see this one coming your way. She looks like a fucking clown." This practice came to a quick end when one of the callers left the PA on.

"Rouge will help protect you from the dry air inside the cabin during the flight," said the instructor. Caroline passed a note to Paula that said, "Yeah, but it won't help protect you from the headhunters at Barnum & Bailey." Paula lost it.

"Is there a problem?" asked the instructor. They might as well have been in junior high school.

"No, Tracy," said Caroline to the instructor, covering her mouth. She almost said "Miss Tracy."

But it got worse when Paula and Caroline took their seats and were fawned over by dueling makeup artists. They made eye contact, and their mirrored expressions were like two people on the bow of ships sailing in opposite directions. And then they smiled. Then they laughed, and then they really lost it, a laughing fit that brought them to the point of tears, leaving the makeup artists helpless, their newly applied makeup running as they fell out of their chairs in stomach-aching hysterics.

The pact was signed. Paula and Caroline were camouflaged warriors amidst an alien world of Stepford stewardesses. If only their tears of laughter hadn't washed away their camouflage.

Caroline was relieved to get through training, not because it was necessarily challenging for her, but because of the continuous and subtle feeling that she and Paula were outcasts. They passed their written tests, their verbal tests, their drug tests, their weigh-in, and then it was time for graduation, something neither of them wanted any part of. This was for the virgins anyway, the ones who equated the completion of flight attendant training with the attainment of a Ph.D. She didn't need this and nor did Paula. But it was non-negotiable.

"Attendance at graduation is a strict requirement, a tradition that demonstrates the solidarity of the in-flight group, and if you choose not to attend, you will not be eligible to fly," said Tracy with all the firmness she could muster. Her speech went on to include a few more historical notes, a welcome soapbox to preach the gospel of being a flight attendant.

"Got it. We'll be there," said Caroline, interrupting her instructor. She didn't need to hear anymore propaganda.

Graduation was held in the ancient Atlanta hangar that once housed DC3s. To Caroline's surprise, there were a few thousand well-dressed people in attendance—lots of parents, friends and relatives of the graduates.

The festivities opened with a speech from a retired flight attendant who told a few stories about her first flight and how excited she was. She went on to share a couple of whimsical tales from the fifties and sixties and closed with a testimonial: being a flight attendant was an honorable career that gave her great memories.

Caroline's cynicism seemed to melt away as she listened. This was a woman of obvious intelligence, sincerity and pride.

Then Barbara Lewis spoke.

"We work in an industry that is essential for the U.S. and the world economy. So many jobs, jobs well beyond the airline business, count on the ability to travel, to trade, to communicate with each other. You, ladies and gentlemen (she gestured to the graduates), are about to become a fundamental part of our industry, just as your predecessors have."

It was always difficult for Caroline to place "flight attendant" into any context that included the word "essential." *She* wasn't doing it to help fuel the economy of either the U.S. or the world. She just needed a new job. From a skeptical New Yorker's point of view, this claim to flight attendant fame was a big stretch, but at the same time, she couldn't dispute it. And as before, Barbara Lewis impressed her. She was a leader who seemed to work for her people when so often it was the exact opposite.

Finally, another surprise for Caroline. Wesley Arnold stepped up to the podium and delivered a short but clearly heartfelt congratulatory speech. The last time Caroline had seen him in person, a ribbon was wrapped around his face. This was a much better performance. He was, she had to acknowledge, a good speaker who loved his company.

"I don't think people out there fully understand how important the in-flight group is to our success, but I can tell you that whenever I talk to customers, they always point to our flight attendants as the heart and soul of our organization. And that is something we will never take for granted. You, the newest graduates of the Alta in-flight class, are the chosen few, and you have been selected because we saw something in you, something special, a standard of excellence that so few can meet. On behalf of our entire company, let me say to all of you, congratulations, and welcome to the best in-flight team in the world!"

Caroline looked out into the crowd and caught sight of Danny, an appreciative grin fixed on her. She and Paula were standing side by side, a few rows behind the podium, and while the rest of the class cheered and cried, they simply looked at each other. And then they smiled and hugged.

They found themselves to be unexpectedly proud.

38

By the summer of 1994, Alta was suddenly the third largest airline in the world, having completely digested the assets of Global Airlines. They now had over 5000 flights a day to over 400 cities. Nearly a quarter of a million passengers boarded an Alta flight every 24 hours. They served 53 countries, and they were the dominant carrier to Europe. Their hubs were perfectly placed across the United States, and their gateway cities funneled passengers to every continent. As they approached mid-decade, the Alta empire had successfully transcended its Southern roots and now sparred with the biggest of the big boys for control of air travel around the world. In July, when Wesley and his management team posed for the annual photograph in front of mahogany row, the rusted red tractor was gone, severing for eternity the last visible thread to Marty Willman's small crop dusting operation that once served the Mississippi delta.

Like all of the frontline jobs in the airline industry, one's "position" is decided by seniority. Choice of routes, home cities and schedule are determined on a first hired—first served basis and in the case of the in-flight group, the high seniority of the Global flight attendants was now added to the mix. The resulting glut of New York based flight attendants that came with the acquisition was enough to bump both Caroline and Paula to positions in Atlanta. They decided to share an apartment and endure the transition together. They would be "on reserve," meaning their schedule was fluid and they could be called at any hour of the day or night with just two hours' notice to get to the airport.

Still, there were enough days off that Caroline could commute back to New York and her beloved apartment on the beach. But the travel took its toll—especially since she was now doing it for a living—and the money for two apartments just wasn't there, so in June she reluctantly eased her way out of her lease up north and had her stuff shipped down to her. She was philosophical about it. This is what you asked for, she said to herself. You wanted change, you got it. The South, a roommate, a new job—yes there were some adjustments, but fortunately Paula was more than a roommate. She was her new best friend.

They rented a two-bedroom apartment in an area called Vinings just north of the city, and shortly after they were settled, Caroline put in some phone calls to past acquaintances. She had cordial but relatively short conversations with both Danny and Shawn. Danny was happily dating another flight attendant, and though he didn't seem serious about it, she sensed his contentment. Shawn was now a regional marketing manager.

To some degree, Caroline and Paula were interlopers just like the Yankees who preceded them, and it was clear they'd always be slightly out of sync with their surroundings. It was tougher for Paula, especially on the job. So many new rules to deal with, some legitimate, but some just legacies of antiquated traditions. Worst of all were the company weight restrictions for flight attendants.

Each month, Paula waged a battle that culminated in an official Alta weigh-in that would determine whether she was "compliant." This, Caroline thought, was certifiably ridiculous, a custom that traced its roots back to the unspeakable practices of Southern female submissiveness. But it was all there in black in white, spelled out in tables of maximum weights to heights within Alta's standard practice manual and the in-flight handbook.

Paula was not a tall woman, about 5'3", but she was required to maintain a weight that never exceeded 125 pounds. Caroline weighed 127, but she was 5'7". And men had the advantage of an additional 25 pounds simply because they were men. Caroline was aware of the weight thing going in, but perhaps because of the silliness of it all, it never occurred to her that weight restrictions would be anything more than un-enforced recommendations. She was wrong.

"This is bullshit!" she said to Paula one night. "We need to fight this."

"Fight it? How are we going to do that, Caroline?" Paula was not good with conflict, and Caroline's battle cry only served to bring her roommate to the edge of tears, so she pulled back.

The weigh-in routine was increasingly disturbing for both of them. Each flight attendant had to visit the corporate scale at least once each month, and as long as they met their weight requirement any time during the calendar month, they would have until the end of the following month to do it again. If they failed to meet their weight requirement two months in a row, they were to be suspended without pay. Paula struggled, but not as much as some of the others she'd observed, many of them making a customary practice of purging just before they reported to their base, where, in their underwear, they would file in like cattle to be weighed.

As an act of misguided sympathy, each base stayed open late into the night on the last day of each month. Just before midnight, a crowd of flight attendants would frantically get themselves weighed and their weight recorded for the month. Then, just after midnight, they would all get weighed again to cover them for the new month that had just arrived. This would give them a full two months before they would likely need to purge themselves again. Anorexia and Bulimia became so commonplace that phone numbers for recommended doctors and counselors were posted on the bulletin boards, but the company refused to acknowledge any connection between their archaic practice and the physical and mental destruction it wrought.

◆   ◆   ◆

In August, an interesting bit of gossip filtered through the ranks. In response to a lawsuit made by former Global flight attendants, Alta was under investigation for improper hiring practices. Paula and Caroline cackled over the tabloid TV interviews.

"Doggy style? They didn't ask me that," said Paula.

"Don't these people have any good healthy pornography down here? We were just interviewing for a friggin job! Why do we have to be their fantasies?" said Caroline.

"Well, good for the Global girls! I thought there was something wrong with those questions," said Paula.

"Of course there was. They should have known they weren't going to get away with it. They just wanted to find some way to get rid of people they didn't like. Global people. Serves'em right. I hope they take'em to the cleaners."

"You're talking about your company, Caroline."

"*Our* company, Paula. Our fucked up company."

"Then why do you work for them?"

"When I hear this stuff...I don't know, Paula."

A few weeks later, a memo was distributed to all flight attendants, and although it didn't list all of the terms of the settlement, it was easy to read between the lines. The opening was a characteristic attempt to convince the naïve that their latest moves were an act of moral revelation rather than legal dictate. In a mock Southern voice, Paula read the memo to Caroline over a beer in their apartment.

Our in-flight group is an important part of our operation, and Alta recognizes the need to continually improve the overall quality of life for our flight attendants.

Caroline had to interrupt. "Funny how their recognition seems to get a lot better when the only other option is paying up. They make me puke. Oh, wait, that's what they want me to do," she said. Paula laughed before continuing.

Effective immediately, all in-flight crew members will have a 20% increase in their meal allowance.

"What the hell are we going to do with it if we can't eat!" Paula said. Caroline responded, "Wow, what a break! Quick, what's 20% of seven dollars?"

A new advisory group of flight attendants will be created. This group will be charged with communicating the issues and needs of the frontline on an ongoing basis.

"Sign me up!" said Caroline.

And then, they came to the last change, a policy change that appeared almost as if it was added on reluctantly, or at least with the hope that it would not be completely noticeable to the workforce.

Also effective immediately, all flight attendant weight requirements and related procedures are discontinued until further notice; however, there is no expectation of resumption of these requirements anytime in the future.

Paula and Caroline erupted in screams of joy, a fist pumping foot stomping joy of victory and vindication.

"The assholes finally saw the light!!" said Caroline. The relief was plainly evident on Paula's face. Relief that was far beyond what any person should have to feel for something so unfair.

"Let's go out and celebrate," said Caroline.

"Oh...oh yeah, Caroline. Oh, let's go!" There was a passion to Paula's voice, as if she was alluding to sex. Under their immediate circumstances, it would be something better: Tex-Mex in Buckhead at a place called Rio Bravo. It was Paula's favorite food at Paula's favorite place, but up to now it was a place she only ate under a cloud of guilt and apprehension. Tonight, however, it would be a full plate of fajitas for each of them along with the margaritas to wash them down. Caroline now allowed herself a drink or two on special occasions, and this was certainly one of them. Never before and never after would the food taste better than it did that night, a night that ended with far too much to eat, more than enough to drink, and a giddy cab ride home.

For Caroline and Paula, the night was the highlight of their summer, one they would remember fondly as "The night of a thousand margaritas."

39

As 1994 drew to a close, Danny's job had run its course. The Global Airline acquisition and the thrills and spills that went with it spanned nearly three years, but now the beast had long been swallowed, and Danny was bored. If it wasn't for Cathy, he was sure he'd be in a state of depression. Even after two years of dating, she was in the background of every thought, carrying him through the day, softening his irritation and lightening his mood. She was "in" him, and it made him a better person. Over the course of each day, when his mind was free to wander between phone calls, meetings and other consuming tasks, he asked himself if he could now imagine his life without her in it. With her trips and his schedule they rarely saw each other more than twice a week. Parting, even for a few days, felt increasingly unnatural to them, as if something was always being severed each time they said goodbye.

The recent drudgery of his job didn't help. He was growing needy, reliant on Cathy to balance the pain of his job with the pleasure of her presence, and that, he remembered, was how he ended up losing Caroline. Then, one blustery October day, Wesley called him in for a closed door meeting.

"Danny, I've got something I need you to handle."

Nothing new about this. This was how Wesley assigned tasks when he was in a good mood. When he wasn't, it was simply an absence of politeness that distinguished the assignment of one task from another.

"Whattaya got?"

"It's big."

"How big are you talking?" Wesley paused for dramatic affect, and then with a sneaky smile, he delivered a description that sent a surge of energy into Danny.

"Let's say, the greatest peacetime gathering in the history of mankind, and it's only 400 and something days away."

The Olympic Games were coming to Atlanta.

Danny's assignment wouldn't start until January, giving him some time to wrap up the remaining loose ends of his current position and spend a holiday week with his parents up north. His selection to manage Alta's Olympic sponsorship restored his internal balance and allowed him to take a fresh look at his relationship with Cathy. They had settled into a comfortable routine, something Danny didn't want to give up, but he also needed to understand what kept them together. Was it the miserable job he had but was now leaving behind? Was it just plain inertia? Was it love or was it need? He'd find out, because now he was much less needy.

When the week drew to a close, the answer was clear. Each night as the stream of his thoughts flowed into the ocean of his sleep, he let his mind wander back to this woman he loved, and each morning he missed her more. He loved her, he missed her, and he wanted to be with her, now and perhaps forever.

He returned a few days before New Year's, and though he had been invited to parties, gotten e-mails about $100 hotel packages and found flyers at his door for restaurant prix fixes, he and Cathy had yet to settle on a plan. It didn't matter; all he wanted to do was be with her, wherever that was.

She picked the spot, a hole in the wall bar in a dense cluster of buildings just east of the Atlanta city limits—an enclave known as Decatur. He drove to her house and they took the subway two stops south and five stops east. They knew they'd take a cab home, but at least they didn't have to worry about leaving their cars anywhere.

He held her hand on the subway and thought about how good it was to see her. No tuxedos and gowns for them tonight. When they found their way out of the subway station, she paused, momentarily disoriented, and then led him up around the station and along a walkway lined with restaurants and shops. Then into a town square, toward a nondescript doorway with a weathered wooden sign that had ceased to be legible.

"Here it is."

There were large wooden barrels outside that served as tables, but they were understandably empty in the frigid air. The street, which was actually a half circular parking lot on the fringe of the square, was vacant. All was quiet but the rustle of the trees along the courthouse. Danny was all for a quiet New Year, but this seemed to be a ghost town.

The door was all wood, a giant medieval hatch, rounded at the top and with a slab of smoothed oak that served as a handle. She pulled it open and a blast of hot air hit them. It was full of people, and buzzing. They squeezed in at the urging of patrons so the door could be quickly closed. It was as if the place was vacuum packed, and any breaking of the seal that was the door sent a jet stream of arctic air across the room.

Danny took in the establishment, a dimly lit nest of rusticity, filled with new and existing regulars. The ceiling was high, giving the place an airy, almost exterior feel. To his left and right, everything around him was either wood or brick, if not human. And straight ahead was the bar, a wondrous fortress of aged and lacquered timber, encircling the bartenders, whose demeanor was frenzied but not harried. He could tell this from their smiles. They obviously liked what they were doing. They were certainly not bartenders of the Buckhead type, who trumpeted their brusque behavior as their sacred privilege. Those were the ones out to make a killing. In contrast, these people were sharing happiness. Even if it was New Year's Eve, one had the sense that these bartenders were where they wanted to be. And that's instantly how Danny felt.

"I like this place!"

"I thought you would," she said.

They made their way to the bar and ordered a couple of perfectly poured pints of Guinness. As they turned from the bar, they spotted a space along the wall, a bench behind a table.

At 11:40 p.m., the waiters and waitresses began making the rounds with plastic glasses of champagne, all of it on the house. Others handed out noisemakers, party hats and tiaras. Danny had the sense that he was at a party rather than a bar. He grabbed a tiara, placed it regally on Cathy's head and delicately smoothed her hair. When the countdown to midnight ended amid a crescendo of cheers and noisemakers, he gave his girlfriend a lengthy and spirited kiss and then he leaned close, his mouth to her ear.

Smack in the middle of the decade, on this final night of 1994, there was no diamond ring, no fancy restaurant with fine crystal, no getting down on one knee. This was as pure and simple as the core of their relationship.

"I love you and I want to marry you," he said to her. She looked at him for an instant, suddenly serious, and Danny's stomach tightened. She removed the tiara, cradled his head in both hands, kissed him on the cheek and then replied, close to his ear so he wouldn't misunderstand.

"I love you and I want to marry you too." She smiled and noticed that he had tears in his eyes and it brought tears to hers.

"Happy New Year, Daniel".

"Happy New Year, Cathy."

PART IV
1995–2001

40

Danny was swept away in a flurry of excitement and activity that marked the preparations for the Games. As an Olympic sponsor, Alta invested $30 million dollars just for the rights, and they'd spend about twice that just to make legitimate use of it. At first, the sponsorship announcement generated an uproar from many Alta employees, most of whom were not based in the Atlanta area. This was not unexpected, considering that Alta still had negative cash flow and a financial hangover from the Global acquisition. Naturally, the Olympics were perceived by many to be a boondoggle—just another extravagant hospitality party for corporate kingpins.

But as the Games drew closer, the voices of dissension were drowned out in a wave of local excitement and employee events. There were pep rallies and countdowns, pin trading and celebrations with medalist athletes, and even a visit by the strange blue mascot that had become a worldwide laughingstock beyond the confines of Atlanta.

Danny had been named General Manager of the Olympic Sponsorship for Alta, a promotion that immediately vaulted him into one of the highest profile positions within the company. He was given a nice office with a window (something he'd never had before), a share of a secretary and three staff members. Still, the demands were enormous and the pressure was now only shifted, as he moved from beneath the CEO's thumb to the glare of the world. As the official airline, Alta would be responsible for successfully transporting much of that world to the Games. Any incidents would be highly visible.

In the meantime, how was he supposed to get married to Cathy in this vortex of activity? And even then, if he could squeeze it in, would their first year of marriage be anything like it should?

Cathy had the same worries, and since they hadn't planned on anything large, they debated together whether they should put it off. It wasn't going to be a big deal either way. In the end they decided to go forward with the wedding, and in October of 1995 a small gathering of 20 friends and family convened at the courthouse in Decatur. They had a boisterous dinner in a nearby restaurant, and the next day it was back to work. With 250 days of frantic preparation ahead, the honeymoon would wait until after closing ceremonies, when they could both enjoy it to its fullest.

Danny moved his essentials to Cathy's place, but they both knew it could only be temporary. They needed something big enough for the both of them, and Cathy wanted a house in the suburbs. Neither of them had a whole lot of time for house shopping, and besides, they all looked pretty much the same to Danny anyway. But they did want a place they could both call their very own. In November, they put some money down on a house in a subdivision that was still under construction. A couple had backed out on a piece of property, and Cathy wanted it.

"How do you know you're going to want this if it's not even built yet?" he asked her.

"Because then we can build it exactly the way we want to," she said.

This was exciting for Cathy, and Danny enjoyed watching her immerse herself in this creation of the world around her. The paint, the carpeting, the fixtures, the doorknobs, the appliances—all of these were carefully selected with minimal input from Danny, which is the way he wanted it.

"Aren't you excited?" she asked him.

"Not as much as you."

"Why not?"

"I don't know. But I'm excited. I am." She grabbed him around the waist.

"You're lying to me," she said.

"I am excited. You know what I'm most excited about?"

"What? Tell me, tell me."

"The best part about this house?"

"What? What!?"

"…is that when I come home…"

"Yes?"

"You'll be in it," he said.

"Oh, you are *so* sweet. Too bad I'll probably be on a trip somewhere," she said with a laugh and a hug.

41

Suddenly it was the summer of 1996. With two weeks to go before the Olympic flame was to arrive, the frenzy inside and out of the office was beginning to hit its peak. The saving grace was the knowledge that it was going to end. Danny felt as if he hardly saw Cathy at all, and each time they tried to plan something quiet and isolated, his beeper would go off and the latest crisis would sweep him away. At the same time, there was a euphoria that fueled the energy, endless energy as they hit the ten-day mark.

Atlanta, the once modest Southern city that built an airplane hangar for Marty Willman, was about to welcome the world.

Wesley Arnold soaked up every moment. He was the personal host to the board of directors, all of whom were pampered beyond belief. In some ways, it was hard to believe that the Olympics had finally gotten underway, but once they did, the machinery of the program hit its stride, and Wesley basked in the glory of his fellow bigwigs. Alta employee volunteers were released from their jobs to drive wives of the directors to upscale malls for shopping trips, days of beauty, or whatever else they wanted if it wasn't an Olympic event.

Danny lurked in the background, barely distinguishable from the people who worked for him, but he remained the only point of contact whenever Wesley whispered one bizarre request after another out of the side of his mouth.

"Can we get one of those Olympic flags?"

"She wants one of those banners from the swimming venue. Get one of those, would you?"

"See if you can get one of the athletes up here to say hello to us."

"Get us four dream team tickets for tonight. You can do this, can't you?"

The problem for Danny was that he was only as good as his last favor. Failure to deliver, no matter how strange or unreachable the request, meant sustained disappointment. Conversely, success meant fleeting happiness. He couldn't win.

He also realized he could only control so much and that led him to the conclusion that he had a duty to himself to have a good time. Midway through the Games he negotiated a day off for himself, something his loyal staff had heavily encouraged. His one mandate to his troops was to make sure they were always accessible but that they enjoyed themselves, and now his subordinates were holding him to the same standard.

It was a Saturday night, and after most of the guests were off to bed, Danny slipped out of the hotel, into his car and off to his home to get his wife.

"Let's get outta here, doll. We're going to a big party."

"Please, not Wesley and the board again?" Cathy had served time as Danny's beautiful wife amid the crappy hors d'oeuvres and half-intoxicated hospitality guests, but after the second visit to the governor's mansion, she bowed out, realizing there would be no quality time under such conditions.

"No, just you and me. Let's head downtown."

The traffic was unusually sparse—a pleasant surprise for the locals who had expected the worst. Most everyone appeared to have been scared into not driving and the result for Atlanta was the cleanest air quality in years.

They sped down I-75 and exited at Northside Drive, which took them the back way into Centennial Olympic Park, the unofficial social hub of the Games, complete with a stage for free concerts, numerous sponsor pavilions, pin trading tables, a striking set of fountains and other festive, but sanctioned attractions. Encircling the park were the unsanctioned attractions: tables and tables of knock-off hats and T-shirts, pins and merchandise. The mayor had sold out every slab of bare sidewalk to the get-rich-quick crowd of petty merchandisers, and the result was a bazaar of third world proportions.

Danny paid $20 to park his car, something he'd have no problem expensing, and they found their way through the gates. It was a pleasant evening by the standards of summer in Atlanta. He led his wife past the spouting fountains and the children playing in them, then onward up a short flight of stairs to a field of bricks that served as the Olympic Plaza. He had marked out his steps much earlier, so he knew exactly where to go, and as he towed his wife behind him, she began to wonder what he was up to. There were people swarming all over the park and music was blaring from the stage, so he kept her very close to him.

"Here it is!" he said, looking at her.

"Here is what?"

"Us." He moved his foot to reveal the engraved brick with their names on it:

CATHY AND DANNY
FOREVER

"Oh, Danny!"

"Not very imaginative, I know. But it says it all if you ask me."

"I don't need to ask you. I agree with you." He grabbed her in his arms and leaned forward to kiss her.

And then it happened.

Never before had they heard a noise quite as loud as this one, and it froze everyone in their tracks. It was a single giant explosion of incomprehensible power, a blast followed almost immediately by a wave of air pressure that washed over the populace like the fury of a storm. There was first shock, then a few distant screams, then panic and then bedlam—a disoriented bedlam as people backed away, then walked fast and then ran, all of them running away from where they thought the danger was.

Danny gripped Cathy's hand as most of the crowd began running in their direction, and then swept them along, elbows and legs flying around them, buffeting them as they tried to maintain their balance. As the wave of humanity picked up speed, Cathy's hand was torn from her husband's and she was knocked to the bricks. Danny fought and pushed aside the people until he could stand over his wife and deflect the oncoming swarm to the left or right of her with his forearms. The children playing in the fountains began to scream in terror as parents scooped them up and lugged them toward the streets away from the source of the blast. But no one, including Danny and Cathy, really knew what it was, where it was centered and if there was another one that could go off at any second. The horror swept through the crowd with the conductivity of a lightning bolt. There was a tense silence of people trying to get away, people screaming for their children, an orchestra of car alarms, and then within a half minute, the wail of sirens—confirmation that something really had gone terribly wrong.

Danny caught a break in the flow that was long enough to lift Cathy to her feet. Her face was scratched, but her eyes revealed the real injury, a catatonic glaze that was the imprint of terror. She didn't speak, and Danny felt every part of her body that didn't keep her standing go limp. He grabbed her around the waist.

"Come on, Cathy. Come on, let's get out of here. We're going to be all right."

She looked at him as if she'd never seen him before, but then as she came to, she began to move her legs.

"That's it, come on, Cath. Good. Let's go."

She picked up speed, and then she started running, the fear overcoming the shock, the legs kicking in. She ran away, as fast as she could in one direction, leaving Danny in her wake. He didn't try to slow her down; he just kept up with her, right behind her, weaving through the crowd, careful to make sure that she didn't run across a street with oncoming cars.

But in the confusion, no cars were moving. She ran past the CNN center and on to Martin Luther King Boulevard, a stretch of road that had been closed off from cars. The crowd was now entirely behind her, but she kept running and he kept following, into the darkness and the deserted space along the rail yards. The street made a turn to the left, but she kept going, climbing over the concrete barrier and on to the tracks. She kept running, away from the light, the noise, the crowd. Away.

"Cathy! Cathy, stop!!"

He was right behind her, but she didn't hear him. Every action, every movement was involuntary and instinctual. She was as much in flight as a gazelle from a cheetah.

He caught up to her in the darkness and placed his hand on her elbow as he overtook her. She screamed at his touch, a fearful and agonizing scream.

"Cathy! It's okay! It's okay."

"No!! No!! Let me go. Lemme go. Lemme, Lemme go!!"

"Cathy, we're safe!

She broke free and began to run again, but she was out of breath now and weak, and Danny caught her again.

"No no no no no no no no," she said and collapsed into tears

"Cathy, we're safe! We're okay. It's okay! I'm here. I'm here!"

She crossed into another level of consciousness, an awareness that her husband was there, and then she grabbed him and hugged him—hugged him as if she were hanging onto a cliff by her fingertips. She cried powerful tears in his arms, tears driven by a fear that believed all efforts at self-preservation were futile.

For Cathy, it was a hopeless and helpless confrontation with seemingly certain death. What Danny had once thought were trivial quirks were actually symptoms of a fragile soul.

And now that soul had been shattered.

42

Cathy cried all night and into the next day. And that's when Danny felt as though he might as well have had his body torn in half. He had to go back to work, back to manage the whims and desires of Alta's inflated egos. But how could he leave his wife? He bought himself a few hours with a phone call and then called a neighbor. Peggy would be glad to stop by and spend some time with Cathy. Still, he was worried. Cathy had her arms wrapped around her knees, a tank top on and flowered pajama bottoms. She was quietly staring into space. He noticed that she seemed to be rocking slightly, rhythmically trying to subdue whatever it was that haunted her.

"Peggy, thanks for coming over."

"No problem, Danny. Glad to help. Where is she?"

"She's in the bedroom. I've gotta go, but I'll be back as soon as I can."

"I'll handle it, Danny. I'm here for both of you. You go to work now and everything will be fine when you get back."

He had never really liked Peggy and her husband, Cliff, that much. They seemed a product of the worst qualities of suburbia, but now she was like an angel from heaven, and he felt guilty for not appreciating her. Her generosity seemed bottomless.

"Peggy, thank you. Thank you so much. So much."

"Don't think of it, Danny. Get going, you've got an Olympics to run."

An Olympics—is that what it was? Is that what it was supposed to be? He recounted the last 10 hours. The city, if not the world, was in a state of shock. Every shred of Olympic idealism had been blown to bits, and Danny had no idea what was going to happen next. The first thing he did after he got Cathy into bed was call every person on his team and make sure they were all safe. Next, he called Wesley and said he would feed information to him as it became available, but for now, the plan was to get everyone back to the hotel (if they weren't there already) and wait to see what would happen. Worst case, he could send all the women to the mall and all the men to the golf course. Fortunately, none of the guests had wandered into the park the previous evening so they also were all accounted for.

The team members were beginning to get calls from the guests, a few that started with the simple phrase: "Get us the hell out of here!" Fine. A mini exodus of 70 or so caught morning flights out of Atlanta.

The death toll at Centennial Olympic Park was two, and since the blast felt as if it had the power to kill hundreds, Danny was actually relieved to hear this. There were also reports that they had caught the person who had done it, and a frenzy of media had already closed in on the alleged bomber, despite the fact that the man, who was later exonerated, could not possibly have carried out the attack.

By noon that day the dust was literally beginning to settle, and a declaration was made that the Games would go on. Wesley, who was also on his own mental spin out of control, called Danny throughout the morning, asking for guidance. He was clearly disoriented; his own personal party had been wrecked and that was something that never happened to Wesley Arnold. But then he would come back to reality, pledge his undying support and respect to Danny, and resolve to patiently await instructions. There was no scapegoat for these events, making this one of the rare times when Danny could tell his boss what to do.

A track and field session was scheduled for the afternoon, the first event that would take place since the bombing. Danny considered the possibility that no one would show up. Why should they? What could remain of the so-called "Olympic Spirit"? He just wanted it all to be over. If they decided to cancel the whole thing, it would actually be a relief. But nothing was canceled. Once they knew everything was still on, Danny gathered his team at the hotel.

"I know you're all tired and nervous. I want you to know how proud I am of all of you. The Games are going to continue, and we've still got a lot of guests. But if any of you want to bail, I want you to know I understand. I totally understand."

Danny looked over his team, and where he expected to see tears, he saw only resolve. Nobody bailed. The team unanimously pledged to stick it out until the end.

Sunday, July 28th was an unusually beautiful day in Atlanta. Not too hot, and crystal clear. Danny had a mild case of shell shock; every loud noise touched a nerve, a flight response that had to be reined in long enough to realize it was just a loud noise. With each one he'd say a prayer to get through it all without another casualty and then he'd say a prayer for his wife.

There were about 100 of them in the group he was chaperoning, and they got to the stadium early, their finish line seats the best in the giant stadium. It was virtually empty an hour before the session, confirming Danny's expectations. No one was coming. Everyone, it seemed, had left.

In reality, security had tightened, and people were just waiting to get in. Danny engaged in chatty but subdued conversation with many of the guests, and this raised his spirits. The people who had stayed on were no less enthusiastic, and underlying it all was a feeling of determination. When he looked up from one discussion, just a few minutes before the first event would begin, he realized this resolve had been multiplied by 100,000.

The stadium was full.

He had been in Atlanta long enough to assess it as a city largely driven by fear. A city of impenetrable SUVs and gated communities, of cul-de-sacs and gun ownership. But here they were in the face of a great unknown. Who could say that another bomb wasn't ready to go off at any moment in any place. It would have been so easy to just stay home and safe. As for Danny, he had the typical naïve and unsupported biases toward the south—prejudices that had diminished over the years as he began to feel more at home, but in this instance, in this defining moment of Atlanta, he had grossly underestimated the collective courage of his city.

Danny's mind wandered as the event began. He was trying to put this experience into context. He wasn't much of a historian, and at times he grew impatient with acquaintances that had yet to put the Civil War behind them. Still, over the years he had developed a better understanding of what happens to the character of a city that has come through a war, and Atlanta was the only American city that had ever done so.

For the true natives, the pain, and in extreme cases, the feelings of vengeance seemed to have been passed down through the previous five generations with great efficiency. But there was another feeling that surpassed the negative. It was this determination, a will to prove, perhaps more to themselves than the rest of the world, that the place was worthy. Even the symbol of the city, the Phoenix, rising from the ashes of destruction, still resonated with many. Everything in the city seemed new, in part because everything old had been burned to the ground. Ever since the burning of Atlanta, the city had built and bustled its way to prominence, first in the South, then in the country, and now in the world. Whatever fears he may have attributed to the community as a whole were nowhere to be found on this sunny summer day.

The city of Atlanta had shown up.

Danny felt a giant paw of a hand on the back of his shoulder. It was Wesley.

"Danny, how's everything going so far?"

"Good, Mr. Arnold. So far so good. Beautiful day."

Wesley gave a nod and a smile that Danny returned. There wasn't much else to say; it was like spotting a familiar face in the trenches through the smoke of the last attack. Survival was its own reward.

Danny broke the silence. "Come meet some of our guests here, Mr. Arnold. Richard, Richard Quinn, this is Wesley Arnold, our CEO." Wesley leaned across and extended his hand to the man and his wife, shaking theirs with both of his.

"Richard, thanks very much for coming out today. We really do appreciate it," said Wesley, the smile replaced by a solemn look of gratitude, as if Richard Quinn had stepped up and joined the battalion on the front line.

A starter's gun went off, and Danny jumped in his seat. He still wanted it to be over, still couldn't wait for everyone to go home from the Olympics and peace to return to his head and stomach, his heart and especially his wife. But as the runners galloped around the far turn of the track and the crowd oohed at the magnitude of the exquisite human effort in front of them, Danny sat back and let a small flood of relief enter his soul.

Everything was going to be okay.

43

Mercifully, the Olympics ended without further incident, and the bombing faded into the shadows. Although the crowds returned and the amazing feats of athleticism retook their rightful place in the foreground, the bombing would remain one of the unfortunate legacies of Atlanta's Olympic Games.

The guests of Alta departed, gushing with gratitude for Wesley Arnold. This was expected, for even though Danny had engineered the entire hospitality program, had assembled the pieces and worked around the clock for over a year at great personal sacrifice, the kudos always went to the CEO. Wesley accepted credit as a king would for the soldiers who died so he could live. No surprise, but it didn't matter to Danny. Making it to the end was the best reward he could ask for, and he wasn't alone. The city seemed to be in a giant state of exhalation. After a half decade of anticipation followed by its head-spinning two week culmination, an emptiness settled over Atlanta. Danny didn't know what he would be doing next, but now with the frenzy behind him, he had one thing on his mind. He needed to reconnect with his wife.

Cathy's improvement was slow. Her periods of composure increased, but there were still stretches in which she seemed lost. Danny would move his head into her field of vision and fill the vacancy in her eyes.

"Are you all right?" Her eyes would slowly capture his face.

"I'm fine," she'd say slowly.

But she wasn't fine. In September, they went to a doctor who referred them to a neurologist, who referred them to a psychiatrist, who referred them to a pharmacist. Cathy recounted the evening of the bombing to the psychiatrist, and she was quickly diagnosed with PTSD—Post-Traumatic Stress Disorder. He wrote out a prescription for something called benzodiazepine and something else called paroxetine. While she was relieved to have both a label for her problems and a "cure," it seemed like just another HMO band-aid to Danny. No options for further investigation or analysis. The job of the in-network practitioner was to slap a diagnosis on the problem, write out an instant cure and send them on their way. Next please.

"I don't know if I want you taking all that stuff," he told her.

"What the hell. What else am I going to do?"

"I might have a better cure," he said.

"What's that?"

"How about a honeymoon?"

"A honeymoon? You really want to go on a honeymoon with your wacked out wife?"

"Stop it!" he said. He hated when she did this, but it was something she'd drop into their conversations now and then.

"I'm kidding," she said.

"Don't kid about that. It's not funny."

"Okay. Where are we going?"

"We're going…far away."

He wanted to make their destination a total surprise. The ideal would have been to have her wake-up there, and considering the medication she had been given, this didn't seem that far out of the question. In the end, he told her how to pack and held his secret as long as it took for them to get to their departure gate.

Hawaii. Not the obvious tourist spots like Waikiki or Maui, but a remote locale. They went to Lanai, the smaller, sparsely populated island across the channel from Maui's Kaanapali Beach. This was the island once dedicated exclusively to growing pineapples, but now the first hotel had been built on the beach, a rambling pristine expanse of rooms that opened toward the distant Maui volcano of Haleakala.

The medication and time change left Cathy sleepy for a good part of their trip, but there were moments of great enjoyment. Their room was up on a bluff and secluded from the other rooms. It had a small patio and just beyond that was a stretch of thick bladed tropical grass shaded by two palm trees that angled wildly in the direction of the pacific winds. The illusion was one of having their own island.

One late afternoon during their stay they pulled two chairs out onto the grass to face the ocean. The sultry air thickened into an approaching storm, their view giving them front row seats to the spectacle of thunderheads piling upwards against the blue sky. They pointed out to each other the rain in the distance, the isolated shadow of gray torrents beneath the column of white. They held hands and didn't talk, but instead just watched the storm come slowly toward them. And when it arrived, they let it wash over them, a baptism of sorts, the drops cooling and pounding them with the force of a vigorous massage.

"I don't want to go back," she said. She almost had to shout in the downpour.

"Back to the room?"

"No. Back to Atlanta."

He leaned over and kissed her, his chair tipping against hers. The shower suddenly strengthened, beating into them and slapping in the fresh puddles on the ground, enveloping them in a sensory experience that made her kiss him with a vigor equal to the monsoon. They went inside just as the storm let up and made soaking wet love on the floor. When the chills came afterward, they warmed each other in a steaming shower and made love again. They ordered room service for dinner and finished a third session just as their food arrived. And then they ate face to face on their patio in their terry cloth robes, their escape complete.

"I love you, Cathy."

It was as if a thousand thoughts were exploding through her head when he said this, all of them anxious and humiliating, none of them believing that he could love her. She felt so deeply ashamed of her condition, of her "flaws," that the tears welled up.

"What is it? What's the matter?" he asked, but she couldn't talk, and each time he asked her what was wrong, it only further pointed out that something was wrong. There seemed to be nothing that Danny could say that wouldn't make it worse. As she cried, he quietly came around to her side of the table and held her.

◆   ◆   ◆

Of course, they did go back to Atlanta, back to their cul-de-sac and the next stage of their lives. The trip brought long stretches of normalcy to Cathy, but re-entry was rocky. She would take some time off from work and become absorbed in her immediate surroundings. Danny felt that work might be just the thing she needed, but she was resistant, and he was not going to argue with her about it. He would avoid conflict with her at all costs. Anything to bring her back to normal.

Over the next few months, out of the summer and into the fall of 1996, it became apparent to Danny that only one thing would bring her back. It was order, in every sense of the word. He had joked with her about her perfection, always on time, extremely neat, excessively ordered, but it was never an issue. Now it would be her chosen path out of disorder and away from the anxiety that went with it. She would kill her fears by making her world so permanently predictable that nothing could reach her.

The house was still new and immaculate, but somehow she managed to make it more so. There was always a project, no matter how small, like repainting the trim in each room so that the definition between wall and ceiling and floor was perfect. Or steam cleaning the carpet, which didn't seem necessary in a house so new, but Cathy had heard of the presence of toxins in the carpeting of other new homes and they needed to be vanquished.

She cooked for him almost every night, serving meals with the artistic presentation of a restaurant, with sprigs of parsley grazing marinated cuts of pork or chicken. Danny showered her with appreciation, but he sensed she was driven by a fear of not making him happy, this at the expense of her own mental health. He struggled with the idea of discussing it, but he was afraid she would misinterpret this as a sign of dissatisfaction, and this would only push her into an ever deepening abyss of anxiety. So he left it.

44

Wesley Arnold was under siege. The board of directors had their Olympic fun and Wesley did a fine job, but now it was time for a change. Except for the acquisition of Global, Alta was a constant follower, but things were different in the late '90s. The industry had reached a new level of volatility. There was no room for error and being a follower meant being at risk. Sound bites would circulate informally among the board at quarterly meetings. "Leadership" meant being "proactive" and controlling the corporation's "destiny." But the storm clouds of dissent were gathering, and this was Wesley's biggest blind spot. Things were slipping out of control.

The largest cloud was the pilot union. Their contract was almost up, and negotiations were not going well. They'd already marked their calendar for a strike date, and Jeff had taken to paging Danny as a reminder. Why he did this, Danny wasn't totally sure, but the messages consisted of frenetic union incantations and ominous warnings.

"123 days till the walkout. Don't let it happen!"

Maybe Jeff thought Danny still had influence and would pass these tidbits on to Wesley. That seemed plausible. A guy like Jeff—a pilot who kept the same job and only moved up to bigger aircraft—would have a hard time grasping the concept of movement across different departments of a corporation. That wouldn't have made any sense to him. Either way, convincing Jeff that he could negotiate with Wesley was about as likely as Alta rewarding Danny for his loyalty. The company took on a dark, pre-war mood, and now things were about to get much worse.

Informational picketing was a favorite tactic of the union, presenting to the public the appearance of a strike. There were several great ironies to this: one was the belief that the public cared more about the pay of pilots than it did about the threat of a shutdown. Another was the fear that it managed to generate, scaring people over to other airlines and effectively reducing the future bookings that would be needed to pay the pilots what they were demanding. Third was the ongoing proclamation by the union that contract negotiations not take place "through the media." all while they posed for photo ops with their poetic signs that said things like "Alta pilots—We'll never rest until we're paid the best!"

The bookings for the summer of '98 were looking strong, but the latest contract would expire in the heat of it all, on August 1st. If agreement wasn't reached, the pilots would vote to authorize a strike, and if after a 30-day cooling off period they were still unable to come to terms, the airline would grind to a very sudden and tumultuous halt.

The day of reckoning was coming, and Jeff was going to make sure there was no confusion among Alta management about the role of their most important work group. On a certain level, he wanted a strike. He was sure they didn't take him seriously, especially now, years after they had promised to resolve the past issues. He even lobbied to authorize mid-contract picketing right before the Olympics—a time of maximum visibility, and therefore, maximum leverage—but the moderate factions of the union overruled him. Still, the internal discussions among the union leadership were so contentious that Jeff had now been elevated to one of the chief negotiator seats. With his union activity at such a high level, he only flew once a month.

His personal life was of minimal importance. The cycle with Jeanine was nearing its end—she asked way too many questions—and so he moved out and got an apartment near the airport. Once in awhile he would head over to a nearby bar where a new flock of flight attendant trainees would be debuting, but he had no desire for a relationship. He'd chat up a few of them and see where it led to, and hopefully they would understand that one night was enough. There was no reason to complicate things. Of course, not all of the trainees were this pliable.

"Jeff!" it was a familiar voice. He turned from his conversation at the bar with one of the trainees.

"Caroline! What are you doing down here? Great to see you!" He gave her an affectionate kiss on the cheek and a hug. Maybe too much of a hug.

"This is Paula. We're here to help with training."

Caroline expected an introduction to the girl Jeff had been speaking with, but he ignored her right out of existence and she faded into the background.

"You're a flight attendant? I can't believe that!"

"Why not?"

"I just never thought of you like that."

Caroline knew Jeff well enough to understand his limitations. No use exploring his thinking on this topic. She wanted to bring Paula into the conversation.

"Yeah, been doing it for a few years now actually. Paula here came over from Global."

"Ah, Global." Jeff's face seemed to twitch with a thousand little thoughts, as if the right reaction was in a slot machine, finally coming up.

"We've had a lot of problems with the Global pilots," he said.

"Oh," said Paula, nodding politely. Caroline felt the tension in her back. What the hell was he talking about?

"Seniority. They think they should have higher seniority than us." Jeff added.

"Jeff! Do we need to talk about this?" Caroline broke in.

"Why not, what's the problem? She's a Global person. Don't you think she'd be interested?" He was pointing at her, thrusting a finger from the hand holding his beer bottle.

"She's an Alta person now. Who gives a shit?"

"I give a shit. It's my life and those guys have been trying to screw us from the start! We saved their ass!"

"Great to see you, Jeff." She grabbed Paula's hand and they walked off.

"Still an asshole," she said to Paula.

"What?"

"A fucking asshole. Long story. I'll tell you all about it some time."

For Jeff, these encounters were commonplace. He seemed to thrive on conflict and in his mind, he always won. There were no exceptions, only a lack of understanding or capability on the part of his weaker opponent. And his biggest opponent, the chief executive officer of Alta Airlines, would soon be among the defeated.

◆   ◆   ◆

By the spring of 1998, Caroline realized it was time for her to do a self-assessment. She had come a long way and done more for the company than Alta's management would ever know. She saved the Global acquisition, she inspired others, she was independent, she was smart, she was knowledgeable and she was strong. She was no cosmetology graduate, but at the same time, she was not a college graduate either. Despite all of her capabilities, despite her strength, she felt locked away from her aspirations. If she was going to make things happen, big things, being a flight attendant was not going to cut it. This was not the career path to prosperity. She knew there was only one way to unlock new opportunities. She needed to go back to school.

This was not a new thought for Caroline. She'd been pondering it for some time, but there were two major hurdles and they were the obvious ones: time and money. Her seniority now afforded her the ability to choose her schedule, so that was manageable. Money was the bigger problem, but her slow climb up the pay scale had now given her a slight cushion.

She did some research and found that she probably could take two classes each semester and get by with a hefty student loan and the modest bit of financial reimbursement that Alta provided. The loan wouldn't be payable for several years, and by that time she should expect to be paid enough to make it tolerable. She applied to Emory, fairly certain that she wouldn't be accepted, nor be able to afford it. But a month later, she received acceptance to an evening undergraduate program that would start at the end of August, one that had flexible schedules and tuition by class. Still, it would be very tight. She'd have negative cash flow until her next raise a full year away, and by her initial calculations, it wasn't going to work, but with Paula's help, they managed to trim their expenses and map out a way for Caroline to squeeze through.

◆   ◆   ◆

Jeff met her during a layover in Los Angeles. Her name was Olivia, an undeniably beautiful woman, a Latin who truly understood the man-woman thing. It was about time. She dressed impeccably and was smart enough to look nothing less than perfect each time he'd seen her. To this point, he had only seen her twice, but he had a good feeling. A gut feeling that finally, here was someone, a woman who would accept him for what he was and not try to change him. A woman who gets it.

She was in the bar of the hotel near LAX when he met her, probably trolling for pilots anyway, but he didn't care. If anything, it was a relief to meet a woman who knew what she wanted for a change. She was exotic, with a perfect combination of subservience and passion. The salient remembrance was her hair: dark cascading Latin locks that snapped as she threw her head back and forth atop him.

She worked in a department store on Rodeo Drive where she was a makeup artist. Her face was mannequin perfect, but with a dose of Hispanic life in it. He felt lucky to have her, and with a week-long break from beating the bushes of his union membership, this trip would be a welcome escape.

When they first met and he gave his pilot spiel, her eyes opened wide. She hadn't traveled that much and always wanted to.

"Where would you like to go?"

"I want to go to the pyramids," she said. "I've always wanted to see them."

The conversation picked up exactly where it left off after the sexual interlude. It was a comfortable conversation—travel. Not that Jeff gave a crap about silences, but at least this topic was easy to sustain for him. And this being the first night with her, he wanted to be talkative, because women liked it when you were talkative after you fucked them.

"Why do you want to see the pyramids?"

"I saw the one in Las Vegas. That one that's a hotel, and ever since then I've always wanted to see the ones in Egypt." For a second, Jeff considered the possibility that she might not know which was older.

"Have you been to the pyramids in Mexico?"

"No no. I've never been to that part of Mexico, but I've seen pictures."

"Where have you been?" he asked her, looking for another thread.

"I've been to Las Vegas!"

"I'll take you to the pyramids."

"You will?" He knew this would excite her. Her eyes lit up again and she rolled back on top of him.

"You really will take me!?" She put her hands on his abdomen and slid her hips back and forth over him. Jeff considered that maybe she thought she could impregnate herself with this trip and there'd be no turning back.

"Yes, I will take you. I've never been there. We'll have fun."

She let her breasts and her body come down on him and kissed him, plunging her tongue deeply into his mouth, and then sliding it along his neck and then to his chest, before finally submitting to the guidance of his hands on the back of her head, softly but firmly pushing her downward. He held her head in both his hands, his arms extended, his fingers deeply awash in her hair. She would be a good companion.

45

"We're off!" Jeff announced.

She sat next to him in first class, her smile wide as the horizon. She wore a sun dress that fell a few inches short of her knees. Jeff had flown her to New York the night before, and now they were on their way to Cairo following a short stop in Paris.

"I am sooooo excited," she said. They left the ground on an early evening in late August. Jeff's mood was buoyant. He felt as if he was on the threshold of a sustained winning streak, ready to declare victory on several fronts.

There was the battle for his son. After many years and thousands of dollars paid to his lawyer, he was on the verge of gaining full custody. The string of Joanne's "anomalous behavior" was now long enough that at least one judge had taken notice in Jeff's favor.

There was the battle for his profession. He'd made great progress cultivating his union's resolve and he knew he'd be even more energized for the ensuing war with Wesley Arnold when he returned. They were going to choke the golden goose of Alta until management truly understood who was in charge.

And there were the spoils that he could once again claim. He had Olivia on his arm in the first-class seat beside him, and they were flying toward the pyramids.

◆　　◆　　◆

7:25pm

Danny was still ten minutes away from his driveway. Cathy would be waiting for him. Dinner would be waiting for him. The place would be perfectly clean. She would greet and kiss him as she had now for the last two and a half "perfect" years.

Despite, or perhaps because of the perfection, there was a feeling of lifelessness all around him. The neighborhood was built out now; the lawn had taken hold nicely, the tree line had been pushed back to a safe distance and a few of the more reclusive neighbors had erected fences around their property. His life and his yard were clearly demarcated. There was so much to be thankful for, but so little to remind him of it. It was as if he had no pulse and there was nothing to arouse him. Even his sex life had eroded into a smooth, barely perceptible heartbeat. He loved his wife, but scheduling sex—something she insisted on if they were going to have it—seemed to deflate the entire endeavor. The idea, he had always thought, was to make sex good enough that she'd want to have it even if it wasn't scheduled. Lovemaking had descended into a sorry state of obligation, another task on the to-do list for his wife, and he had only himself to blame.

On this evening, as he finally pulled into his driveway, his state of mind, his entire state of being, crawled from the subconscious into the conscious. He realized he was slowly dying.

7:30pm

Jeff looked out the window, past Olivia's excited eyes to the setting sun behind them as they began to pull away from the East Coast. The plane banked to the left over the Atlantic. Jeff noted that the bank was a little steeper than he would have done it. The cockpit door even flopped open, which was unusual. Normally the door would have been closed.

7:40pm

Now the plane was banking the opposite way. Jeff could see the tip of Long Island, Montauk Point, through the window. He seemed to be looking straight down at it. They had to be at about 15,000 feet, he calculated. Too low for a trip across the pond. Why they were banking, he wasn't sure, but for some reason they seemed to be heading back toward New York City.

7:45pm

Danny trudged up the walkway, the perfectly manicured, perfectly gardened walkway to the front door of his so-called castle. Cathy was vacuuming when he came in and didn't hear him. He knew he'd probably scare her and even considered leaving the house until she was done so that he could re-enter within earshot. He knocked on the door from the inside, but she still didn't hear it, so he took to yelling.

"Cathy!"

Still, she was deafened by the roar of the vacuum until her head followed its path to Danny's feet and she screamed in terror before she recognized him.

"I'm sorry," he said.

"You shouldn't do that!" she said.

"I didn't mean to."

She was more upset at being scared by him than she was angry, and it frustrated him that he couldn't do anything about it.

"I'm sorry, Cathy. I am."

"It's okay."

But it wasn't. There was a lot that wasn't okay.

7:47pm

Caroline managed to talk Paula into Mexican in Buckhead. They went to Rio Bravo and sat outside on the patio. This would be Caroline's last night out for a while. School would be starting up and the obligation had imposed a higher standard of discipline on her routine.

"Last chance for a summer romance," said Paula.

"Yeah, right. As long as we break up next week, it might be worth it."

"Most of the guys here would probably break up with you the next morning."

"Aren't we too old to try and figure them out?" Caroline asked her friend. The margaritas had just arrived.

"I always wonder what guys are thinking. I can't help it," said Paula.

"It's just so exhausting. I feel like I've been doing it for decades."

"You *have* been doing it for decades. Me too!" They laughed.

8:07pm

The normal state of mind creates a barrier between conception and understanding that something terrible is happening. One resists believing in the cataclysmic until one has no choice. But for a pilot, and especially one of the best pilots in the commercial airline industry, the worst case scenario is always "top of mind." Whether in combat or a furious storm, the best pilots react before they need to because that's what works, and *that* more than anything is what separates them from the lesser men.

Jeff's body tightened as his survival mode took over. The plane was now flying way too low, and far too fast. And it was flying in the wrong direction. The cockpit door was still open. He sprung from his seat and headed toward the cockpit.

Just as he was crossing through the galley he was hit, blindsided by a huge set of forearms that slammed him with tremendous force into the forward door of the aircraft. His head hit first, knocking him into a state of semi-consciousness that slumped him to the floor. For the few seconds that it took the guy to grab him by the shoulders, he was unable to move. Jeff was instantly flipped onto his chest. His arms were pulled behind him with a violent wrenching before they were bound with duct tape. His face was pressed sideways into the rubber coated floor near the door. He couldn't see the man's face, but he could hear him breathing heavily and he could smell him. A drop of blood slipped into his eye, the salt burning him and obscuring what little vision he had left. He felt the guy's knee on the small of his back, pinning him down as he wrapped his wrists with the tape. Then, as if he'd momentarily lost his balance, the guy's hand came down on the floor and into Jeff's field of vision. Tanned skin and a dark jacket with three light gray stripes on the cuff. He was in uniform.

He was one of the pilots.

Jeff heard a deep breath and felt the knee leave his lower back. Then he was painfully pulled to his feet by his arms and half carried back into the cabin.

"Everybody stay in your seats. Stay in your seats, please. It is no problem. This passenger has had too much to drink."

The man spoke with a calmness that couldn't possibly be associated with the act of violence that wracked Jeff's body. He deftly spun Jeff down into his seat and began to extend another length of duct tape. He lowered to his knees and prepared to bind Jeff's feet to the footrest.

Olivia's face was blank with fright. The pilot gave her a quick and reassuring smile.

"Its okay, miss."

Jeff began to struggle as he felt the guy grab his ankle. This triggered a sudden and explosive blow to the head from the pilot, knocking Jeff back into delirium.

Olivia screamed.

"Quiet! Quiet! This man needs to sleep!" he said to her. The smile was gone.

"Do you need to sleep too?" She shook her head and burst into a quiet convulsion of tears.

8:20pm

"I am absolutely and perfectly happy, Danny."

"Are you really, Cathy? Don't you want to go back to work?" There was a long silence. Danny thought he picked up a range of fleeting emotions in her face.

"I don't want to go back to work. I'm not ready."

"But aren't you bored, being here all day."

"I am not bored. I have everything I need here."

"I know we have everything we need, Cathy. But what do you want?"

"Can't we just eat dinner? That's what I want."

"Talk to me, Cathy."

"I don't want anything. I just want everything to be like it is. Can't we just be happy like this?"

"You're afraid, still, aren't you?" he said. She threw her silverware onto her plate with a rattle. Her face reddened and the tears began to flow.

"Why can't this be okay? What's wrong with this?" she cried, her hands outstretched. She looked skyward for the answers to her questions. Danny came around the table to hold her.

"I'm sorry, Cathy. It *is* okay. I love you. I'm just thinking there's got to be more for us."

"Well then, if this isn't enough, if I can't do enough, then why don't you just leave me?" She pulled away from his embrace.

"No! No, Cathy. I just want us to get better."

"You mean me. You want me to get better. You want your crazy fucked up wife to get better, that's what you're telling me."

He didn't reply.

8:31pm

Jeff regained consciousness. Olivia had both hands on his head, wiping the blood off him and smoothing his hair.

"Olivia, reach into my pocket. Get my pager," he whispered. She looked up to make sure the pilot wasn't watching them. They were in the second row of first class, so her hands were hidden from anyone in the galley. She slid her hand into his pocket and pulled out the pager.

"Open it."

It was one of those pagers that had a small keyboard on it.

"I want you to send a message for me, and then I want you to cut me loose."

8:34pm

"We'll find a way, Cathy."

"Why don't you just leave me? If you're not satisfied, why don't you just give up?"

Danny's pager suddenly went off, a piercing tone. It was in the pile of stuff he normally unloaded upon his arrival at home, keys, wallet, watch and pager. It never rang after hours anymore, not since the Olympics. He turned it off the moment he heard it.

9:27pm

Whenever they were out in Buckhead, they never failed to be approached by the latest in a long string of "bim-boys," as they liked to call them. The innocuous conversations were devoid of substance but almost always entertaining thanks to Caroline and Paula's low expectations. In the midst of one, Caroline's attention was diverted to the television suspended from the ceiling, beyond the shoulder of the man talking at her. She squinted to see it. The lower fifth of the screen was ablaze with the words "Breaking News." Above that, a map with a circle on it over the Atlantic, just below what looked like Long Island. Her beach house back in Long Beach would have almost been inside of the circle.

At the very bottom of the screen, words scrolled across.

"Alta flight 66, en route from New York to Paris crashed at approximately 8:48 Eastern Daylight Time this evening."

"Excuse me," she said. She stood up, walked over to the TV and camped below it. Paula broke free from her conversation to join her.

"Can you turn the sound up?" Caroline said to a waiter. He began to shake his head until he saw the story on the screen.

"Yeah, just a sec."

Other people stood and gathered under the TV. The music was shut off and replaced by the booming volume of the news.

"...minutes into the flight, air traffic control lost voice communications with the aircraft, although there is a report that they could still hear sounds in the cockpit. The flight was tracked in what appears to be a large figure-eight that crossed and re-crossed the eastern portion of Long Island before apparently plunging into the Atlantic."

10:05pm

It had been a long and sometimes volatile discussion with Cathy, but now there was no turning back. The tangle of Danny's thoughts, as a matter of last resort, had finally boiled down to a single request.

"I want us to go back to counseling."

"Why us? Why not just me? I'm the one with all the problems," she said. She had been swinging between tears, panic and now belligerence.

"It's about us, Cathy."

"What am I doing wrong? I've done everything I could. I've tried to be just right for you and it's still not good enough."

"I don't want you to be perfect, Cathy. I just want you to be happy." He knew he'd made a mistake as soon as he said it. The word was a hot button.

"How many times do I have to say it?! How many times?! I'm happy! I'm fucking happy!" Maybe if he could lighten things they could find their way out of this mess of a conversation.

"Yes, my love, you seem very happy!" He put both hands on her arms and softly tried to shake her into laughter. Her face was red and streaked with tears, her eyes tired as she looked up at him before letting her mouth lapse into a trace of a smile against her will.

"You think I'm crazy."

"No! No, Cathy. I'm crazy."

"You're crazy?"

"Yes. I'm crazy…about you," he said. Then she laughed, and then laughed some more at his vain attempt at Patsy Cline, which was gratefully interrupted by a ringing phone.

"Oh, you better get that," she said. Normally, they would never answer the phone at home, but it was late and so Danny thought it might be important. Besides, she told him to get it, so he did.

"Hello?"

"Daniel Woodson?"

"Yes."

"This is the Alta Care Team coordinator. This is not a drill. Are you available to deploy?" He looked at his wife, his face going grim before answering.

"Yes, I'm available." He covered the receiver.

"Turn on the TV," he said. Cathy turned the TV to CNN.

"Flight 66," said the voice on the other end of the line. It was as if he was talking into the TV; the same numbers were flashing onto the screen just as he said them.

"Got it."

"Went down in the Atlantic about an hour ago."

"Okay."

"Passenger Veronica McManus."

"Yes."

"You'll have her family."

"Okay."

"Age 29. Husband Donald. Other family members are scheduled to meet him in Atlanta around midnight. We need you to meet him and his family at the airport."

"Got it."

10:10 pm

"Goddamn it!" said Caroline.

The gathering under the TV had begun to loosen. People were dispersing, but not Caroline and Paula. Her cell phone rang.

"Caroline Douglas?"

"Yes."

"This is the Alta Care Team coordinator. This is not a drill. Are you available to deploy?"

"Um…ah, yes. Yes, I'm available."

"Flight 66 went down over the Atlantic a little over an hour ago."

"Yeah, I saw. I mean, I saw the report on TV."

"Passenger Jeffrey Palmer."

"Jeff?"

"Do you know him?" Of course Caroline knew Jeff, but she also knew that she would not be assigned to his family—meaning Joanne—if the coordinator knew this, so she lied.

"No. No, I don't know him."

"Do you have something to write with?"

"Hang on just a minute." She flagged down a waitress and borrowed her pen. She tried to write on a napkin while holding her phone, but she couldn't.

"Paula, write what I say," she told her friend.

"Wife, Joanne. Alta employee—works in New York." She didn't need to write this down.

"Need you on the first flight tomorrow morning up to LaGuardia."

"Okay. I'll be there."

10:40pm

Danny grabbed a garment bag and a small suitcase out of the closet. He didn't know where he'd be staying or what exactly he'd have to do, but slowly his own feelings, his desire to be with his wife, to spend an intimate Friday evening together, to build on the warmth that he was feeling for her and the progress they had made—all of this suddenly had to be pushed aside and replaced by the duty that he had hoped he'd never have to fulfill. He packed three suits into the garment bag and some casual clothes into the suitcase, along with his shaving kit, passport, cell phone and finally his Care Team handbook, the metal bound accumulation of instructions, scenarios, phone numbers and contingency plans that would guide him through his upcoming experience. As an afterthought, he grabbed his pager, flipped it on, and then noticed the two words spelled out in bold capital letters on the tiny screen.

NO ACCIDEN

46

Caroline called Joanne from the bar and woke her.

"It's me."

"Hey. What's up?"

"Do you know what happened?"

"What do you mean?"

"A plane went down."

"Ours?"

"Yeah."

"Oh my God!" Joanne was awake now.

"Joanne, have they called you?"

"Who?"

"Alta."

"No." Just as she said that, there was the beep of call waiting in Joanne's ear.

"Hang on," said Joanne. Caroline knew that was the call, and she knew that when she spoke to her friend again, it would be with the knowledge that the father of her child was dead. It took several minutes before she came back on the line. Caroline spoke first.

"You there?"

"Yes. I'm here."

"You heard?"

"I heard."

"How are you?"

"I'm...okay. Jamie doesn't know yet, of course."

"I'm coming up tomorrow, Joanne. I'll give you a call as soon as I get in."

"Caroline?"

"Yes?"

"Caroline, I'm glad you're coming."

"I'll see you tomorrow, Jo."

◆   ◆   ◆

Danny got to the airport earlier than he needed to and that was a good thing. It gave him some time to collect his thoughts and review his handbook. On paper, the job was simple: do everything he could to help the family of the victim get through the next few days.

He thought back on why he entered the program. Why volunteer for a job like this, an assignment that you prayed you'd never have to take on? His ultimate conclusion was simple: He would do it because he *could* do it. He was emotionally strong. *He could do it.* He could share his strength if the time ever came to do so. And now that time had come.

An airport page broke into his thoughts and Danny heard his name.

"Daniel Woodson, please meet your party at the International Ticket counter."

It was a bit of a walk, and with each step, he got closer to the reality of death. How would this man react, this man who had just lost his young wife? Would he be angry with him? Would he hold him responsible for killing his wife?

Donald McManus was easy to spot in the terminal, the only man in his line of sight whose posture betrayed his grief. He was holding himself up, his arm outstretched on the ticket counter. A tall man, he was well-dressed, with short dark blond hair and angular features. Probably in his early 30s.

"Donald?"

"Yes. I'm Donald. I'm Veronica McManus's husband." It seemed to take all of Donald's strength just to speak the words. He extended a disembodied hand to Danny.

"I'm with Alta. I'm going to try and help you." Donald seemed puzzled by this, and Danny was sure the same thought was running through his mind. What could he possibly do?

"What happened? Why did it crash?" Donald asked.

"I don't know. I'm going to try and help you find out," said Danny.

47

The morning after the crash, Danny got a call from Caroline.

"Where are you?"

"I'm up in New York. I'm with Joanne," she said.

"What are you doing with Joanne? Did you get activated?"

"Yes. That's why I'm with Joanne?"

"What?" asked Danny.

"Danny, Jeff was on the flight." In the few seconds that followed, the dots connected.

"No accident!" he said

"What did you say?" asked Caroline.

"I got a page from Jeff. It must have been right before the plane went down."

"What did it say?"

"It said 'No accident.'"

"No accident? That was the page?"

"That's what it said."

"We've got to tell someone. Tell Alta, or the government or something!" Caroline said.

Danny agreed, and so he fed his information up the line in the hopes that it would get him the details he needed for the family of Veronica McManus. But there was no sense in sharing this piece of information with the family, at least not right now.

◆   ◆   ◆

Caroline moved into Joanne's house for the week and together they searched for details. Word had already worked its way north to Caroline that Jeff's last girlfriend, Jeanine, had retained a lawyer in an attempt to claim some portion of an inheritance—money that she felt she deserved as Jeff's companion.

"It's over," said Joanne.

"What do you mean?" asked Caroline.

"I don't have to worry about losing my son. After all these years, I can relax."

There was no point in Joanne covering up this feeling. The years had been tortuous, and though she felt a certain degree of sadness over the tragedy, it couldn't match the feelings of relief that went with the end of court dates and fears. She felt some sympathy, but she could not say she was grieving. Jeff had done little to deserve her grief.

"And I don't want his money." From the looks of her place, it was clear to Caroline that she didn't need it. Joanne was a saver, the rare individual who diligently put away her money into short and long-term buckets of investment, a skill she'd developed over the years simply to keep her head above water. She wasn't affluent—this was no stately mansion—but she had done well enough to keep her home in Garden City, a nicely aged neighborhood on Long Island. The elimination of legal fees to defend her custody status was a windfall in itself that would soon put her well into the black.

"Well, I'm going to make sure you get it anyway. Or at least that your son does." This came down to simple communications. Caroline gathered the required documentation, the marriage certificate and divorce decree, the birth certificate, the title to the home and the last three months of child support checks. Joanne had all of this at her fingertips, neatly filed in a plastic box with a lid on it. Caroline took these with her to the library and made several copies. She then faxed them to the Family Assistance Center, the emergency operation that Alta had set up to manage the flow of documents, money and information.

By the end of the second day, bits of information about the crash were finally starting to come in. It took less than twenty-four hours for the activity to go from "Search and Rescue" to a salvage operation. There were no survivors. The plane had hit the ocean so hard that the largest piece of anything was no bigger than the hood of a small automobile. "Like a bottle being dropped off a skyscraper," was how one televised expert described it as he held the little model plane in his hands. There was a lurid quality to it all, especially when one or two distant relatives consented to tearful interviews about the dead.

One headline blasted, "*PASSENGERS KNEW THEY WERE GOING TO DIE.*" What was the purpose of a statement like this? Danny thought. It was the first time that he could see the devastation of a crash directly through the eyes of a family. Something like this only brought more pain.

Contributing to the stress level was Alta's occasionally inept handling of the media. Wesley Arnold was nowhere to be found. Corporate Communications was "on point," but real or imagined, Alta was not out front enough to gain any public favor for their actions in the wake of the accident.

Then he remembered and it all made more sense to him. The State Department had stepped out in front, or at least directly behind the National Transportation Safety Board representatives who would be conducting the investigation. The FBI had also entered the fray, literally bumping the Alta representative from the microphones after each brief statement. There was only one reason Danny could attribute to this: It was *not* an accident.

The routine continued for the McManus family: twice-daily conference calls, errand runs and meetings with the family.

"What can you tell me today, Danny?" Donald would ask. He was naturally soft spoken, but as the shock began to wear off, his strength started to trickle back into his body and voice.

"Not a lot. The black box has been recovered but they're not releasing any information yet." Danny could read in Donald's face the immediate inclination to press him on this, but it was quickly followed by the realization that there was little to be gained.

"So there was nothing wrong with the plane?"

"We don't know. The maintenance reports are routine. I'm afraid we're going to just have to wait and see what they find out."

They were seated at a coffee table with a scattering of papers, bills, documents and letters. It was a comfortable townhouse, carpeted and painted in the muted colors of a standard unit. The window shades were pulled, giving the room a subdued quality. It was as if Danny and Donald were in a sanctum—a place that was close to death without being in danger. Sunshine was the enemy, as was anything happy or routine. There was another world going on right now just outside the window, a day-to-day world of people going to work and being with their families and not caring as much as they should. That other world continued in its natural state, taking itself for granted, ignorant of ever-proximate tragedy.

Danny knew his assignment did not require him to grieve, but being within the sanctum made that impossible. He considered how tragedy is read about in the newspaper every day, but it can't be fully understood from that distance, from the day-to-day world—a good thing because the alternative would bring society to a halt. But from where Donald stood now, it was hard to accept that this outside world didn't care. Let's face it, Danny thought to himself. Nobody *really* gives a shit.

He moved into a hotel near Donald's house, close enough to deliver whatever he needed to. Flexibility was important; a volunteer needed to "flow" toward the completion of their tasks, getting done what had to be done through the paths of least resistance. It was only the third day of his assignment, but it seemed like a week. Danny would fall asleep first from exhaustion, but then he'd wake up in the middle of the night, his mind racing through his responsibilities. They told him this would happen in training, his mind moving into survival mode, sensitized to every clue and nuance that would protect him. In effect, his own existence had unconsciously become aligned with Donald's survival. He had become a soldier under siege, with failure being equally unacceptable.

Or at least that's how his brain was operating, and that was another tidbit of wisdom his training had told him. Under these circumstances, you can't always control your own brain. Some people would feel guilty, a survival guilt that twisted into an obligation to feel pain, to torture oneself so as to share the pain. As if that were really possible. What good could come of that?

Absolutely nothing.

48

It had been a week since the crash and there was little to show for it. The salvage operation was focused on scraping items off the ocean floor and transferring them to a secure rented warehouse on the south shore of Long Island. It was a jigsaw puzzle of massive proportions that included shards of aircraft along with piles of individual minutia, poignant connections between the day-to-day world and the owners who had suddenly left that world behind. Wallets, business cards, cigarettes, lighters, nail clippers, watches, eye glasses, photographs, gloves, bracelets, rings, makeup, tape players, books, keys, cell phones. All of it the stuff of life where there was no longer any life to be found.

The question of bodies was irrelevant. There were no bodies, only "material," as they called it. Human material, a benign term meant to soften the reality of explosive dismemberment and decapitation.

There were 273 passengers and 14 crew members on board. The Alta Care Team had fanned out across the country and a good part of Europe to help the families and now it was almost time for them to be reeled back in. Memorial services were planned; you couldn't really have a funeral without a body.

◆　　◆　　◆

Danny made his way down the country road as part of the procession and then took his place at the rear of the church in the small town in central Georgia where Veronica McManus had grown up. He watched as the family and friends filled it to capacity. Donald read a poem, the ode he first read to his wife on the night he asked her to marry him. These words would be engraved in the small granite memorial outside.

The service ended and then it was time to say goodbye. *Disengagement* is what they called it in training, which seemed more appropriate for a spacecraft than people. A cold term, but intentionally so, because it had to be this way. As a volunteer, Danny had performed his service and given everything within his power. Now it was time to leave them with the phone number for the Family Assistance Center and say farewell. He made the rounds and received tearful and sincere thanks, the most heartfelt from Veronica's mother.

"Please come and see us some time," she said.

"I'll try," which was really the only way he could tell her that he couldn't. He had to let go.

It was late afternoon and a light rain had begun to fall as he drove north on I-75. The road and sky opened up in front of him, 80 miles to Atlanta, and he realized he was going back, not just to the city he lived in, but to that other world. The day-to-day world. That's when he cried for the first time.

And that's when he knew that life had grown more precious.

◆   ◆   ◆

It had been a few years since Caroline and Joanne had seen each other, but the visit brought their friendship to a new level of closeness. They recounted their individual experiences of Jeff (except his advances toward Caroline), and the rift that had come between them for a time before she married.

"Do you wish you hadn't married him?" asked Caroline.

"Sometimes, but then I wouldn't have had Jamie. Out of evil, comes goodness, I suppose." It was a conversation that explored each of their thoughts, hopes and beliefs over the years.

"I can't believe how much we've changed," said Caroline.

"No kidding. I used to feel sorry for you, because you weren't married." Caroline laughed before answering.

"That's funny. I used to feel sorry for you because you were," and they both laughed. There was little discussion about the details of the crash. As each day passed, it faded into the background until it was time for Jeff's memorial service.

Jeff's parents came up from Florida since most of the extended family still lived in New York. Caroline and Joanne attended with Jamie in tow. It was a military ceremony that included the presentation of a flag to Jeff's distraught mother. This was the most painful moment of all for Joanne; she had remained relatively close to her former in-laws and now she was with them. She draped a sympathetic arm around the matriarch. There was no sign of the girl named Jeanine that they'd heard about.

Caroline spent an evening with her family the night after the service and then flew back to Atlanta the following day. She could think of nothing better than seeing Paula and returning to her schoolwork. The fall semester had started without her and she needed to catch up. Fortunately, she was given a full week off, a "decompression" week, as they called it, before she would be expected back to work.

49

It was time for one of Wesley Arnold's annual rituals—an assessment of his achievements as Alta's leader in preparation for the upcoming shareholder's meeting.

It was easy to pick out the highest point of the last few years: the Olympics. Even with the turmoil, he was the host with the most, the easy winner in the battle of the giant egos. There were few things more satisfying than watching premiere athletic events in the front row of a venue with those who accepted his invitations, and looking back fifteen or twenty rows to wave at those who hadn't. The board of directors was given everything they asked for. They couldn't have forgotten that, especially if they wanted the same treatment at the Alta sponsored 2002 Olympics in Salt Lake City.

But the crash of Alta Flight 66 over the Atlantic the previous summer changed everything. Wesley did finally step forward into the spotlight in the wake of the disaster, but there were suspicions that he had to be prodded. Many of the board members had already aligned against him and were on the hunt for tangible reasons to move him aside. Yet their real reason was the intangible: they just plain didn't like him anymore. He was arrogant, vain and isolated, having wrapped himself in the consolidated power of chairman, chief executive officer and president. Though he had pledged to select a president as second in command, he had stalled for years, his vanity not letting him even consider a succession plan. At least not for the near future.

Paradoxically, the crash also sheltered Wesley from criticism. There was consensus that this was not the time to shift leadership. There were too many uncertainties, and as much as Wesley's enemies didn't like him, everything about the enterprise needed to point to stability. As with every major crash of a commercial passenger aircraft, there is an immediate drop in traffic that lasts only as long as the traveling public's short memories. But now that it was back to normal, the other monsters were beginning to raise their heads.

Immediately after the crash, the pilots agreed to an unusual one year extension of their existing contract. This was positioned as a show of support for Alta management in a time of crisis, but the reality was the union's chief negotiator had been killed in the crash, and the negotiating committee felt the risk of getting a bad long-term contract was too high. They needed to get their strategy in place, and by the spring of 1999, they were ready. At the top of their list: A pilot seat on the board of directors with voting rights.

The shareholders' meeting was an annual demonstration of Alta's most immutable customs. Each and every year the chairman and CEO would convene the shareholders at the Oak Ridge Hilton, an unpretentious but sufficient hotel that sat on the original site of Marty Willman's house, or so the legend said. When their founder was alive he didn't say much about it, but even if it wasn't true, it was a lovely piece of corporate folklore.

The town of Oak Ridge reveled in the attention and posted "Welcome Alta Shareholders" signs throughout the small airport and along every road entering the town. But of course, the chief advantage of having the meeting in Oak Ridge was its remoteness. The less people in attendance, the better. Lower attendance meant higher predictability, and that meant lower risk of embarrassment. Ironically, the warmest welcome was traditionally reserved for one particular shareholder.

Gwendolyn Dobson, or Gwendolyn A. Dobson as she preferred to be called, stepped out of the aircraft from her first-class seat and was led to the elevator by a cheerful skycap. A white Cadillac—it was always a white Cadillac—waited on the tarmac, the driver pulling the passenger door open at the sight of her.

"Hello, Ms. Dobson."

"Hello, Willie. I hope you have had a good year," she said with a half salute.

She was an elderly woman in a pink and white flowered dress with a matching purse and gloves. Her white hair lost some of its shape in the gusts of the tarmac, something for her to fix up on the ride to the hotel. Her osteoporosis was severe—she didn't have to bend down to get into the vehicle. Her most profound feature was her eyes, large and dominating, almost like a chameleon. There was even the illusion, as described by a few haunted VPs, that her eyes worked like a chameleon's, capable of focusing in two totally different directions at once. Being locked into conversation with her was a frightening and far too frequent experience for the most powerful of the Alta leadership.

"What do you think they'll come up with this year, Willie?" she said.

"I don't know for sure, Miz Dobson, but I'm sure you'll be able to handle it. What do you got in store for them this year?"

"Oh Willie, you know I can't tell you that. You come to the meeting and find out."

Willie and Gwendolyn only saw each other once a year, but they had something of a "Driving Miss Daisy" relationship, a patron/servant kinship that had preceded them by at least a century. The routine was always the same. Willie would ask her what she was planning and she would never tell him. But at least Willie had fulfilled his duty and that was always enough to receive the $200 check that Alta slipped to him each year even if he had nothing to report. It was just another small piece of the annual choreography.

"The 1999 meeting of the Alta Shareholders will now come to order." Wesley Arnold's deep southern voice cut through the murmur in the room. People settled quickly into their seats.

"Let the record show that the meeting of shareholders came to order at exactly 10:00 am central daylight time on Thursday, April 17, 1999. Please find the agenda on your chair. This morning I will begin with some introductions and opening remarks. We will then present the proposals set forth in the proxy statement and conduct the balloting. I will then give my annual report to the shareholders followed by the preliminary results of the balloting. Finally, we will entertain questions and comments from you, the shareholders."

The room held the distinction of being the second largest indoor space in the "city" of Oak Ridge, the largest being the high school gym. It was thickly carpeted and heavy on the gold trim, with perhaps one too many mass produced chandeliers. Wesley stood at a podium in between two long white-clothed tables.

"To my right is our general counsel and secretary, Mr. Randolph W. Condon. To my left are the representatives of Arthur Andersen, our independent accounting firm. They will tally and announce the preliminary results of the balloting."

As planned, there were only a few hundred of the shareholders in attendance, but a surprisingly strong contingent of pilots had commandeered a block of seats in the center of the meeting room. Wesley would not be intimidated. They could send all 7000 of them into the same room as far as he was concerned and they wouldn't be as powerful as he was. Still, it was important that Wesley convey a tone of responsiveness. Technically, he was speaking to the owners of the company and therefore must sustain the posture of accountability and politeness. In his very first shareholder's meeting he had miscalculated the importance of this and his arrogance leaked through.

Alta CEO grows Testy in Front of Shareholders was the headline, followed by a story that got considerable local attention, but because shareholder's meetings are rarely major events, it didn't go much beyond Oak Ridge. Nevertheless, it was enough for the Board to require Wesley to complete a secret full day consultation with a public relations specialist. This was humiliating, but it was also well in the past and now Wesley Arnold knew the dance steps in his sleep.

"Our first proposal has been brought forth by chief pilot Tucker 'Tuck' Richards. Captain Richards is a 20-year veteran with Alta Airlines. The proposal is to grant a voting seat on the Alta Board of Directors for calendar year 2000. The board of directors recommends a "no" vote on this proposal. Captain, the floor is yours."

The contingent of pilots erupted in applause as Richards stepped up to the microphone standing in the center aisle. He read directly from his prepared notes.

"Thank you Mr. Arnold, Mr, Condon, our board of directors, distinguished guests and my fellow Alta shareholders.

"It has been a difficult year for the airline industry in general and Alta in particular. We are still recovering from the horrible accident that occurred last year, and the investigation continues into the cause. Fuel prices remain highly volatile, distribution costs are still above reasonable levels, and consolidation among the major air carriers appears to once again be on the horizon. Never before do the words of our founder, Mr. Martin Willman, ring truer than they do today. It is our people who are our strongest asset, and with that said, it is our people who should have the greatest say in our destiny. We must weather the changes as we have in the past: together. And in that spirit, Alta's most dedicated employee group is ready to step forward and represent the interests of Mr. Willman's most important asset, the people of Alta Airlines. And so I would urge each and every shareholder to recognize the necessity of teamwork and unity that is now before us. Vote yes on Proposal #1. I thank you."

The pilots burst to their feet in a standing ovation peppered with hurrahs and cap doffing. A sparse few non-pilots joined in, but the excellent acoustics and the location of the pilots in the geographic center of the room amplified the applause to the level of thunder. Arnold stood at the podium, stone still, waiting patiently for it all to cease. And then when it was totally silent he began.

"Thank you captain. The board of directors believes this proposal will dilute the objectivity and accountability of this as a governing entity. It therefore recommends a "no" vote on this proposal.

"Proposal number 2…"

"Wait just a minute!!"

Unlike the applause, the acoustics managed to twist this high pitched voice into a screeching sound. Gwendolyn A. Dobson had been among the first to take her seat, as she always was, and she only needed to shuffle a few steps to the microphone. One of the assistants quickly arrived, adjusting the microphone stand to complete the parabola with the woman's hunched body.

"First, let me say welcome once again to the shareholders of Alta and to you, Wesley, and to all of the board of directors and to also tell you that even if you have this meeting in Oak Ridge every year, it will not keep me from coming here because the people are always so nice and friendly and because every time I'm here I visit new friends and old that I have made and……"

This was the way Gwendolyn A. Dobson spoke. Everybody knew it, and every year everybody in the room expected it. She spoke in one long sentence, usually covering her own noble past as a survivor of a German concentration camp, her eccentricities, and inevitably, one or two pet peeves that, for the sake of accountability, found a voice in the clipped German accent that managed to dominate the shareholders' meeting each year. She tended to speak in absolutes, using words like "always," which she pronounced as "al-vays."

"…and the seats on the plane are far too small for the average human and, if you look at me, I am smaller than the average human and they are too small for me, so much so that it is like I am always back in the concentration camp, and I should know because I was in one, Wesley, and I know about profitability and that you always have to get as many seats on the plane as you can, but you don't want to concentrate your passengers so much that it is like a concentration camp because that would be inhumane and just wrong, and…"

The script for Wesley was simple: restraint, reserve, deference, politeness. Try and get a few words in edgewise, but let her shout you down. Don't be defensive. Don't engage too deeply. Let her pummel you to the point where the shareholders, the media and the board can do nothing but sympathize with you and worship you for the upstanding and dignified manner in which you've handled this cantankerous, eccentric, bug-eyed gadfly of a bitch.

"…the pilots are nice smart people that are the best there is and they should be able to vote and they should be supported and so I would like to know what you have to say to that!"

Wesley had tuned out for a moment and wasn't quite sure what "that" was referring to, but he took a guess it was the proposal.

"I agree with you, Ms. Dobson; our pilots are the best in the business. Your comments are appreciated as always, and we will let the shareholders weigh the issues."

Wesley had become adept at toeing the line of condescension. She would of course spring to her feet for the other proposals as well, but he was on his game today.

What Wesley Arnold did not know, however, was that an ambush was well in the works. The board had already decided to accept a non-voting pilot as a board member, setting in motion a domino effect that, if all went according to plan, would lead to the resignation of their president, their chairman and their chief executive officer in one fell swoop.

50

"There is *no* way this is going through! I don't want one of those guys within a hunderd miles of my board!"

Wesley's Southern accent always got a little thicker when he was angry. He stared coldly at the man across the conference table from him, a Texan by the name of Calvin Piersall. Piersall was a big man, and perhaps because of a subconscious fear that the meeting could come to blows, the board tapped him to give Wesley the news in the privacy of the Oak Ridge Hilton's "Cottonwood" conference room. Grandson of Marty Willman's original benefactor, Piersall maintained a relaxed matter-of-fact attitude toward the enraged executive. Wesley Arnold had become so accustomed to creating tension in those around him that Piersall's calm parental demeanor only drove his anger higher.

"Wesley, I'm sorry, but we've already made a decision."

"Well, I'm the chairman, and we're just going to have to change that decision." Bylaws were not one of Wesley's strong points.

It was now late afternoon in Oak Ridge, and the shareholders had had their say and departed. The resolution to accept a pilot on the board was announced at the very end of the meeting, leaving Wesley Arnold flustered as he adjourned the gathering. What was once an unfathomable possibility to the chairman had suddenly come to pass as all of the directors voted their shares in favor of the resolution. Jacques Dion, the former Global Airlines chairman, played a key role in engineering the resolution. His actions were the fruition of an unspoken grudge whose seeds were sown many years earlier during the acquisition of his company. He had not received the credit for the deal that he'd expected, and on top of that, the confirmed first class travel privileges that had been guaranteed to him as part of the acquisition had been downgraded to standby in the past year. All of this pushed him into a state of festering bitterness.

But the greater reality, based entirely on circumstances that the board felt had escaped the attention of their leader, was that the pilots were about ready to walk out and shut down the airline. Pilots had very long memories and the Global seniority issue had rankled them for seven years now. Something had to be done and the board seat was the perfect high visibility gesture.

Those on the board closest to Wesley Arnold knew he'd never go for it. He didn't negotiate with pilots and his inability to understand why they weren't the happiest flyboys in the sky created in him a perception that pilots were a bunch of spoiled power-hungry brats. The board predicted that Wesley would choose to do battle, and the attrition from the conflict would be far too costly for the operation. When he was led into the conference room, he found the entire board of directors seated in front of him, a surprise party of the worst kind: a corporate execution.

"Wesley, the decision stands." It was Russell Pate, the now elderly son of Marty Willman's first underwriter, Stanford Pate. He was the senior director, but unlike most board members around the country who wither away during their service, Pate was a sharp and wily old man with a pragmatic business sense.

"The decision does not stand while I'm still running this company," yelled Wesley.

And then there was silence. The plan had worked perfectly, and Wesley realized that he had fallen into the trap. It had been inconceivable to him just an hour earlier that anyone would let him step down from the helm. But in the soundless vacuum of support that he now found himself, the reality he'd been so blind to was now shining in his eyes. He would have no support. The board of directors fully agreed with his last statement, but not in the way he would have preferred.

"Goddamn it! Goddamn all of you! You fucking bastard assholes! None of you know a fucking thing about running this airline! Not a fucking thing!"

He was screaming, filling the room with a vicious rant that ended once again in stone-cold silence. Then just as quickly, he became conscious of himself. He straightened his tie, smoothed what was left of his hair, and walked out of the room without another word.

◆   ◆   ◆

Things moved fast in the hours and days that followed, as they often do when there is a vacancy at the top. A severance package offer had already been drafted and placed on Diane's desk in a large sealed envelope. Attached to the envelope were strict instructions from Pate to open it at a specific time unless otherwise directed. When the moment arrived, the same evening as the meeting in Oak Ridge, she did so and left the letter on her boss's desk, exactly as instructed. The letter also provided Wesley with forty-eight hours to tender his resignation publicly to avoid setting in motion a less desirable chain of media events. And because there was a legacy to protect, he would comply.

Wesley Arnold's resignation letter was glowing with gratitude and fond farewells. He recounted his origins: A humble man who joined a humble Southern airline. He touted the high points of his tenure, but he was careful not to overdo it. Finally, he thanked "the people of Alta" profusely before closing with the ever conciliatory "but now it is time for a change."

And just like his predecessor, he vacated far earlier than was absolutely necessary, before his spotlight of leadership decayed into one of glaring humiliation.

◆   ◆   ◆

After a year of shrouded investigation into the crash of Alta Flight 66, the transcripts from the black box were finally released. But even then, it was still unclear what had happened. Somewhere in the mix, Jeff's voice had been identified and the flight data recorder—the mechanism that tracks each function of the aircraft—showed a curious divergence of the tail flaps. It was as if one of the pilots was pulling up to climb at the exact same time that the other pilot was pushing forward to dive. Jeff had made it into the cockpit, and from the struggle that was obviously going on, he appeared to be the one pulling up, all in a cacophony of screaming and mysterious references to Allah. The prevailing but not yet public theory was that the plane was being intentionally flown back toward New York City, but the speed of descent was far too fast to have anything to do with a safe landing. Complicating the matter were the divergent flaps, which eventually put the aircraft into a tragic death spiral.

All of this lent further credence to Jeff's final message, which, along with the pager that carried it, became buried in the muck of the investigation once it had been confiscated from Danny. Anticipating the worst before it happened, Jeff had clearly signaled that it was not an accident. It was all very obvious, and neither Danny nor Caroline nor Joanne had any doubt that this member of their once youthful foursome had died a hero. If the plane was intended to be crashed into a building, then Jeff Palmer had probably saved thousands of lives, but no one would ever know it, and even if there were those few in the dark corridors of government who did believe it, the facts were long disposed of down a memory hole. Danny pursued channels both inside and out of Alta to find out what had happened on board, but the doors had been slammed shut, and any further efforts to uncover the truth would have labeled him as a delusional conspiracy theorist.

The final summary that was deemed fit for public consumption stated that the crash of Alta Flight 66 was an accident resulting from "an unforeseen and deadly combination of aircraft malfunction and human error." All aircraft of the same make and model would be investigated for flap irregularities and research would continue into the failure of the pilots. But the book was effectively closed. There was nothing more that Danny could do.

The completion of the investigation in 1999 coincided with the announcement by Wesley Arnold that he was stepping down. Danny found this surprising. Nobody loved the company more than Wesley, and under his leadership, they had become one of the dominant carriers in the world. How could they make a change like this now? Even more ominous, the board of directors was setting out to do something they had never done before: select an outsider to run the airline. For many of the old guard, especially the 30-year relics still stuck at the airports and in Reservations, this was the beginning of the end. Of course, this attitude aligned neatly with their usual state of pessimism anyway, but a change of this magnitude dealt them a rich new source of gloom and doom to ponder.

Within a month, the board had selected a professorial product of the banking industry by the name of Maynard Brennan. He was anything but the physically imposing figure that his predecessor was. Not only was he from outside of Alta and outside of the industry, he wasn't even a Southerner. In fact, he was a true New England Yankee, right off the Revolutionary War battlefields of Massachusetts. This would have been unthinkable a few years earlier, but the board had successfully created a party line built on change and urgency. Alta was on the verge of becoming the greatest airline in the world (whatever that meant), and Maynard Brennan was going to take them there.

One by one, the executive VPs, followed by the senior VPs, were slowly moved out of the company, replaced by a cadre of outsiders from leading fortune 500 companies. The days of leadership fed by inbred seniority were dying. Brennan would accept nothing less than the best and the brightest.

Everything was changing in 1999, and Danny's own career was no exception. He took a position as a manager in a small department called Electronic Commerce. This is where they ran the clunky website that only recently had begun to process bookings. The future looked bright, and within just six months of his arrival, the department began to get attention and funding in line with the growth of the Internet. This was the future, and Danny had been lucky enough to get in on it. He liked what was happening, where he was, and where they were going.

In the context of what he'd been through, the corporate upheaval swirling around Danny was of little consequence to him. The experience of working on the crash had permanently changed his life, leaving him with a deep-seated faith in the course of events. While others struggled and whined about the size of their paycheck, their bonus, their car and their office, Danny was at peace. He had borne a tremendous burden and realized an undeniable, if unspoken, gratitude from a family that he had served in their time of greatest need, and no material reward would ever come close to the contentment that this brought to him. He had succeeded in a way that defied both definition and appreciation from his superiors and it didn't matter at all.

This, however, did not mean that Danny had settled into eternal passivity. On the contrary, the growth of his appreciation for the moment and tolerance for change gave him the courage to step back and take inventory of his life, to assess what was important and what wasn't, what was succeeding and what was failing. He was acutely conscious of the natural state of avoidance in himself and the world around him, of the inclination to deny that anything was wrong. This led him to a firm conclusion: If he continued to live his life avoiding and accepting his failures, he would be ignoring the obligation he now felt he had to live his life with the immediacy of the moment. Ultimately, this led him to his most painful acknowledgment of a failure in his life in the fall of 1999.

His marriage was a failure.

It had taken a year for Cathy and Danny to broach the subject, and the trigger was not a critical mass of tension between them, but rather a complete lack of it. They had lapsed into a long-term state of conflict avoidance that had evolved into emotional separation. This was followed by awareness, then admission, and then finally agreement to go to counseling.

The tears flowed heavily, but they were purgative tears. Nobody was to blame, and they had long ago subconsciously sacrificed their passion for stability, but this latter condition had progressed and was now draining the life from their souls. When the tears dried, the prospect of separation lit a spark in each of them that needed to be kindled, because the physical act of separating would only bring their spirits into alignment with their actions. They were already separated in every other way.

Still, it was hard to get started. Danny suggested they go out to dinner together. It would force them to talk and they could cover the logistics of the separation among other more distracting topics. They both found it surprisingly easy.

"How do you want to do this?" Danny asked.

"I think I want to go back to Texas for a while. I can stay with my parents and then we can work out all the other details later."

"You sure you don't want to stay? I don't mind finding a place."

"No, no. You stay. It will be good for me to get out of town. I should be able to get a leave of absence."

There was a slight temptation to reel her back in, to reconcile and start over, to make it all better, but they'd done that many times before and their counseling brought to light the patterns of destructive behavior that had only continued to hurt both of them. They needed to push on.

"Okay. I'll stay," he said.

Danny came home one evening to an empty house that still resonated with Cathy's presence. Immaculately clean, the carpet just vacuumed, the kitchen and bathrooms sparkling, and the bed, the king size bed that he would now have all to himself, perfectly made. There was a note on the kitchen counter.

Danny,
There's a sirloin marinating in the refrigerator for you for dinner. I'll call you next week. Love, Cathy

He opened the refrigerator and then he closed it. He turned on the TV and then he turned it off. He took his work clothes off in the silence and put on a pair of sweat pants and a T-shirt. And then he sat down on the couch, put his head in his hands, and let himself cry.

51

Caroline's first year at Emory was revitalizing. She narrowed her focus and determined what she needed to do over the coming years to get a business degree. This would open up the doors she needed to become the leader she knew she was.

She could see the climb she'd made so far, and it was easy for her to admit that she'd never felt quite so confident as she did now. Of course, she could only laugh at the disposition of her love life. At some point, she did want a husband and children, but up to now, no one was even close to meeting her standards, and she wasn't about to lower them. Meanwhile, the post-crash edginess of air travel had faded after a year. Caroline humored herself by considering how the traveling public, out of fear for their lives, would resist flying in the wake of a crash, but only until the fares went down low enough.

"Everyone has their price," said Paula. Through the summer and into the fall, the planes were once again packed.

Caroline's schedule for the month of October 1999 included a run that she hated, but the price of controlling her schedule meant taking on the table-scrap trips that others shunned. This one went from Atlanta to New York, LaGuardia and then back down to Fort Lauderdale. From there, she'd work the return flight to New York and then back to Atlanta. She had now become accustomed to bringing a textbook with her on trips, but this journey afforded her little downtime, especially once she got to New York. Maybe she had softened a bit in her few years down South, but even as a New Yorker, there were times when she was never quite prepared for the unending string of petty demands she might get on the flight out of LaGuardia. This was what they called a "whole can" flight, which meant the normal procedure for distributing soft drinks ran counter to the cost-saving policy of filling two cups per can. You didn't do that on this flight. It was understood that you gave the passenger the whole can of soda to preclude the inevitable accusation that Alta was trying to "rip them off."

A good number of these passengers were the people who often perceived airlines on the same level as utilities. Making a profit was a crime, the fares were too high and abuse of reservations agents, ticket counter agents, gate agents and flight attendants was far from improper, but instead an entitlement that might as well be part of the "contract of carriage" on everyone's ticket.

"Have you had a burrito flight yet?" Paula asked Caroline

"Not yet. What's that?"

"That's when they leave a full diaper in the seat pocket. Cabin Service calls them burritos," said Paula.

"Delightful."

The consensus among the many flight attendants who had done a tour of duty on the New York—Ft Lauderdale run came down to two words: expect anything. But on this Friday night, Caroline felt fortunate. She was blessed with the more civilized assignment of working the first-class cabin. The flight was overbooked, meaning every coach seat of the MD90 would be filled five across, and because there were still vacant seats in first, there would be a few lucky coach passengers who would be bumped up to the front. One in particular appeared as though he had won a sweepstakes.

"Gimme a Crown on the rocks," said the man. He was a big red-faced fellow, probably in his early 40s. Dark, stringy hair flattened across his scalp, but not enough to cover the sunburned redness of it. It looked like a tanning bed accident. He wore a green New York Jets sweatshirt, something Caroline thought must have been a holdover from his adolescence until she discovered that it was the adolescence itself that had held over. He was chatty and friendly when she served the drink before the aircraft pushed back from the gate.

"Hey, I like it up here in first class. I'll never fly coach again." His smile was brimming, a smile of someone who has suddenly discovered that all limits to his desires have been removed.

"No charge, right?" he asked, pointing to his drink. He wasn't necessarily a loud person—this was likely his normal voice level—but he was one of those people whose verbalization naturally carries. No one within the first-class cabin or the first few rows of coach (his real target) was out of earshot. Caroline tried to modulate the effect with the softness of her own voice.

"That's right, sir," she said, just above a whisper.

"Great! See you later!" Modulation had failed.

Outside the jetway, the shuffling of overbooked passengers delayed the departure by 20 minutes, enough for Alta Flight 518 to lose its take-off slot, and at LaGuardia Airport, that is the board game equivalent of "go back to start."

It was a typical Friday night in New York, and Caroline could see the long line of aircraft merging and snaking their way to the runway like a motley school of fish. Large widebodies interspersed with small props, unrecognizable charter flights, a Learjet, a cargo plane, 727s, 767s, an ancient DC-10, and the hottest thing in the sky, the sleek RJs as they called them—regional jets that promised to be the profitable savior of the industry.

Caroline didn't really mind delays when she worked in first class because it gave her more downtime and a chance to discreetly crack open her textbook in the jumpseat up front. She heard the tone of the call button, a rare occurrence in first class. Maybe this was due to the proximity and attention they already gave these passengers, or some unwritten ethic among those who frequented this part of the plane. Regardless, the sharp tone of the flight attendant call button in first class was more analogous to the blare of a car horn, especially when it was being hit repeatedly, as it was right now.

Caroline leaned over and looked down the aisle to see the guy in the sweatshirt looking right at her, his arm half outstretched, rattling the ice in his empty plastic cup. She closed her textbook, stood up, smoothed her skirt and waited an extra second before walking down the aisle.

"Another one?" she asked him.

"Absolutely."

He seemed okay; nothing to be worried about yet. At least he was still smiling. But now she was ready for the flight to leave. Just as she was pouring the liquor, she felt the muffled jerk of the plane pushing back. Relief.

"Here you go."

"Thanks. Hey, tell the captain there's no hurry. Not if I'm up here in first class." Caroline just smiled and nodded. She didn't want to engage him in conversation, one that would prick the ears of everyone around them. She already sensed an awareness among the other passengers. Granted, people rarely if ever dressed up to travel anymore, but on most flights, including this one, those few who did were sitting in first class, lending a greater degree of alien status to sweatshirt guy.

The in-flight crew turned on the safety video, but the blare of the call button sounded again. Caroline didn't look right away. She didn't need to. These were the times when she needed to tap her reserve of professionalism and put all thoughts of irritation aside. She made her way back to him and crouched down in the aisle next to his seat. She didn't need to do this, but it was a way of calling attention to the safety video, as if she needed to avoid obstructing any view.

"Nother one please?" he said, loud enough to shout down the safety instructions.

"Sir, we need to wait until we take off first." This wasn't necessarily true, and Caroline knew it wasn't true—not when you're number 17 for takeoff. She also knew that the passengers around her, the regular first-class flyers knew it wasn't true, but they weren't going to say anything because they knew what she was trying to do. Adding to that, she knew that sweatshirt guy would never have had anything close to a previous experience in first class that could refute Caroline's statement.

"Well, I hope we're taking off soon," he said, and for the first time his grin vanished, a sudden disappearance that made what he said all the more frightening.

"I'll be back later," she said, with a radiant smile that she hoped would protect her.

52

"Ladies and gentlemen, we're now number one for take-off. Flight attendants please prepare the cabin for departure."

It had been another 30 minutes, but Alta Flight 518, now 74 minutes behind schedule, was finally speeding down the runway. Caroline and one other flight attendant would serve dinner and within just a few hours they'd be back on the ground. As soon as the wheels were up and the MD90 had begun its steep climb over the Long Island Sound, Caroline heard the latest proclamation from sweat-shirt guy, this one a sing-song version.

"Ooookaay, we've taken off now." Did the guy want her to bring him a drink *now*? She ignored him.

"The captain has turned off the seat-belt fastened sign and you are now free to move about the cabin, however if you are seated we ask that you keep your seat belts fastened in case we encounter any rough air."

Caroline looked down the aisle as she completed the announcement into the PA phone. This time the guy's arm was stretched all the way out. Normally they would start taking drink orders from the front, but she had no choice. She hung up the phone and made the walk down the four rows directly to him.

"Bout time!" he said.

"The usual?" she asked him. This was a phrase that fell outside the lines of standard practice. You never wanted to call attention to a passenger's drinking if you could help it, but this was another subtle calculation on Caroline's part. He wouldn't know the difference, but the surrounding passengers, if they didn't know it already, would pick up on it, and she was beginning to consider the possibility that she might need their help. She went light on the Crown.

"Thank you very much!" he said.

"You're welcome," she said.

"Hey, where you going?" he asked.

"We're getting dinner ready for you."

"Oh yeah! Dinner. Okay, you can go."

"Thank you," she said.

The exchange was taut with tension. Maybe dinner would calm him down a bit. He could marvel at the opulence of a first-class meal, and then maybe he'd get all smiley faced again.

As they brought out the trays for dinner, she made eye contact with all of the other passengers, and three of them, purely by the tone of their voice and their quiet display of gratitude, provided her with the assurance that they would be watching out for her. This was not unusual. It was as if flight attendants and their best customers had their own invisible airwaves of communication between each other, finely tuned to sense danger and unite if and when the time came.

Before he finished slobbering his way through the meal, sweatshirt guy handed his cup back to Caroline.

"That drink was weak. Can you pop it up a notch this time? Please!"

She took the cup and nodded. This was a question with no right answer—one that presented the dilemma that every flight attendant faces at least once in their career. Contrary to the guidelines for alcohol service, sometimes it just made sense to keep the drinks flowing, get them drunk so they fall asleep and avoid the confrontation that always came with the cut-off. Unfortunately, this guy seemed a long way from sleep. When she picked up his dinner tray, she noticed he'd taken the small glass salt and pepper shakers—souvenirs to remember his one and probably only visit to first class. He would use them to prove to his friends he had flown in first class, and if anyone needed proof, this guy did.

"Nother one!" he said. The smile was gone. Caroline turned back to him, a tray in each hand.

"Just a minute, sir."

It was almost decision time. She cleared the other trays first, which only served to increase his belligerence. She was going to lie to him and see if that worked on its own. If it didn't, she was going to have to cut him off anyway. She returned with a warm smile on her face, an expression that was the polar opposite of the tension she felt.

"Sir, I have some bad news." She gave him a little pouty face.

"What? How could there be any such thing as bad news in first class?"

"We're all out of Crown Royal."

"No way! Can't you get some of those mini bottles from those sorry ass people back in coach?"

"Sir." She crouched down and lowered her voice. Everything she was doing was also for the passengers around her. No flight attendant could ever underestimate the importance of witnesses in a situation like this.

"What!?"

"I'm afraid I can't give you another drink." There was silence, and then there was tension. The man's face turned redder, his teeth became clenched. Others were tuned in, ready to jump to Caroline's defense.

But they would be too late. They would all be too late.

"That's bullshit!!" The man suddenly uncoiled, the full force of a powerful punch landing on Caroline's face, crushing her nose and knocking her into darkness. She didn't hear the rest of what he had to say, and she didn't feel a thing when he hit her again and again in the space of three seconds as she crumpled to the floor.

"Fuck you, you fucking stewardess whore bitch! This is fucking first class!!"

53

When Caroline awoke in a hospital the following afternoon, she had no idea where she was until a nurse told her.

"Who?" she asked. A sharp bolt of pain hit her jaw when she asked.

"Charlotte. You're *in* Charlotte, North Carolina."

Caroline's emergency contact was Paula. As soon as she got the call, she flew up on the first flight the following morning. She would later be thankful that Caroline was sleeping when she entered the room. The sight of her friend brought her to immediate tears. Caroline had suffered a partially shattered cheekbone, a severely broken nose and a still yet to be determined injury to her neck. Her head was partially wrapped and held rigid to her shoulders in a shiny metal brace—a halo is what they called it—that kept the vertebrae in her neck aligned. Most of her face was streaked with deep purple and black bruises. The force of the blow had pushed the bone and cartilage of her nose upwards toward her brain, barely avoiding penetration of the membrane.

"She's stable, but she's also probably lucky it wasn't much more serious," the doctor told Paula.

"Don't call this lucky! This is not lucky!" said Paula. The grief had been replaced by anger with no logical target to take it out on. Paula grabbed her sleeping friend's wrist and accepted a tissue from the doctor. During her second visit later that afternoon, Caroline was awake. Paula took a peek through the small glass window of the door, got herself together and then entered with a beaming smile.

"Hey kid. So you wanna be a flight attendant, eh?"

"Yeah, right. I feel like I'm in a fucking birdcage." Caroline could only speak very slowly.

"What happened?"

"This guy just punched me."

"Let me guess. New York to Fort Lauderdale. Coach."

"You're half right. He was in first. Got bumped up."

"Figures."

Another man entered the hospital room, a clean-cut man in a jacket and tie. He quietly approached her bedside before introducing himself.

"Hello, Caroline, I'm Dean Gage from Alta Legal."

"Hello."

"I wanted to share with you what happened and see how you're feeling."
Paula's antenna went up.

"Yeah, and what else? See who's going to sue her for putting her face in the
way of a fist?" said Paula.

"I'm sorry, and your name is?"

"It's Paula. I'm her best friend and roommate. And guardian!" she threw in.
Paula wasn't even totally sure what the word 'guardian' meant but she knew it
was a legal term, so he'd understand it.

"Paula, we want to press charges against this man and we need Caroline's help.
Were you on the flight?"

"No. I was *not* on the flight. I'm just trying to look out for my friend. Obviously our damn company could not do the same!" she said.

"Paula," said Caroline.

Gage replied calmly, "I know. It's horrible. But we're going to try and make
up for it."

Caroline was not up for another confrontation. To her, the sight of Dean
Gage was a pleasant one. Just someone to come to her side from Alta was encouraging, even if it was too late. He recounted the events that followed Caroline's
last memory.

"The captain was given immediate authorization for an emergency landing
and brought the plane into Charlotte. The flight was on the ground in fifteen
minutes. Paramedics got right on board first and got you out of there."

"What happened to the guy?" Caroline asked.

"He's in almost as bad shape as you are. According to the other flight attendants, a number of passengers jumped on him and landed several blows of their
own. They put the plastic cuffs on him and actually hog-tied him. He screamed
all the way to the ground, so another passenger stuffed a napkin in his mouth as
soon as the plane landed. They've got him in the city jail here in Charlotte. We
have most of the first class passenger's testimonies."

"What's going to happen to him?" she asked.

"We want to keep him in jail until trial so we're going to ask that there be a
very high bail."

She nodded, but then realized she couldn't nod.

"Now, Caroline, I need to ask you a few questions when we can have some
time alone. I'll come by a little later."

"Why don't you ask them now?" asked Paula.

"Yeah, go ahead," said Caroline. "Let's get it over with while I'm still awake. I might fall asleep again and wake up in fucking Kansas."

"Alright. But remember, this is purely to strengthen our case. Do you remember how many drinks he was served?"

"What the fuck do you need to know that for?" asked Paula. Gage recoiled.

"I served four to him and then I cut him off. And then he slugged me."

"That's fine. Just so you know, the witnesses on the flight said you handled everything as perfectly as it could be handled. More than one of them volunteered to testify for us, so please don't worry about any of this being questioned."

"Then why are you questioning it! Damn right she handled it perfectly. This woman is a graduate student. She knows her job better than anyone," said Paula.

"Paula, it's alright. Nothing else is going to happen to me."

He politely resumed. "It's just that we have to be prepared for this guy to counter sue. He may try and claim that you served him too many drinks and he's therefore not responsible."

"How the hell could he possibly do that?!" asked Paula.

"Granted, he would be stupid to try, but we just need to be prepared."

"How bout we just have the guy killed. Alta should have hit men for people like this," said Paula. Caroline smiled.

"Paula, don't make me laugh. It hurts."

Gage stood up.

"Here's my card. I'll be in town as long as you're here," he said.

"I don't think we'll be going out dancing tonight, eh Paula?" Paula's oscillation between anger and tears was now swinging toward the latter. It was hard for her to fathom that her best friend could still have a sense of humor. Gage continued.

"Let me know what I can get for you. Paula, let me get your number too in case I need to reach you. Believe me, Caroline, the company takes these kinds of incidents very, very seriously. This man may make bail before the trial, but we're going to put him right back in jail for as long as we can." He patted her gently on the hand and left the room.

This didn't do much for the pain that was beginning to set in. Caroline's IV was on empty, she was tired, and soon after the next bag was hung beside her and plugged in, she was ready for more sleep.

"I'll be back later on tonight," said Paula, as Caroline drifted off.

Caroline woke up again just after sundown, and a new face was standing over her. A new face that was an old face.

"Danny?"

"Caroline." He held her hand lightly. She curled her fingers around it and squeezed.

"Danny."

"I brought you something." He held up a small paper wrapped bouquet of flowers for her.

"Were you, like, expecting a funeral?"

"No, I just wanted to bring you something, and I didn't really know what to bring."

Oh so Danny of him. It wasn't that he meant anything to her anymore; he was married and part of her long-past history. But at this moment, under these conditions, the tears welled up quickly in Caroline. For all her pride and independence, for all her cynicism and distance from past relationships, it was now suddenly so meaningful to be cared for. She cried and then apologized for crying.

"I'd love to smell them if I still had a fucking nose," she said through her tears. The reality of her injuries had come to the fore.

"I'll get you some more when your nose grows back." She laughed and then let loose a small scream of pain from the laughter.

"You can't make me laugh. It's a hospital rule, and besides, you'll make me snap my spinal cord."

"Cathy, I mean, Caroline…"

"Okay, that's all the time we have for today, thanks for coming."

"*Caroline*. I'm sorry."

"No, I'm sorry, Danny. I forgot my name tag, but I'll be sure and hang it on this bird cage for the other visitors…"

"Stop it, Caroline."

"And don't forget to bring Cathy her flowers."

"Stop it! These are for you, Caroline." They both stopped talking. She realized she'd pushed the limit.

"What is it, Danny?"

"Cathy and I have separated."

"*Real*-ly?

"But that's my problem. I would have been here anyway. I can't believe this happened to you."

In the past, this would have been her opening to harp on his opportunism. Whatever the real reason for his presence, she just didn't have the energy to critique the flaws of Danny that she'd come to know over the last decade. She was the one who needed caring now, and he had come to her. The small details of cause and effect were irrelevant. She reached for his hand again and he squeezed it with both of his.

54

Caroline remained in Charlotte for three more weeks. Her parents drove down to see her (the previous year's crash in New York had infected them with a chronic fear of flying). Danny and Paula shuttled back and forth from Atlanta, sometimes together on their free days, and sometimes tag-teaming so the time that Caroline was alone was minimized. Even Shawn came to see her one day—thoughtful, sensitive Shawn.

"You look like shit!"

"Great to see you too, Shawn."

"Why didn't you kick his ass? You used to kick my ass?"

"I never kicked your ass."

"I'm kidding. About how you look of course. You look as beautiful as ever."

"Cut the crap. Shawn, I'm not in the mood for this?"

"Sorry. How are you, really?"

"I've been better."

Behind Shawn's smart-ass façade was a sincere feeling of pain for his friend Caroline. He just hadn't ever learned how to express those feelings, but when the conversation finished an hour later, they both recognized the bond between them. In the end, the visit from Shawn was a high point, a sign of a special friendship that she could reflect on and preserve in her haloed head.

She needed these high points because her lowest point came when she first saw her face. The damage would require reconstructive surgery for her cheekbone and her nose. In the meantime, sweatshirt guy was sentenced to a year in jail; there was no need for a trial. Dean Gage had apparently convinced the defense attorney that any jury hearing the witnesses' testimony and seeing the list of the injuries inflicted on his client would most certainly put him away for a much longer period of time. It was tempting to go through with it, but Caroline didn't want to relive the events, and she accepted the sentence as just, especially since it would increase her chances of reaping a larger settlement in a civil trial. She picked one of the parade of lawyers that passed through the hospital and let him go at it. Any money she received would probably not get to her until after the guy got out of jail anyway, so she might as well forget about it for now. And forgetting about it was high on her list of priorities.

The surgery was reasonably successful, but the nose would never be exactly the same. She had been scarred, her beauty now permanently flawed. This alone brought her to a deeper understanding of herself. First, the revelation that her appearance, her natural beauty, had always been important to her, and on further reflection, much more important than it should be; second, that her self-confidence and independence were fleeting. This brought her to an epiphany: she wanted someone to love and protect her. But then, what if they just left her, like Danny did, or got themselves killed, like Peter did? Yes, she wanted to be with someone, but now more than ever, she also wanted to avoid making still another stupid decision about a guy.

After Caroline's return from Charlotte, Danny began turning up on the edges of her life, sending her an occasional e-mail or leaving her a message. There was nothing insincere about his communications—he genuinely seemed to care about how she was doing—but she was not ready to take it any further. The temptation was strong. Why not just let go, she thought. Let him take care of her. They're friends and he's got himself a nice empty house. They were lovers once, so that whole sex-with-someone-new thing would not be an issue. But then she would come to her senses and realize that settling was a mistake. She was aware enough of her own neediness to recognize that her judgment was impaired.

Soon after her return home, Caroline was informed by Alta that she would receive a full year's paid leave of absence and the option of unlimited professional counseling. This was, of course, a transparent attempt to prevent her from suing the company, but she had no desire to do that anyway. She actually wanted it all to be over with, although the counseling would be worth trying. After what she'd been through, there was no stigma attached to seeing a shrink. She decided to take full advantage of it.

Her therapist—a middle-aged woman named Margaret whose soft warm voice and homey office provided a haven for her thoughts—raised her awareness to a level she never thought possible. The most tangible outcome was a formula for contentment that answered an important question: What did she need to do to overcome these doubts about herself?

She knew that most of the answers could be found in pure recognition. There was really nothing wrong with her, but to push her forward, Margaret and Caroline agreed that finishing school and some other outside activity would put her over the top. Through their animated and sometimes tearful conversations came clarity, and soon the appropriate path was solidified against the backdrop of the alternative: a romantic relationship with a former boyfriend named Danny.

"Not gonna happen."

"That's not what you said during our first session," said Margaret.

"Yeah, I know."

"Why?" Long pause.

"I wasn't thinking clearly. I couldn't have been. I was weak. I mean, Danny has been great and all. He's really been there for me this time."

"This time?"

"Yeah, he left me once."

"When did that happen?"

"That was like, thirteen years ago."

"And you still think about this?"

"No, no I don't. Well, not a lot. Very little. What might have been is long gone. Its all water under the bridge. I'm not mad or anything. It's just that, Danny is Danny."

"Is Caroline still the Caroline of twelve years ago?"

"Noooo, no way. I'm a lot different."

"But he's the same?" There was another long pause before Margaret continued.

"Caroline, I don't necessarily disagree with you. I think you are wise to stay out of any serious relationships in the short term. Work on yourself; work on Caroline before you think about someone else. But when you are ready, I would recommend that you stay open to all possibilities. You have been through an experience that very few people can relate to. It can't *not* change you."

The tears came. *Damaged*, that's how she felt. She had changed all right. Margaret pressed on.

"The only question is, will it make you weaker or stronger, and if you do come out of this stronger, and I think you will, then you will be able to handle almost anything. Don't be afraid, Caroline. You've already overcome so much. You should be proud of yourself."

"Myself?" she said. "Who the hell is that? The one with the smashed nose or the one who was around before it got smashed?"

"Caroline, when I talk about change, I'm not speaking of your nose. Right now I know it seems very important and very upsetting, and that is completely understandable. But I think over time you will find that you haven't lost anything of real importance."

Margaret didn't have all the answers, but the routine of seeing her each week helped get Caroline to a healthy plateau. From there it would be up to her.

◆   ◆   ◆

Regrettably, Caroline was far from alone in what she had experienced. The reality in the industry was that "air rage" had become a growing phenomenon. Flight attendants were naturally in harm's way and the Flight Attendant unions of the other airlines were blazing a trail toward protection of their membership. In response, Alta established voluntary self-defense training and asked Caroline to be their poster child. She declined. There was no pride in recounting a war story that she found more humiliating than courageous, but it did at least give her the other activity she was looking for.

In the summer of 2000, she and Paula enrolled in the self-defense class. Her target date for returning to work was the fall of 2000, so the few months ahead were a good time for her to master these skills, and there was no way she was going back to work without being a master.

The instructor was a woman, a black belt and silver medalist in the Judo competition at the Atlanta Olympics four years earlier. This immediately infused the class with a level of confidence in her skills. Although not total confidence.

"Why can't we get the gold medalist?" Paula whispered to Caroline.

"She's probably busy training the passengers," said Caroline. The instructor brought everyone to attention.

"Why don't we go around the room and have everyone tell us a little bit about yourself, what you're looking for in this class and why you're here."

"Great," said Caroline under her breath.

"My name is Cathy Woodson. I wanted to enroll to build my confidence. I had a bad experience a few years ago, and this will help me."

That must be Danny's ex, thought Caroline. Pretty girl. Nice nose.

The rest of the introductions were chirpy, interspersed with words of encouragement from the instructor. Caroline decided that she wasn't up for a replay of her experience when they finally got to her. She really didn't know what she was going to say. When her turn came, the instructor gave her a nod and all heads turned her way. She paused for a second before speaking and then it came out:

"Yeah, I'm here because I got the crap beat out of me eight months ago, and if anyone touches me again I plan on ripping their throat out and shoving it up their fucking ass."

The class fell silent. The emotion in Caroline's voice brought a lump to her throat and Paula could see the tears beginning to fill her friend's eyes. She decided to break the silence with a war whoop and applause for her best friend.

And then everyone clapped. Caroline smiled at Paula and then laughed through her tears as she tried to wipe them away. Paula stretched her hand out to Caroline and they linked fingers.

"Okay," said the instructor. I can't promise you that we'll teach you how to do that, (laughter) but we will make sure that you can protect yourself from anyone on board your plane."

The sound of her own voice resonated inside of Caroline's head. She had never felt this way before, but right now she was angry—a burning anger that had caught up to her now that she was as healed as she would ever be. In a way, her words were as shocking to her as they were to all of the people around her and she was angry about that too. How could this have happened? How could someone cause a statement like that to come out of her mouth? He made her this way! How could he have done this to her? He had damaged her body *and* her mind!

She just wanted to punch something.

55

Danny busied himself in the months ahead with changes. He and Cathy had finalized an amicable divorce and sold the house for a nice profit. He took an apartment in midtown and cautiously dipped his toe into the Atlanta social scene with a group of friends he had met at work. On the one hand, the whole idea of this was vibrant and exciting, bringing back memories of past freedom. There was a near constant stream of attractive women for him to meet and charm. But it wasn't long before he was tired of it all. He resisted being bitter toward the many women who were interested in the money that he didn't have, and he accepted the possibility that he might not have the energy and drive to find that one person out of the hundreds that he could connect with.

He had re-established his friendship with Caroline, and had hoped that it might lead to something more, but she had consistently rebuffed him. They still did things together—she took him out to dinner on the depressing night that his divorce was final—but it was always platonic.

◆　　◆　　◆

On Labor Day weekend of 2001, Joanne invited Caroline and Danny to a beach house she had rented on the Jersey shore. This fit Caroline's schedule perfectly. She had the following week off, and they agreed to spend it with Joanne and her son Jamie doing "touristy" things together in the city. But first, a few days at the beach. It would be a reunion, absent Jeff of course. A few acquaintances from their shared history in Reservations were also in the house for the weekend, each of them, including Joanne, older and grizzled from a barrage of phone calls that had never let up. This was the living they'd long ago resigned themselves to and the physical effects were clearly etched on their faces.

"Let's go to Point Pleasant," Joanne suggested. It was a Saturday night, hot and sticky and thick with the threat of a late summer thunderstorm, but the idea seemed irresistible.

"Okay, let's!" said Caroline.

"Let's!" said Danny.

"You guys are mocking me!" said Joanne

They filled two cars and maneuvered into parking spaces a few blocks from one of the Jersey shore's classic old time boardwalk amusement parks. Point Pleasant was an arcade of lights, food, games and kids mixed with harmless packs of drunken New Yorkers. This pack washed down their dinner with various tropical drinks and started a zigzagging stroll down the boardwalk. Danny spotted a line of wavy blinking lights a hundred yards in the distance.

"Come on, Caroline, we're going to ride the roller coaster. You remember when we used to do that?"

"No, I don't remember."

"You do too remember."

"No, Danny. I completely...don't remember!"

"Yes! I know you remember." Caroline was too buzzed not to smile. He grabbed her hand and ran toward it with great leaps like the scarecrow heading for Oz.

"Come on! Come on! We're going to ride the roller coaster!!"

"All right, slow down. It'll still be there when we get to it."

They waited on line with the kids and teenagers all around them and then they squeezed into a seat, a seat meant for couples in love, lovers who should be close together, shoulders and hips snug against each other for the ride.

"You do remember the last time we were on a roller coaster together, don't you?"

"Yeah yeah, I remember. I remember a lot of things, like when you said we'd stay together and then..."

And then he kissed her. She kissed him back and let the memories of Danny flow back into her. The seat jerked forward, ending their kiss. He laughed and then she laughed.

"Maybe you shouldn't remember everything," he said to her.

"Well maybe you should!"

A few minutes later they were sharing a scream, because although it was a modest little boardwalk roller coaster, it packed more punch than either of them expected, and they laughed together all the way back to the end of it, laughing at everything and nothing. It was a moment and an evening as simple as the joy of a roller coaster, of lightness and exuberance, of the rare occasion when childlike wonder reaches into the hearts of grownups and reminds us why we live.

For many hundreds of people, it was the last weekend that they would live.

56

"You've reached Caroline's cell phone. I'm not available at the moment. Please leave me a message and I'll call you back as soon as I can."

Danny would wait another sixty seconds and then he'd try her number for what was probably the tenth time. It was only about 10:00 on a Tuesday morning, but the last hour defied explanation. He had been in a meeting at work, when descriptions filtered in on what had happened. Planes crashing into buildings, buildings falling down—it sounded absurd. This is when panic set in for Danny, because all he knew was that Joanne and Caroline were set on doing all of the tourist activities that they'd never done growing up in New York. His second message to her was one of unrestrained panic.

"Please call me, Caroline. The second you get this, call me."

In the meantime, the country was sent out of a blissful summer and into a state of reeling shock and confusion.

"What the fuck is going on?" someone shouted.

"Are any of our planes missing?"

"The Pentagon?"

"Pennsylvania?"

"Did our people get out of the World Trade Center?"

"It's what? It's down? The building? The whole building?"

And then, "Both of them?"

There was a sickening feeling of unprecedented disorientation. The entire office packed into the conference room to watch CNN on the wide screen video conference TV, to gaze at the unimaginable replayed before their eyes.

By 10:30 that morning, Alta had determined that all of their aircraft were accounted for, all of them either on the ground or within minutes of landing. This did little for Danny as his thoughts were consumed with Caroline. Thousands were dead or dying and she and Joanne could very well be among them. Fourteen years they had known each other and now he was beginning to feel as though he'd taken every one of them for granted.

Between his calls to Caroline, Danny did what everyone else was doing. He called his family and they exchanged vague reassurances in the face of an undeniable truth: Nothing like this, nothing even close to this had occurred in their lifetimes and all they could do was stumble forward at the mercy of the next uncontrollable event. By noon, Danny had slipped into a trance in front of his computer when his cell phone rang.

"Danny, it's Caroline."

"Caroline! God! Caroline…"

"I'm okay."

"Where are you?"

"I'm walking uptown."

"Joanne?"

"Yeah, she and Jamie are with me. We're okay. It was close."

"Are you safe now?"

"Shit, I don't know. Is anyone safe now?"

"Are you out of downtown?"

"We're in the Village. We're covered in dust, but we're walking. Us and about a million other people."

"What happened? Where were you?"

"I don't want to talk about it. I've got to try and make some other calls, but do me a favor. Call Paula and tell her I'm okay."

"Call me later," he said.

The entire commercial air transportation system was locked down in the hours that followed. Danny walked outside his building and encountered a sensation he'd never before experienced from the place he was standing: complete and total silence. One of the busiest airports in the world, just a few hundred yards away from him on this beautiful September afternoon was as frozen as a photograph. Hundreds of aircraft were now scattered around the continent in a state of suspended transportation.

When Danny drove home later that afternoon, the electronic signs over the highway declared a "NATIONAL EMERGENCY." It wasn't as if the Department of Transportation could do anything to make it better. The reality was that any human interaction that failed to acknowledge the death that humanity had witnessed on this day would be considered trivial.

She called him that evening, as she had promised.

"Do you want to talk about it?" he asked her.

"It was bad, Danny. We were on the boat coming from the Statue of Liberty and…we saw the first plane…"

Caroline was lapsing in and out of tears, one moment her strength taking over, the next dominated by her realization of what she'd seen. He let her talk as much as he felt it would help her. He'd seen what happened too, over and over again, but all he cared about right now was that she was okay. When the tears began to overwhelm her, he interrupted.

"I'm going to come get you."

"What?"

"I'm going to come get you. I'm coming up to New York."

"I can stay with Joanne. I'll fly back."

"There are no flights, Caroline. Nothing is flying."

"For how long?"

"Nobody knows, but I think it's going to be a while. They don't know what happened, and you know they're not going to take any chances."

"Then how are you going to come get me?"

"I'm driving up."

"Danny, you don't have to do that."

"Caroline, you might not understand this right now. I'm not even sure I understand it, but I *do* have to do it." She didn't have the will for an argument. Logistically, it didn't make sense to her, but she hadn't the strength to figure it out now.

But for Danny it was clear. There was one single most important need in his life—perhaps stronger than anything he had ever felt before—and that was the need to see Caroline. He stopped off at his apartment, put on some shorts and his favorite T-shirt, stuffed a few days' worth of clothes in his duffel bag and he was on the road before sundown. He grabbed a large coffee at a convenience store just before the entrance ramp of I-85, and minutes later he was heading north.

As darkness fell, he listened to the radio and the endless reports of the tragic events. He crossed into South Carolina by 9:00 p.m. and left the bad news behind in favor of an 80s CD that brought back better memories of New York. He drove fast—nobody seemed to care on this particular night—and made good time up through the South.

He was in North Carolina by 10:00 p.m., rolling past Charlotte and Greensboro and on to Durham through the night.

He hit the Virginia line just after midnight and the long straight shot to Richmond. At 3:30 in the morning, somewhere south of Washington DC, he pulled into a rest area and reclined his seat for a nap. He was up and back on the road just after 5:00 a.m., circling Washington on the Beltway. In the distance he could see a plume of smoke from the still burning Pentagon and he could hear the fighter jets patrolling the skies.

Through Maryland and Delaware there were no people on the road. He crossed over Delaware Bay into New Jersey just after 7:00 on the morning of September 12th. Another hundred miles and the monotony of the turnpike began to gradually give way to the refineries and factories of northern Jersey, and then, where he would have expected to see the twin towers in the distance, there was just billowing smoke. He didn't need to see any more than that. Not right now.

"Caroline, its Danny."

"Hi Danny."

"I'm almost there. Give me directions to Joanne's."

"Where are you?"

"I'm in Brooklyn, on the Belt."

"No, you're not."

"Yeah, I am. I'll be there in half an hour. Just gimme directions."

It was almost nine o'clock now, and Caroline hadn't slept more than two hours the entire night. She put Joanne on the phone to pass the directions to Danny and then she started instinctively throwing her things together. She was ready to get out of town.

As for Danny, she had to admit to herself that she couldn't wait to see him.

57

"You'll be okay?"

"Yes, of course," said Joanne. "I've got my man Jamie here to protect us." She gave her son a smile and a thumbs up. Joanne was smart enough to know that this was a time when children needed to hear and see the confidence in their parents, even if it didn't really exist. Keep the spirits high.

"Oh, that's right, I forgot. What am I worried about? Jamie's here!" said Caroline.

"Well, I'm glad Jamie's here," said Danny. "Jamie, you sure you don't need me?" he asked.

"It's all under control!" said the nine year old.

With that, they hugged and kissed and cried a little, and then Caroline and Danny were back on the road. Fatigue set in within a few hours, their sleep patterns thrown off by the previous night, and they decided to grab a motel room off a turnpike exit in the flatlands of south Jersey. They closed the shades and were asleep before their heads hit the pillow.

For Caroline and Danny, the days and nights were now running together, their periods of consciousness severed from the daylight hours. Time had become less relevant. There was light and there was dark, and now it was dark. She awoke; he was awake, on his back, looking upward at the pattern of the ceiling tiles.

"Hey," she whispered.

"Hey."

"You see anything up there?"

"I didn't wake you, did I?"

"Yes. You shouldn't stare at the ceiling so loudly." He smiled at this. She unconsciously rolled toward him and laid her arm on his chest.

"Whattaya think?" she asked.

"I don't know. It's just so weird."

"That's not the word I was thinking of." He didn't say anything, but then he felt her shudder and pulled her closer. He had taken off his shirt, and now he could feel the moistness of her tears spill down his chest.

"Oh Danny, it...it was so horrible." She was crying now, talking through her tears.

"I saw people jumping. I saw them die. And then the buildings...I saw them all die."

Time had finally made Danny smarter. He wasn't going to say something stupid like, it'll be okay, because the truth was that it was not okay. He let her cry and softly rubbed her back. She slowed down and then stopped. He could feel her breathing get heavy, and then after a single big deep breath, she raised her head and looked directly at him.

"Let's get out of here," she said.

It was still dark, and the roads were empty. They had fallen asleep so early that now it was only just after midnight. A morning fog arrived with them in North Carolina. They stopped for coffee even though they were wide-awake, and when they got back on the road, she talked through the entire ordeal in detail with the dispassion of a reporter.

"We were on the boat coming back from the Statue of Liberty. We got to the dock and heard the first plane. It hit the far side of the building so all we saw was the smoke. We couldn't go up town from where we were so we headed down along the river. That's when the second one flew right over our heads and into the building. I could feel the heat. We kept moving toward Battery Park." She went on to describe the sound and the sight of the buildings falling, and then the horrible cloud of concrete dust that swallowed them. Through the account, Danny had the strong sense that this was Caroline's way of controlling what little she could. It was as if she were getting on top of it, objectifying it in a way that would keep her as sane and separate from the event as humanly possible.

"And that's what happened." There was silence for several miles, before Danny spoke.

"I was scared."

"You? Why?"

"I was scared that I wouldn't see you again." He was staring straight ahead at the road. But she could see a tear starting to well up in his eyes, and then one break free.

"Caroline, I was so scared I wouldn't see you again. So damn scared." She grabbed his hand, and he let a few sobs escape. He checked his rearview mirror and then pulled the car over to the shoulder. When he came to a stop, they embraced, and he let his tears flow.

"I'm so sorry, Caroline. I am so so sorry for what I did."

"What do you mean?"

"I left you. I should have never ever left you."

"Danny, that was so long ago."

"Doesn't matter."

"Its okay, Danny."

There was a sign up the road in the distance:

Welcome to Georgia, The Peach State. We're Glad You have Georgia on Your Mind!

58

Alta Airlines was one of the luckier ones. It had been spared an attack by terrorists and some believe this was purely by virtue of its non-nationalistic name. It had also secured enough working capital to carry it through the lowest points of the post 9/11 era. But the industry as a whole was sent plummeting into the worst period of its existence, and for Alta, the stage was set for unimaginable challenges marked by episodes of shameless corporate greed.

For Danny and Caroline, the subtle forces pushing them together were initially more powerful than the pull. This was a time to take stock, to appreciate the sincerity of the moment, to transcend the myopic pursuit of perfection in favor of the immediacy of a new reality, and Caroline now recognized the reality of Danny's love. In the months ahead, their history and their future were spliced together, and all of the events between faded into the background of their memories. They realized they were not the same people who had said goodbye to each other back in the 1980s, except perhaps for a core love that they had once shared, a soul mate bond that re-emerged, a mutual feeling that could now be fully appreciated without the distractions of impatient youth.

◆　　◆　　◆

Midtown Atlanta had been experiencing a renaissance for the past few years. Dilapidated houses had been claimed, refurbished and turned into restaurants and nightclubs, giving the area a homespun but sophisticated atmosphere that became a magnet for flocking clubbers. On a warm spring evening in the year 2002, Danny and Caroline squeezed into a parking space along 13th Street and walked down to Crescent Avenue.

Caroline pointed up a hill to a house with a wraparound porch.

"Hey, how about that place?"

There were neon accent lights along an awning that stretched down the porch stairway. Beautifully dressed people were spaced along the railing on the porch, most of them holding martinis or glasses of wine. A buzz of laughter and conversation rolled down to the street.

"Let's do it!" he said.

As they approached, Danny was able to decipher the name of the place spelled out in the neon. It was called "EmDouble-u's," whatever that meant. They were waved in, and even though there was no cover charge this early in the evening, the gesture by the bouncer made them feel important. A beautiful young woman welcomed them as she grabbed menus.

"Two?"

"Yes. Do you have an outside table somewhere?" Caroline asked.

"Sure, follow me."

She led them straight back through the main room and on down a hallway that opened up into a large canopied outdoor deck. There was a bar to their immediate right. Tables set with white linen tablecloths and fine china lined the perimeter of the deck, and century old trees provided a lush green background beyond the railing. The dogwoods were out, and clusters of whiteness accented the green.

"Wow, this is nice!" said Danny.

They took one of the tables and ordered glasses of chilled white wine from the extensive list.

Danny looked at some of the childlike carvings in the wood railing right next to their table. Hearts, with the name "Pearlly" in it. "Pearlly + Joseph." Then another one with "Pearl luvs Stephen Taylor," and then what Danny thought was a reference to a year: "1953."

The wine arrived, and his attention returned to the woman across from him. Caroline and Danny were on a date together—a date that had the aura of their first one so many years ago.

"To the future, Caroline. Our new future."

"How about we make it better than our past," she said.

"That's a promise."

Danny's eyes again wandered around the room until he saw something on the far side of the deck up on the wall. There was a large plaque of some type that he couldn't make out. He rose out of his chair, his eyes locked on the three-foot square of iron.

"Where are you going?"

"I've got to look at this. Come with me."

They walked over to the wall, and Danny read the inscription aloud.

"ALWAYS MAKE YOUR CUSTOMER FEEL IMPORTANT"

This is the former home of Martin Willman, founder of Atlanta based Alta Airlines. Alta Airlines began as a small crop dusting enterprise in 1922 in Oak Ridge, Louisiana. Through wise business decisions, and the help of a loyal family of employees, Mr. Willman grew his small company into one of the largest airlines in the world. Alta Airlines has long been an engine of commerce in Atlanta and the Southeastern United States.

Mr. Willman and his wife Candace purchased this home in 1939 when Alta moved its headquarters from Oak Ridge, Louisiana. Martin Willman died in 1992. His home was presented to the city of Atlanta as a gift on behalf of the estate of Martin Willman and executors, Candace Willman and Pearl Louise Willman Taylor.

Dedicated, 14 June 1995.

Of course, the city of Atlanta seemed to have no problem selling their gift right back to some entrepreneur so it could be turned into a nightclub and restaurant. But there was one consolation: at least it was tasteful place. Now it made sense. "EmDouble-u's" was a clever phonetic spelling of the founder's initials.

They returned to their table and ordered dinner. She, the pan seared salmon, he the grilled filet mignon, and with it, a bottle of champagne.

Danny pondered the obvious.

"Wonder what Martin Willman would think of his home now."

"I think he would be happy," Caroline said. "After all, it is the kind of place that makes people feel important."

"Yes. Yes, it is, isn't it."

Acknowledgements

I have been extremely fortunate to have the faithful support of friends and family. Chief among them are my unofficial critics and editors: Melissa Grossman, Bill Tatman, Bronda Wetteroth, Stan Graboski, Tom McGelligot, Melissa Weston, my sister, Kim Keady, and my parents, James and Sally Donovan.

My *official* editor, Susan Kelly, provided valuable expertise and encouragement throughout the painful process of getting the manuscript into a manageable form. Cherrie Bevers lent her tremendous creativity and inspiration to the cover design, in addition to being a valuable source of feedback. And Dave Paule gave me his time and guidance with the publishing process. I am also grateful to the fine people at iUniverse for their patience and consideration during the editing process.

Thanks also to my brother Tom Donovan, for the catchy title, and to my friends at the Brick Store pub, because almost all of them know my name. And for their ongoing friendship and encouragement, I must also convey my sincerest thanks to Greg Adamo, Karen and Troy Burns, Terrence Burns, Angela Chiodi, Margie Fischer, Janice Hoover, Kim Koopman, Debbie Lilly, Wendi Mayerson, Tim McCarthy, Toby Pratt, Suzanne Rolon, Cheryl Rousseau, Kerry Stegeman, Travis Werner, and several others who indulged me by letting me read to them.

Finally, thank you to my former co-workers at Delta Air Lines for their dedication and commitment to this noble industry. They are the true inspiration for this book.

0-595-33751-1

Made in the USA
Lexington, KY
25 August 2018